Praise for

Blues Dancing

"Delving into the Philade... ...novels (*Tumbling*; *Tempest Rising*... ...psodic performance in this story ... ...moves seamlessly between the early '70s and ea... 9Us. . . . Pitch-perfect dialogue and a keen eye capture the spirit and cadences of the early '70's. . . . Flashbacks to the early days of the erstwhile lovers' relationship shimmer with the intoxication of first love, while their later encounters powerfully reveal their vulnerability to old desires . . . readers (become) passionately involved in the fates of these winning characters."
—*Publishers Weekly* (starred review)

"Diane McKinney-Whetstone has a gift for secrets—personal secrets, family secrets, childhood secrets. She excels at the art of imitation, allowing tensions to build to a breaking point before clearing the air with a dramatic revelation . . . *Blues Dancing* is no exception, with multiple secrets and drama to spare."
—*Philadelphia Inquirer*

"Novelist Diane McKinney-Whetstone makes readers settle in and get comfortable. Closing her latest book *Blues Dancing* is reminiscent of moving from a beloved neighborhood and leaving behind friends who are like family."
—*Emerge*

"Johnson steals this stirring novel."
—*Baltimore Sun*

"In an era when most writers bank on hype and hook to grab a reader's attention, McKinney-Whetstone has amassed an enthusiastic cadre of readers by writing engaging characters supported by enchanting language."
—*BET Weekend*

Praise for
Tempest Rising

"McKinney-Whetstone solidifies her position as a writer of well-crafted, serious popular fiction. . . . McKinney-Whetstone is masterful at rendering the spaces between people, giving to the air that separates them a taste, a texture, a soul."
—*Philadelphia Inquirer*

"McKinney-Whetstone's gifts as a writer continue to fascinate."
—*San Francisco Chronicle*

Praise for
Tumbling

"Even the air is palpable in *Tumbling*. . . . The story moves forth on the power of Ms. McKinney-Whetstone's characters. Ms. McKinney-Whetstone captures the formidable struggle to protect both a community and a family."
—*New York Times Book Review*

"A densely textured narrative that proves as rich and filling as a well-cooked meal. McKinney-Whetstone's remarkably skillful first effort should place her at the forefront of a generation of emerging African-American women novelists. McKinney-Whetstone is clearly a smart, careful writer who's created a page-turner of a novel with abundant style and irresistible charm."
—*Washington Post Book World*

Blues
Dancing

ALSO BY DIANE MCKINNEY-WHETSTONE

Tumbling

Tempest Rising

Diane McKinney-Whetstone

Blues
Dancing

a   n o v e l

Perennial
An Imprint of HarperCollins*Publishers*

A hardcover edition of this book was published in 1999 by William Morrow and Company, Inc.

BLUES DANCING. Copyright © 1999 by Diane McKinney-Whetstone. All rights reserved. Printed in the United States of America. No part of this book may be used or reproduced in any manner whatsoever without written permission except in the case of brief quotations embodied in critical articles and reviews. For information address HarperCollins Publishers Inc., 10 East 53rd Street, New York, NY 10022.

HarperCollins books may be purchased for educational, business, or sales promotional use. For information please write: Special Markets Department, HarperCollins Publishers Inc., 10 East 53rd Street, New York, NY 10022.

First Perennial edition published 2000.

Designed by Jam Design

Library of Congress Cataloging-in-Publication Data is available.

ISBN 0-688-17789-1

00 01 02 03 04 ❖/RRD 10 9 8 7 6 5 4 3 2 1

For Greg

Blues
Dancing

One

_____

THIS NIGHT AIR was filled with low-hanging clouds. The kind that softened everything they covered with a smoky blue haze that felt like a dream. Like this neighborhood way west of the river that had declined over the years from a place of majestic three-storied rows to intermittent blocks of good and bad and devastated; like the too-young boys in too-loose clothes hanging on these corners doing deals that would make the devil beam; even memories of a time when a girl becoming a woman had thrown away her promise as if it were a tattered rag, and descended into a drain lined with syringes, bent spoons, and long-sleeved shirts dotted with her innocent, middle-class southern blood. It all took on a floaty, shimmering effect inside these clouds and became appealing in a way that was both sultry and safe. Especially through the back window of this yellow cab. Especially to Verdi as she gave in to the softening powers of the fog.

She nestled against the cracked leatherette seat as the air swayed in and out through the window. Two-faced March air, chilly yet impatient for spring, so it had a filmy warmth to it, she picked it apart for the warmth rather than close the window, siphoned through the myriad aromas trapped and kept close by the low-slung clouds as the cab rolled past the gone-to-bed homes and businesses of West Philly: someone had liver and onions for dinner here, turnips there; she could smell chicken grease from the take-out wings place on Fifty-second Street; curry from the Indian restaurant as they got closer to the University City section where Verdi lived with her life mate, Rowe; nutmeg, thyme, from the House of Spices. And there it was. Butter. No mistaking it, the smooth milky aroma concentrated under this fog. It went straight to her head, swooned her because her aunt Posie was superstitious about things like that, said that a whiff of collards on a Wednesday means you're getting ready to get paid, or the scent of lemons when it's snowing means somebody close is pregnant, the hint of fish frying on a Thursday means you're having overnight guests for the weekend, and the smell of butter on a foggy night means you're getting ready to fall in love.

"You smell that?" she said excitedly to the back of the cabdriver's head.

"I don't smell nothzing, my cab clean, lady."

She yelled at him to stop then and she rarely yelled at people like cabdrivers, elevator operators, the ones who vacuumed the carpet at the special-needs school where she was principal. Figured she'd be working thus if Rowe's large hands hadn't rushed in and broken her fall when she'd tumbled from her heightened station in life. Told the cabdriver to stop right now, let her out, she needed to get out.

"You sure, lady? Here? That lady who tip me said I wait till you in your door."

"She worry too much, I'll be fine," Verdi said, talking about Kitt, her close first cousin, her aunt Posie's daughter with whom she'd spent the evening, who'd walked outside with Verdi and stuck her head in the cab as it was about to pull off.

"You call me if that arrogant pompous professor you shacked up with gives you any shit about staying out so late," Kitt had said.

She'd waved Kitt away like she was trying to do to the cabdriver now. But he just sat there reluctant to leave her out here like this. She didn't know what it was about herself that made people want to watch over her, thought maybe it was her eyes with their downward slant, or how she wore her hair relaxed bone straight and cut close the way Rowe liked it, or her thinness, he liked her thin too though she preferred herself when she'd had a curve to her hips.

She leaned into the cab window, whispered into the driver's face, "My aunt says if you smell butter on a foggy night you're getting ready to fall in love." She made her eyes go big, lowered her voice even more the way her aunt would do. "And if you're walking alone when you smell it—"

"Yeah? Yeah? What happen?"

Verdi didn't know the rest, when her aunt got to this part her face would glaze over in an oily sheen, she'd start fanning herself and shaking her head. Lord have mercy is all her aunt could say after that. "It's just better that's all," she said to the cabdriver as she turned and started walking toward home.

She took measured steps though she knew she should be rushing if she were going to stick to the story she'd fed Rowe earlier. She hated that she'd lied, such a harmless thing too, spending the evening at Kitt's house. But Rowe despised her cousin so. Went on and on about her lack of degrees and couth whenever Verdi let on about her visits there. So rather than hear him rant about her first cousin with whom she felt closer than a sister, Verdi told him that she was going in town to get her nails done, to get chocolate-covered-coconut eggs for the baskets she was doing for the younger ones at her school. Not Godiva but better than the Acme brand; ran around after work then to at least get the eggs, then begged Kitt for a manicure after they'd pushed back from another one of Kitt's culinary masterpieces.

This air was too creamy to rush through anyhow as it settled on her forehead now, stroked her, slowed her steps even more. She needed to walk, not for the sensation of the buttery aroma swimming around in her head, nor for falling in love, she'd been in love once, loved Rowe most of the time now. Right now she walked because, because why? she asked herself. Because. She just wasn't ready to go home yet.

And already she was close to home on this quiet street of ornate wood-and-stained-glass doors where the houses were big and old on the outside, newly restored on the inside with center-island kitchens and updated wiring to accommodate home offices and theaters and sophisticated security systems because crime had increased sharply in the 1990s in this once cushy part of Philadelphia. Rowe wanted to move, wanted to get more upscale and live in town, but so far Verdi had resisted, she preferred living on the fringes where the cluster of blocks like hers inhabited by university bigwigs and offspring of original old-money Philadelphians almost met the not-so-affluent blocks, the war zones, Rowe called them. How livid he would be if he knew that she was walking alone out here now as if she were taking a Sunday stroll through Rittenhouse Square.

The air was getting thicker the closer to home she got, making like a corset around her, binding, still soft though, enticing. She didn't blame Rowe for being the way he was, reasoned that he needed to be so protective for himself as well as her, he truly believed that without him she'd fall again. So she inched along now, allowing the air to do to her what Rowe usually did: feel so good, even as it bound her up.

She stopped at the corner, waited for the light to turn green though the street was absent traffic. She was the newly appointed principal at a private school for special learners and was careful about things like crossing the street, staying between the lines, making sure that the temperature on the hot water heater was set to below eighty-five, the kinds of things to keep her students safe. Especially the ones like Sage, Kitt's beautiful seven-year-old who'd yet to speak her first word, whose mutism was a puzzle to the medical community because speech was controlled by such a small part of the brain and damage there rarely existed in a vacuum. Except that although Sage suffered some developmental delays, she'd far surpassed even the most optimistic prognosis. Her slice of sunshine, Verdi called her. Was seeing Sage's face all over again as she'd tickled her chin earlier today and unpinned a note from Sage's pearl-buttoned sweater sent by Kitt, who often communicated with Verdi that way. Was just about to see her cousin's loopy handwriting again too, sprawled across the red construction-papered note, the contents of which had tilted Verdi off her center, but right then she heard a rush of tires, felt a set of head-lights drench her back.

She kept walking, balled her hands tightly around her briefcase, the chocolate eggs; could fling one or the other and then run if she had to. She wasn't afraid though, in these kinds of situations that had the potential to be life or death, she was rarely afraid, exasperating to people who cared about her, like Kitt, like Rowe.

"Hey, hey," the driver of the car called and she was both relieved and disappointed that it was the cabbie's voice. "I feel too guilty. Wolf packs hang around here. I ride next to you till you get to your house. Maybe I smell butter too, you and me, we fall in love."

Cute. She didn't laugh though, didn't try to dissuade him either. Let him roll along with her and at least enjoyed the play of his headlights against the three-storied twins and singles that looked like castles with their gabled tops poking through the tops of the blue-gray clouds. And now the cabdriver was whistling an off-key, offbeat "Strangers in the Night," and Verdi had the thought that what if he were really a serial killer who did his victims in in the most heinous ways? Her breath quickened at the notion. That was frightening to her in the way that encountering maybe some gangbangers was not, evil cloaked under the guise of doing good. She didn't dwell on it though, didn't want to get herself all riled up, and now she was in front of her house anyway. She threw her hand to tell the cabdriver she was home, listened to the remnants of his tune hanging as the cab drifted on through the fog.

She just stood there then. Looking up at her own ornate door, and all those steps she had to climb as if they led to some tower where Rapunzel was kept. Tried to push through the air that had gone from cream to molasses, strapping. Couldn't. It's almost midnight, she told herself, what are you doing, get your ass on in the house, even as she stopped, put down her briefcase, the chocolate-covered-coconut eggs, then sat down herself—ordinances against step sitting where Rowe wanted to move. She folded her hands in her lap, focused on the castle across the street, comfortable as the butter-tinged air stroked her forehead, told her to go ahead and think about him. No harm in just thinking.

"HE'S BACK," Kitt had whispered in the note Verdi unpinned this afternoon from Sage's pearl-buttoned sweater, "Johnson's back in

Philly, girl." And the blood rushed from Verdi's head and bombarded her heart at the thought of his return, her long-ago love who'd helped her navigate the wiles of city campus life more than twenty years ago when she was freshly here with her downward-slanted eyes that he called enticing, and the southern smile that he said sweetened all that was bitter about his life; the one who introduced her to *Soul Train* dances and encouraged her to pick her pressed hair out into an Afro and gave her patient instruction on the art of holding her liquor. The one who'd gotten all inside of her head, between her legs, transformed her perspective. She cultivated in him an appreciation for gospel music, he took her to see Santana; she strung him out on caffeine, he introduced her to Boone's Farm Apple wine; she insisted he dine with a napkin in his lap, he taught her to roll a joint. And before things went lumpy between them like vomit from too much drink, he was saying yes ma'am to his elders and she could say fuck you without a drawl.

She saw a light jump on in the third floor of the house across the street. Hoped they were just going to the bathroom, hoped they wouldn't look out the window, see her, then call Rowe, tell him Verdi was weirding out sitting on the steps alone this time of night, only March after all, chilly out. She didn't know why Johnson's presence here was affecting her like this. He'd been back before; she'd refused to see him each time even though Kitt had begged her, prodded her, reminded her that in all these years Rowe hadn't even married her so what was the harm, an hour, an afternoon with a former beau. But Verdi knew that she wasn't strong enough to see Johnson and resist him, a host of angels wasn't that strong. Plus Kitt hadn't been privy to the darkest scenes in Johnson and Verdi's togetherness when they'd cha-chaed with the devil. Didn't know the particulars of how he'd sat next to Verdi on the beanbag pillow in the center of her dorm-room floor, cooed cooed his love in soothing bursts of hot breath against her face, tied her arm above her elbow, taught her how to ball her fist, how to find her vein, hit it, plunge it, how to nod off into the milky blue. Miraculously Verdi had kept the shades drawn on that descent into hell thanks to Rowe and to her family's entrenched denial that wouldn't allow them fathoming such a thing about their Verdi; they'd instead gobbled up excuses about the stresses of school, or a bad case of mono, impacted wisdom teeth, even dehydration, sleep deprivation, rather than accept the truth of how Verdi had spent her junior year.

So Verdi refused to see Johnson again. Even though Kitt had let Verdi go through three entire courses of her meal and hadn't mentioned the note she'd pinned to Sage's sweater and it was only as they languished over a dessert of Jell-O and angel food cake that Verdi couldn't stand it anymore and said, okay, cousin, stop being coy, spill it, the note, you know you want to push me straight into his arms.

And Kitt sighed and twisted her locks and said that nothing would make her happier than seeing Johnson and Verdi together again, but that she would respect Verdi's feelings on the subject that she assumed hadn't changed, had they?

And Verdi forced out an emphatic no, no, she wouldn't see him this time either and Kitt said that it was settled then, no pressure from her, she promised. And Verdi told herself that it was settled too, even now, sitting on her front steps feeling the chill in the concrete work its way through her trench coat.

Except that there was something different about this time, maybe because when she'd read Kitt's note she'd just ended a harrowing meeting with her staff that had her questioning her ability to be a leader, and thoughts of Johnson right then were like a salve rubbing her in the places where she'd just felt so attacked. No. More likely it was that his visits were getting fewer, more spaced out—it had been almost eight years since the last time he was here, she was sure because

Kitt had just birthed Sage, was in the hospital, weak with severe post-partum depression, and Johnson had flown in to see Kitt. What if he waited ten more years before he came again, or twenty. She felt a brick drop in her stomach at the thought, she'd be sixty in twenty more years. She stopped herself. Felt silly, felt guilty too because once she started with her obsessive counting she'd have to factor in Rowe's being twenty years her senior, meant Rowe could be dead the next time Johnson came back, felt as if she were betraying Rowe, he'd been so good to her. Really. Grabbed her hand and held on tight when she was slipping into hell.

She should go in the house now, she told herself as she watched the room in the third floor window across the street return to black. She swallowed a final gulp of the butter in the air, pushed through the fog to get up the steps even as she sensed Johnson's presence back in town with a mix of titillation and dread the way an abandoned lover feels unforgotten footsteps in the middle of the night getting closer and closer to the bedroom door.

Two
_____

V ERDI EASED INTO the bedroom and listened for
Rowe's snoring, an enormous incongruity about Rowe
was his snoring, as if he'd let loose at night in ways that
he never did during the day; his snoring had a raucous quality that
should bellow from a drunk sailor, or a bad-boy rapper, not this highly
respected professor of history at the university with his polite unob-
trusive features, and proper academic speech patterns, and mannered
pretensions that lent a deliberateness to everything he did, even when
he blinked it was as if he had first given the matter careful consider-
ation. But right now, as Verdi pushed the door all the way to open,
Rowe wasn't belting out those inharmonious sleeping breaths even
though he believed in early to bed, early to rise and it was just about
midnight.

A mild orange warmth crackled from the fireplace in this expansive room that was originally the living room. They'd turned it into their bedroom at Rowe's insistence, though, because of the fireplace, and marble-topped mantel, and chair rail and crown molding that were never-ending, and the oversized built-in mahogany bookcases, and the floor-to-ceiling picture windows that looked out on a centuries-old beech and a trio of Victorian singles—that scene through the windows was such a postcard when it snowed that they actually took a picture one year and used it as a cover for their holiday greeting. Back then they'd agreed that this room was too perfect to be formal; had far too much capacity for a hearth-type ambience to be wasted on an occasional wine-and-cheese gathering, the intermittent burst of company, maybe a Christmas Eve by the fireplace. No, no, they would sleep in this room, and watch TV and listen to music, and read and study and compete with the fireplace to see which could give off the most heat because back then, when Verdi was so needy and Rowe so competent, they made their own fires dance.

Right now it was the slow bluesy dance of the real fire that Verdi focused on as she stepped all the way into the bedroom and looked at the back of Rowe's head and tried to keep the oh-shit, I'm-caught grimace from taking over her face. She hadn't even planned out what she would say to Rowe until right now as she walked all the way into the room.

There Rowe sat wide-awake in the forest-green velvet chair, his shadow billowed to twice his size on the wall behind him and then shrank and went amorphous in the fire's dance. His feet were propped casually on the ottoman, his robe open revealing his plain white boxers and matching sleeveless undershirt, his chest muscles taut under his skin that didn't know whether it wanted to be light or dark. The edges of the robe touched the neat stacks of journals extending up from the floor like a gate—or fortress—on both sides of the chair.

His reading glasses were riding the tip of his polite nose, the glasses were black and picked up the black in his hair that hadn't yet gone completely to gray, like most things about him were showing evidence of the slow, steady trek from young to old, though he worked out with religious regularity, was careful to eat mostly by-the-book heart-healthy foods, even dabbled in melatonin, and chromium, St. John's wort and ginseng on the side; he was getting to sixty, could feel the increased pull of gravity trying to force his shoulder muscles to the ground, his waist, his abs, even his manhood threatened to take part in the descent made all the more dreaded because Verdi was younger than him by a full twenty years.

She walked across the bedroom and leaned down and kissed his brow. "You still up, babes," she whispered as she peeled her lips from the soft creases in his brow. She couldn't tell if he was grimacing out of anger or concern or maybe the creases just came up as a question mark with no particular emotion attached. Something about the feel of his wrinkled forehead against her mouth caused her to decide right then that she'd tell him where she'd really been. She'd brace herself for the spewing out of bad adjectives about her cousin that would surely follow, but she at least owed him her honesty. "I tried to slip in so I wouldn't wake you, isn't tomorrow your early class with all the smart-asses?"

"Now, how can I go to sleep without my pet next to me," he answered. He hadn't called her pet in years. It was the nickname he'd used when their love time was a secret, when she was still a student, when he still lived with his wife, when everything about them being together was so inappropriate that she couldn't stop herself from shaking she'd be so nervous, he'd tease her, call her his teacher's pet while he squeezed and caressed and loosened her up so that her natural desires could come down. He grabbed her hand now and held on and pulled her down to sit on his lap. "After twenty years with me, you must know my most important bedtime rule, I never ever close my eyes until I know where you are?" He unbuttoned the cuff of her left sleeve as he spoke. "So if you ever want to cause my demise, just stay away from home around bedtime, I'll quickly succumb to sleep deprivation, because trust me, Pet, I won't sleep. No, no, I won't sleep."

"I—I was going to call you, Rowe," she stammered as he began to roll her sleeve up past her elbow.

"Don't explain, just tell me where you were." He worked his ability to modulate his voice regardless of the maelstrom that might be kicking up on the inside. Right now his voice was soothing, gently persuasive, an acute contrast to the thunder moving through his body. He pressed his thumb against the inside of her arm and dragged his thumb the length of her arm right along the vein. He had to grit his teeth to hold himself at bay so that he wouldn't break her arm because in that instant he wanted to wrench it from its socket, hurl it around like a baton on fire for making him worry like this. The past three hours he'd almost exploded with the fear that finally she'd gone and done it, she'd reverted to the ways that he'd saved her from back in the seventies during her undergraduate days that culminated, or descended, to that day when he'd found her in the men's bathroom of the history department, her prizewinning face kissing the vomit sliding down the base of the urinal. And he'd scooped her up and rushed her home with him, where he and his then-wife, Penda, spoon-fed her clear broth, and coke syrup, and turned the heat up and down in response to her fever and chills, and finally resurrected the cherub-cheeked girl she'd once been. And even though Rowe fell in love with the restored version of her, he'd never really let go of the impending-doom kind of anxiety that Verdi might leave him—after all he'd done for her, given up for her—that she might relinquish it all for that powerful call that had dragged her down the first time. But her veins were smooth, no raised places like there used to be during their early time together when he'd rub her arms nightly with cocoa butter and kiss her veins, and tell the marks to be gone. He tilted her arm toward the light of the goose-neck lamp just to make sure. He glanced at her but she was looking away, a humiliation falling off her face that made the skin on her face seem to sag. He hated to have to inspect her like that, hated to have to remind her of what she used to be, what she still had the potential to be. But he had to know, he reasoned. He was her protector, after all. But now he was sorry seeing the skin on her face fall, and he pressed his lips against her unblemished vein and kissed and licked at it and told her how much he loved her arms, how much he loved her, now where was she, just tell him where she'd been from this afternoon until midnight.

And now she was crying; not sobbing, but a soft quiet kind of cry. He knew it was because of the way he'd just examined her arm. And her soft tears falling on the arm that he held under the lamp melted him and he pulled her against his chest and covered her up in the robe, and told her that it was okay, wherever she'd been, it was okay. He just had to know. Certainly she must understand that she was the only weakness he had on earth.

Her skin beaded in chill bumps at how he'd just prodded her arm as if she were a patient at a methadone clinic, better that he had asked her to pee in a cup. Her shame at his thumb tracing the familiarity of her veins turned to anger, and now just as quickly as her resolve to be honest with him about how she'd spent her evening with Kitt and Posie and Sage had come, it dissipated, cloistered now in the chill bumps in her skin, and she didn't feel like listening to him rail against her only cousin after all. "I went in town," she said as she sniffed and tried to dry out her voice.

"Until midnight?" he asked, his lips coming up from the space between her shoulder and neck so that he could see her.

"Actually, as it turned out, yes." She sat up and let the edges of his robe fall against the journals. She rarely lied to Rowe. Rarely had to. Occasionally she'd tell him that a suit cost two hundred dollars that actually cost four, or that the mayo in the tuna salad was nonfat when it was actually a hundred percent real grease; she'd lied more by omission than commission often about visiting Kitt by just forgetting to mention it as something she'd done on a given day. But she'd never fabricated an entire scene after the fact as she was getting ready to do, ad-libbing detail along the way. Never looked him straight in the eye as she was doing now, propped on his lap, making her own eyes go innocent and girlish in that downward slant to distract him from her words. She began to feel the manifestation of the lie in her body. Not as a shame, or embarrassment even, but as a ripple building and spreading out like foreplay, an excitement racing through her, softening those chill bumps on her skin to an oily sweat.

She started unbuttoning her blouse. "I had to hunt for the candy eggs for my little ones, you know how special they are to me. From one store to the next I trounced until I found some nice ones already in cute little flowered boxes. And then I couldn't decide on lipstick shades, maybe it was the rain, baby." She put a moan to her voice as she yanked the edges of her blouse from her skirt. "Honestly, I went from Fashion Fair to Clinique to Chanel, everything was too red or too purple or too shiny. How 'bout you go with me Saturday, I just couldn't make up my mind tonight."

"Well, the stores close at nine-thirty," he said, trying not to be distracted as Verdi undid her other sleeve cuff and let the blouse fall from her shoulders.

"Then I got a manicure, don't my nails look good." She played a piano in the air under his reading glasses, grateful that Kitt had taken such care with her nails.

He looked at the buffed, straight-across evenness of her nails, and she felt the prodding of his eyes against her hands and dared him in her head to put those under the light too. "I got them done at Topper's, before you ask, since I feel like I'm being interrogated here." She hadn't meant for her sarcasm to slip through.

"Look, Verdi, I was out of my mind with worry," he said. "You come in here this time of night without any empathy for the torture you put me through, without at least even trying to understand all the wretched places my mind must have gone after nine-thirty came and went."

She fixed her eyes on him again. "I'm sorry," she cooed, "God knows I am."

"I was just out of my mind with worry." He said it with finality, as if to convince himself as much as her. Told her that she would have every right to act as he just had if his history with her had given her cause for such concern. Her eyes were starting to well up again and he could no longer retain his weakness where he held it now, deep in his belly muscles that were sore from him contracting them so. He let his belly go flaccid, unhinged his arms. "My sweet, sweet Verdi," he said as he put his lips to her fingers. Then he took her fingers in his mouth. "Mnh, they do look so good," he said as he made sucking sounds against her fingers. "Everything about you is so good."

She felt his manhood rising against her as she gently urged her fingers from his mouth, pulled her bra straps down one at a time, streaking his spit down her chest as she did. She reached behind to her back to undo the clasps. She stared straight at him as she did, beyond the tip of his nose where his reading glasses still hung, right into his eyes that had that sweaty, starved look. "Well, while I was getting my nails done I heard them saying that the last full-body massage scheduled for nine-thirty had just canceled. And I said what the hell, mnh, you know, baby. I work hard. You do too, you know you should treat yourself to a full-body sometime."

She was purring now as her bra fell and landed on the journals and he grabbed at her chest with his hands, and pulled her down to continue with his lips what he'd just done with his hands.

"And then it took me forever to get a cab, mnh, baby, the cabs are so slow, mnh, so slow around Topper's."

He fought to stay focused. To hear the rest of where she'd been, to pick her words apart for signs of deceit, but her voice was going right in his ear, hot like her breath, and now she was moving against him in slow, hard circles. And now she lifted her skirt up to her waist and straddled herself over him and made the circles faster and more intense until his manhood protruded through the slit in his boxers. She pressed harder against him, and he thought, Topper's, of course, she was just at Topper's getting a manicure and massage, Topper's kept later hours on Wednesdays after all. And in that instant right before he exploded he would have believed her if she'd said she'd just gone to the moon.

And later that night, after they moved from the green velvet chair to the bed and had fallen asleep wrapped up in one another pretzel-style—at least Rowe had fallen asleep—Verdi was wide-awake listening to Rowe's raucous, inconsistent snoring, and thinking about what she'd wear to work, and her agenda for the next day's staff meeting, and how she should handle her backstabbing vice principal, and a new teaching technique she was going to start using with Sage, and the budget projections due to the headmaster, and the exact color of purple and green grasses she wanted for her children's baskets, and damn, wasn't that some good corn bread Kitt had made just like that from scratch; deeply padded between all of those can't-get-to-sleep middle-of-the-night thoughts, when the trifles take the same weight as the grave as they all crowd for space in her head, she untangled herself from Rowe. She kissed his chin because she truly cared for him, owed him so much, owed him her life.

She shifted and yawned and turned her back to Rowe, felt clammy and warm and threw the covers to Rowe's side of the bed, pressed her eyes trying to hurry sleep, but instead felt that dip in her heart that she thought had callused over years ago since Johnson had left Philadelphia, but now, suddenly, pulsed with an intensity and a beat that she thought must be what her aunt Posie felt when she'd break out into a sweat as she described the smell of butter walking alone through the nighttime fog.

Verdi and Johnson were connected from the start the way that the leaf and the root of the same plant are connected. She was accustomed to catching the sun with her welcoming southern ways, the pampered only child of a prosperous preacher and his wife. He was more at home pushing in the dirt, a city boy, clinically depressed mother, father who'd left when Johnson was ten. She was adept at sustaining a blossom, used to being pointed at, look how pretty she is, how smart, how sweet, isn't she sweet. He knew things though, tentacled underground, knew things in a deep way.

She'd met him back in 1971 her first evening on campus where she'd felt isolated and strange all day with her white hall mates, in small but significant ways. She had a single room and they'd knocked on her door incessantly to introduce themselves, said if she felt lonely not having a roommate just yell. And they were friendly enough until one of them asked if she could show her how to iron a pillowcase, and Verdi said she didn't know how, and then she asked Verdi if she could please call her mother surely she must know how. Another one asked her if she could just comb her hair over the third sink, her hair was so thick surely it would repeatedly stop up the drain and that way there would still be open sinks while they waited for a plumber.

So she felt a sense of falling into place as she sifted into the meeting of the Black Students' League. The air was warm and close to her skin as she edged along the wall looking for someplace to sit, or at least stand. There were a minimum of seventy people crammed in here, mostly huge-Afroed; mostly wearing frayed, wrinkled jeans topped with dashikis, or tie-dyed shirts adorned with red, black, and green beaded chokers, or peace signs; T-shirts hollered out from all over the room emblazoned with maps of Africa, or fists pointing skyward, or Huey Newton sitting stalwart in that wicker chair. A few were dressed like Verdi, polite short-sleeved cotton shirts, neatly cuffed denim shorts, pressed hair, tiny post earrings, cheeks still wet with their mothers' kisses. Verdi found a seat on the floor next to a version of herself, they smiled at one another in recognition of their sameness.

The current speaker was just finishing up as Verdi caused a ripple across the row as she settled into her spot on the floor, was just introducing Johnson to give the welcome to the incoming freshmen as Verdi shifted her hips to cross her legs lotus-style.

Johnson took to the front of the room, stood there and waited for Verdi to get still, and was struck by how smooth her knees were. She looked up then, saw him looking at her, felt the entire room focused on her. Her face pulled back in embarrassment but then he let loose a smile, nodded at her and said hello, looked up and took in the entire room. "And hello to you all." He knocked the table three times with his fist. "All of you freshmen will hear such a sound against your door in the next days," he said. "It will be me, or another member of my freshman orientation committee, all sophomores because we're close enough to have not forgotten how it feels to land in a place like this, but we've survived a year and hope you can benefit from what we'll pass on of our experiences."

He began talking in expansive sentences then and Verdi was further riveted by his voice. After she'd been captivated by the way he'd just smiled at her, by his energy, his sense of motion in his thready-cut clothes, even his tall, dense Afro seemed to sway as he did; the asymmetrical tilt to his eyes that were even darker than his skin and made him look simultaneously threatening and tantalizing, as if he were accustomed to keeping people at bay or enrapturing them with his eyes depending on his mood; after all of the visual depictions, it was aural, his voice that affected her now, the baritone of it, the citified bad-boy edge to it, the way he stretched it and filled the room with it now with his intelligent and explosive sentences.

"The BSL isn't just here to throw parties," he said, "though it cannot be denied that we throw one hell of a party." He paused for the laughter and applause, then turned serious. "There is tremendous need for the defragmentation of our voices," he said as he went on to talk about the power black students have when there is a focused, unified approach. "The university can turn a deaf ear to ten of us, but let's see them do it to a hundred, they'll try, but our raised collective voices can and will drown their best attempts at not hearing us, at not responding to our requests that through the university's own subjugation rise up as demands."

"Speak, brother," and "You telling the truth," and "Power to the people" punctuated his sentences and then his phrases and soon the entire room was participating in the rousing back-and-forth rhythm. For fifteen minutes he went on like that without benefit of script or notes, making his points and then building on them, then bridging effortlessly to shaping his next point, rounding it, making that one whole as well. And then as his talk was winding down, he focused right on Verdi again. "Don't feed into the way that they'll look at you that challenges your right to be here, don't contribute to their accumulation of a standard deviation that justifies the choking of financial aid for those who will follow, avail yourselves of all of the resources that will help you to make it. Remember, unfair though it is, inordinate amount of pressure though it may be, it's not just you alone occupying a seat in that chem lab, or Psych I course, or Intro to American Lit lecture, it's your entire race, my brothers and my sisters, it's that ten-year-old playing half ball up in West Philly where I come from, who's already figured out the physics of what happens to a ball in flight when it's cut in half as opposed to how it behaves when it's whole, he's in class with you black people, because if you don't make it, they can justify preventing him from ever having the view of Walnut Street from the inside of one of these buildings over-wrought with ivy, and let me tell you as a Philly native, it's a different view, a pretty damn sweet one too."

Verdi met his gaze when he looked at her, held on to it, surprised herself at the grip with which she held on to it. Though she hadn't opened her mouth when his words called for a verbal affirmation, she went with the tempo, felt her arms bead up in chill bumps as the substance of his words went right to her head and her heart, but it was his voice, the feel of it resounding through the room then pushing through her ears that got under her polite cotton shirt, made her breaths come faster the more he talked, until by the time he was finished she had unfolded her legs from their lotus position, had straightened them and crossed them at the thigh so that she could squeeze herself, hold herself in because she felt a dropping inside of herself like she'd never felt before, as if his voice had gone between her legs and done to her what she'd never allowed the boys from home to do with their fingers.

She wondered then if he was the type her cousin Kitt had warned her about when she'd called Kitt panting and wheezing she was so excited as she told her she'd been accepted to the university, and Kitt went stone silent, and then in a voice that almost slurred it was so low and absent anything that resembled happy asked, why you want to live here? It's okay if you just coming to spend the summer with me, but live, shit, you got the run of the country to choose from for a school, and you coming from Georgia to this city with its sharp-edged corners and cold, no-speaking, eye-rolling women; and jive-talking two-timing men; and racist flat-footed, humped-belly cops; and bigoted low-income whites with their tightly zipped pockets of slums? Here?

Verdi was not deterred though. She'd spent enough alternate summers here to allow her attraction for the place to percolate into a strongly brewed passion so that she was not even the thinnest thread disillusioned when Kitt rushed her with admonitions. The high crime rate around campus, the city slicksters who prey on young girls and boys living away from home for the first time, the tear gas likely to be inhaled during student demonstrations, the no-good men, the filth, please, cousin, go to Spelman, Tuskegee, Fisk, Hampton, please spare yourself the filth of northern, so-called integrated city campus life.

But Verdi came anyhow. Bolstered by her prosperous preacher father who couldn't see beyond the swell of pride that his daughter had gotten accepted into the Ivy League. It was a way to extend his family's reach beyond the familiar and entrenched soil of southern black schools. Isn't this what he'd marched nonviolently for in the last decade, why shouldn't his daughter sample the intellectually liberal leanings of northern whites. Wasn't she a National Merit finalist, top tenth of her class, seven hundred on the verbal portion of the SATs. And wasn't he funding ninety percent of her tuition out of pocket. He'd shut down all protest by his wife Hortense, who'd been frightened by Kitt's late-night phone calls whispering, "Don't let her know I'm calling you, but, Auntie, this is a bad town for a young girl living alone, especially one as naive and trusting as Verdi, don't let her come, Aunt Hortense, please don't let her come." Leroy overruled even Kitt who he knew wanted only the best for their girl. Promised Hortense that whether or not Kitt was there, he'd make sure their baby girl was getting along. He was an office holder with the National Baptist Convention and a sought-after preacher and lecturer so his travels took him to Philadelphia often enough anyhow. Between that and the protective reach of the university over its own, and their fervent implorings to the God they both called a personal friend, Verdi would do fine, he'd calmed his wife in the end. Just fine.

She thought then that Kitt's admonitions had nothing to do with the likes of Johnson when he knocked on her door later that evening, said, "Hello, Verdi from Georgia, my name is Johnson and I just stopped by to say welcome."

Three

JOHNSON PUNCHED THE dashboard in the rented maroon
Grand Am trying to get the radio going, to intercept the up-
holstered quiet inside this car, to blot out the crunch and squeal
of chain-reacting brakes on the outside. Heavy traffic today. It was a
Friday afternoon in Philadelphia, he reminded himself, Philadelphians
drove stupid on Fridays. Even in the 1990s he still knew Philadelphia
after all; born here, died here too in a sense. Had had to leave here
in a jones-induced flourish more than twenty years ago to shed his
skin, to reemerge as he was now, a restored version of his better self.
He was back here this time on business. The advance man for a
Chicago-based Institute for Human Potential that raised funds for
nonprofits. He was the mission maker, a master in fact at recasting,
or even formalizing organizational missions that could yield hundreds

of thousands of dollars for deserving entities willing to write his employer into the contract as an administrative cost. Here it was a from-the-grounds-up program benefiting boys at risk, like he'd been a boy at risk, even though he'd been finger-pointed as a boy with promise.

He jumped at the chance to come back here, live here for the next two months. At least his heart did: he'd be closer to Verdi's cousin Kitt, his true and abiding friend; and Kitt's mother, Posie; and maybe, maybe even Verdi. Foolish to wish for closeness with Verdi he told his heart as he slammed on his brakes and then switched lanes and then cursed because he'd ended up behind a SEPTA bus. Hadn't she refused to spend some time every other time he'd been back he reminded his heart as he turned the radio up loud to drown out the thought that this time it would be different. How could it be? Wasn't she still with him, Rowe, her once college professor who'd swooped in like such a fearless knight to save Verdi from herself, and from him. And hadn't he, Johnson, been responsible for her tasting hell after all.

He sighed and adjusted the volume on the radio and resigned himself to being behind this bus and the fact that he was going to have to bump and grind through this rush-hour traffic all the way back to his City Avenue apartment. A dose of Johnny Hartman blaring through the radio singing "Just the Thought of You" melted down his throat like a cherry-flavored lozenge and took the edge off of his trek through West Philly near where he used to live. He looked beyond the bus to try to picture this corner before this Amoco gas station was here. When it was a three-story apartment building where his dead brother's best friend Bug lived. Dealt drugs. OD'd. Saw himself there on Bug's orange vinyl couch under the Jimi Hendrix poster. Shook the thought. Concentrated instead on the mixer he needed to attend tonight with an association of probation officers. They'd be valuable stake holders, and could attract significant dollars.

Troubled Waters Foundation. That's the name change that had

been swimming around since he'd taken this assignment. Hadn't voiced it to his bosses yet. But he liked the sound of it, so did the woman he'd sipped ginger ale with two nights in a row at the hotel lounge across the street, she'd talked about the possibility for metaphor for whoever had to write the ad copy. He'd tried to explain that it wasn't ad copy, but she was a burned-out copywriter so that's how she thought, she told him.

He pulled into the underground parking lot and took the long way around to get into his building. Turned the key and pushed the door open on his one-bedroom efficiency that smelled of day-old Chinese takeout. He'd complained twice about the cleaning service, they wouldn't do a white boy like this, he muttered. He sat on the side of the bed and picked up the phone and hit the numbers to retrieve his messages. Kitt's voice pushed into his ear.

"Good news bad news, Johnson, baby. Verdi said that she won't see you. Surprise, surprise. But I still want to invite you over for Sage's eighth birthday party. Next Saturday, the day before Easter. No she won't be here. Call me and tell me what you want special for me to cook for you. And Mama said you've avoided her each time you've been back before and if she doesn't see you this time somebody's getting their butt kicked. My words not hers."

He lay across the bed and drew his hand down his face. Had to just accept that it wasn't their season. That's one thing the brutality of his past had taught him. Everything happens right on time no matter how long it takes.

It appeared that everything was happening right on time as Johnson sat at his mother's oppressively sad kitchen in October of 1971 thinking that he'd always had only two options: college or death. At least that's how it had been staged out among his three older brothers. The oldest dead in a metaphoric sense, in jail, the result of running a package for a friend; the package was filled with two ounces of uncut heroin and Johnson's brother refused to name the friend he was running for, where he was running it to. The next oldest brother dead for real, when his helicopter was brought down in the U Minh Forest of the Mekong Delta. The third brother, Thompson, closest to Johnson in age, had navigated the land mines in their West Philly neighborhood and avoided jail, gone to college instead, Cheyney, majored in secondary education and ended up teaching phys ed and coaching the award-winning chess team at Vare Junior High until he fell away and moved to San Diego with his bride and didn't visit often because he couldn't breathe in his mother's sadness.

Johnson followed in that brother's footsteps easily, even as he made his own tracks to surpass him, to do what he could to patch up the shredded lining in his mother's heart that showed so in the creases around her mouth when she tried to smile.

He'd always been certain that he would go to college. Before he was picked out by the guidance counselors at West Philly High to be part of a special program that sent him to enrichment classes at the computer lab at the university, before his soaring SAT scores that had recruiters licking stamps to him from Bucknell to Holy Cross, before every other program for the disadvantaged scrambling in 1971 for lucrative federal matching dollars tried to claim him as their poster boy, the success story, the one raised by a poor single mother in the impoverished, intellectually devoid slums of the city who triumphed after all. He knew he'd go to college much before the helpers swarmed.

He'd always excelled in geometry. Gifted when it came to shapes: naming them; measuring them; positioning them; predicting changes in them over time; determining their functions on a graph, in an equation, a schema, a room. "I'm gonna build you your dream house, Mom," he'd told her after he'd been accepted to the university. "I'm majoring in architecture, and opening my own firm, and then I'm gonna design and build houses for you and all the hardworking beautiful black mothers just like you."

He'd actually been building her houses of sorts since he could remember. Out of wooden building blocks that he'd sneak home, one or two a week from his kindergarten class; out of Popsicle sticks and Elmer's glue in the third grade; out of pinocle cards, a game that he played like a pro from the time he was twelve; out of cut glass and clay, a solar-powered house that had been his science project and took second place in the all-city competition his junior year in high school. And now out of his textbooks as he sat at his mother's kitchen table this Friday evening itching to get back to campus, to Verdi's room, to her cheerful naïveté that so begged for him to teach her things. He piled two books horizontally on top of the spines of two more and asked his mother if she could cut his meat loaf extra thick, and sop it in gravy because there was someone he wanted to share it with.

"Who?" she asked. "Turtle? Rev? Counselor? Moose? Tower? Medic?" She knew them all by their nicknames, these other scholarship students who'd crowd around her table during semester breaks when they couldn't afford traveling fare home and wolf down her good home cooking as if they didn't know when their next meals would come.

Sometimes they didn't, Johnson told her, melting her heart with stories of how this one couldn't buy a ticket to get back to Oakland over Thanksgiving nor could that one who lived outside of Cleveland, and they were going to have to dine with the skid rowers at a soup kitchen on Ridge Avenue because they were out of money. So Johnson's mother, who had a throbbing soft spot for young men, having already lost her second son to the war, insisted that they all come to her house, and even overspent so that she could cook twice the volume and send each young man back to the dorm with mountainous go-plates to tide them over until the university started feeding them again. But after she lost her oldest son to prison, and her third to a new wife and geography, she would sift in and out of depressions that had Johnson stroking and kicking to keep from drowning under the weight of the air in her house.

"So which guy is it?" she asked again. Her voice distant and tired as she talked into the pan she'd just pulled from the oven.

"It's not a guy," Johnson said to his mother's back. He unstacked the books he'd been building and laid them out end to end.

"Not a guy? Then must be a girl," she asked and answered at the same time as she glanced over her shoulder at him and then turned back to spoon continuous clumps of white rice onto a plate.

"Yeah, some girl from Georgia. Verdi's her name," he said as he reassembled the books to bring them to a point.

"Verdi. From Georgia, huh? And she's not cooking for you? You taking food to her?" She laid two thick slabs of meat loaf over the rice and washed the top with brown gravy. "Southern girls learn how to cook early, you know."

"Come on, Mom, she's a freshman," he said as he watched the gravy edge to the crust of the meat loaf and just hang there as if deciding whether or not to fall.

"Well, why haven't you brought her past?"

"No big deal, Mom, she's just a friend." He moved the books around some more as his mother walked the plate to the table and just stood there looking down at him. He didn't return the look; didn't want to. He knew that her expression would be a fatigued hurt, as if even her sadness was tired of being sad, the skin under her eyes thick and sacky, her mouth turned in an upside-down U, set, like a plaster-of-paris mold. He couldn't remember when she'd lost her beauty, her ability to take over a room with her smile. But sometimes lately he'd look at her and her face would be so sallow, so drained of faith and hope and the robustness that used to make her brown face so inviting to gaze upon. Sometimes her despair was so exposed and magnified on her face that even in his manhood it frightened him and he'd want to run and hide himself in the pleats of her skirt the way he did when he was a child. He guessed she'd have that effect on him now so he rested his head on his arm and fiddled with the books.

She set the plate down on the table. Waited for him to look at her as she watched him playing with the books, shuffling them one way then another. Sighed then to the top of his head when he still didn't look up at her. "She must be a big deal seeing as how you bring all of your other friends past. Especially when they're hungry." She yawned as she went back to the stove. "I'll put the string beans in a separate dish, a good-size dish," she said, "that way I can load her up on them, nothing beats hunger like some fresh string beans in a cornstarch-thickened base the way I do mine."

"She's not exactly what you would call hungry, Mom," he said, struggling to keep from getting defensive about not bringing Verdi by. It was true, he had ushered all of his friends in and out of his mother's house since he'd been at the university, her house just a ten-minute bus ride from campus, a half-hour walk if they were quarterless. Even the ones from money he'd not hesitated to show the modest house where he was raised; he reminded himself of that now, bolstering himself so that he wouldn't have to admit to the unforgivable in his mind, being embarrassed about his mother when it came to Verdi. Now he looked at his mother's back as she stirred around in the pot of string beans. She had a pink crocheted sweater over her shoulders, the silver beads that held her glasses around her neck peeked unevenly through the top of the sweater's open-weave stitch. Her black-and-gray hairline was tapered in an oval and a few strands hung longer than the others and poked against the sweater's yarn. At least her back was easier on his eyes; the pink sweater made her appear soft and young.

"Well, why am I sending her half of my good meat loaf if she's not hungry?" she asked, reaching for her slotted spoon from the Maxwell House coffee can she used as a utensil holder.

" 'Cause I'm always bragging about the culinary skills of my dear, sweet mom." He tried to make his voice go light to deflect the heaviness sighing in the air. "And she's always talking about her cousin who lives somewhere in West Philly too, and we just have this silly bet, you know, I told her that my sweet generous mom could probably cook her cousin under the table any day of the week."

"Well, I just hope she's nice," she said as she spooned string beans into a bowl.

"What's nice got to do with meat loaf, Mom?"

"Can you see to it that I get my good dishes back, please, she's a rich girl from Georgia, I know she'll appreciate that this is good china."

"Who said she's rich? And don't switch subjects on me, Mom. I'm talking about food and you're asking me if she's nice and now you've even decided that she's rich. How in the world do you make those leaps?"

"Well, for starters you just sat there and formed and re-formed those books a half a dozen times and you keep coming back to the letter *V*. Secondly, you keeping your face from me like you got something to hide. I agree, don't have a thing to do with meat loaf. But it does have everything to do with being known by the company you keep, so like I already said, I just hope she's nice. And as for the rich part, I can just tell. Am I right?"

"She's nice, Mom; she's very, very nice."

"And rich?" Her arm hung in midair between the pot and the bowl as she waited for him to answer.

"I think her people have a little money, yeah." He didn't know why a lump came up in his throat when he said it. As if he'd betrayed his mother somehow, or why the air in the kitchen was bearing so heavily on him he felt a tightness in chest as if the air was getting ready to close in on him and cause him to suffocate. He thought about just leaving the plates, just running through the house and out of the front door so that he could breathe, so that he could have respite from his mother's hurting wrinkled face that he couldn't do a thing about. He couldn't be the son she buried in the ground, nor the one she buried in her heart; couldn't be the man who walked out on her; and right now, being her last-born child, a shining sophomore at the university espousing all that being young, gifted, and black entailed, right now being who he was, Johnson, wasn't enough.

She set the bowl of string beans on the table next to the plate of meat loaf and rice. The skin on her hands was still smooth and tight the way he'd always remembered her hands, efficient as she tore off plastic wrap and covered the plate and then the bowl.

"I first thought you might stay and have some dinner with me, but since this is a girl, from Georgia, that you taking this to, I won't put any pressure on you."

"No, I'll stay, Mom." His voice was pleading. "Come on and take us both up plates to eat now, I'll stay." She'd always had a gift for doing this, getting him to beg to do something for her that he really didn't want to. Like now. More than anywhere right now he wanted to be in Verdi's dorm room sharing the meat loaf and rice with her. Had even picked up a dime bag of joint to introduce her to. Had Isaac Hayes and Otis Redding albums packed and waiting on the chair by the front door. Had two fresh condoms tucked into the seam of his wallet. Had hopes for this Friday night with Verdi that after they went to a BSL and faculty advisers–sponsored party at the high-rise and then tipped back to her dorm room buzzing from wine and cheese, she might let him all the way into her moistness. So close, so very close they'd come the weekend before, and the one before that; and before that even. The past five weekends he'd spent Friday night at her dorm, easy to do because she had a single room so no roommate to displace. They'd even come to be known as a couple around campus. But instead of grabbing the food up, his albums, his sadness, and scurrying like a squirrel at snow's approach running, running to catch the D bus that would zoom him down Chestnut Street and into Verdi's presence, he was pasted in the kitchen chair, begging his mother to let him have dinner with her.

"No, no, you get on back to school, now, I insist. How you gonna keep you and hers food hot if you sitting up here having dinner with me?"

"They have toaster ovens in the lounge."

She ignored him, though she was grateful for the gesture, really. But she truly didn't want to burden him more than he was already burdened being her youngest son. What could she share with him right now save her grief that was welling up in the corners of her eyes. "Let me get you a couple of bags," she said, walking quickly to the shed kitchen so she could turn her eyes away from him.

"Mom," he said again, drawing the word out in a long breath that wanted to cry. "Come on, please, let's have dinner together."

"No, you go on, now. Not tonight," she called from the shed kitchen. "We'll have dinner together another night."

"Why not? What? Do you have plans or something?" he asked, hoping that she did, that maybe she had reconnected with friends she used to have, or met a man, or joined a church, a Bible study group. He thought about the oversized black leather Bible that Verdi kept on her desk. He suddenly wished that his mother had forced him to go to church when he was growing up. Then at least he'd have something to offer her right now, he could tell her to pray for the return of a little joy. Verdi was always talking about praying for this and for that as if praying was something she did as easily as breathe.

"I'll double these bags over so the juice doesn't leak through," his mother said as she walked back into the kitchen. "You sure don't want your clothes smelling like string-bean juice and you're on your way to see some rich girl from Georgia."

"Verdi, her name's Verdi, Mom."

"I'm sorry, son, I didn't mean to disrespect her by not calling her by name. I know those southerners are big on respect." She pushed one bag into the other and stood it up on the table. "How you planning on carrying all this plus your books on the D bus."

"I'll manage, even though I want you to know that I could be carrying half the amount of food if you'd let me eat my dinner right now, here with you."

"Hand me that plate here, please." She talked right over him. "Maybe I should use two separate bags," she said as she sized up the food on the table as if this was the most crucial decision she'd ever have to make.

He passed her the plate and she lowered it into the bag and then followed with the bowl of string beans. "Okay, this works out fine," she said as she rolled the top of the bag down. "Just try to support the bottom as best you can."

He didn't say anything, just looked down at the bag. He could feel his mother's eyes on him, it was warm in here. Wasn't she unbearably hot in that sweater? he wondered. Then he met her gaze, her eyes were moist and the moistness was spreading out and getting lost in the thick folded skin around her eyes. He grabbed her to him, then.

Squeezed the tops of her arms and then circled all of her against his chest, whispered, "Thanks, Mom, for the meal. Love you."

He could feel her head nodding against his chest. Now she was pushing him away telling him to go, telling him to go right this minute while the D bus was still running with regularity. Telling him to support the bottom of the bag and don't forget his books. Telling him to work hard. Telling him to say hello for her to Tower and Turtle and Medic and the rest. And the girl from Georgia. "Verdi. Tell her your mother sends her regards too."

Johnson had not planned on such a lengthy stay at his mother's kitchen table this Friday evening and now he was late getting to Verdi's dorm room to accompany her to the party in the roof-top lounge of the high-rise dorm where the black students and their faculty advisers were supposed to connect. He'd just made it to the corner of Chestnut Street to see the D bus rolling by, yelled and ran behind it to no avail somewhat slowed down by the heavy bags he carried. He cursed and waited on the solitary corner and tried to scatter the image stuck in his mind right now of his mother in that house all alone where the air was heavy and still. It was dark out already and that made the scene in his mother's kitchen even more cheerlessly fixed in his mind so he decided to keep moving, move his body and his mind would have to become unfixed and follow, he reasoned.

He walked the three blocks quickly down and over to Market Street to catch the el. Had to argue with the cashier to get him to accept his transfer; the transfer actually being from the day before but often the fare takers didn't care enough to check. This one did check and Johnson was severely agitated because the man was a brother and violating the unspoken practice that unless one was a severe Uncle Tom, a brother always let another brother slide in such a harmless case as this. Johnson held his agitation at bay so that he wouldn't blow up and instead was able to offer up a tearjerker of a story that begged for violins about being a broke university student trying to get back to campus. True though it was, especially now that his father was on a new wife and pleading poverty, had barely advanced Johnson money for books, Johnson heightened the melodrama so there would be a hint of doubt. Even though this was the early seventies and the rejection of material excess was often a lauded and fashionable trait, and even though he wore his poverty around his neck as if it were his heavy silver-toned peace medallion, he was sometimes deeply embarrassed by how lacking were his financial resources, particularly surrounded by the relative opulence of the university. He reminded himself to check where he was on the waiting list for a minimum-wage-paying work-study job, if nothing was forthcoming in the immediate short term he'd be forced to look off-campus where an employer wouldn't be as sensitive to a student's time constraints, he made a mental list of places to apply as the el jerked him back and forth and carried him swiftly to within a short walk of Verdi's dorm.

More fast talking to do to the security on the front desk at Verdi's dorm who at first wouldn't let him through because whoever had answered the phone on Verdi's hall said she wasn't responding to their door knocks. He tried Cheryl, the sister who lived upstairs from Verdi, whenever Verdi wasn't in her own room he usually found her there. Not tonight. Went through the list of the few black students who he knew lived in this dorm, no answers from them either. He finally reached a white girl he knew fairly well because she'd been active in black causes, she okayed Johnson up and he went straight to Verdi's room and found a note on the door telling him that she'd tried to wait but had decided to walk on over to the high-rise dorm with her history professor and his wife who'd had dinner in her dining hall as part of a University Life–sponsored student-faculty mixer. He went into the lounge and left his bag with books and crammed his mother's meat loaf and string beans into the tiny refrigerator, thought about it, pulled a Hi-Liter pen from his bag and wrote on the food bag in huge block letters DO NOT TOUCH IF YOU LOVE TO LIVE.

He got to the high-rise dorm and more security to go through where he had to leave his matric card at the front desk to gain entrance to the party that was in the roof-top lounge. This party was already in high gear, he could see that as he stepped off of the elevator and angled himself through the double glass doors. Though the food was sparse, a little celery and dip, cheese and crackers, deviled eggs, the drink cascaded bountifully as the faculty advisers went blind to the bottles of wine being quickly emptied from the cases stacked neatly under the skirted table. The lights were dim and the walls were sweating and all sizes of Afros nodded and bobbed as intelligent brown bodies swayed and bounced to War and Sly and the Temptations in a Mellow Mood. They were loose and laughing with abandon in the way that people do when they've spent all week fighting to be seen as more than a special case, a slot, aid recipient, the product of a partnership with the city, state, feds. At least that was how Johnson felt most of the time; for all of his rhetoric about not allowing the racist tactics to make them have a diminished view of themselves, he often did.

Johnson squinted through the dimness trying to find Verdi; stopped every few steps to do the elaborate Black Handshake with "his boys," and to give the ladies a peck on the cheek. He was well known here, respected as a Philly man, tough and intellectually gifted, worked hard, partied hard, got in the faces of people who offended him, but always fair. Never flung on his hard-core, urban-boy street attitude unless it was absolutely necessary—and never did at all to people from New York City.

"You seen that pretty Georgia freshman?" he asked Tower, the six-four basketball player from the boonies in upstate Pennsylvania."

"Yeah, yeah, man, I did." He laughed and slapped Johnson's hand. "Fucking real, man, over there at that other end of the room, or the middle of the room, or some fucking where." He laughed again, this time doubled over he laughed so hard.

"Hey, man, what you been doing?" Johnson asked, his face halfway between serious and amused.

Tower leaned down and whispered in Johnson's ear, "A little of this, a little of that."

"Little of what, man, wine, weed, speed, what?"

"Just a little killer smoke, man. From my little killer pipe."

"Well, you keep it a little, you country bastard. And you make sure you know what you getting and who you getting it from." He reached up and shook Tower's shoulders. "You with me, man."

"Lighten the fuck up, Johnson my brother man. And then maybe you should light the fuck up your damn self so you can shut the fuck up." More bent-over laughter. "In case if you didn't notice, there's a party going on in here and shit."

Johnson slapped Tower's palm. "Solid, man," he said. "Advice well taken, except I hope I don't get as silly as your wasted, country ass." He was getting ready to ask him who'd he copped from anyhow, but right then he spotted Verdi and he surprised himself at the surge he got when he finally saw her face.

She was bubbling over with laughter like everybody in this roof-top lounge seemed to be laughing. Standing between her history professor and his wife, her solid softness molded into tight black jeans, thick leather belt with an oversized silver peace-sign buckle cinched in her waist, white cotton shirt added dimension to her slightly formed top and gave her a wholesome crispness so contradicted by the seductive fit of the jeans that it was exciting to him right now. Verdi was saying something to the wife that made her throw her head back and show the fillings in her molars; the professor smiling at Verdi as if she were his protégée and she'd just done something to make him very proud. Johnson got a tinge of an emotion that he couldn't define watching the professor watching Verdi so, at first he thought it was jealously, but he shook that off as ridiculous and settled on that maybe it was Verdi's ability to captivate these two. How seamless was Verdi's interaction with them right now, like matching patches of silk stitched end to end with a delicate thread. Johnson felt like the odd patch right now as he walked toward them, like flax, or burlap; corrugated with an itchy roughness, and poor. Until Verdi looked his way, and their gazes met, and her eyebrows arched as if to say, Johnson, is that you? And even in the darkened room he could see her face opening up for him, her smile going beyond the gracious and polite shared with the professor and his wife. This smile for him right now was effusive, her healthy lips stretched all the way from earlobe to earlobe, her downwardly slanted eyes almost closed she grinned so. He felt his chest swell when she smiled at him like that. He was dignified right now. A worthy man. An honest man. A weakened man right now because he knew for sure that he was a man falling in love.

She waved him over, called out his name, laughing as she did. "Hi, Johnson, 'bout time you showed up."

"Now, you know I was going to show up," he said as he entered their circle. He pulled her gently, loosely in his arms and kissed her cheek, then extended his hand first to the wife then to the professor.

"So this is the Johnson you've been telling us about?" the wife asked. "So nice to finally meet you." She nodded approvingly at

Johnson and he caught a glint in her eye that told him that she was sincere enough. Plus her attire, a tan suede western-style vest with fringes topping bell-bottom jeans topping more tan suede on the boots, also fringed, gave her a casual air that didn't smack of the I-am-a-professor-and-I-control-your-fate image being cast around by her husband right now who was excessively tweeded down from sport coat to button-down vest to pants.

He told her how much he liked her vest and she shook her head, thank you, said she'd picked it up down at Sansom Village. "I just love the revolutionary energy in that place. Don't you?" she asked.

The professor cleared his throat then, threw his head back and drained the sherbet and 7UP punch. "Well, speaking of revolutionary energy," he said, clearing his throat again and reaching his tweeded arm between Johnson and Verdi to toss his cup in the trash can that was beginning to overflow, and then moving all the way between them to mash the cup solidly in. "It seems as if you've given this freshman some bad advice."

"That's debatable, Rowe." The wife cut him off.

"Anything's debatable, Penda," he said, his jaw muscles shifted, and he made a sound that was somewhere between a sniffle and a snort, as if an unpleasant aroma had just wafted by.

"Later, please, Rowe," Penda said as she tried to lock eyes with Rowe and Johnson could tell that she wasn't the type of woman who was likely to just roll over in public to spare an argument with her mate.

Rowe didn't look at Penda though, didn't look anywhere in particular, just looked out into the room as if he were about to begin lecturing to an auditorium filled with eager, terrified freshmen who'd heard how demanding he was. His voice was pointed, as if it were his finger going right to Johnson's chest. "All of this, this business we've been hearing from Verdi about the white professors at this institution wanting to pick somebody's brain, is nonsense, just nonsense," he said.

Verdi looked at Johnson apologetically. "I was just saying to Rowe and Penda," Verdi rushed her words, "when they asked me if I'd gotten to know any of my professors that I was honestly a little hesitant of letting them pick my brain, which led me to tell them about the conversation we'd had about that, you remember, don't you, Johnson?" She held Johnson's gaze as she spoke, which he took to mean that she hadn't quoted him in a negative way.

Johnson did remember, knew exactly what Verdi was talking about. He had warned her that the white professors often wanted to get inside of the heads of the black students, as if they were at the university not as students trying to get a degree like everybody else, but as guinea pigs, research subjects, a valuable source of data, and since the university was footing the bill for many of them anyhow, they should be willing to give back in this way. He'd insisted to Verdi that she shouldn't feel obligated to put out a whole lot of excess effort helping them to understand her, or by extension all black people everywhere, that she didn't owe anybody shit.

"I'm inclined to agree with your wife, Professor." Johnson looked at Penda and smiled when he said it. "It is debatable."

"Let me give you my perspective, young man," Rowe said, this time he did look at Johnson, his tone more conciliatory. "Not engaging professors in meaningful dialogue because one is afraid that one's brain might be picked is a practice that borders on being a negligent student. One passes up the opportunity to get a greater insight into the teaching community here at the university, and also, quite frankly, a shot at a better grade."

"Uh, well, Professor, I guess you would have had to have been privy to the entire conversation, you know, before and after we got to that part in order to get the full gist of what I meant."

Rowe didn't answer. He just looked away and scanned the room and moved his shoulders slightly to the beat of the music and smiled as if he suddenly realized that he was enjoying himself.

"Hey, you missed my cousin, Kitt," Verdi said brightly. "I wanted you to meet her, but she couldn't stay. I've been trying to get her down on campus for the longest and when she does come she only stays for ten minutes."

Rowe cleared his throat again. "Probably uncomfortable."

"Oh Rowe, that's not true," from Penda, agitation clouding her voice. "That young woman didn't seem uncomfortable in the least."

"I'm willing to bet that she was," Rowe said mildly, trying but not really trying to hide the disdain running through his voice. "How would you feel on a set like this, some of the best and brightest young black people on the planet gathered in this room, and you're from one of Philadelphia's rougher neighborhoods with no real aspirations to be part of this set in the first place, now you can't tell me you aren't going to experience a level of discomfort. Look at you, and you." He motioned first to Johnson, then to Verdi, kept his eyes on Verdi then. "You're in a different league, a very select league, and it's unfortunate, but you're on a track where often people can't follow you, even someone as close as your cousin seems to be to you in an emotional way."

Verdi didn't know whether to be flattered or insulted, Johnson could tell by the confusion trekking across her forehead. "Well." Johnson reached across Rowe and touched Verdi's elbow, her cotton shirt was soft and stiff at the same time and more than anything right now he wanted to feel all of her against him. "Uh, that's a provocative notion, I guess. Definitely more grist for the debating team, I guess. But if you'll both excuse me, it's a Friday night and this is a party." He emphasized "is." "And I came to dance, so how 'bout it Lady V."

He led Verdi away from the wall where his self-restraint had just gotten a good workout farther into the center of the room that had become the dance floor. "Hey, hey," he shouted playfully as he inched between the throngs of moving arms and shoulders and hips. "Can't a brother get some place on the floor to get a groove on with this sweet, sweet freshman from Georgia?"

Verdi blushed and her cheekbones went so round he just wanted to pull her close and kiss one then the other.

"Awl, Johnson, if you want some room now you got to take it," someone called from the center of the circle.

"Dig it," from farther along the edge, "isn't that what he's always telling us when he gets his James Brown thing going, talking 'bout don't nobody give him a thing, just open the damned door and he'll get it his damned self."

The room exploded in laughter and they did make room for Johnson and Verdi but the fast song was over and now the Temptations were singing "With These Hands I Will Cling to You." And Johnson realized that this was his first slow dance with Verdi. They both realized it simultaneously, it seemed, and they went stiff and just stood there giggling nervously. And she put one hand out and he reached for the opposite then she extended her other hand and he reached for the first. And they laughed some more then he took both her hands in his and they swayed to the beat and only their hands touched and their eyes and that's how they danced their first slow dance together, almost two feet apart.

When the song was over he squeezed her hands, said, "Thank you, pretty freshman from Georgia. That has got to be the most unusual and by far the most satisfying slow dance I have ever taken part in."

She blushed through her cheeks again and this time he did lean in and kiss her right on her fleshy lips; it wasn't a long kiss but definitely intense and then they just stood there communicating with one another with their eyes and he didn't even have to ask her if she was ready to leave as he covered her hand in his and led her away from the dance floor in the center of the room. And if people said anything more to him as they headed for the double glass doors, he didn't know it. Didn't stop to do another black handshake or lightly kiss another young lady on the cheek. And though he did want to turn around and look back in the direction of the professor and his wife, see if the professor was watching them—watching Verdi really—he didn't. Just squeezed Verdi's hand harder inside of his and led her; he so loved—so needed—to lead her and rightly sensed that she thrilled in his being her guide. And he knew this for sure tonight, that Verdi was his for tonight, and he was hers and whatever she wanted, if he could, he'd do.

Johnson was surprised at how easily, how quickly Verdi came. He'd never been with a virgin, even his first time when he was in high school was with a woman four years his senior whose flat tire he'd changed late one night when he was walking home from a party. She was so grateful that he'd come along and rescued her on that deserted stretch that she offered him a ride to wherever he wished, plus a half-hour detour through the park where she'd more fully expressed her gratitude by drowning him in her experience. After that episode there had only been two others, one had been a grade-school crush who was rebounding from a relationship with a running-around football player and used Johnson to take out her revenge. He didn't mind being exploited in that way; he was eighteen and perpetually aroused and though this was the seventies the sexual revolution hadn't made an impression on the girls he knew. His only other conquest had been nicknamed Scamp, and he'd felt sorry for her and spent time with her only to give her some relief from the brutish treatment she'd become accustomed to from the more low-life neighborhood thugs. At least that's what he'd told himself the summer between freshman and sophomore year when they'd do it standing up in the alley behind her house where ivy grew wild and curtained them. He was glad that none of his couplings prior to Verdi were virgins because of the low-level emotional attachment. He'd heard often enough what an arduous time it could be when it was the first time for the girl; that they'd cry and bleed and just want to be held.

Not Verdi. Though she'd started off shyly enough, squeezing his hand and giggling the four-block walk from the party in the high-rise back to her dorm, blushed each one of the half a dozen times when he turned her face to his and gave her an openmouthed kiss and said that he just needed momentary relief from the October chill and her lips were like a furnace. She giggled some more when they got to her room and as soon as she closed the door he had her all up against the wall breathing double time as he whispered how badly he needed her, that she filled spaces in him that he never even knew were lacking; that she had gotten inside of his head, put a spell on his mind, that he was emotionally ensnared and all he did anymore was think about her, that he didn't throw the love word around lightly, "But damn, baby," he said as he started undoing the buttons on her soft and stiff white cotton blouse, "did I forget to tell you that I'm falling in love. Verdi Mae, I'm falling in love with you."

She got really innocent then; blushed and looked away as he undressed her, didn't want him to see all of her at once, even coughed nervously and sighed out a "I'm so fat," as he clumsily attempted to peel off her tight black jeans. But then she caught his face; it was so unconnected at that moment, as if he couldn't control his mouth that was drooping to his chest, and his eyes that were threatening to bulge from their orbits, even his nose that she loved because it was such a strong nose, defiant, was flaring uncontrollably. He looked so shamelessly vulnerable, so starved as if he was about to break out into a pant. And seeing that her bareness was affecting him so gave her confidence that began as a dot glowing from her center and then spreading out in ripples and then waves until they were both standing on top of their clothes, lips and fingers finding each other's pulsations, their passion lifting them up and tossing them all over the blue-and-white-flowered bedspread that had been handpicked by her mother to match the rug.

And they got a rhythm going then, a back-and-forth that he was sure must have been the primal rhythm before there was music, or sound, or the universe. And she thought a similar thing. And he didn't know how much longer he could hold out as they kept tasting each other's mouths. He was just going to have to burst, he told himself, didn't even know if his condom could contain it, it would likely be so profuse. But right then it happened for her; felt as if her center had shattered into a burst of iron filings so that there was no longer a rhythm, just chaotic spasms as the iron filings shimmered throughout her being, from her toes to her scalp to her soul, and she cried out then. "Mercy Jesus," she cried. And at first he thought that he was hurting her so he eased up until she mashed her heels into the tops of his thighs and then he exploded and cried out too.

Her shyness returned afterward. As they lay facing each other on the dorm-sized single bed tingling all over and limp, she pulled the blue-flowered sheet that matched the bedspread up around her shoulders. He breathed out a laugh at that move and when she asked him what was funny he didn't tell her that she'd just worked him like he'd never been worked before, hollered and squeezed and held on as if her *raison d'être* was to bring a man to unsurpassable ecstasy, and now she was covering herself up like a timid neophyte. He didn't try to explain that it was the contraries of her nature that attracted him so, the tight black jeans and demure white shirt, her unbridled self and then covering with the sheet, that she was both virgin and harlot, and such a surprise package that he just wanted to be with her all the time to see what other sides she could show. He didn't say any of this. Just kissed her nose, traced the outline of her lips with his tongue, then got under the blue-flowered sheet too and they kissed and touched until they were both pulsing all over again, and got back to that rhythm that was primal and loud.

They were famished after the second time and Verdi asked if there was a chance that Ronnie's Sandwich Shop might be open, said that she'd take the half-a-mile walk up there with him right now if it meant that she'd be able to devour a big fat juicy cheese steak with sweet peppers and fried onions and ketchup.

"No need, baby," Johnson said as he jumped up and pranced across the room to where he'd kicked off his jeans. "I've got a surprise that I'm going to whip on you right now and the timing couldn't be better."

Verdi marveled at how comfortable he seemed with his nakedness as he slowly unrolled the condom that hung like a sac filled with heavy cream. He took his time as he balled it up in a Kleenex and then wiped himself meticulously. She'd never seen a man's naked front before and now she was staring so that she would be able to describe it to Kitt who, when she asked what did he look like—as she was bound to do—wouldn't be referring to his face. She hoped Kitt wouldn't be angry, she thought as she tried to memorize all the ridges and textures of Johnson's manhood; she had promised her that she would take her time. "Always make a man wait a year," Kitt had insisted over and over since they were thirteen. "That way you can tell whether it's real love or bullshitting horny." This may have been horny but it certainly wasn't bullshit, she smiled contentedly to herself as she watched Johnson step into his jeans and heist them up in what seemed like slow motion. This was love, she wanted to sing right now, wanted to jump out of the bed and dance around the room the way her aunt Posie used to, wanted to stare at his manhood forever.

"Hey, what you looking at, baby?" he asked softly as he noticed her staring. "You looking at Andy, huh?" he said as he walked toward her, his jeans wide open.

"Andy?" She laughed and blushed and looked away. "Come on now, Johnson, you can't be telling me that you actually have a name for—for—um—for—"

"For my penis?"

"Yeah, for your penis." She was propped on one elbow and when the sheet fell and exposed her breasts she held back the impulse to cover herself again.

" 'Course I do, got to know what to call him when I'm trying to talk him into behaving." He jiggled it around playfully. "You know, when I see your face in a crowd, ol' Andy gets all riled up, and I have to tell him, 'Hold on, now, Andy, calm down, just calm down.' And hell, don't let my eyes even begin to fall on your beautiful behind." He sat on the side of the bed, leaned over, and squeezed her butt. "Then I have to leave the room so I can yell at him you know, 'Andy, sit your rebellious ass down right now.' Then he embarrasses me, starts pouting so the whole world can see he don't know how to behave."

Verdi laughed hysterically and he savored the sight of her right now. Though he wanted to touch her some more, to feel her unrestraint drip between his fingers, he wanted more to watch her, sprawled back on the bed, the sheet kicked almost completely off she laughed so hard, her brown-on-gold skin glistening with muted perspiration, her hair out of the barrette and standing every which way and making her appear wild and tameless, almost erotic.

He did watch her until her laughter settled down to a cough and a sigh and a smile. And she reminded him then about the surprise.

"Oh yeah, shit," he said as he got up and zipped his jeans. "I guarantee that you'll love them both."

She turned into a little girl then, wrapped herself up in the flowered sheet and looked like a Roman goddess at a toga party as she jumped up and down on the bed, begging excitedly, "Tell me, let me see, come on, Johnson, tell me, let me see."

"Okay, give me a minute, baby, just get comfortable." He laughed as he pulled his undershirt hurriedly on. "I'll just give you two hints, one of the surprises is stuffed in the fridge in the lounge. And the other, aha, my little pretty, the other one is tucked inside the concealed pocket of my safari jacket."

He ran out of the room and took a quick detour into the men's side of the dorm to use the bathroom, used the toilet, scrubbed his hands, sang out loud as he worked up a lather that he must be falling in love. He laughed and did a two-step out of the bathroom, bumped into a white boy on his way in. "Yo, sorry, man," he said, still singing and dancing back down the hall into the lounge. The lounge was chilly, a marked lowering in the degrees, he thought as he smiled to himself at how warm Verdi's room was right now, how burning up that sturdy twin bed. "Bed's damn sure sturdy," he said to the chilly lounge air as he whistled and pulled the double-bagged food from the refrigerator. He found baking tins under the sink, a small pot to go on top of the stove, really more a one-burner hot plate than a stove, but it would do for the string beans he thought as he turned the electric burner to high. He whistled louder as he assembled utensils, a knife to cut the meat loaf, a spoon for the rest, two forks for them to eat with. He stuffed the meat loaf and rice and gravy into the baking tins and got them warming in the toaster oven; filled the pot with half of the string beans and set it over the glowing circles of electric heat. He rubbed his hands together and blew into them and warmed them over the pot that started to bubble almost immediately. He stirred around in the pot and suddenly felt his mother's sadness billow through the lounge and take over. He swallowed hard. "Not now!" he said to the lounge air. "Not here, not now. Shit! Damn! When do I get a chance to be happy?"

He headed back to Verdi's room, loaded down with the food, saw Verdi's next-door neighbor going in her room hugged up with the white boy he'd just seen in the bathroom. "Hey, Johnson, let me get that for you," she said as she turned the knob to Verdi's room. He just nodded, couldn't say thank you trying so hard to hold the lump in the way he had been holding it in since he'd said Verdi's name to the back of his mother's pink crocheted sweater, and then later when he exposed his poverty to the el cashier, the way he had held it in at the roof-top lounge party when he was struck by how easily Verdi fit in with the professor and his wife, and even as he and the professor sparred academic phrases. And now when he should be the most ebullient, having just consummated his love in a divine way with the woman that would have been his dream woman had he ever given himself over to dreaming, at the point when he should be running across the campus shouting through a megaphone that he was in love, so much in love, with a sweet southern miss named Verdi Mae. He was fighting to restrain this lump in his throat that he thought was his mother's sadness. He was all the way in the room now, Verdi wasn't here, and he put the food on the desk and now he realized standing in this empty room that this wasn't his mother's sadness he was feeling, it was his own.

Happy-go-lucky, gregarious as he appeared on the exterior, he'd always had a side to him that was so lonely—even before he lost his brothers—so absent anything that looked like joy, that he sometimes worried that he'd be consumed and taken over by this forlorn self.

But he'd always been able to distract himself: his studies, his BSL activities, a bottle of wine and a good party, always moving, had to be doing something, or on his way to doing something. But tonight he was in love. And with this sadness that was threatening to drizzle down his face right now as he plopped on Verdi's bed, was an enveloping fear that his dispirited self might destroy his round at happiness, and in the process, destroy him. And Verdi too.

He sat down on the bed and shook convulsively at the very thought. He mashed his head in his hands and cried like he hadn't cried since he was a little boy and stood at the radiator and looked out the front window and watched his father load his suitcases into the generous trunk of his brand new '58 Chrysler. That's how he felt right now, like a little boy, and so abandoned.

He got himself together, then. The pepper-and-onion aromas wafting from the smoke rising off the food on the desk helped. He started talking to himself, telling himself that it would be okay, his mother, he and Verdi, his brother doing time. Everything that he cared about this night would all be okay he told himself over and over as he started taking up the food from the tins and stacking it on his mother's brown-and-white-printed china plate.

He heard Verdi's voice floating down the hall, heard her laughing, saying yes I've got company, I hear you do too. I won't tell if you don't. He wiped at his eyes trying to think of something funny to say so that he could laugh right away and distract her from his eyes. He hoped they weren't wet looking or swollen. Maybe he'd return to his Andy jokes, yeah, he thought, feeling better as he remembered how hysterical Verdi had gotten over Andy.

She looked almost angelic walking through the door, wrapped up in a pink quilted, satin-collared robe, her hair repulled back into the barrette, her face freshly washed with a dab of Noxema dotted over a pimple on her chin.

"Okay, what you got for me," she said as she hung her washcloth and towel on the bar outside of her closet.

He stood in the middle of the floor. "Drumroll, please."

She smiled broadly and hit against her thighs in fast succession.

"Thank you, my lady," he said as he bowed and extended his outstretched arm toward the desk. "May I present to you my mother's very own world-famous meat loaf with rice and gravy and string beans."

She jumped up and cheered and put her fingers to her mouth and attempted to whistle. "Bring it on, sir." She preened, at the thought that this was her man and he was about to serve her up a meal. "Hungry as I am right now, bring it all on."

He inched the desk out some, held back the chair, and bowed again offering her the seat.

"Ooh, ooh, we need candles," she said as she went to her desk, rummaged through the bottom drawer, and came up with two pink tapers and two crystal candleholders. She held them up and he looked at her, them, in amazement.

"My mother is so proper," she said as she put them all on the desk and went to the other end of the room and into the closet. "She insisted that I bring these in case I needed to entertain." She emerged from the closet with cloth napkins. She stuck the candles in the crystal holders and lit one then the other.

He dragged the other chair over for himself and positioned his mother's good china dish between them. "You don't mind if we eat from the same plate, do you, Verdi?" His voice went soft and uncertain when he asked it.

"I don't mind if we eat from the same fork," she said, and then clapped her hands together and said, "Okay, napkins in our laps." She smoothed a napkin over her pink quilted robe. "If my mother walked in here right now and smelled the scent of our natures, you know what she'd do, she'd put her gloved hands on her hips and she'd snap at me, 'Verdi Mae, how dare you begin a meal without saying grace and affixing your napkin in your lap?' "

Johnson smiled and covered her hand with his. "Why don't you, um, say it, baby."

"Say what, cutie pie?" She reached over and pinched his cheek.

"Um, you know, a prayer, I mean, um, grace." He took the other cloth napkin from the desk and put it in his lap. He didn't know if it was that this napkin was so heavy, or if that's just how cloth napkins felt.

She bowed her head and said a quick grace, then took a fork and dove into the meat loaf.

"Oh my goodness," she blurted as she closed her eyes and tilted her head and allowed a dreamy smile to take over her face. "This is so good. I mean this is so good." She took another forkful, and another, chirping in between about how delicious it was, how divine, how damn good, how she already loved his mother just by her food, how she loved him, told him that at least half a dozen times as she plowed through the bowl of food, taking two forkfuls to his one, stopping every so often to dab at her lips with the napkin, to look at him and smile a soft smile through the candle flame dancing from its orange-and-yellow center with a hint of blue. She looked like an angel to him sitting there in the pink quilted robe. So unspoiled. He felt himself getting filled up again as he put his fork down and just sat back and watched her eat.

Four

ITT CREAMED HER fingers for the new back she was about to do. A licensed pratical nurse by training, she'd scaled down to part-time years ago so that she could be there when Sage got home from school. Replaced the lost income by doling out massages from the mauve-colored room off of her kitchen. Business was good though, thanks to her regular clients, mostly cops from the eighteenth district, and she really only held on to her LPN job at the Care Pavilion Nursing Home for the health insurance and retirement benefits.

This was her last back for the day and she thought that when she was finished she would call Verdi and see how she'd made out getting home so late last night. Kitt was maternal toward Verdi, even though they were both the same age, forty; both only children born to fraternal-twin sisters, Posie and Hortense, who, fortunate for the cousins, had passed down their good looks: their unstoppable cheekbones and fleshy ear-to-ear grins, brown-over-gold complexions, downwardly slanted eyes. Fortunate too that the cousins didn't inherit their mothers' relationship that had gone to tin years ago when they parted ways over a man, when Hortense ran away to Atlanta with the smart, upwardly mobile young divinity student that Posie said had first had eyes for her. Posie stayed in Philadelphia and married down, often, each husband filled with more promise and less resources than the one before, and even though Posie's men made up for in passion and excitement what they lacked in bank balances, she blamed Hortense each time one of her men went bad, said it was Hortense's conniving ways that had snagged the one who would have been a keeper in her life. But Verdi and Kitt filled in the canyon of sisterly affection their mothers left and managed to spend summers and extended holidays together through all of their growing-up years thanks to the Greyhound bus. And Kitt fussed over Verdi, instructing her as if Verdi's moneyed upbringing in the cultured mannered traditions of the Georgia black middle class had detracted years from her chronological age and left her too soft around the edges to fend for herself, while Kitt believed that her own raising that happened in the financially varied neighborhood of West Philadelphia added onto her years and turned her into a wise woman even in her youth. An old soul, Kitt called herself.

Right now Kitt promised herself that she wouldn't say anything more to Verdi about Johnson being back than she'd already said at dinner last night. She'd decided to just go ahead and set up a meeting between them and not even say anything beforehand, decided to use Sage's birthday party as the venue. That's the other reason she needed to call Verdi, to tell her about Sage's party, if she could ever get to the phone, since she was starting much later than she'd planned on this new back.

Usually when she came into the massage room on the other side of her kitchen, they were already face down in the chair or on the table, depending on whether they were getting a neck-and-back or a full-body, but usually they were her regulars, this one had been referred by one of her regular cops from Pine Street. He wasn't a cop, an accountant, or middle-management something at the university. Had tried to stand there and take off his blue-and-white-striped heavily starched shirt right in front of her. She never watched them take off their shirts, too personal a thing to do. But when she started to turn around and leave the room, he'd called her name, said, "Miss Kitt, where did you say I should hang my shirt?"

She came all the way into the room and closed the door and showed him the hanger and hook on the back of the door. He was doused in some unisex cologne that smelled sweet and musky and she reached into the deep pockets of her soft pink jacket for her cigarette lighter and set it on the table next to her vanilla-scented candle.

He was out of his shirt now, his undershirt too, and hung both on the hook without using the hanger and she was left staring at his buckskin-colored-shade-of-brown chest. She looked down, focused on his shoes, nice leather oxfords with a hand-stitched look to them.

She looked quickly past his chest to get to his face, saw how big his pupils were, like silver dollars just dipped in pitch tar as he stood there waiting for her directions. She dismissed the eyes, didn't want to acknowledge that he was affected by her, that could really skew a session. She cleared her throat, said, "I'll help you into the chair since this is your first time; next time, if there is a next time, when I come in here, this is how I'd like to find you."

"Whatever you say, Miss Kitt." He half laughed as he unconsciously (seemingly) stroked the hairs on his chest. "I mean, you come so highly recommended, I've been told that your massages put a man in the mood for some nighttime frivolity."

She took a deep breath, then let the room go completely still. She pointed to the certificate hanging over the specially designed massaging chair made for kneeling onto with a foam-backed face rest at the top of the chair. In a low, even tone she said, "Sir, I'm not at all concerned with what you or anybody else does before or after you take up time and space in my room. My massages are the result of an associate's degree worth of training and are completely by the book. I hope we understand each other."

His face got all sheepish then and he apologized, said he'd meant no disrespect. She softened; he looked so drawn around the mouth, tired.

She pointed to the knee rests and guided him by the elbow to help him get into position in the chair. "Comfortable?" she asked after she manipulated the foam inside of the face rest so that it wasn't pressing too tightly against his skin. She leaned down to say it in his ear. "Because this face rest adjusts if you're not."

He shook his head, yes.

She mashed a button on the boom box resting on a shelf above her head. "I'm just turning on a little jazz on RTI. If that doesn't suit you, I can pop in a tape, or if you'd rather no music, that's fine too. Just let me know."

The back of his head nodded in agreement.

"I don't usually talk during the session, most just like to go with the music and what I'm doing to the muscles in their back. But if you got something on your mind, I can listen." She turned the dimmer switch down and the mauve-colored walls in this room took on a muted brownish tone. She lit the vanilla-scented candle and waved at the flame to get the scent moving through the room. She flexed her fingers one more time, squirted cream in dime-sized puddles at various points from his shoulders to his waist. She leaned then with her whole body into this wide, thick back.

He released a whispered ooh as she started at his neck. She mashed with her whole weight into her thumbs and dragged them down the length of his frame on either side of his spine. His oohs got louder the harder she pressed and she could feel the muscles in his back expanding, stretching out in response to her fingers. She needed that. Needed to know that what she was doing felt good. She'd always thought backs rendered more grief than any other body part. If you had time to dwell on someone's back, she reasoned, they were in the process of walking away from you, leaving. Hadn't she seen her mother cry over the sight of countless backs, shirted, bare, broad, humped, wide, with varying degrees of spine? Hadn't she cried over one? So what she did with the backs seemingly to generate income, she also did to mitigate her rage at the sight of them. She could either rub them down, or hack them with a carver. On this she was definite, there was no middle ground.

She breathed in deeply through her nose. The vanilla radiating from the candle swam to her head and she felt a giddiness descend as Sarah Vaughan blared "Misty" through the radio. This one's oohs had graduated to oh Gods and she added her other fingers to her thumbs, and at certain points mashed with the heel of her palm. She closed her eyes so that she could really palpate this back and even absorb its electrical charge. Some backs were like that; they just opened for her at every possible hairline crevice, allowing her to send her touch to radiate even beyond the bones, and in gratitude the muscles offered up their own impulses that entered through her fingertips and rushed to her brain and affected her like endorphins flying around in a runner's head. She was buzzing now as she squeezed and pressed and kneaded and hacked and went deeper and deeper and now she couldn't even tell where her fingers ended and this back began, so fused were the two. And this session was everything it should be, the way she wished they all could be. And when it got to this point, she was no longer starved and afraid at the same time for the companionship of a man, lonely; and her beautiful daughter Sage was no longer mute and could speak fluent sentences like any other seven-year-old. And his sighs of Lord, Lord, oh my Lord filled the room and even flooded out the sound of Sarah's voice, and now she lived in a center city town house that was better even than Verdi's house, and she'd been born to Verdi's sagacious mother Hortense who knew how to do more for a man than keep him stirred up in her pheromonal thickness the way that her own mother Posie did all of the men she loved. Have them half-crazed over her, ready to dispense with whatever they did in their practical lives and kick her door down to get to her until she saturated them in her brand of womanhood that oozed like liquid silk. And once they'd had their fill of her, after a month, two, three, rarely more than a year, they'd disengage from her shaking their heads, asking themselves what had come over them to have them laying up so. Kitt hated that about her mother, that she always allowed them to be the ones doing the leaving. Her aunt Hortense, on the other hand, knew how to make the man do the pleasing, at least she'd done it with Verdi's father, had him pastoring one of the poshest congregations in Georgia, and at the same time treating her as if she were a queen. Kitt always figured that if the story about Posie and Verdi's father, Leroy, even had any truth to it, that it was better that he'd favored Hortense in the end, that Posie wouldn't have known what to do with the likes of a Leroy anyhow.

But even that didn't matter, her hands were so on fire as she pushed into this back, as if she'd pummeled all the way through to some other side and was up to her elbows, covered in his buckskin-colored-shade-of-brown back. But right then she felt a change in the air behind her diluting the charge this one was sending to her brain, the creak of the door opening, turned, and there Posie was.

Kitt grimaced when she looked at Posie standing there, head tilted to the side like a five-year-old, baby blue eye shadow swathed over her generous lids, frosted mocha lipstick like the kind a prom queen would have worn in 1968, hair way too long for a woman her age, hips too rounded, too pronounced, pushing from under her waist-cinching belt.

She stretched her mouth wide, told Posie to get out without allowing a sound to come from her mouth. She didn't want to have to stop now, especially since this was his first time; she knew that once she stopped, she could never pick up and get it to be as good as it was where she'd left off. She jabbed her finger in the air, pointing beyond Posie; Posie just stood there with her head tilted, her expression midway between delight and confusion. Kitt scowled at Posie as she kept her other hand moving in wide circles against this back, and then, to her great relief she saw Sage approach the door, walking on her tippy toes, pulling her grandmother by the arm, her finger against her mouth. Gingerly pushing the door all the way closed. My God, Kitt thought, and they say Sage is the one with the limited brain, they never met Mama that's for sure.

"Everything okay?" this one asked.

She tapped his back to let him know that it was.

"My God, you're good," he whispered between his moans of satisfaction. "Damn."

She squeezed his neck in response.

"Shit, I want to marry you, and after my last wife I swore I'd never do anything as emotionally destabilizing as promising to live in relative harmony with anything that raises as much hell as a black woman."

She slapped his back then, it was almost a playful slap and she surprised herself that she felt the need to giggle. What did he say his name was? Bruce. That was it. He looked like a Bruce in the face with his poppy eyes and bulldog nose. Cute though. She did remember that she liked the way his face rounded out when he'd fixed it to apologize. She stopped her thinking. Prided herself on the detachment she maintained with all of her clients. She could quickly kill her business if she ever let a session turn into something it wasn't by viewing a client as anything more than a back, by allowing her thoughts about a man to ooze through her fingertips. She returned to using her thumbs. Her thumbs were toughened from years of lifting hot pans without an oven mitt.

"Married?" he asked.

She stiffened at the question. She didn't answer though, didn't tell him that she'd been married once to the father of her daughter but that he had a roaming eye and unfortunately the bulge in his pants tried to keep up with his eye; she just kept working the base of his neck with her thumbs.

"That's right, you said you don't talk, sorry." He sighed, then added, "Damn, I've apologized twice in a very short time frame, anybody that makes me do that ought to at least let me take them out to dinner."

She still didn't answer. She'd been come onto less in the past year than she had even when she was round with Sage in her womb. She thought it had something to do with twisting her hair into locks that the unenlightened still associated with MOVE or Jamaican Rastahs. No matter, her locks certainly weeded out the bullshitting men.

His voice was muffled and low pushing through the face rest and that took some of the charge out of his words and made them easier for her to ignore. Anyhow, she had a firm do-not-date policy when it came to these backs. And now this one's time was up. She did one more sweep of his back in wide circles. Worked the pressure points in his scalp for thirty seconds. Whispered that he could take his time putting his shirt on as she snuffed the vanilla-scented candle. She left the light on dim, then closed the door on the room off of the kitchen and went to wash her hands and come out of her jacket and give Posie hell for barging in on her like that.

POSIE WAS squeezed up with Sage in Kitt's newly reupholstered wing chair that sat at a slant at the living-room window. She rubbed her hand up and down Sage's back. "Uh-oh, baby, your grandmama's just in a little trouble."

Kitt let go an exasperated sigh. "Mama, please, how can you be in trouble with me, I'm the daughter, you're the mother, remember."

"Oh, I just said that to joke with Sage, but you are upset with me. I mean, look in the mirror and see how your veins are popping."

"You darn right I'm upset." Kitt cut her off, snapped at the air in a hushed tone, and then quietly spit her words back at Posie. "How many times have I told you that you can't just come and barge in here on me when I'm working. I mean it takes time to set a mood, this was his first time and I depend on repeaters, furthermore I don't even talk, and here you come ready to start blabbering all loud about a bunch of nothing probably having to do with your latest gigolo—"

She stopped herself. If not for the hurt look coming up on Posie's face then surely for the way Sage stared at her not even blinking.

Posie lifted one of Sage's soft and thick wheat-colored braids, studied the braid so that she didn't have to look at Kitt. "Mama's sorry, darling," she said to Sage's hair. "I was so caught up in what I wanted to tell you, I completely forgot you were working. You know I wouldn't hurt your livelihood for anything in the world."

Sage reached up and put her arm around her grandmother's neck and patted the back of her neck.

"Shit," Kitt said under her breath. "Shit, damn, shit." Not only did her mother make her feel as if she'd just tied her to a railroad track whenever she corrected some inappropriately immature thing she did, now her daughter was staring at her as if she'd just shot an arrow through Posie's heart.

But right then Bruce reemerged into the living room, remnants of the vanilla scent still hanging to him, and she had to swallow what was left of her outburst, even as she watched Posie wriggling her hips and struggling to sit up on the edge of her seat, and pulling her stomach in so that her chest protruded just so.

Kitt turned her back on her mother. "I'll look to hear from you should you like to schedule another appointment," she said as she started leading him quickly toward the door to the enclosed porch, ignoring Posie who was clearing her throat in the most audible tones. But then she couldn't ignore Posie when she yelled out, "Kitt, doll, aren't you going to introduce us?" She sighed and stopped and rolled her eyes.

Bruce turned around and bowed slightly and smiled.

"Uh, Bruce, this is my mother, Posie, and my daughter, Sage," Kitt said, trying not to let her agitation slip out in her tone.

"Police officer?" Posie asked as she stood and extended her hand.

"No, Mama. He works at the university."

"Teach there?" Posie was all smiles, and even laughing between her words when she noticed his wedding-band finger was bare, had been bare, skin tone nice and even going up and down the entire finger.

"No, uh, I work in development; may I call you Posie?"

"Well, if you don't I'm just going to hit you, I am." She slapped his arm playfully. "I hope you enjoyed my daughter's massage. She's the best, I want you to know that."

Kitt rolled her eyes in her head. Bad enough when she thought Posie was coming onto the man for herself, now she was realizing that this embarrassing scene was on her, Kitt's, behalf.

"I agree, Posie," Bruce said as he held on to Posie's hand. "I already proposed, but she wouldn't talk to me."

"Now, Bruce." Posie preened and let her eyelashes go into a flutter. "That's only because she was working. Tell him, Kitt, you talk, can't stop talking once you get going good on a subject you like, cooking for instance, now, Bruce, my daughter can sure 'nuff cook, can outcook me any day of the week, tell him, Kitt."

Kitt didn't answer.

"I mean even my grandbaby loves her mama's cooking and my Sage is one picky eater, don't you, baby?" Posie tickled Sage in the small of her back. "We're just so proud of our darling, Sage." She poked Sage, propelling her. "Show your mama how much you love her cooking."

Sage ran to Kitt then and grabbed her around the waist and burrowed her head in her stomach, and as sometimes happened, Sage caught her mother off guard and Kitt lost her footing and they both would have landed on the floor except that Bruce was standing right there, arms opened like a wide receiver, so that Kitt ended up pressed against his heavily starched blue-and-white-striped shirt inhaling his unisex cologne with remnants of vanilla mixed in.

Posie stood back now, satisfied at the scene going on in the middle of Kitt's living room. Kitt struggling to get her balance, Bruce pulling her off of her center so that she'd have to lean on him, Sage holding on to her mother, which amounted to pushing her even more against Bruce. Go 'head and push, Sage, Posie thought it so intensely that it was more a prayer than a thought. Because she reasoned that her daughter needed a man in her life so badly right now that Posie could taste the need herself and her own mouth would get dry and she'd roll her tongue around and get ready to find herself something soft and wet to quench her thirst until she remembered that she had a man, always someone coming and going in her world even at the age she was, that what she was feeling was just a sympathy dry mouth for her daughter's needs. Just wasn't natural to swear off men the way Kitt had done, probably why she was fixated on putting Verdi and Johnson back together, confusing her own nature with Verdi's. And this one who Kitt was peeling herself from now, and apologizing to, and saying Sage is just sooo demonstrative sometimes, this one Posie could see had some nice arms under that blue-and-white-striped shirt, the best arms: strong, unmarried, holding-down-a-good-job kind of arms.

She was so filled with anticipatory excitement over this desirable potential of a mate for Kitt, she forgot all about what she'd wanted to tell her when she'd barged in on Kitt's session. That Johnson had called. Asked that Kitt please call him first chance she got. She braced herself for the telling-off she was about to get as Kitt walked back in from the enclosed porch and Posie ran and grabbed Sage and fixed her eyes on Kitt to go wide and sad with a pleading to them. And Kitt just stood there and stared at her mother with that look that said that she couldn't decide whether Posie was a blessing or a curse.

Kitt just shook her head and said, "Mama, you are just so pitiful."

"I just can't help myself, Kitt." Posie rushed her words and made a steeple of hands and pressed them to her mouth and whispered, "Forgive your mama for being the way she is."

Then Kitt looked at her watch, told Posie it was almost time for her breathing treatment. Then focused on Sage, tried to hold a stern face when she looked at her and said that before she took her grand-mother's side again she should remember who feeds her.

SAGE BARRELED for her mother, arms outstretched, mouth wide open as if she were about to take flight. Undaunted. Many things were still a puzzle to her, especially why her thoughts melted into the bumps on her tongue no matter how hard she tried to make them stand up and march through her lips into words, but this one thing she knew for sure, the fiery glow around her mother when she set eyes her way, a warming blaze of colors that leaped and danced and chased off the cold, steely things like silvers and icy blues. She saw her mother's love as a flame, felt it too as she pressed her head into the soft heat of Kitt's stomach and closed her eyes tightly and allowed her mother's glow to surround them both, all yellow and orange with a hint of brown and red. Posie joined in the hug and Kitt put her arm around her mother too, even as Posie's hair that Kitt thought was way too long for a woman her age rubbed against her face, it was so soft against her face.

———

Kitt was the first to notice a change in Verdi that fall of '71. Noticed it in the profound dearth of her contacts. Noticed that she and Posie had been eased out to the periphery. Knew that it was unlike Verdi to go for so long without calling and begging for Kitt to come visit her, or inviting herself over for a meal, or just calling and sighing into the phone, trusting that Kitt would be able to interpret the sighs and say something that would give her relief. But Verdi wasn't calling and even when Kitt would call her and try to entice her over with mouthwatering descriptions of the pot of this or that she had working with Verdi's name on it, Verdi declined, begging it off on all the booking she had to do. Kitt had even taken to sending covered plates down to Verdi's dorm via Posie's latest man. Felt as if the reasons for her dread over Verdi coming to school here were blooming to fruition, that Verdi would shut her out, defer to her charm-school upbringing, and begin to see Kitt as an embarrassment, a practical nurse with a basic high-school diploma in home economics who had never even been presented at a debutantes' ball. She could have accepted the ouster from someplace far, had Verdi enrolled in a school in the south, but from right in the same city, almost down the street only two miles away, was too close, so close that just the thought was breaking Kitt's heart.

"I wonder why we haven't heard from Verdi Mae," Kitt had been saying to Posie almost every day for the past month, unable to disguise the hurt in her voice. But in what Kitt considered a rare bout of wisdom coming from her mother, Posie had cautioned Kitt that once Verdi became entrenched in university life it might feel as if they were losing her for a while, that Verdi was in fact embarking on a lifestyle that they didn't, couldn't know. That they had to allow her space and time and not make her feel as if she had to choose campus or them, that Kitt and Verdi would always be close as sisters, but for right now Kitt had to let Verdi be.

And Kitt had let Verdi be. Never mailed the letter she penned telling Verdi to just forget they were blood if she insisted on ignoring her so; didn't demand otherwise when Verdi's floor mates kept Kitt holding on the phone for five, ten minutes at a time only to return saying that Verdi couldn't come to the phone right now; refused to go down to that campus even, especially after the gathering in the high-rise dorm when she'd suffered through fifteen minutes of Verdi's history professor eyeing her up and down with a discernible upper-crust disdain. Kitt had decided that socializing with her cousin would have to happen on her home court so that she could have the advantage of familiarity.

But now she discarded that resolution. Decided about seven one Friday evening that she could no longer stand the torture of waiting to hear from Verdi. That she'd have to examine her in the flesh herself and allow Verdi's eyes to tell her what she thought the dearth of contact already had told her, that Verdi no longer wanted Kitt in her life. "Tomorrow morning," Kitt told Posie, "I don't care what you say, Mama, I'm getting on that D bus and going to check up on our girl." But then she remembered that she didn't have anything to wear, remembered how incongruous she'd felt at that gathering in the high-rise when she'd worn one of her pleated kilt skirts from high school, one of Posie's low-cut ruffled blouses. Moaned as she piled her bed high with her closet's offerings of doesn't-matter-what-they-look-like clothes because she wore a uniform to work, the rest were clothes for wearing to church, an occasional sequined number for being dragged to a cabaret in when Posie got it in her mind every so often to help Kitt find a boyfriend.

Posie sauntered in and out of Kitt's now disheveled bedroom every fifteen minutes or so offering her oversized pearls, or tight mohair sweaters, or rhinestone-studded belts. And after a string of "no," "no thank you, mama," "no way you've got to be crazy if you think I'm wearing that, Mama," Kitt tried to explain to the confused look in Posie's doe eyes that she needed something collegiate looking. "You know, kind of hippieish, but toned down."

And then Posie sighed and said that if she really thought that it was that important, even though personally she thought that Kitt could show up in a burlap wrap and Verdi would still be thrilled to see her, but if it would make her feel not so sad about herself, she should just have to hop on the el and try to catch Lit Brothers before they closed. And Kitt said that she didn't have that much money, that she had put most of her paycheck in the bank. And Posie left the room and came back then and pressed three twenties in her hand, told her to hurry so that she would make the store. And when Kitt asked if Posie's boyfriend the limo driver could give her a fast ride up there, Posie lowered her head and flashed a smile that vacillated between embarrassed and naughty, said, "Mama got to keep him here with me, baby. You know, got to give him a proper thank-you for those twenties he was so generous and easy about giving up."

"Mama," Kitt dragged the word out, "why you put yourself in that position on my account?"

Posie fingered Kitt's collar, moved her hand down to let it rest over Kitt's heart. "I really do feel it here, baby. What I'm doing is not so bad long as I feel it here. Mama hopes one day you'll understand what I'm saying, then maybe you won't think so poorly of me."

Kitt couldn't respond. Was too filled with the mix of pride and disdain that her mother's actions aroused in her, her ability to melt her and harden her at the same time. She wanted to hug Posie for her motives, slap her for her deeds. Settled on a quick peck on the check but no verbal thank-you as she rushed out of the house to catch the store.

She shivered at the bus stop on her way to Sixty-ninth Street and wondered what college must feel like, to have your smartness constantly reinforced by being surrounded with ivy and books and the right to protest the war. Kitt thought herself to be smart, though in a different way from Verdi. Thought it was a shame that there wasn't a campus for people like her, gifted when it came to knowing how to survive. Thought that she'd surely have gone to a major university had she been born to Verdi's mother, Hortense. So gathered up Hortense was in her mind; like a vase of show roses—Hortense had vision, knew the paths to take where the best blooms were, knew to carry her shears for snipping them off. Tried to instill some of that vision in Kitt when it was her turn to spend summers in the south. Would pull her aside maybe at night when Verdi was asleep, would whisper, "Aunt Hortense would love to see you learn the piano, or take a ballet class, or go to Paris, or wear white lacy gloves, would pay for it myself but your mama's so hard-hearted when it comes to me, we're fortunate she lets us have you every other summer." She'd go on then to give Kitt instruction on men, how necessary it is to train a man how to treat you, she'd tell Kitt, and how to spot the ones who weren't even worth the instruction. "A man who doesn't melt over you like hot wax, so that you can remold him into what he needs to be, will bring you nothing but frustration," she'd insist. "Like a man who walks on the inside and allows you to walk next to the curb is never worth your time," she'd insist as she stressed to Kitt over and over the importance of always keeping her head even if her emotions were in a spin. "That's your mama's problem," she'd say. "Poor thing just loses her head over and over again. You got a good head, Kitt. I see in you what I don't even see in the one I birthed, promise Aunt Hortense you'll always keep your head." Kitt so valued her private time with her aunt, wished that her aunt Hortense had been her mother instead, would daydream about it even, until Posie's breathing condition scared her so, filled her with guilt that it was her wishing that had caused it, banished those fantasies about being raised by Hortense to the deepest pouches in her mind, except that every now and then she opened the pouch just a sliver; she did right now, just for a minute or two, as she made it into Lit Brothers with twenty minutes to spare.

She found her way to the department where *Jesus Christ Superstar* was pumping through the speakers. Hurriedly selected a tan suede jacket with fringes and a pair of bell-bottomed jeans with an American flag seared on the knees. Walked through the shoe department on her way out of the store and tried on a pair of tan suede boots, also fringed, they fit like skin and she bought those too, even though the salesman was flirting overtly, asking for her number, telling her how her beautiful legs really made the boots. And she tiredly told him unless he was giving the boots away to please stop, that she didn't believe in playing and paying. She tried not to think about her mother as she counted the change, probably upstairs wiping her bedroom walls with the limo driver right now.

She was nervous the next morning as she sat at a booth in the back of a restaurant just up the street from Verdi's dorm. Had called Verdi and told her to get her butt over there right that instant so that she could look her over and make sure that some evil campus witch hadn't cursed her and made her grow two heads or some such thing long as it had been since she'd heard from her. That she'd promised Aunt Hortense she'd look out for her. "So come on, right here, right now," she'd demanded.

She'd listened for signs of disappointment in Verdi's voice when she'd shouted, "Kitt, oh my gosh, you're here, right up the street, sit tight please, I'll be right there." Had to admit that she'd heard only a shocked gladness. Was relieved, really.

And now she sipped her coffee and took small nibbles from buttered toast iced with Concord-grape jelly. Then she heard a throat clearing, followed by that familiar giggle filled with naïveté that would make Kitt want to rush in and protect, and Kitt looked up and there Verdi stood, groggy, half hung over after another night of stretching her parameters with Johnson, but obviously excited to see Kitt. And Kitt took one look at her, sleep flaking from the corners of her eyes, hastily put-on tam covering her uncombed hair, face naked of lipstick or blush, and saw not just her cousin, but this beautiful woman, all grown up and beaming, as if the heavens had just opened and spilled light all around her as she grinned down at the booth where Kitt sat sporting her new suede jacket.

"Lord have mercy," Kitt said, shaking her head slowly, letting the toast drop into the saucer as she studied Verdi down to her sockless feet, who right now couldn't keep her teeth behind her lips, nor stop the reddish tinge from pulsing beneath her brown-over-gold skin. "You're all messed up in the head."

"Huh?" Verdi said, unable to contain a stream of giggles.

"In love, girl. Strung out, nose wide open, heart on your sleeve, feet off the ground, head in the sky, infatuated, probably sex-saturated. How else can I say it. You are seriously, dangerously, not-keeping-your-head in love."

"I am, Kitt." Verdi squeezed into the booth next to her and banged the table and threw her head back and laughed. "I am, I am, Lord help me because I am. I am. I am. I don't even know what to do with myself, you know it's like I'm in a perpetual dreamy state. I wake up, I go to class, I eat, I study, I go to bed at night, and his presence, whether or not he's with me, you know his presence is with me, prominently, he's just on my mind and all I really want to do is just be with him." She took a sip of Kitt's coffee, a bite from the toast, and spit crumbs out as she talked so fast and excitedly. "He's so, he's different, Kitt. Not corny like the boys back home, you know, not all materialistic. He's got substance, you know he's into the BSL. Not hardly the type of man Mama would choose for me, or even you." She stopped then and looked at Kitt, as if prior to now she'd just been talking to the bacon-scented air in this restaurant that felt cozy and safe because it was nearly empty, being before noon on a Saturday and rarely did students start flowing in until one or two. And Kitt's face was guarded like she'd never seen it before, as if she had to defend her face from some hurt that was threatening to shadow it, and she realized then how she'd been shutting Kitt out, barely returning her calls or dialing her number unprompted to say hello, to ask how her aunt Posie was, to invite herself over for a meal, or even to thank her for the hot plates she'd send down by Posie's man a couple of times a month. She felt herself getting filled up at the thought of how long it had been since she had unburdened herself to Kitt. Nowhere else had she experienced the type of honesty and trust that she'd known with Kitt and now it was affecting her because she'd been so distracted since she'd been at the university, worse than that even, she'd been stingy, miserly, with her attention when it came to

Kitt of all people, the one whose generosity toward the people she cared about had always been amazingly boundless.

"Kitt, Kitt, I really want you to meet him, you know," Verdi said as she coughed and took another sip of Kitt's coffee to untighten her throat. "I hope you'll love him because that's important to me. And I'm sorry I haven't called, honest." She stopped and swallowed and tried not to cry. "It's just that my time, my focus, I'm—I'm just so scared because I feel like I'm not in control, you know, like is this something I shouldn't even be doing, and yet I can't stop myself. I just want him, you know what I mean? I just want to be with him, I'm just so, I'm so wide open and it's so scary. It is. And on top of everything I miss Mama and Daddy and Aunt Posie, and you, I especially miss you." Now she was crying. "I didn't even know how much I've missed you until right now." She covered her face with her hands and then fell into Kitt's arms.

Kitt just listened and then patted the hiccups that came up in Verdi's back as she sobbed. She didn't nudge her away even though Verdi was raining on her new collegiate-looking jacket, the one that she'd hoped would keep her from embarrassing Verdi in front of her Ivy League friends, keep her from showing up looking like her uneducated cousin from the slums. She rubbed circles in Verdi's back thinking how relieved she was now that she had popped up on Verdi unannounced to see for herself. Now she could concede that Posie had been right. It wasn't that Verdi had become so enthralled with the university after all, it wasn't that she no longer felt enamored of Kitt and Posie, it wasn't that she looked down on them, or was embarrassed by them. She was simply, wildly in love.

"What you do, girl, get drunk last night?" Kitt asked finally as she continued to sweep Verdi's back in wide circles. "You know that cheap fruity wine you college students drink will make you cry when you should be laughing, laugh when you should be crying. Have you praising the devil and cursing the Lord and trying to figure out which is which between your ass and a hole in the ground." She felt Verdi strangling against her as her sobbing tried to turn to giggles and then back to sobs. "See what I tell you. You don't know what to feel, and once you figure that out, you don't know how to act appropriate to what you feeling."

Verdi lifted her head and rubbed her eyes. "You're right, Kitt, I don't know how to act, but it's not from wine, it's from everything being so new, you know living on my own, making my own decisions, I mean there's so much freedom here, no curfew, you know, the dorm rules such as they are aren't enforced, I mean it's a coed dorm as it is and there are, you know, couples who actually live together right in the open. You know, there was some comfort in all the structure Mama put on me; and she's not here to tell me what to do, what to wear, who my friends should or shouldn't be, even though I have good friends, one sister, Cheryl from Texas, lives upstairs from me, we're close, and actually, Barb, the white girl who lives next door to me, is very cool, we've actually hung out—" She stopped midsentence as she fingered the collar of Kitt's jacket. "My goodness, Kitt," she said, her voice going up a full octave, "this is a really nice jacket, I mean really nice, you must have caught some sale because I know you don't believe in spending money on clothes. And look, I cried all over it," she whined as she picked up a napkin and dabbed at the wet parts. "And it's a good suede too, why you let me do that?"

"It's just a jacket." Kitt brushed off the compliment, embarrassed now that she'd gone to such an extreme as rushing out to buy a new jacket just to venture down on campus, as if such a gesture had even been necessary with Verdi. She pushed Verdi's hand away. "Well, don't go getting all comfortable about being so much on your own," she said to redirect the conversation. "I talked to Aunt Hortense this morning; she called from the airport; she's on her way to campus right now. Probably be waiting for you in the lobby when you get back."

"Huh!" Verdi gasped and shrieked at the same time.

"Gotcha," Kitt said. Now she threw her head back and laughed. "I wish I had my Polaroid to snap that horrified look that just came up on your face." She gasped and coughed. The laughter felt good even as it choked her. Meant her chest was opening up. "What? That Negro's probably laying up in your bed right now, isn't he?"

Verdi fell heavily against the booth and let out a loud relieved breath. "Damn, Kitt, you ready to give me heart failure. I was thinking I was gonna have to call Barb or Cheryl, tell them to knock on my door—"

"So he is up there, isn't he? Don't lie to me, girl, or I'll tell on you. You know you can't lie straight anyhow."

Verdi blushed and hunched her shoulders and looked at Kitt undereyed and then couldn't contain the smile that took over her face. "Oh-oh, Kitt, why don't you come up and meet him right now, come on, I really want you to."

"Girl, please." Kitt drew the "please" out to three syllables and took a gulp of coffee. "What are you talking about, you're talking crazy. Shucks, If I want to see some half-sleep man who's spent the better part of the night getting his rocks off , all I have to do is go back home and walk in my mama's bedroom."

They both laughed and then Verdi got quiet, serious, fingered the fringes on Kitt's jacket. "You know, I really understand what Aunt Posie was experiencing when I used to spend summers there and she was in one of her enraptured states and floating instead of walking, sighing instead of breathing, just agreeing absentmindedly to everything we wanted."

Kitt rolled her eyes up in her head, said she sure as hell hoped Verdi wasn't turning into Posie. "I mean a really great love should come only once or twice in life, maybe three times to a die-hard romantic, but not over and over and over again like it does with Mama." They both grabbed for the coffee cup at the same time and Kitt told Verdi to go on and finish it since she'd already slobbered and cried in it anyhow. "And order me a fresh cup," she said as she swirled a crust of toast around in the dish of jelly. "And if you really want me to meet this man that's got you laughing and crying at the same time," she said, "go get him. I'll wait right here. We all three can have a proper get-acquainted breakfast. He can treat." She saw Verdi's face dent in and out when she said the part about him treating. She realized then that he couldn't treat. That Verdi had come all the way from Atlanta on her parents' good graces and money to one of the most prestigious schools in the country and fallen head over heels in love with a poor boy. Aunt Hortense will just shit over this, she thought as Verdi drained the coffee cup and then jumped up saying that they'd be right back. "But my mama," Kitt said out loud as she watched Verdi's back go through the restaurant door. "My poor misdirected, overly hormoned, melodramatic mama will be so very proud."

Kitt and Johnson did take a liking to each other. As Kitt watched Verdi and Johnson float into her view through the restaurant's storefront windows, and after she took note to make sure Johnson walked on the outside and protected Verdi from the curb, and then saw them almost saunter through the restaurant door hand in hand, she appreciated Johnson's scuffed-up leather jacket, his faded sweatshirt where the U emblazoned on the chest had washed out from red to almost brown, and though she could tell that he had the potential to drag one foot behind him and stroll like a jitterbug as he stepped aside to let Verdi walk first through the narrow aisle toward the booth where she sat, his walk right now was straight, tall, respectful with a tenu-ousness about it like his face was tenuous; his face handsome though in an asymmetrical way, with his long chin made longer by his goatee and mustache and slightly off-centered nose, and his dark eyes that were dashing this way and that, moving through the restaurant, she could tell, looking to find her.

Johnson was struck by Kitt's pleasing features as well, knew immediately that was her even before Verdi stretched out her arm from Kitt to him and back again as if she were presenting royalty, could tell by the stark resemblance between Verdi and Kitt. Both with those deeply etched cheekbones, and downward-cast eyes, and soft-looking cushions to the lips. Except that Kitt appeared older, stronger than Verdi, especially now as she sat leaned back against the booth, arms folded tightly across her chest, one eyebrow arched way up that gave a half scowl to her face as she looked beyond Verdi to get to him; he guessed she was thinking something like, Let me check this Ivy League Negro out and see what he's up to with my cousin. He liked that, was glad that Verdi had at least one other person in this town watching her back. Still he figured he'd better pull his best manners from his pocket and wear them like kid leather gloves if he were going to have a shot at maybe causing her to lower her eyebrow and softening that scowl on her face. He knew the importance that Verdi attached to Kitt's perceptiveness when it came to reading someone's character, knew how badly Verdi wanted Kitt's blessings, knew she'd probably pressured Kitt as much she had him to be nice. "Please," she'd begged on their walk over. "My cousin is the most honest. generous, down-to-earth person I know. You'll love her, I'm sure of it, so just please be nice."

Kitt and Johnson didn't need to be pressured. There really was a natural energy between them as they shook hands and looked each other up and down and confirmed that neither was threatening to the other. Then suddenly, in the same instant it seemed, they both recognized that they'd known each other briefly but significantly in their childhoods.

"Didn't you go to Hamilton?" they asked simultaneously?

And the anticipation of this first meeting melted into the memory of the powerful slice of history they shared at Hamilton Elementary School. Kitt was in fifth grade, Johnson was in sixth. And a rumor was whipping through the upper grades about Kitt's mother and Johnson's father: Johnson's father had recently left home; packed his bag and told his wife simply that he needed to be free. He took a room over top of Punchy's Seafood restaurant on Fifty-second Street, and one Friday—so the elementary-school kids said—at 6:30 P.M. sharp, Posie slunk into Punchy's wearing spiked heels and a fake three-quarter-length leopard coat, and sat at the counter and ordered two dozen batter-dipped fried shrimp. Johnson Senior emerged from the darkened staircase that led to his room, and whispered in Posie's ear loud enough for the waitress to hear—an older sister of a Hamilton sixth-grader—that if she wanted to maybe listen to some Lou Rawls while her shrimp was frying he had a stack of 45s sitting on his spindle upstairs just waiting to fall. And according to the sixth-grader's waitress sister, the two dozen shrimp got cold waiting for Posie to come down from Johnson Senior's room even though they'd been double-wrapped in foil and kept next to the flame of the gas-burning stove. And the rumor got so hot, so inflated, that it bounced around the chipped plastered ceilings of the third floor of Hamilton School where the fifth- and sixth-grade classes were. And after a few more Fridays passed they were saying that Posie had taken to coming into Punchy's earlier, four o'clock, before the rush-hour crowd came with their orders for fried fish. And Johnson Senior was already sitting at the counter waiting for her, had already placed her order, and they'd sprinkle their shrimp with pepper and hot sauce, and feed each other until they were down to nibbling on each other's hands. And by the time they were done a crowd would have assembled, egging them on in the distinctively loud voices of those who've worked hard all week and can finally let loose in a Friday-evening, eagle-flying, scotch-and-soda-and-shrimp kind of way. And according to the sixth-grader's waitress sister, Posie seemed to glow in the attention, would get more outrageous during their feedings, even licking Johnson Senior's arms up to the elbow. Until one Friday Posie walked through the door in that three-quarter-length fake leopard only this time the spots didn't stop with the coat, her legs were also spotted, her hands, even her face. This time, they said, she made purring sounds while she and Johnson Senior fed each other batter-dipped fried shrimp to the cheers and jeers of just-got-paid happy onlookers. And then after she had tasted Johnson Senior's sweat as much she could, having gone beyond his elbow this time, and growled while she devoured his neck with both teeth and tongue, this time, the sixth-grader swore that her waitress sister swore that Posie unbuttoned the three-quarter-length fake leopard, and was butt naked underneath, except that it was hard to tell at first because leopard spots that matched the coat had been painted over her entire body. But when Punchy's other men patrons realized the nature of the cat woman before them, they told Johnson that if he didn't go for it, they surely would. And a few even started coming out of their jackets and even shirts until Johnson Senior beat them to it, and according to the waitress, who swore to her sixth-grade sister on a stack of Bibles, Posie and Johnson Senior did it right there on the middle of Punchy's Seafood floor. The rumor became like air at Hamilton Elementary; it was everywhere, just inhaled by the older students who understood what a nasty thing had happened between Johnson's father and Kitt's mother. When either Johnson or Kitt walked by a group of assembled classmates they were met with "meows" and purrs, and scratching sounds, because these children were avid Batman fans and had studied well the sounds that Cat Woman made. Then one day Johnson saw Kitt on the landing in the back stairwell that was reserved for fire drills but Johnson had started using it to avoid the throngs of teasers who crowded up and down the main staircase. Kitt was moving quickly down the stairs and she looked so strong and lonely from the back and he had to take the steps three at a time to catch her. "Hey, hey, Kitt," he'd called, but she kept her swift descent going. "I want you to know that my father's allergic to shellfish, so they're lying, or my father would be dead right now." She'd stopped then, turned and looked up at him; they looked at each other with a straight-on directness that was unusual for children their age.

"And my mother doesn't own a leopard coat, fake, three-quarter-length, or otherwise," she said. And they both just stood there, silence reverberating between them, chests heaving, tears welling up. They both knew it to be a fact that their parents had taken up with each other, not at Punchy's over batter-dipped fried fish, but Kitt had walked in on Johnson Senior and her mother holding hands in the living room of their second-floor apartment; Johnson had seen Posie leaving Punchy's through the side door that led up to his father's rented room. And even though Posie and Johnson Senior broke it off after less than a couple of months anyhow, and the rumor dissipated and dissolved into the next salacious story to titillate hyperactive prepubescent fifth- and sixth-graders, and even though Johnson and Kitt never really interacted after that afternoon, they had connected in that darkened stairwell in a way that their youth would not permit them to understand. It was a connection that resurfaced now as they marveled at the uncanniness that they should have Verdi in common.

"You're Johnson's son," Kitt said with certainty.

"You're Posie's daughter." Johnson matched her confident-she-was-right tone with his own brand of voice pulled up from his stomach.

They laughed then, slapped hands. Hugged. Pointed at each other and laughed some more. And when Verdi bounced up and down because she couldn't contain her excitement over Kitt and Johnson finally meeting, and asked, "What? What is it?" Kitt and Johnson both paused, as if they both sensed how easily they could slip into a fractious, contentious vein even growing to hate each other forced to compete bitterly for Verdi's affections if they didn't have some other point of alliance between them that had nothing to do with Verdi. They read in each other's eyes at that moment the need to keep their original bonding scenario unspoken, and in so doing undiluted.

"It's nothing," Kitt said as she squeezed Johnson's hand and laughed some more.

"Well, how do you know each other's parents?" Verdi asked, looking from Kitt to Johnson, amusement and confusion competing for expression on her face.

"Just that your aunt Posie was the, um, pretzel lady at our school." Johnson said.

"And your, um, boyfriend? Is that appropriate college lingo? Anyhow his father bought a lot of pretzels."

Johnson chuckled and winked at Kitt and kissed Verdi on the lips. And Verdi decided that it didn't matter, that all that mattered right now was that two of the people she cared most about were seeming to be beyond the uncomfortably stiff formality that could kill a friendship even while it was budding.

"Well, let me tell you"—Kitt rushed her words—"Johnson here had one hell of a funny-shaped head back in elementary school."

"And I mean no disrespect," Johnson said then, "but your cousin was kind of, you know, fat."

Kitt punched Johnson's arm as if they'd been close for years and they all three laughed and spread themselves out in the back booth and sealed their closeness over omelettes and grits and mounds of breakfast meats.

And Kitt liked Johnson so much that she insisted on paying for breakfast that morning, told them to just pretend that the breakfast took place at her kitchen table which she'd been planning to do anyhow if she could get an occasional callback from Verdi. Framing her paying in those terms made it acceptable. Saved Johnson the embarrassment of having to spend money no doubt slipped to him by Verdi; Kitt had been on those kinds of dates before when the man was nice as Cooter Brown and twice as broke, and she'd want to at least split the bill but their maleness took it as a personal affront that the woman should pay and she'd sit there and watch them squirm and even pull up nickels from the lining of their pants to piece together enough to cover the tab.

But Johnson seemed not to mind that Kitt was paying, seemed not to mind most things Kitt suggested, even when she'd call and tell Verdi to send Johnson up to her house when he got some time, that Posie's limo driver had bowed out on her, "surprise, surprise," she'd say jokingly, and this new man of Posie's was blind in one eye and couldn't drive and she'd cooked way too much of this or that and could they help take some of it off of her hands. Johnson was glad to go. And he'd feel a calming need to open up descend as he and Kitt always started off talking about elementary school while Kitt spooned out the plates and double-wrapped them in wax paper and carefully taped the sides. And before long the topics would turn to things more contemporary, sometimes Posie would even be in the kitchen, would join in with her odd mix of wit, wisdom, and immaturity that tickled Johnson so. It wasn't uncommon for them to chatter for an entire hour after the bags of food were packed. And sometimes Johnson would stop by there even if there was no offer of food as an enticement, if he'd just been to see his mother and needed to thin out his sadness before he went back to campus. And Posie and Kitt welcomed him with laughs and hugs and made much over his arrival as if Johnson was becoming the son Posie should have had, the brother Kitt needed.

Kitt and Johnson were spawning such a pure honesty between them and they'd find themselves telling each other things that heretofore had remained caged and locked in their own minds. Johnson and his feelings of inferiority when it came to being able to treat Verdi in the first-class kind of way she'd grown up with. Kitt and her regret that she'd never had a shot at college, at least that's what the guidance counselors told her when they placed her in the home-economics track. Johnson and the call he sometimes got for the street, that as much as he had an aversion for the type of lifestyle that brought his brother down, he was still drawn at least to some of the people who'd been friends with his dead brother; he was so fascinated by their honor-among-thieves credo. Kitt and her fear that she'd never fall head over heels the way Verdi had with him, the way Posie did every other month; she loved her mother dearly, she told him, but was so afraid of becoming like Posie that she'd hold back even with decent prospects; always she'd hold back.

And sometimes after they'd talked so long until they were drained in a satisfied kind of way and Johnson would linger over a Kool filter tip, they'd pick up each other's eyes through the smoke, and something that would approach a physical attraction would try to taint the air between them and make it go common and low. They knew to disregard it, to not even dignify it by heightening it to a stature that would make it worth considering. They both loved Verdi too much to let the bad air form itself into a thought to be pondered, the commission of a low-down act to be considered. And as they were beginning to realize, they loved each other too in a way that was so honest and so pure that they'd never risk toppling it because some nefarious stream of chemistry decided to show itself in the smoke of a Kool filter-tip cigarette.

But even with all of his self-disclosures, Johnson still kept to himself the taste of thunder, that manifestation of the storm cloud that would start in his stomach and rise up into his chest like reflux from a too-spicy meal until the hot embers regurgitated and singed the skin along his jaw. It was especially strong during the three-and-a-half-week Christmas break and Verdi had gone home, even though she'd begged her parents to let her stay on campus and had almost had her father ready to relent until Hortense grabbed the phone, voice cracking, insisting that she needed her baby home, that she'd get physically ill if she had to endure the holidays without her, that it was enough that they'd allowed her Thanksgiving with Kitt, but she'd rather she just pounce on her heart than deny her Christmas with her only child. And it was a teary good-bye when Johnson loaded Verdi into the cab headed to the airport that Christmas Eve, and his dorm felt like a mausoleum with Tower and Moose and everybody else he might interact with gone home too. And he felt like the right thing to do was to go home and spend Christmas Eve with his mother, not that he wanted to, but that was certainly the right thing to do. And he put a sweater on under his scuffed-up leather jacket and decided to walk. Had walked past the empty frat houses and the closing-early hoagie and steak shops that serviced the campus, and the off-campus apartment buildings with their iron-gated windows, and the Acme and the Presbyterian church, and then the blurring that happened between the campus and the neighborhood where the structures looked the same but the people scurrying in and out were now worlds apart, one being trained to take over the world—or at least to take it on; the other, well, to the other this small patch of the city was the world. And he felt so wide-legged at this point on his trek up, strad-dling the worlds, when he was fully on campus he was sure West Philly was where he belonged, and when he was at home, he was sure his rightful place was on campus, but right around this spot where

[84]

the boundaries overlapped he was at home nowhere. He hurried across the imaginary divide and now had another mile to go and the sun was beginning to drop and the air out here was growing teeth and he pulled his skull cap farther down over his 'fro to at least meet his ears, and he wasn't wearing gloves, he didn't own gloves. And now he was right in front of the three-story house where Bug lived, his dead brother's best friend, and he thought what the hell, he'd extend holiday greetings and in the process thaw his hands.

Bug's real name was Anthony and when he was small everybody called him Ant for short but as he got older, bigger and tougher and delinquent, and learned how to fight with banister posts, he changed his nickname to Bug because he thought Ant sounded girlish and threatened to kick ass if anybody called him that again. Bug and Johnson's brother Fred had been best friends from kindergarten. They were supposed to go to Vietnam together under the inducement of enlisting under the buddy system that assured they'd be platoon mates, but Bug failed the physical, was diagnosed with hepatitis, and they wouldn't let Fred unenlist.

Bug repeated that story to Johnson now as he ushered him into his dimly lit third-floor apartment and hugged him and clenched his teeth in the middle of telling Johnson how much he looked like Fred standing there. "That should have been me in that chopper with him, you know that don't you, Johnson. We was bloods, man, seriously, man."

And Johnson nodded and was not as adept as Bug at holding back the tears and asked to use his john. When he'd gotten himself sufficiently together he walked back into the living room via the kitchen where the table was loaded down with a balance beam scale and plastic Baggies and a shoe box filled with weed. He got a flashback then of the first time he'd smoked a joint sitting on a crate in the empty lot around the corner from his house. It was the summer between tenth and eleventh grade and it was Bug who'd turned him on, taught him how to roll it, how to hold it in until he coughed. And then Fred came up on him, knocked him in the head so hard the joint flew out of his mouth, told him to take his ass home, told Bug, "He's going to college, man, he don't need to be doing that shit."

Bug and Johnson were on the same wavelength because he repeated that story to Johnson as he offered him a seat on his orange vinyl couch under the Lava light–enhanced Jimi Hendrix poster. He was bursting in fact with stories about Fred that had Johnson in stitches and then tears as he and Bug passed a continuous stream of joints between them. And Johnson was so caught up he lost track of time as Bug introduced him to dimensions about his brother that he'd never known. For this space of time that he sat on Bug's orange vinyl couch and smoked joint and laughed through Bug's vivid recollections about all the hell they raised, his brother wasn't really dead. And especially when he wasn't laughing, when Bug's stories turned searing in their revelations about his brother's true nature, it was as if his brother was sitting right next to him on the couch, telling him to move the fuck over, that real men didn't sit so their bodies touched even as he had his arm around Johnson's shoulder. He was enraptured by the time Bug told the story of how he and Fred were caught shoplifting model airplane kits from the five-and-ten when they were in their early teens, "only caught our asses because your softhearted brother stopped in the middle of our getaway to chase down some common thief who'd just snatched some old lady's purse. 'Why? Why you do such a foolish-assed thing?' I asked him all night that long night we spent in the Youth Study Center. And you know what he said, told me he had principles, that he was just liberating that model airplane, that everybody paid for that stolen airplane and what's twenty-nine cents split a million ways, but if that woman would have lost her purse that probably held her expense money for the month, only she would have paid, and that ain't right, ain't fair worth a damn.

You know he turned it into a political act. That's what I loved about your brother, he had a heavy understanding. You dig where I'm coming from, Johnson?"

Johnson did, even appreciated his brother's ambivalence when Bug related how his brother had dabbled in the Black Panther Party, but knew he'd have to commit with his life and wasn't sure if he was willing to give his life for it. "Aint that a shit," Bug said, choking on sobs. "He still ended up giving his life, just that the movement he gave it for wasn't even his own."

Johnson got up to leave then, asked Bug how he planned on spending Christmas.

"I'm hanging around and dealing a little weight, man. Christmas is so much bullshit but it's good for business, especially with all you college students converging again on the neighborhood. That pound I got on the table be gone by this time tomorrow night, man. So I'm just hanging and selling. Stop on through if you of the mind to over the holiday. Or anytime, man. You my young blood. Anytime."

And Johnson knew he would stop back again. Thought that Bug might even step in and fill the oversized shoes his brother wore. Especially after he got home and his mother had already gone to bed, a card for Johnson propped up against her tabletop Christmas tree, the tree leaning, all the heaviest bulbs on one side. He tenderly re-arranged the bulbs to balance them. The bulbs were thin-skinned and fragile in his weather-worn hands and he took his time. When he finished he sat down in the plastic-covered armchair facing the tree. Plugged the tree in and watched the lights blink on and off. The bulbs reflected a near-perfect symmetry. He thought about Verdi. Cried.

Five

ALREADY VERDI COULD feel the levity inside of her that happened whenever she approached Kitt's house. Even though the fine drizzle was keeping the air more gray than yellow today, the clouds seemed not even to be as heavy when she turned onto Sansom Street. Partly because this block was such a diamond even in the 1990s, thanks to Kitt's tenaciousness, her political activism. Though portions of West Philly had slid in property value like skis down an icy slope, there were no abandoned houses on Kitt's block, no litter or graffiti, no peeling paint, no hedges out of control, no drug corners or Stop 'n' Cop Beer Marts within a two-block radius, and the empty lot on the corner had been transformed into a vivacious urban garden that made Kitt's house such a joy to approach.

Not that Verdi was unhappy when she approached the house she shared with Rowe; she filled her space nicely with Rowe; was happy the way air inside of a voluminous crate is happy, protected, right angle to right angle. Not buoyant though. At Kitt's she was buoyant. Especially now as she started up the steps to Kitt's house, and here was her slice of sunshine, Sage, jumping up and down and clapping when she saw Verdi and squealing and trying to say her name, gasping as spit dripped down her chin as she blew out the V sound, forcing it out, trying to make the whole name come out with the "Ve." But the whole name wouldn't come out, and Sage stomped her feet in frustration.

"That's okay, Sage," Verdi soothed as Sage bounded onto the enclosed porch, her arms wide open, and Verdi dropped her briefcase and scooped Sage up and squeezed her as if it had been weeks since she'd seen her. Though it had just been hours, just since 2:45 when she'd escorted Sage's class to the waiting school bus, the way she escorted all of her students at the end of the day, and greeted them all first thing in the morning. Had been criticized for being too hands-on as a principal by the vocal few who resented Verdi hurtling over the vice principal already in place to get the principal's slot, had been told to her face that she was interrupting the emotional attatchment that the children needed to have not for her but for their teachers. Wanted to do like Kitt would have done, wanted to tell them to go fuck themselves, but she was a consummate professional, told them it would take her time to retrain herself, after all this was only her first year out of the classroom and the tug to spend time with the children was stronger than her managerial inclinations.

"How's my sugar lump?" Verdi said as she kissed Sage's cheek with an exaggerated slurping sound and then eased her back down on the porch. She stooped to Sage's eye level; what a perfect face this child had with that same grin as the cousins and the twins that involved her entire face and enchanted people so and shocked them too when they realized that Sage was different, special, that she hadn't yet spoken her first word though she was seven, but even still she had surpassed all predictions of severe developmental delays, could point to her eyes and ears, and nose; if her mother said go upstairs and look in my top drawer and bring down my pink eyeglass case, she could do that too. Though she couldn't yet read and write, and had a tendency to keep her fists balled, and sometimes reacted emotionally to strangers, she remained a puzzle to the medical community by how dramatically she'd surpassed their predictions, and yet she couldn't talk.

Verdi put Sage's hand against her jaw so that Sage could feel her muscles working. "Sugar," she said, drawing the word out. "Sugar."

"Verdi," her aunt Posie said with the same exaggeration and then a laugh as she walked out onto the enclosed porch.

Verdi giggled and ran to Posie the way Sage had just greeted her. She mashed her lips against Posie's cheek that smelled of Ponds cold cream and reminded Verdi of the chunks of her growing-up she'd spent with Posie and Kitt where she'd felt a sanctity she'd known in few other places.

Posie squeezed Verdi to her, felt the sharpness of her shoulder blades even through the taupe-colored trench coat. Stretched her back to arm's length. "I hope you're trying to hold on to what little weight you're carrying, darling. Looks like you shed a few pounds in the couple of days since I last saw you. I mean you look good, don't get Aunt Posie wrong, that brown highlights to that pixie haircut, I personally like you with a little more hair but you wearing that short style well now, looking good baby, like a piece of raspberry cheesecake, you do, sweet and well adorned, just sliced a bit too thin."

"Oh Auntie, I know, I know, but everybody can't be the stacked figure eight like you and Kitt," Verdi said as she kissed Posie's cheek again.

"True," Posie said, and did a little twirl and a curtsy followed by Sage imitating her grandmother and they all three laughed. Though Kitt fussed often about her mother's inability to age, to accept that she was no longer a twenty-year-old temptress, Verdi loved this about her aunt, was awestruck by how alluring Posie still was even at sixty.

"Kitt's with her last client of the day and I'm sure not gonna be the one to go back there and tell her you're here, so you might as well come on in and get comfortable, darling, and what may we thank as the reason for being graced with your presence two evenings in one week?" Posie said as she opened the door and held it and waited while Sage ran back to try to scoop up Verdi's briefcase.

Posie nudged Verdi to tell her to look at Sage. "Told you that chile got plenty of sense," she whispered to Verdi. "I do believe she's gonna talk soon too. Keep working with her, Verdi Mae, I see the improvement just in the short time you been principal at her school."

"Oh Auntie, you know I will now," Verdi said as she went to help Sage with the briefcase, asking herself why was she back over here again this Friday anyhow; told herself that it was for the grilled salmon Kitt did on Fridays; wouldn't admit to herself that it was for conversation about Johnson, so many questions she had about him: Had he married yet? Children? What about his eyes, did they still get that stony intenseness that used to move rapids through her?

"And how are things going on your job anyhow?" Posie sliced into Verdi's stream of denial about why she was here. "You feeling more settled in with your new position?" she asked as Verdi shook off her taupe-colored raincoat and sank into the couch, and a more satisfied version of herself emerged like always when she got here, got to the easy unencumbered feel of this green corduroy couch, the peach flowered wallpaper that Kitt had hung herself, the lacy curtains she'd pleated from the tablecloths Verdi had brought her back from Mexico, the spotless coffee table, the sense of order here, not strained and calculated, but free-forming like a cha-cha that's always on beat even when the feet misstepped.

"Gorgeous suit, Verdi Mae," Posie said, before Verdi could answer. "You really looking the part of a principal in that navy silk suit, I tell you that much. 'Course I know it's got to be hard making the switch like you did from teaching to leading. I remember when I was working at the dry cleaners, before my lungs started acting up and I had to go out on disability, and I was made the lead presser, and let me tell you, Verdi Mae, those other girls I'd been promoted over really showed their behinds, some used to be my friends too. Lord yes, went as far as accusing me of sleeping with the boss. People surely change up on you when you become the one in charge, even try to make you doubt your own fitness for the job you were selected to do."

Verdi's mouth dropped as she sat on the couch stroking Sage's braids. It was almost as if her aunt knew the tussle she'd been having with herself over her new position. Was about to tell Posie about the blowup she felt she was building toward with her vice principal and her clique of supporters when the phone rang and Posie went to answer it, had her back to Verdi as she laughed out loud and walked into the dining room with the phone. And Verdi had the thought what if it was Johnson on the phone? She shook the thought, felt like she was betraying Rowe to think about Johnson, especially when her thoughts boarded a run-away train and she was seeing them together all sweaty and fused. Right now she focused on Sage instead, who had stretched herself out on the well-padded Berber carpet and was rolling her fat barrel-shaped crayons over construction paper. Verdi got down on the floor with Sage and said each color as Sage picked them up, scarlet, she said about the red one, and Sage held it up again, and Verdi laughed at herself, said it's red, baby. Red. Though it was scarlet. The same color as the two dozen velvety roses Rowe had brought home last night apologizing for running his finger along Verdi's vein like he'd done. He was so sincere and seemed almost shy, certainly embarrassed, and Verdi had melted, that softness pouring off of him reminded her why she had such great affection for him anyhow. She almost admitted then that she'd lied, that she wasn't getting a manicure and a massage. She didn't admit it though. Did resolve within herself to be honest from here on out when she spent time with Kitt. Told herself that she would call Rowe as soon her auntie got off of the phone to tell him where she was. Resolved to pluck Johnson from her fantasies. Convinced herself now that she was here for a taste of Kitt's grilled salmon.

Verdi was always able to discern Rowe's softness. Even back when he taught her history. She'd gotten in the habit of sitting up front in the large lecture halls so that she wasn't looking on the backs of the heads of the continuous tides of white people that sometimes made her feel as though they might rise up in a great wave and have her flailing around struggling not to drown, and the feeling was so intense that sometimes her chest would even go tight and from then on she was severely distracted from the lectures, so she was always right there within two feet of Rowe's lectern for his course called the Crisis of the Union. And this one day as he held the lecture hall in his grip as he went around the room and pointed at people and in his bellowing voice asked them questions in order to determine whether they'd been listening, whether they'd done the readings, and he pointed at Verdi then, though his voice lost a degree of its menace: "According to the slave narratives, what was one of the most compelling psychological weapons used against the African male?"

Verdi looked first at her desk as her heart pounded in her ears, then at him, saw the loosening in the muscles of his jaw that were usually clamped so tightly together. "The emasculation factor," she said, and after she'd spoken realized that she'd whispered.

"I'm sorry, what did you say?" he asked as he moved from behind the lectern until he was standing almost directly over Verdi.

"Well." She cleared her throat, forced herself to speak up, to look directly at him as she spoke. "It's not stated explicitly in the narratives we've read, and is also conjecture on my part, but even worse than what is stated explicitly, the male slave being forced to watch other slaves brutalized, to take part in the brutalization, is the far more devastating weapon of the African male lying down with his wife knowing that she's been with another man, albeit in a forced way, and that the other man is also his captor and has rendered him powerless to do anything about it. The fact that descriptions of those kinds of feelings are absent at least in our assigned readings leads me to believe that it was too devastating to even verbalize."

He was quiet when she finished. Just stood there looking at her as if he'd been hypnotized, his jaw so slack now his mouth hung open slightly. "That was a courageous conjecture," he said finally as he walked back to the lectern. "More of you should sit up here in the front row and absorb similar kinds of insights."

He stopped Verdi on the way out, told her again how much he appreciated her comments. "Forgive me if I'm crossing the line," he said as he folded papers into his briefcase. "But my wife's nephew is visiting this weekend, a freshman also—Moorehouse man, but we won't hold that against him." They both laughed as he held the door open for Verdi to walk through. "Anyhow Penda and I were thinking about who we could invite over for dinner this Saturday, and Penda was so dazzled by your performance in her intro-to-ed-psych course last semester that we both said your name at the same time. But, Verdi, please don't even look at this as a blind-date situation or anything that approaches that, and you can even think about it, let me know after class on Wednesday."

And Verdi was thinking that it sounded benign enough, and she liked his wife Penda. And they were outside now, walking down the steps from College Hall, and there was an antiwar demonstration going on down on the grass with placards waving and people talking through megaphones. And Verdi easily picked out Johnson in the mostly white assemblage, and she knew how ambivalent he was about these demonstrations, having lost a brother who'd willingly enlisted. And she could see his distress all the way from where she was by the way he had his hand propped in his chin. Knew that he needed her. That he'd feel rejected if she spent Saturday evening with some Moorehouse man. She turned back to Rowe and smiled. Said, "I'm sorry, I have to decline, I already have plans for this weekend. But, well, I guess tell your nephew that I said hello anyhow."

She shook the look of disappointment that came up in Rowe's eyes as she ran down the steps to get to Johnson, to put her head against his chest, to warm his chest. It was chilly out here and he had his jacket wide open. Even as Rowe clenched his jaws again and watched her running, knew who she was running to. Thought it was such a waste.

———

But no matter what Rowe or anybody else thought, Verdi and Johnson had taken on glows of two people fiercely in love as they became increasingly like interlocking wood carvings, where one protruded the other dimpled to better accommodate the fusion. Johnson was spending so little time in his own dorm with Tower and the rest, and so much time in Verdi's room that the night security just let him sign himself in without making him ring her room first. Verdi's next-door neighbor, Barb, joked that Johnson should be allowed to attend the hall meetings since for all intents and purposes he lived there too. Verdi's best friend Cheryl started seeing Johnson's roommate, Tower, she said, just so that she might maybe catch a glimpse of Verdi if she happened to come by. They accepted the comments breezily though. Laughed, waved good-bye, closed the door to Verdi's room where they had become accustomed to sharing one scrumptious meal after the next complete with candles and linen napkins. Sometimes they mmmed and aha'd over spaghetti and meatballs or livers smothered in onions carefully prepared by Johnson's mother and packaged and contained in her slightly chipped china for Johnson to transport on the bus ride down. Sometimes they languished over a turkey-and-stuffing plate piled high sent from Kitt and hand-delivered by Posie's latest beau. Sometimes they picked at a bowl of chili con carne pilfered from the dining hall hidden under one of Verdi's oversized textbooks. Sometimes Johnson hopped a bus to Whitaker's in Southwest Philly and brought back hoagies so substantial that the mayo and onions and cheeses and meats soaked perfectly circled holes through the brown paper bags. But their real appetites transcended even these palatable treasures; it was each other that they hungered for most. Craved. As if they satisfied in each other intense yearnings due to some elemental lacking in themselves.

For Verdi it was the knowledge of things edgy: the marijuana cigarettes Johnson had taught her how to smoke, a trip into West Philly to a card house and speakeasy posing as a dimly lit cellar party just before it was raided; a midnight snack where she and Johnson wolfed down hot buttered yeast rolls at Broadway on Fifty-second Street to quench reefer-induced pangs of famish where Verdi was mesmerized by the late-night mix of laughter and chatter coming from whores and cops and young boys trying to be old in outdated processed hair, and old men trying to be young boys in Afro wigs and gold medallion chains, and middle-aged choir members who'd just left a worship-and-praise service, and the drunks trying to keep some coffee down, and the legitimate club goers just outside Broadway's window scrambling like carpenter ants before a storm in and out of red-and-blue-aired establishments on the Strip. It was all so thrilling to Verdi as Johnson exposed her to pieces of living she'd never before imagined. She felt herself becoming smarter, sharper, growing angles where she'd typically been round; muscle where she'd been flaccid and soft. She felt leaner and at the same time expansive, fit, as if she were not only working out academically, intellectually with the intense smorgasbord of university requirements, but also being acculturated in the opposite direction, developing that tiny dot of herself that she'd never really nourished that longed to straddle the line between comfort and security, danger and intrigue in the dichotomy of good girl–bad girl, scholar–street-smart. Sometimes she even yearned to cross the line and wade for a minute in the treacherous and forbidden muddied rapids Johnson was introducing her to.

Verdi and Johnson crisscrossed each other in their awakenings to leanings that were opposite their original selves because Johnson was beginning to feel the nudges of transformation as well. He was going to church regularly, having been introduced to a congregation not far from the campus where an old classmate of Verdi's father was the pastor, and though he complained to Verdi about so-called middle-class Baptists, "They're extremely Uncle Tomish when it comes to the struggle," he'd say, "No offense to your father, baby, but those church people have power out to way wide with their economic base, and it's just not being funneled in any collective and therefore effective way." Yet, on the Sunday mornings when she might have otherwise overslept because they'd been up half the night playing pinocle with Tower and Cheryl and smoking "the killer," as they called the really potent weed, and drinking wine and sometimes even graduating to vodka and orange juice, he'd still kiss her awake and put on a borrowed sport jacket over his jeans, and feed her coffee so that she could make the six-block walk to the church, and once there he'd even occasionally clap during the choir's rendition of a particularly energetic and rousing tune. He actually trod inside of a Bonwit Teller store when Verdi went to buy a birthday gift for shipping down home to her mother—and Bonwit Teller had always symbolized gross opulence to him where the socially negligent would pay three dollars for a cotton handkerchief and scoff at being levied a proportional amount to fund the war on poverty—but he strode through the marble-tiled floors of that place and even stuck his Afro pick in his jeans pocket instead of as an ornament growing out of the center of his hair; he kissed her behind the ear when he did, whispered, "This is only for you, baby, might keep the security guards in their three-piece suits—as if I don't know they're rent-a-cops—from walking on our heels while you try to shop for your moms." He experienced theater for the first time with Verdi under his arm. Sat through the Philadelphia Orchestra on tickets sent by Verdi's piano teacher from back home and never admitted to Tower and Moose and the rest how the violin concerto stirred something someplace so deeply planted under his layers and layers of city-street-poor, revolution-now affect that it frightened him at first. Desisted admitting to any kind of transformation when his dorm mates challenged him over spit-tinged marijuana cigarettes. "You getting so establishment we got bets on how long before you strut through here in a Brooks Brother pinstripe and leather-soled oxfords," they teased.

Where Verdi would openly express the thrill of all that she was experiencing; she would beam and laugh and hop excitedly and beg, "Oh please, Johnson, let's go off campus and cop some really good weed and then trip off of the drunks on Fortieth Street," Johnson could not. Felt that indication of any acquiescence on his part meant that he was selling out.

"I'm nobody's Tom," he'd remind Verdi even as he accompanied her to tea at the Mount Airy home of the descendant of the founder of the social club that at her mother's insistence had been a part of her growing-up years. Had to pretend that his entry into Verdi's world was solely for her, that it was even painful for him to take certain steps. Would maintain to his boys as they guzzled cheap wine and told pussy-chasing stories that he was forced to accompany his lady to the *Nutcracker* suite or else she'd hold out on him at night, then he'd go on to chronicle how Verdi would let him curl up in her tiny dorm bed all next to her and as soon as his manhood went hard as granite and swelled and throbbed she'd remind him how he'd refused to participate in what he called some wannabe activity and then she'd close up tighter than a clam protecting a gleaming oversized pearl. "Do you know how that shit feels," he'd say, "like hey, man, just put me on ice in a freezer someplace so I'll go numb because that laying up hard all night next to a warm soft body is some painful shit."

He'd get their concurrence then, their sympathy, though of course he lied. Verdi was perpetually hot and brimming, it seemed, just oozing sexuality once they got to her room and locked the door and dimmed the lights and got some Stylistics going on the record player. Lately she had even started making the first moves, showing her nakedness unabashedly, jostling to be on top, wanting to try things, always always wanting to try something new. He sometimes thought that it was a good thing that she was so straitlaced, that she might otherwise suffer from nymphomania if not for those cultural and religious controls that were so glued to her sense of who, what she was. So he was more than grateful for that shy and blushing churchy side to her because it kept him from worrying about some other brother tapping on her door when he wasn't around—especially since she didn't have a roommate and the brothers always went after the ones with the single rooms. All he'd have to do was remember her manners, her politeness, her ability to say something like, "The Lord is my shepherd, I shall not want," as quickly as he was prone to take the Lord's name in vain and the thought would relax him, confirm in his mind that Verdi wasn't some temptress just passing the time with him until the next pair of pants came through, that it wasn't just a nonspecific maleness that she responded to when they were together and she turned to cream, it was him, Johnson, who aroused her, who she adored. She was his lady, his African-American queen, and he'd topple mountains to keep her so.

Except that he couldn't topple the mountain of his sadness that had slithered through him so quietly without even calling attention to itself, until it was so deep on the inside that he couldn't even tell from where it emanated, couldn't single out an event, or remark, or thought, or memory—no cause, it seemed, to the depression that would start with a pounding fist from the inside of his chest and then billow until even the air that surrounded him accumulated itself into a bleakness that he could barely see through. It was worse during the summer. And this summer of '72 was the worst of all because Verdi wasn't here to give him relief.

Though she'd pleaded to be allowed to stay in Philly just as she did every break, her parents said no. Her father had secured her a paid summer position in Maynard Jackson's campaign for mayor, so staying in Philly this summer wasn't negotiable, not at all. And even though she'd managed to finagle two weekends back in June, and one in July, the stretches without her, without being able to draw on her infectious good spirit, her intact benevolent philosophy that believed that through it all everything would work out fine, made

Johnson feel the way he imagined a broken-down racehorse must feel just before it was shot.

And it wasn't just the missing Verdi. It was all of his school activities that had kept him occupied so that his sadness had to be thunderous before it captured his attention. He'd worked incessantly on a committee to plan a black dorm on campus, and now that was going to happen; he'd studied hard otherwise, though he'd missed the dean's list because of a C in a lit course, Romantic Poets, not even part of his major architecture concentration, blamed the grade on the racist professor who told Johnson that although his paper comparing Wordsworth and Coleridge was brilliant, he'd misplaced semicolons, that he'd never make it through an institution such as the university if he didn't master the use of semicolons. But even fighting the racism when he was on campus involved a certain directed energy that he didn't have to draw on at home. Had to draw on only enough to make it to his assembly line–like summer job at UPS, and stop by Bug's third-floor apartment on the way home because at least that way his mother would already be asleep when he stumbled in and he wouldn't have to torture himself trying to think of something to say to drain the heaviness from her sighs.

And Bug's orange vinyl couch brought Johnson relief this summer. Bug's stories about his brother mixed with the marijuana and the wine, even filled a corner of the hole Verdi's absence left. And when Johnson confided to Bug that he missed his old lady, Bug laughed, said my young blood I got just the thing to cure a lonely heart and turned him on to a little speed in orange juice. And by July he was also popping Quaaludes to counteract the hyperness brought on by the speed, and then he was smoking opium to smooth it all out, and he was on the countdown to when school would start, when he'd have Verdi's head against his chest again, and it was within ten days, the middle of August now, and by now Bug's orange vinyl couch had the print of Johnson's substance etched into its cracks. And Bug asked Johnson if he was ready to taste heaven.

"Taste heaven?"

"No shit, man. I swear to you man, but you got to be prepared because it's some powerful shit, man. Better than pussy, man. I wouldn't lay this shit on just anybody, but you my young blood, man."

And Johnson said that he wasn't about getting strung out.

"One time don't string nobody out, Johnson, man. But hey, it's cool. It was gonna be turn-on but I ain't got to beg nobody to turn them the fuck on."

And Johnson's defenses were already down, the wine, the reefer, his sadness snaking him the way that it was, and ten entire days before he'd see his Verdi Mae. "Bring it on, man," he said, "let's see what the fuck you talking about. Bring it on."

"You sure, man?" Bug said even as he cooked it in a Vaseline lid on the coffee table. "This shit is without sin that's how pure it is. Get ready to see Jesus," he said as he showed him where to tighten the belt, and the vein they were going to hit: the thickest vein, that showed on the underside of his arm and shimmered with sweat and pulsed like a sex-starved woman. "That one, we gonna hit that one," Bug whispered, and he pumped it into Johnson's arm, and Johnson didn't even feel Bug pull it out because a pipe organ started issuing forth its vibrations from the center of his chest and sending its smooth tones to his head bursting note by note and melting, coating his brain with liquid music that was thick and sweet as sap. And he started to sing along with the organs. And now he knew how it felt to be transformed into a note and given pitch through the air and soar and dip, freely, uncaged, no longer internally bound. This night he sang all night long and nodded as spit dripped from the side of his mouth.

And even in this liquid condition he knew that he would have to feel this pipe organ again. Damn.

Remarkably Johnson kept the heroin part hidden at first by just staying away from people who mattered; he was only partaking once a month anyhow, light doses, and after each one, when the rush was over and the liquid music dried, leaving only its irritating thickness, he swore to himself that he wouldn't do it again. That the posthigh lethargy was too momentous a price for him to pay with all that he was trying to accomplish. School, Verdi, the BSL, the good-paying part-time job at United Parcel. Except that at least while the pipe organ was vibrating, he wasn't sad. It was the absence of sadness that he sought when time and again he'd return to the orange vinyl couch at Bug's. Once a month on Thursdays, his payday—though this rippled progression from one substance to the next had started off as turn-ons, freebies, gifts from Bug, now Bug would often proclaim, "My young blood, if it were up to me I wouldn't charge you a dime, but you understand I have suppliers to pay, though I swear whatever you want will always be at a price not a penny higher than my cost to procure it."

But with this regular, monthly use came a certain boldness, that he could do it and nobody would know, and surprisingly, nobody did notice at first; more surprising, at least to Johnson was who noticed first.

Posie was between men this Saturday evening and spending more time outside of her bedroom where she could think clearly. She couldn't think at all in her bedroom. Her bedroom was designed for feeling over thought with its perfumed air, and lacy antique curtains, and softly textured and flowered wallpaper; her night tables were skirted, her pillows covered with satin cases, her bedspread such a hot, bold pink that it bordered on red. But the kitchen where she was right now was a mild yellow, Kitt's favorite color, and expansive and cozy at the same time, organized, functional, no excesses like the boudoir vases, and lamps, swatches of silk here, velvet there that permeated Posie's bedroom and ensured that any brain activity was merely as the conduit to explode impulses to other body parts. Posie was thinking about how she really needed to spend more time outside of her bedroom, that she probably wouldn't have been with half of the men she'd been with if she'd picked and chosen surrounded by the kitchen's mild yellow thought-provoking walls. Right now Kitt stirred around in a pot on the stove, and Johnson had his face in a book, and Posie's thinking was so clear that she could feel the crisp, smacking sound of her thoughts as if they were being shuffled around like a deck of new cards. No man was coming to call this Friday evening so no need to pull away from the settling sounds of the kitchen to bathe and oil and dust herself down and sweeten her crevices and swathe herself in her silky lounging robe that fell open to her waist when she sat in her pink velvet chair just so. No need to light an Essence of Nature candle and inhale deeply so that the oil on her skin would mix with her own womanhood rising out through her pores and have him—whoever was the object of her infatuation at the moment—begging to do anything, whatever she wanted, just let him be against the feel of her skin. Instead tonight she inhaled the steam rising out of the pot of chicken and dumplings Kitt was stirring, and something about that aroma hitting her nose brought out her maternal side as she picked at the ends of Johnson's dense Afro and told him that his ends needed a clipping, that his bush would turn shaggy and unkempt looking if he didn't take special care of his ends.

And Kitt agreed and commenced with a description of the worst 'fro she had seen yet. "It was all matted and so filled with lint that I swore a whole family of rats could have been living in that hair, so I stood up the whole bus ride home rather than sit next to that man."

Posie laughed and fingered Johnson's hair and enjoyed the card game going on in her head that was unencumbered by her bodily sensations.

That's when her thoughts moved beyond Johnson's hair to his hands. His hands were still. They were rarely still. He was always tapping them or patting them or strumming them, always palpating something, fidgeting in ways that she thought so charming and little-boy-like. But he wasn't fidgeting now, hadn't been lately now that she thought about it. Lately he'd been dragging, even talking slowly when usually his words splashed out like typhoons. Big intelligent words especially if he was preaching to Kitt and her on the unseen ways that black people were exploited; many Posie hadn't even given thought to. But he wasn't talking as Posie squinted over his shoulder to catch a glimpse of the title of the book he was reading. *The Underside of American History.* She repeated the title out loud. "That sounds interesting, Johnson," she said as she walked around to the other side of the table to look on Johnson's face.

He sat there smiling slowly even as Posie prayed for the typhoon, for his words to gush out and indict the white man and his history. Anything to show some pointed understanding. But Posie saw that his face wasn't showing any real comprehension of the words on the page, that he seemed ready to fall asleep in the middle of his smile. And now he yawned, took what felt like to Posie a full minute to stretch his mouth to an oversized O, and just as long to fix it back to a line that sagged at the corners. Posie felt her heart drop. "I said that book you're reading sounds interesting, Johnson." Her voice was loud and insistent and Kitt turned around from the stove to see why her mother was speaking in such a tone.

"It is, Posie. Very interesting," Johnson said, his head still in the book.

He started laughing then, and if Posie's heart dropped just a minute ago, now it froze. She knew only one thing that would have an otherwise hyper person like Johnson laughing like he was laughing now, a slow series of low erratic cracks coming from his throat that sounded to Posie more like a death rattle than a laugh. It was true. She hadn't wanted to admit it to herself how off of his rhythm he'd been. And just at that second of insight when the airiness of her feelings might have transformed itself into a concrete thought, she'd get distracted, pulled to her bedroom by her latest beau so that her thoughts went amorphous on her. And then Johnson would show up a few days later with his movable nature intact, talking in gushes again, following Kitt and Posie's every word.

"Johnson," Posie said, in that voice of hers that was high and flat and belied the seriousness plastered on her face. "Do you feel all right, I mean you seem not altogether with it, if you know what I mean."

Johnson closed his book and let it fall against the table. He looked at Posie then and tried to smile, but what felt like syrup was caked to the sides of his mouth and was impeding his smile, so he scratched at the corners of his mouth and then scratched his neck, his eyes closed now, and then he realized he was scratching all over and sat up with a jolt.

Posie's expression had gone from serious to horrified as she watched him scratching like a common street junkie. Why? With all he had going for him, why? Why would he flush it down the toilet like this? She almost asked him, almost demanded that he explain the why to her. But she couldn't form the words against her tongue even as she groped with her hands to try to help the words along and ended up doing with her hands what she couldn't with her mouth. She slapped Johnson with the back of her hand soundly across his dumb-struck face.

"Mama," Kitt blurted as she turned around this time to the sound of skin against skin and saw Johnson grabbing his face, blood dripping between his fingers from where Posie's cocktail ring had ripped across his cheek. "What did you do to him? What's wrong with you?" She walked toward Posie, the wooden ladle spoon in her hand dripping a cloudy-colored liquid on the floor that smelled of dough and onions. "Mama, are you going crazy or something, look at what you did to his face."

Kitt ran to the sink and exchanged her wooden ladle spoon for a wet paper towel and in a flash was dabbing Johnson's cheek all the while asking, demanding an explanation from her mother, even as Johnson told Kitt that it was okay, he was fine, just fine. "Just leave it alone, Kitt," he begged, "I'm fine, just fine."

But Kitt wouldn't leave it alone, couldn't as she stood eye to eye to Posie and was struck by the righteous defiance in Posie's eyes. In Kitt's mind there was only one thing that would make a woman slap a man, draw blood the way Posie just had, and then stand back look-ing justified and vindicated. The man would have had to have just squeezed her butt, or pinched her breast, wet her ear with his tongue, slid his finger in her crotch, rubbed his manhood against her thigh. Kitt couldn't even fathom that Posie had just slapped Johnson as a mother would a son, because she rarely saw Posie as a mother in a terrycloth robe and mismatched wool socks, or cotton duster, or pin-afore apron making chicken and dumplings. No. Kitt was the one who made chicken and dumplings while Posie sauntered in and out of the kitchen whenever she felt like it wreaking her womanhood like a whore wearing too much perfume. And since at this moment she couldn't see Posie's maternal side, she totally misread the scene and didn't even notice Johnson trip over nothing but his own feet as he pushed himself to standing, or the lagging to his words when he mumbled out that he didn't mean to cause any confusion, that he would just leave, he was fine, just fine.

"Don't leave, Johnson," Kitt said, even as she continued to stare Posie down. "Mama owes you an apology because she's sorely mistaken about whatever it is that she *thinks* just caused her to hit you like that."

"Well, what do you think I *think* it is?" Posie matched Kitt's tough-girl stance with her own but the hand-on-hip, finger-pointing, I'll-kick-your-ass-right-now demeanor was too unnatural for Posie to maintain and she settled for her arms clasped tightly across her chest.

Kitt shook Johnson's shoulder. "Tell her she must be losing her mind," she said, her voice screeching with all the emotion of someone who's positive that they're right even before hearing the facts and feeling so certain without the facts reinforces that the sense of rightness must be coming from some intuitive place and therefore couldn't be in error.

Johnson felt as if he wanted to piss and shit at the same time not knowing what to make of whatever was happening between Kitt and Posie. Even in his diminished state with the fog over his head that always hung around a day or two after he'd emptied the white powdered-filled bag into his arm, he could tell that the argument between them was serious, much more serious than the backhanded slap he'd just taken from Posie. "Please, Posie, Kitt, don't fight on my behalf," he said to the confused kitchen air as he started walking toward the archway of the kitchen door. He let out that death-rattle laugh again. "I just need to get some sleep at night. Whew." He tripped again on nothing but the floor as he continued to walk.

It was too late to ask Kitt and Posie not to argue. Their voices were raised against each other as Kitt told Posie that she was just so self-possessed that she thought every man wanted to come on to her. "Well, you're wrong, wrong, Mother, if you think Johnson wants you, you old woman you."

That stopped Posie. She was just beginning to think that maybe Kitt knew what Johnson was doing, that she was covering up for him and that's why the vigorous defense. Or that maybe Kitt cared so much for Johnson that she was choosing to keep her eyes pressed shut to what he was doing. She was all set to bombard Kitt with the evidence, wear her down with her mother-knows-best offense. But these words that had just left Kitt's mouth and slammed into her with all the force of a Mack truck were not daughter-to-mother. They were woman-to-woman. They were more like words that would have come from her sister's mouth, that had come from her sister's mouth once. How much Kitt looked like her sister now, beautiful and self-righteously defiant and wrong. Posie was without offense, without words, without even breath as she felt herself going into a wheeze. She needed to get out of the kitchen, needed to get to her bedroom and take her medicine, needed to go for a walk in the chilly air and clear her head.

Kitt knew that she'd leaped wildly in the wrong direction when she looked at Posie's face and watched the question mark in her mother's eyes yield to a pained understanding of what Kitt was saying. She didn't know whether to run after her mother, whose silk-paisleyed back was to her now as she walked away shaking her head, or Johnson, who had just closed the front door behind him. She opted for Johnson, called out his name as she ran through the living room to the enclosed porch just in time to see him leaned over, vomiting on the pavement in front of her just-swept door.

Six

ROWE AND HIS estranged wife, Penda, were at it again the day of Sage's birthday party. Arguing. They hadn't traded two back-to-back civil sentences since Penda wouldn't agree to give him a divorce more than twenty years ago. And now they were also trading puffs of smoke on the sidewalk in front of the University City house where Rowe and Verdi lived, because it was chilly for a Saturday afternoon in April, Easter Saturday. This argument was impromptu. Rowe had just stepped out of his front door to run to his car and was on his way back when there Penda was who actually lived only a few blocks away. She was walking right toward him with her purposeful walk no doubt headed to some Saturday-afternoon socially redeeming function, Rowe could tell by the way she held her head, slightly thrown back, her eyes sharp and direct, her mouth hinting at a smirk, exuding confidence in what he'd always called her more-humane-than-thou demeanor. She was still stunning to look at though, even as she came straight at him wagging her finger, saying that she had started to take Pine Street, she'd had a feeling he might splotch her path this otherwise bright and crisp spring Saturday, but since he had interrupted her view, she wanted him to know how irate she was over his refusal to agree to sell a piece of property they jointly owned.

She was aging in an artistically elegant way, multicolored shawl wrapped around her shoulders, fish-shaped southwestern-style earrings dangling in the breeze, black-and-silver braids piled high in a roll atop her head, leather fanny pack cinching her long wool dress around the hips, hands on her hips now as she exploded at Rowe, told him that she should have dissolved all of their financial arrangements way back when after he'd betrayed her so. She never passed on the opportunity to throw his deceit in his face. Though the slant of her attacks changed through the years, what had been a seeming insurmountable rage over Rowe's betrayal had ebbed over time, receding finally to pity for Verdi most days who'd she'd always considered a victim in the sordid affair, and a tolerable disdain for Rowe. But that didn't stop her from consistently barreling into him over the details of their many legal entanglements since they'd never divorced. To this day they still shared ownership in insurances, pension plans, real estate.

She had a heavy voice; he'd always disliked her voice especially when she was angry; it was so throaty and erratic, screeching without warning. Even when they were together he used to try to close his ear to the sound of it when she put it in full throttle like now; the sound was more biting than the words. Except that the word she'd just flung at him about being controlling did bite. Though he'd never believed himself to be any more controlling than the typical responsible man who loved a woman and wanted to keep her safe, he was aware of significant feelings of consternation that seeped through the tight reins he kept on his emotional well-being when his attempts at influencing Verdi failed; such attempts rarely failed; they had today. He thought about Verdi right now, upstairs getting dressed to go spend time with that cousin of hers, Kitt, at her child's birthday party. He wanted to get back into the house now before Verdi left, knew that Verdi would leave through the back door if she looked out and saw Penda boiling over; he'd really only run outside to check the odometer on his car thinking that he would at least insist that Verdi take his car though she hated to drive. Checking the odometer was a habit with him if there was a chance Verdi might be out with his car, something he'd been doing since they first started seeing each other and Verdi was just coming out of the fog of addiction and he'd needed to monitor her every action if he was going to be able to save her, now he did it purely out of habit, just to confirm her honesty rather than catch her lying. He had just written today's mileage on a sheet of tablet paper and folded it into his pants pocket and was headed back in when he met Penda head-on and then the rush of this current onslaught.

"The property's not being sold right now, Penda." His voice was so measured and self-assured despite the fire in his chest. "And I'm not going to continue in this hysterical public display you're making." He almost called her a retro flower child, since he'd heard that she'd been spending time with some washed-out avant-garde jazz saxophonist, and according to one of his postdocs she was actually considering packing up and moving to Northern California in some kind of communal living arrangement. Rowe almost reminded her that this was the nineties, not the sixties. He held back though, bit the inside of his jaw he held back with such intensity. He'd only be miring himself in an even more heated argument and Verdi might leave in the meantime. "We can go over this in a more civilized and conducive venue," he said instead. "Later, next week, please, Penda, please."

His prescriptive and modulated voice was lost on Penda's back as she waved her suede-gloved hand at him as if she were shooing a fly and walked away threatening to force a sale legally. He went back into his house, closed the door with a relatively mild slam considering that he'd wanted to bang it shut.

Verdi was already in their main room dressed for going out, her tan leather jacket already on, her purse over her shoulder. She wore green velvet leggings, a white turtleneck, the four-hundred-and-fifty-dollar Ralph Lauren boots he'd picked out for her at Nordstrom's. She'd gotten her perm relaxer touched up that morning, her ends clipped; her hair was so straight and tapered, the sides meeting her cheekbones in points, a subtle feathering to the bangs. He loved how slim and sophisticated she looked, how desirable, how young. He hated that she wasn't going out with him right now, maybe to some breezily elegant brunch spot.

She smiled at him as she picked her keys up from the mantelpiece, slipped them into the generous pocket of her leather jacket. "I'll be back later on in the evening," she said as she looked at herself in the mirror over the mantel and dabbed her finger to her tongue and smoothed her eyebrows down. "Maybe seven or so. Plans for dinner?"

"No. No plans. I'll wait for you," he said as he stood in the archway between the foyer and their main room with his hands in his pants pockets. His jaw was sore from where he'd just bit it and he rubbed it with his tongue.

"No, don't wait, babes, I'm sure Kitt will have a huge spread."

He grunted then. "Greasy nigger food," he said through the soreness in his mouth, whispered it really.

Verdi pretended not to hear as she leaned down to adjust her boot-strap, though the words went right to her chest, hurt her feelings that he would say such a thing, angered her.

He was sorry he'd said it when he saw how her face tightened. Had promised himself he was going to try to accept her relationship with her cousin since it obviously wasn't going away. "That wasn't a nice thing to say." He hit his hands playfully. "Bad boy, Rowe, why'd you insult that pretty lady?"

"Probably because that's how you feel." She didn't try to keep the ice from her voice.

"Verdi, sweetheart, I never mean to use my, you know, not liking your cousin as a weapon against you. Honestly."

Verdi was unmoved. She just stood there staring at him, feeling as if she wanted to cry, but with a defiance.

Rowe's jaw was really throbbing now, and he couldn't figure out Verdi's look. This was a new look, not really anger, not really hurt, much more direct than was typical for her. "Why don't you take my car," he said casually; though he'd wanted to insist on it, he said it now just to redirect the course of the conversation.

"Mnh, no thanks." She loosened the threaded strips of leather to her pouch-styled purse and dug inside. "I need to run in town first to pick up Sage's gift, and darn, I'm out of tokens too."

"Why don't you just go to the King of Prussia Mall and pick her up something there. I could drive you if you don't feel like driving yourself." He shifted his back against the archway post. He could feel the ridges in the wood molding pressing against his back.

"No way, Rowe!" She almost shouted, thinking how she was looking forward to the bus ride this Saturday afternoon, that the bus ride would be a relief, relief from what she wasn't sure, this house? Him? She just knew that she'd been feeling constrained lately, cor-seted in an ambivalent way as if she were too flabby and wearing a girdle for support, neatness, but itching to peel the tight rubber away from her skin to just let it hang out for a while. "Do you realize the circus that mall will be on Easter Saturday! No thank you. Really. Plus I already have the gift picked out. A talking crayon set, they're holding it for me at Imagioneering."

"Talking crayon set?" he asked. He took his hands from his pants pocket and folded his arms across his chest.

"Mn-mnh. The most innovative thing," she said as she felt a brightness at the thought of Sage slice through her agitation at Rowe. "You pick up a crayon and it says its color, spells its color, names common objects that are that color. Sage will just love it. I can't wait to see her face when she opens it. You know the auditory emphasis I think is what's going to do it for her finally, you know, get her to talk. And she has like this, I don't know, this almost spiritual connection with colors, anyhow it's just the most appropriate thing for her, I'm so excited."

Rowe could see her excitement, felt it as a wave of jealousy that her excitement was directed at something other than him. He went to her and pulled her to him, gave her a peck on the lips. "I'm sure she'll appreciate it; she's very fortunate to have you in her life. So am I." He gave her a more substantial openmouthed kiss, then even started to rub himself against her.

She squirmed and pulled back to look at him. Almost ready to ask him what his problem was. Why he would try to get them both all aroused when she was on her way out of the door. Her face did ask it.

"Naughty me," he said, and held his hands up in mock surrender. "You just look so refined, so beautiful, and I just hate the thought of you in those badlands after dark; please tell me you won't stay long."

"Rowe, it's West Philly, we could darn near throw a stone from here to there, so I wish that you wouldn't call it the badlands."

"Well, it's not like your cousin will have the sense to insist that you get started back home before dark."

"I'm not arguing with you about this," she said as she jingled her keys in her pocket. She was sorry she'd told him the truth about where she was going, but this was Sage's birthday party, she wasn't about to sneak to the party of the child she loved as much as if she'd birthed her herself.

"Don't argue, Pet, just tell me you'll be back before dark."

This was the second time in as many weeks that he'd called her Pet and she couldn't figure out why he was reaching back in his memory for some twenty-year-old nickname that was almost insulting now that she was forty. Plus it reminded her too much of a time when her mistakes circled her like black-hooded she-devils laughing and pointing and closing in on her without mercy. She let it go for now, she was too preoccupied with imagining Sage's delight when she picked up the talking crayons. "I mean I'll try to get back before dark," she said as she put her purse back over her shoulder. "But I can't guarantee it. What's it, almost two, the party starts at three-thirty, so I'll stay till five-thirty, depending on the cab service it could be dark, could be light, I'm not going to box myself in like that Rowe, please don't ask me to. I mean if you're that worried, you could come with me." She held her breath after she said it, Kitt would threaten to fight her if she brought Rowe over there for Sage's birthday party of all events. And in their forty years, Kitt had never threatened to fight her.

"I wouldn't dignify that woman's house with my presence," he said. "That woman with her welfare mentality—"

"Fine," Verdi cut him off without even raising her voice. "I invited you and you declined. I'm certainly not going to listen to you berate my cousin. I'm going." She turned quickly and left the room.

She didn't storm out, didn't mutter out some sarcasm-tinged

words, didn't stop and stash and put her hands on her hips, roll her neck around, call him a motherfucker or at least an asshole. She just turned quickly, quietly, and left the room. Her footfalls were muffled on the carpeted stairway, and he wouldn't have even known she'd stepped into the outside until he heard her turn the dead bolt to lock the door behind her. That bothered him most of all, that she could leave so quietly. What else might she do so quietly, not calling attention to herself, looking so sophisticated and young?

THE HEATER clicked on and the house hummed and sighed and he thought about how he would occupy himself this afternoon. Midterms to grade, journal drafts needing his peer review, a talk to prepare for the opening of a new traveling exhibit at the university museum. He went into the dining room and poured himself a dram of brandy. He dipped his finger in the glass and sucked the brown liquid from his finger and massaged the inside of his jaw that he'd bit when he restrained himself with Penda. The brandy burned his jaw but he just held his finger there sucking on his finger as if it were a red-and-white peppermint stick. Now he turned the glass up to his mouth and sipped the brandy. He held each sip in his mouth awhile before he swallowed, swished it around to dull the throbbing in his jaw. He thought about Verdi as he slowly consumed the now fine-tasting liquor, out there all alone, riding buses with indigents, talking and laughing with God knows who likely to show up at her cousin's. She enjoyed it, he thought. Always had a side to her that resisted the idyllic lifestyle she'd been born into, too willing to wallow with those not her kind based on some notion of kinship, or because they were nice. Huh, she should have been born into a backwoods-shack existence like he'd been, then she'd redefine what nice meant, and family, he thought. He'd tell her how family could hold her back if she really wanted to know, how his family tried to keep him right there with them because he was another strong back to help with the share-cropping that barely kept enough food in their mouths for a good belch. Looked at him as if he'd deserted them when he ran away to join the armed forces so that he could go to college on the GI Bill. He'd always thought that Kitt had ways similar to his older sister, the one who spit in his face when he told her that he was getting as far away from their brand of poverty as he could before it got on his skin and stained him indelibly like it already had done to her. He could tell Verdi some truths about family all right. But he couldn't tell Verdi, couldn't share that part of his past with anyone, not even Penda knew how much he despised being from Tunica County in Mississippi, one of the poorest in the country, because he always joked and shifted into a barrage of the-town-where-I-was-born-is-so-small jokes whenever his birthplace came up. Put Verdi off when she'd ask when was he going to take her to meet his people, he'd disassociated himself years ago, a clean break that he had neither desire nor inclination to repair.

He tilted his head back and drained the glass of brandy and thought about the last time he had visited that place where he was born—he refused to call it home—where black people picked cotton or worked in the catfish factories. It was for his mother's funeral and he'd dreaded going because he and Verdi had just moved in together and she was still so weak and tenuous in her resolve to stop using. He went to his mother's funeral though, more because it was the mature, civilized thing to do than to honor any familiar bonds. He was properly mocked and cursed out by his sisters and cousins and aunts and uncles and got a glimpse of what a hell his life would have been if he'd never broken out. He decided then that not only would he never return, he would never openly acknowledge that place as being a part of his history.

He went into the kitchen and washed out his brandy glass, dried it, took it back into the dining room, and set it on the tray on the sideboard. He went into the bedroom ready to settle in the chaise and start working through his tasks. He would start with the museum talk, get the least favorite out of the way, then move on to the midterms if there was time before Verdi got back and they went out for dinner. He had to break the midterms up anyhow, could only do one or two at a time before he started to question his value as a purveyor of knowledge. She was usually apologetic when she admitted to visiting her cousin. Admitted. He'd gone on and thought the word. Knew one couldn't admit unless one has also lied. What if Verdi was lying to him, what if this whole business about going to a birthday party was a cartload of bullshit? She'd certainly left out of there glowing to be spending the afternoon with a houseful of challenged kids. And since he'd opened the window on this train of thought, he was sure that convoluted massage scenario from the other night was a made-up tale. Suddenly he felt the need to get out too. Go for a ride himself. Maybe allow his car to drift toward Sansom Street. Kitt's street. He'd put a couple of hours in on the work he needed to do, then he'd go get in his car, take in a change of scenery, get from under his own skin for a while.

Rowe always sensed that Verdi's association with Johnson would bring her down. Had tried to talk Penda into mentoring her. But Penda's stance was that one had to show a willingness to be mentored, that she wasn't of the mind of forcing herself on her students in a helping capacity. And Rowe decided that he would, in a sense, force his help on Verdi.

Verdi was coming up on the end of her second year, was living in the high-rise dormitory apartments and this year she did have a room-mate. Charity, at least that's the name she'd given herself, a puffy-haired Woodstock-clichéd, peace-and-love-spewing flower child who smelled perpetually of frangipane and made clanking sounds when she walked because of all the beads and bangles she wore. She was true to her name though, lavishly charitable to Verdi, especially with her pipe that was always stuffed with good weed. She was also polite, respectful of Verdi's space, offering to leave the tiny living room when Johnson came to stay over even though Verdi insisted not, since at least they had separate bedrooms though the walls were paper thin. And Verdi actually grew to appreciate Charity's presence in the high-rise dorm with the pint-sized kitchen that Charity also kept well stocked with fruity wine. Plus Verdi also found Charity and her hippie friends entertaining when they'd crowd into the apartment and smoke and drink and drop acid and trip off of some situation comedy like *I Love Lucy* reruns.

Though this one night, Verdi was particularly restless, a restlessness she felt all the way to her feet that were cold even under the wool sweatsocks she wore. Johnson was late yet again. She'd taken an extra-long shower and creamed her skin with a peach-scented lotion because peach was his favorite fruit, and poured herself into her tightest hip-huggers because she loved the hungry expression that came up on his face when he looked at her in those jeans, she'd put Vaseline to her lips so they'd be velvet when he finally got there to kiss her. And each time there was a knock on the door she was sure it was Johnson, wasn't him though as she'd listen to Charity let in friend after friend of her own. And by the time she went out into the living room it was packed with Charity's friends and she felt such a letdown that she called Kitt to see if she'd heard from Johnson, that Johnson said he was stopping by there to bring down some of Kitt's prize-winning chicken and dumplings. Had he? she asked Kitt. And Kitt told her that Johnson had, that he'd left though, that he'd seemed not to be feeling well, that Posie noticed it too, that she wanted to talk to her about Johnson and his general state of well-being next time she came over, when was she coming over? Kitt asked, concern pushing from her mouth into Verdi's ear, swimming around in Verdi's ear even before her words registered. And Verdi's restlessness ballooned into a stifling dread over the thought of something being wrong with her Johnson. She couldn't even begin to ingest the seed of such a thing. Would tilt her equilibrium and have her spinning like a music-box ballerina gone out of control. She shook off the dread like she'd shaken it off when Moose told her a similar thing, shook it off with an agitation at the one expressing the concern. Said, "Yeah, yeah, yeah, Kitt, whatever, someone's at the door, I got to go." She hung the phone up then on Kitt, rationalized away the worry in Kitt's words as just her cousin's overly obsessive concern for people she held most dear.

So this night when Johnson was so late and Verdi was working so hard to keep her denial intact so that it remained just a restlessness that had her feet cold, Charity and her friends were so gregariously insistent that Verdi join them as they indulged in a smorgasbord of drugs. There were more of them here than usual, Verdi knew the usual ones by name, but there were almost twenty people crammed in here tonight and the living room was hot and they laughed and glowed, and radiated peace and love as they rained out just-conceived poetry from their ever-smiling mouths promulgated by their various chemical mixes. And they were passing around pipes stuffed with hashish, and plastic cups filled with Kool-Aid and grain alcohol, and mescaline dropped on Three X mints, and green pills packed with speed, and pink pills and Darvon, and Quaaludes as they sang from "White Rabbit," told each other to go ahead and feed their heads.

Verdi stood against the wall in the living room right next to the phone, hoping it would ring, picking it up every few minutes to make sure the dial tone was intact. She waved away the drugs being buttered like exquisite hors d'oeuvres and laughed at the crazed and intoxicated acting like performance apes as they swung and dangled from the furniture. Then someone stuck a pipe under her nose and the seeds were popping and glowing orange and red and the smell of burning dried leaves was tantalizing and even though she never ever got high without Johnson because he liked to be there to supervise her indulgence, she felt the need to get back at him for making her wait like this, so she accepted the pipe, but after that first pull on the pipe she said, "Damn!" because this weed was much stronger than anything she'd ever shared with Johnson. And after a second pull that she held in her throat until her head wanted to explode, her defenses were stripped and she was giggling all over the place too, getting ready to recite some poetry of her own and the next time the pipe came her way and she sucked the smoke all the way to her chest she knew that this was no ordinary weed because she was moving her mouth, trying to talk, but no words would come out, and Charity was standing in front of her, smiling her omnipresent smile, saying "Oh-oh my ebony friend, you've gone and gotten yourself good and dusted."

Verdi's good reasoning kicked in like a flash of light and she was sorry then, tried to pull the smoke back up from her lungs, to blow it out. But it was too late, it was down, burning her chest as it went. And she was imagining the scenes Johnson had described to her when people were high on angel dust. "I don't mess with that shit," generally, he'd said. "Too unpredictable, like acid except that it hits you all at once and your reality fades in and out on you. At least acid fucks you up and keeps you fucked up till you come down and you're not cursed with knowing how fucked up you are while you're in the throes."

She was in the throes now though at first she experienced nothing more than a twitching deep in the muscles of her arms and legs. The twitching grew in degrees though and soon she felt as if her limbs were answering to some marionette's strings out of her immediate control even though when she looked down, stretched her arms out, patted her feet, they seemed to do as she wished. If this was the worst of it, she could handle it, she told herself, as she nodded to smiling face after smiling face getting in her face, asking her if she was cool. "Yeah, yeah, I'm cool," she said over and over again, and soon she was walking, squeezing herself through the room too, asking others too until the entire apartment seemed to be chanting, "Cool? Cool?"

But then her eyes started to tear and she couldn't tolerate the light from the television and then it wasn't just the television but the light over the stove, and the table lamp, and soon even the brightness of Charity and her hippie friends had the tiny living room ablaze as they now warned each other not to let the trip go bad. Verdi had to squint and finally dig out a pair of dark glasses just so that the dazzling light wouldn't make her own trip go bad.

They turned the music on high, Janis Joplin, and Verdi's ears were hypersensitive now like her eyes and she thought she needed to find some cotton for her ears because the music was really bothering her. It didn't seem to be affecting anyone else adversely though, they were twirling around and dancing out of sync to the music and touching each other and laughing and squealing. And now she thought that if she couldn't blot the music out, she'd just have to leave the apartment for a while. Not that she was paranoid about them turning on her though there had been published reports of college students killed by drug-crazed roommates and clearly seventy percent of the sweating swaying bodies in this room right now were total strangers to her, it was more the thought that her mother was trying to reach her through the music. Johnson had told her that he knew people who got dusted regularly just so they could see God, or the devil, but he'd never mentioned so that they could communicate across space with the living. But there it was, her mother's voice saying, "Verdi Mae, you put one step in front of the other and you walk on out from that place right now."

Verdi felt queasy and her knees started buckling and she had to hold herself up with the wall as she edged to the door, to get out of there like her mother said, go for a walk, find herself a cup of warm milk to still the twitching in her joints. Charity caught her though just as she was about to slip through the half-opened door.

"Where are you going, my beautiful ebony friend?" she asked.

"Just for ice," Verdi lied. "The Kool-Aid is hot, the air in here is hot, I'm hot, you're hot, I'm going down the hall for ice."

"I'm sorry they're crowding you out like this and making it so hot. Please don't let it blow your high."

Charity's eyes were sincere and pleading and Verdi just nodded because she was afraid that her high was in fact being blown.

"There were only supposed to be four, six at the most, not twenty," Charity continued. "They've multiplied like roaches, and I know any minute they'll be ready to start fucking like rabbits in a cabbage patch. I probably won't even be able to pee tomorrow I'll probably be fucked so blindly."

Charity's words were registering and not registering at the same time in Verdi's head as she tried to tell Charity to just leave with her, she didn't have to be fucked if she didn't want it. But her mouth wouldn't cooperate with her brain, her brain still too shocked from what Charity had just said, and she could only push out grunting sounds. Charity grabbed her in a close hug and Verdi could feel her rib cage through the thin cotton dress she wore. She suddenly felt sorry for Charity that she was so thin, so giving.

She took Charity's hand, was finally able to get her mouth to work. "Leave with me," she was able to say. But Charity just smiled sweetly and waved. "Bye, bye, my ebony friend," she said as Verdi stepped all the way out into the hallway and watched the door close. She was immobilized at first as she just stood there looking at the door as if she were trying to memorize her own address. She thought she would go over to the Quad, try to find Cheryl and Tower. She ran down the hall to the elevator and didn't even notice that she wore no shoes on her feet.

The crisp Saturday night air was dark and smoky blue and filled with activity. She took her hands down from ears, lifted her sunglasses off of her face, and stuck them in her 'fro like a tiara. She felt a horrified sinking in her chest over what Kitt had said about Johnson as she wove in and out of the eight o'clock rush hour of campus foot travelers on their way to and from dinner, or to secure beer for frat parties, or borrow door-knocker earrings to wear to some private set, or assemble in groups to venture downtown to the Bijou Café, or over to Gino's Empty Foxhole in St. Mary's basement to hear some authentic jazz, or to some underground rally, or over-the-top hard-rock concert at the Electric Factory, or like Verdi, on a high that had the potential to go bad as she headed to the low-rise to find Chery and Tower, maybe Johnson might even come in.

Her steps were dragging and she still didn't yet realize her only feet covering was her double-knit sweatsocks. She was halfway to the low-rise when the continuous friction of wool against concrete and now against steel as she crossed the street lined with trolley tracks finally cut through the jittering in her muscles that was getting all the atten-tion and reached her brain and made her say out loud, "Damn, my feet hurt." She stopped right where she was in the middle of the street, though to her fortune the light was green, and lifted one foot, then the other, squeezed and massaged them along the soles and was oblivious to the throngs of students also crossing this street and now blaring car horns as the light changed and Verdi still stood there massaging one foot, then the other, and letting out an aha, over how good it felt.

Such was the scene Rowe happened upon as he headed in from the library, he always spent Saturdays between five and eight in the library. It was emptiest then and he enjoyed the solitude as he reserved reading material for his classes, reviewed journals, did a little of his own writing and research, maybe even graded a few papers. Afterward he and his wife, Penda, would generally go in town for dinner, tonight it would be the Harvey House on Broad Street, then to the Midtown Theater to see *Funny Girl*. Rowe enjoyed the relative material comfort and predictability of his life, especially having survived his financially uncertain childhood. He'd been awarded full professorship and it looked like his wife's tenure was imminent as well. They'd just moved out of the graduate dorm and into their own house just off campus in the transitionally upscale area where many of the professors lived. So he was feeling a satisfaction in his muscles over having completed much work at the quiet Saturday-evening library. He had a smile on his face, a whistle in his mouth, a lightness to his steps, a rousing appetite for his wife as he glanced at his watch to see if there would be time for a quickie when he got in, and it was in that second as he felt a twinge in his manhood over thoughts of being with his wife that he looked up and saw Verdi stopping traffic in the middle of the street as she hopped from one shoeless foot to the other. At first he didn't realize that it was her, saw only that it was a young black woman in a blue-and-red university sweatshirt and tight blue jeans and socks that appeared worn away at the soles. Then he did notice it was Verdi, didn't want to admit that it was the curve of her hips in the tight blue jeans that brought her into focus as he ran toward her, unable to fathom that Verdi of all people, so brimming over with promise and ability, would be in the middle of the street acting like a drug-crazed moron.

"Verdi? Verdi?" he called into the commotion, and then rushed into it himself as he held his hand toward the traffic like a cop and half dragged, half scooped Verdi to the relative safety of the sidewalk. "What is going on with you?" he asked over and over as Verdi leaned her weight on him even as she tried to stand straight and tall unaided.

Verdi's high was blown sufficiently for the moment for her to be deeply embarrassed. "I—I, I'll explain," she said as she looked directly at Rowe, and then unable to conjure up an acceptable explanation save the truth, which was so unacceptable to her at this moment, and she figured to Rowe also, she just hunched her shoulders and looked at the ground.

Rowe peered hard into Verdi's eyes. Had seen enough students wasted off any of a myriad of substances to recognize that Verdi was fired up. He circled Verdi in his arms and told her that she would be okay, even as she got the nerve up to try to explain what she'd done, she didn't know it was angel dust, "honestly," she said, and started flailing her arms and gasping on her words as he told her over and over again that it was okay; it was all okay.

What could he do for her? he asked, whispered in her ear because he was that close as he pulled her over to a ledge and helped her to sit, and then sat himself, his arm back around her shoulder, squeezing, telling her some more that she was okay. "Fine, you're going to be just fine," he said in his most soothing voice, "just tell me what I can do."

He looked her over from head to toe, decided not to comment on her lack of shoes. Besides her behavior right now was mild compared to the outrageous, even bizarre scenes he'd been privy to since he'd been here. Just last year he'd seen a bed in the middle of an intersection every bit as busy as this one, two students snuggled up as if they'd gone to their parents' home for the weekend, though one was so severely intoxicated he nearly died that morning.

She wobbled some on the ledge. He put his foot out to keep her from falling. His knee was pressing into the calf of her leg at first and he shifted his foot quickly. He prided himself on the tasteful professorial distance he maintained with all of his students, even the ones who'd cried on his shoulder the several years he'd been at this university.

"I—I'm fine," she said. "I'm, oh God, I'm embarrassed, I'm just going back to my dorm and putting my head under my pillow until Monday morning."

He laughed out loud. Fingered her chin. "No need to be embarrassed with me, ever," he said. "I want you to feel as though you can come to me for anything, anything at all, Penda too, I mean that, Verdi."

She nodded, but avoided looking at him. Heard Johnson calling her name. Thank God, Johnson, she thought as she looked through the Saturday-evening campus rush hour of foot traffic, saw Johnson crossing against the light, cars blaring at him now as he risked being struck to get to her.

He sucked the air in through his teeth when he saw Johnson approach. Had even remarked to Penda what a mismatch they were, what does she see in that street thug? he'd asked his wife. Probably completes her in some way that you're not privy to, Penda had said. Nor should you be.

Rowe took her hand and helped her off the ledge. Bristled because Johnson was right up on them now.

Verdi stumbled as she tried to get to Johnson. "Whoa, Verdi, you okay?" Johnson said as Johnson and Rowe lunged for Verdi's wobbly body at the same time and almost ended up clutching at each other.

"Actually, no. She's not okay," Rowe said as he straightened up and yielded his grasp of Verdi.

Johnson took her in his arms, squeezed her in a hug, and told her how he'd been looking for her. "Charity said you went to get ice, what's going on with you, baby, out here with no shoes on?" He was whispering now and Rowe cleared his throat.

"Uh, if you'll excuse us, Professor, I'm going to walk Verdi back to her dorm." Johnson didn't look at Rowe as he spoke, looked only at Verdi. Didn't even want to see Rowe's face right now, really. Was still too disturbed from seeing him sitting on the ledge with Verdi, their bodies almost touching they were so close, as if the space between them could have just as easily been filled with an embrace.

Rowe resisted the impulse to grunt as Verdi leaned on Johnson.

"Really, thank you, Professor," Verdi blurted, "I mean for everything." She tried to hold on to this current flash of reality that seemed like it wanted to stay for a while and not fall and lift away. Now that Johnson was here, her refuge, she thought, she could go back to the way things were before she tried to get high without Johnson even as she felt a piercing sense of gratitude toward Rowe. Sweet. Very sweet, she thought as she found more of her balance and leaned less of herself on Johnson.

Verdi extended her hand to Rowe. "I'll see you in class?" She said it both as a question and a statement of fact. Her eyes went big as she said it, her mouth turned up in a demure smile.

He took her hand. Squeezed it. Said, "Verdi, please take care of yourself, you've much too much to offer to risk blowing it." Her hand was warm inside of his; he felt the handshake as a warmth washing over him. Then he dropped her hand abruptly, thinking now of his wife, telling himself that it was Penda he had on his mind even as he looked into Verdi's downwardly slanted eyes and felt a powerful urging for the contact of skin against skin, the kind that would make him rush home—as he was about to do now—to be with his wife.

Verdi and Rowe sealed a friendship after the evening he found her dancing in the middle of the street. He never reminded her how horrified he was to realize that was her stopping traffic like a common drug-crazed lunatic; she never allowed angel dust to touch her lips in any form. He treated her as if she were his prize student; she went to extraordinary lengths preparing for each class to ensure that she was. Occasionally they shared coffee after class and he'd tell her how gifted she was, really. Invited her once again to have dinner with Penda and her sister's son because that young man was more in her league, this time he said it outright. And though she declined, she did it graciously and without insult, took his gesture only as an indication of his fatherly affection for her, even as she talked Johnson up. "Johnson's going to be a famous architect one day," she'd say, eyes shining when she did, or, "Johnson's so devoted to his mother, it's sooo sweet," or, "Johnson got a raise, did I tell you? It's rare for the part-timers to get a raise, but he did and hasn't let his GPA slip in the process." She never let the opportunity pass to praise Johnson's attributes to Rowe.

But when Verdi's parents visited Philadelphia for a national ministers' conference, and Verdi's mother planned a dinner at Bookbinder's so that she could properly meet Verdi's young man, Johnson pleaded overtime at the last minute. And though Verdi was secretly relieved because her throat would get so tight and dry and she'd lose the ability to swallow at the thought that Johnson might fail her parents' inspection of him, she was still embarrassed that he'd bowed out on them with such short notice like that and so to fill the potentially insulting hole that Johnson's absence left, Verdi invited Rowe and Penda, and Penda was suffering with a stomach virus and didn't come and so it was just Rowe.

Rowe charmed her mother, commenting on her jewelry, her wonderful taste in restaurants, her ability to raise a fine young woman. Such an asset to the university, he said of Verdi, and then went on to assure Leroy and Hortense that he and his wife Penda had adopted Verdi in a sense so they could be sure she was well taken care of. Then when Verdi and Hortense excused themselves to freshen their lipstick, Rowe confessed to Leroy that he was quite frankly concerned about Verdi's choice in a steady beau. From one of the city's less affluent neighborhoods, he said about Johnson. Not that he had anything at all against the financial-aid students, some of the university's brightest stars are on full scholarships, he said, but this one is lacking in not only economic resources, but a certain strength of character as well. And Leroy thanked Rowe for his concern, made a comment about youth being wasted on the young, told Rowe to extend their appreciation also to his wife, reminded him that Verdi had an aunt and a first cousin in town with whom she was very close, and if anything ever came up with Verdi and he and Hortense were unreachable, please feel free to go to them, they were Verdi's surrogate family, he said.

Rowe swallowed his opinion of Kitt then since he could see that Leroy held her in some regard. It would be rude, he told himself, to explain to Leroy that he thought Kitt a potential albatross around Verdi's neck. He just nodded and sipped his coffee and then stood and smiled and pulled out Hortense's and Verdi's seat when they returned to the table. But something about the way Leroy raised his eyebrows and seemed to study Rowe as he went into his subtle tirade against Johnson made Rowe squirm. Made him think that Leroy was trying to decide whether Rowe's concern for his only child bordered on the inappropriate. So Rowe spent the dessert-and-coffee portion of the meal talking about Penda, chronicling the accomplishments of some of his other students who were also gems, analyzing the fallacies of the Black Power Movement, and Leroy seemed to loosen up toward him even as Rowe decided that he would retreat somewhat from getting involved in Verdi's affairs, lest his purely altruistic motives be misconstrued.

Johnson was certainly glad he retreated. At times felt himself becoming obsessed with his dislike of the man. When he and Verdi would smoke marijuana through his oversized navy-blue bong pipe and go into their continuous floods of laughter at nothing and everything, just that they were young and high and in love, Johnson would turn his humor on Rowe, say something like, "He walks like he has a broomstick stuck up his ass, either that or like he's trying not to shit on himself." Or, "Why does he talk through his nose all nasal and shit like a white boy?" Or, "What's up with the played-out, diamond-patterned sweater vests? What's he got, stock in an argyle factory?"

It would disturb Johnson that Verdi would sometimes stop laughing, that a seriousness would edge across her face as if that seriousness was always present when it came to Rowe but just too bashful to reveal itself unless provoked by Johnson's semivicious jabs at the man. And Verdi would say something like, "Johnson, that's not nice, really. He's a down brother, a very good brother. You just have to get to know him."

Johnson would want to ask her then just how well did she know him anyhow? Did she know him more than as a professor, did she maybe know him as a man? He never did ask her such a thing though. Couldn't unbridle such an insecurity for Verdi to see, that he felt threatened by the likes of Rowe, stalked by the image of how easily, naturally Verdi and Rowe entered each other's presence.

Would use that insecurity though as an excuse, line it up with all the other excuses waiting patiently to be plucked to justify his using: he missed his brother who'd been killed; or the one in jail; or the one in San Diego; or his mother's grief wasn't thinning fast enough; or he'd failed a big exam; or Tower drank the last of the wine; or he was hassled by a racist cop; or Kitt and Posie weren't at home; or Verdi didn't laugh at his jokes about Rowe; or his stomach hurt; or the sun was in his eyes; or he woke up on an alternate day. Because now he had skidded to nodding on Bug's couch as often as once a week. And though he'd cried like a baby and had gotten back into Kitt and Posie's good graces after the day Posie slapped him, swore to them it had been only that once, that he was experimenting, that it would never ever happen again, and they agreed to keep silent about it to Verdi because they truly adored Johnson so, he was even jeopardizing their adoration. And he avoided them on his days when the pipe organ sang, and his mother, Tower and Cheryl, he avoided everybody except for Verdi. He just couldn't be long away from Verdi.

Seven

JOHNSON GOT TO Sage's party first. Before Posie who had whisked Sage out of the house early and taken her to an Easter-egg hunt at church and then to Strawbridge's to try to find an old-fashioned crinoline slip for Sage to wear under the dress she'd bought for her; before people on the block who didn't want to be the first ones in so they were waiting until they saw some cars parked out front; even before Sage's classmates who lived in all different parts of the city and had to suffer through the bump and grind of Easter Saturday traffic tie-ups wherever there was a mall. So Johnson was the first to ring the bell, the first to step into the scrubbed-clean ambience of Kitt's enclosed porch, the first to smell cloves mixed with the sweet and salty aroma of baking ham, the first to hand Kitt a colorfully wrapped box for Sage, a tissue-wrapped bottle in a bag for

Kitt, the first to grab her in a hug that was so generous in its unconditionality that he didn't want to let go.

He did, though. They both let go as they stared at each other laughing excitedly, and then not knowing what to do with all the energy between them, all the years, they hugged again. Johnson kissed her cheek then. Told her how good she looked, tugged at her locks pushed back with a yellow-and-green-swirled headband. "Told you you were still political." He laughed. "When a sister lets her hair lock she's doing more than making a fashion statement."

"Well what about you, Mr. Johnson? Let's check you out. My, my, my, aren't you the dapper one in your chenille sweater." She took a pensive, analytical stance: hand on her chin, head tilted slightly, eyes squinted. "Let me see now, you still got the mustache, still got that little goatee, of course there's much less hair, you didn't get any taller, not much wider either, which is unusual for someone over fifty."

"Fifty!" he blurted. "Watch yourself, Kitt, if you gonna make me over fifty, then that puts you up there too."

"Okay, stay forty-one, Johnson. But I do have to give you the head-to-toe look-over. You pass, Johnson. Still our Johnson."

"Well, speaking of passing tests, where's Posie, and the birthday girl, where's Sage?"

"Mama took her out to find her a slip. You know Mama and trying to dress people up, like the world's gonna end if Sage doesn't have the exact kind of slip under her dress."

They just stood and looked at each other some more, smiled, and finally Kitt cleared her throat and pulled a bottle of sparkling cider from the bag handed her by Johnson. "Well, I'm just gonna crack this seal and pull out my best flutes and you and I shall toast to you being back in Philly, and back in our home."

"That's sweet of you, Kitt," he said as he followed her into the dining room, and she held the bottle of sparkling cider up in front of her as if it were a trophy, he could see even from the back that she was grinning that ear-to-ear grin that she and her mother were famous for, and her cousin. He cleared his throat, didn't want to think about her cousin right now.

The table was set with a yellow-and-green party cloth that matched the balloons bobbing along the ceiling and her headband and the blouse that she had on, opened as if it were a jacket, hiding the print of her hips. He'd always wondered why she always kept herself shielded under a long shirt, or wide jacket, or loose-fitting dress, built as she was. He'd asked her once. Drunk, and back in town after having been gone for two years and crying on Kitt's shoulder because Verdi wouldn't see him. And he had exasperated Kitt's patience acting like a little puppy, which is what she'd told him, if he wasn't lapping up that cheap wine like a thirsty puppy, and then shitting and pissing like some unhousebroken pet, maybe Verdi would at least meet him somewhere for coffee. And he was so intoxicated, so dented and bruised, that he grabbed Kitt around the collar of her shirt, told her that if she wasn't always covering her ass up she'd have a steady man in her life. "Why you do that, Kitt? Why?" he'd asked with all the melodrama of one who'd gone a full liter of wine past the point when his vision and logic blurred. "You got a beautiful ass and you always hiding it like you ashamed of it or something. Stop doing it, Kitt. Please, please, stop hiding your beautiful ass." He sobbed and shook and implored as if he were asking his mother not to die. Kitt pushed him away. Told him to leave her house right then and go somewhere and pray that he'd wake up the next morning with his memory erased. He did. At least he pretended that he'd forgotten. Called her the next morning and said that he had the taste for pancakes, why didn't they get together at Broadway's for breakfast. Met her hesitant tone with an apology for not stopping by there the night before. Said he must have passed out in his room because he'd come to around dawn dressed to go out but knew he hadn't been anywhere. He had to pretend. No way would he have been to look at her again having treated her with such base disrespect.

She was handing him a flute filled with cider and they clinked glasses and sipped and smiled honest smiles.

"My God it's so, so good to see you, Kitt," he said as he drained his glass and she refilled it. "Makes it feel like I'm really visiting home seeing you."

She asked then if he'd been back to the street where he'd grown up. Chancellor Street. And when he shook his head slowly, hunched his shoulders, and said that since his mother's death, and the scattering of his homeboys from Yale to jail, there was no cause really for him to return.

She told him maybe it was for the best. If he was inclined to cry in his increasing years, he might cry if he rode through there now. "Block looks like a war zone," she said.

"I see you not letting that happen on your block."

"Oh hell no. Our block committee is strong, legal too, we can impose fines if someone's hedges get out of control, or they go too many Saturdays without getting their asses out and sweeping in front of their doors, and don't even let the exterior paint start chipping."

"Kitt, I'm surprised at you. Didn't you used to champion freedom from government intervention."

"This isn't the government, baby, this is communal, this is about a damned-near-perfect block determined to survive. Shit, if the government hadn't hooked generation after generation on welfare, then cut them all off cold turkey without peripheral support like basic medical care, decent schools, an occasional cop to cruise through and at least pretend to be a deterrent to crime, you know, West Philly wouldn't look nearly as bad as it does."

"See you haven't changed, still raising hell like you used to." He laughed when he said it.

"And you have changed," she said as she raised her glass in salute. "It's all good too." She wanted to tell him that she hoped Verdi could appreciate the changed him. But didn't want to break it to him that she'd tricked Verdi there under the pretense of having ice cream and birthday cake in honor of Sage. Just a few of us, she'd told Verdi so that she wouldn't get suspicious, just you and me and Sage and Mama, and Doreen and Nicole and Patrick from school she'd said, nonchalantly. And now she was getting fidgety over what she'd done. Suppose it backfired? Suppose Verdi did something utterly uncharacteristic like convince Rowe to come with her? Or suppose Verdi went so furious that she stormed out, that would damn near devastate Johnson. Now she felt sorry for Johnson standing there, grinning like a choirboy who hit the high note. She imagined how his face would look all contorted with hurt pride if Verdi did such a thing as storm out on him.

She took his empty glass and walked back into the kitchen. He followed her back and said, "Whoa," when the yellow of the kitchen hit his eyes.

"Yeah, yeah, yeah, it's bright, I know," she said, half laughing as she squeezed a drop of Joy dishwashing liquid into each glass and commenced washing them out. "Has that effect on everyone who steps in here for the first time. Specially my new customers, I got to hurry and get them into that back room where I do the massage therapy before they get tired of squinting and turn around and leave."

"How's that going?" he asked as he put his hand to the knob of her therapy room. "Can I peep in?"

"Sure thing, I'll give you a guided tour." She finished washing the glasses and laid them upside down on a dish towel to drain and Johnson opened the door to her therapy room and she walked in first.

"It's small, really small," she said as she clicked on the light.

"Not all that small," he said as his eyes bounced around the room. "Nice color to these walls, really toned down after being in the kitchen."

"Yeah, it's like a mauve. Usually I'm not even a pink person, you know that's more Mama, all lacy and feminine, but mauve has a lot of brown in it, and brown is stabilizing to the flightiness of pink and well, my customers seem to like it."

"What's not to like, looking at these walls, while your fingers hit all the tight spots?" he said, his eyes following Kitt's fingers as she pointed around the room, first to the matching hurricane lamps on the sideboard against the wall that held folded towels and sheets.

"I usually have candles going," she said instructively. "You know candles make a small room cozy and open it up at the same time, plus the way the flames dance makes for a dreamy effect, especially with what they do to shadows against the wall and all of that."

"Mnh, vanilla," Johnson said as he tilted his head and closed his eyes and took in the scent. And now Kitt was explaining how the different parts of the brain were affected by different aromas. "Vanilla is powerfully calming," she said. And then she showed him her table, folded now, and explained how she'd leave a sheet at the foot of the table and walk out of the room while they changed. "I tell them that they can take off as much or as little as they like but that they should be covered up when I come back into the room. Some are incredibly shy, you'd be surprised," she half laughed, "until I get going and then they're tossing off the sheet pointing out the spots that need it most."

"Oh, I can believe that," Johnson said, and then went into an imitation in an exaggerated voice, "Oh Miss Kitt, I'm really tight right here, oh oh ah."

Kitt laughed so hard she almost tripped over the specially designed chair, prompting Johnson to ask what the hell it was. "I know my girl don't be doing no freaky stuff up in here."

She laughed some more and then explained how the chair was configured so that they knelt into it if they were only getting a neck-and-back as opposed to stretching out on the table for a full-body. She got instructive again. Described the music she played while she worked. "I prefer jazz, but I'll oblige their taste, so long as it's not hard rock or something like that that would go against the grain of the mood." Her words came in a rush and she flexed her fingers as if she were about to sink them into some needy back.

Johnson got serious too as he studied Kitt. How competent she appeared now as she pointed out the science behind this and the reasoning to that in the arrangement of her massage-therapy room. She was always smart, he thought, and focused, more focused than he'd ever been, more focused even than her cousin. He shrugged off thoughts of her cousin right now. "I'm proud of you, Kitt," he said, his voice so clear, so absent its infamous joke-making chuckle that Kitt was momentarily startled. "You should have had the opportunities that a lot of us squandered, you know, you just should have."

"Huh, where'd that come from?" she asked as she put the face rest back into the clamps of the folded massage table.

Johnson didn't say anything, just stared at her with a look that was halfway between amazement and affection.

Kitt cleared her throat when she noticed Johnson's eyes locked on her with such intensity. She felt suddenly cloaked in a shyness about being in this tight, vanilla-scented room with Johnson, and Johnson no longer tossing around one-liners to make her laugh. She cleared her throat again and then scratched the inside of her throat because it was really dry, really didn't need clearing, needed some water instead, needed to douse the fire that was trying to edge up her throat.

"I should make sure the party favors are in ample supply," she said as she motioned toward the door.

"Good move," Johnson said, laughing, his laugh forced this time. " 'Cause if we stay in here much longer I'm just gonna have to come outta my shirt, Sister Kitt, you know, and you gonna have to demonstrate your technique and show as well as tell." That was risky, he knew. Trying to make a joke out of something that he felt so intensely at this moment he couldn't even look at her. He subverted the thought. Pressed it down with his thumb and didn't even realize that he was pinching the skin on the heel of his palm until he was momentarily riveted by the pain.

They were back in the bright sun of the kitchen walls and Verdi felt her extroversion reemerge. "Well, stay in town long enough and I might oblige," she said as she reached behind him into her therapy room to click off the light, knowing with the honesty with which she knew most things that Johnson's back was off-limits, she knew him too well. Much too well.

And since they were in the kitchen now, and their closeness had space to spread out and thin and blur against the yellow walls and become nonthreatening again, just an innocent affection between friends, Johnson was able to ask if there was a special man in her life.

"No." She said it with finality, thinking now about Bruce, the new client with the wide back who Posie had been trying to persuade her to agree to date. She'd refused his advances again the night before when he called to make another appointment. She'd been denying to herself though how the man had nudged open that flap she kept securely covering that part of herself reserved for romance. Plus she didn't like the idea that her mother was pushing her so, couldn't stand seeing someone else's hands stirring around in the brew, mixing ingredients before their time. Almost gasped when she thought this as she looked at Johnson's face and realized with a searing illumination that her efforts to put Johnson and Verdi together might be mixing wrong too, putting together flavors that shouldn't even be in the same pot.

"Well, what about Sage's daddy?" Johnson cut in on her thoughts.

"The best thing he did was let go the DNA that gave me my little heart." She turned the glasses right side up that she'd just washed and then filled them with water, she swallowed hers in large gulps while she handed him his. She went to the oven and peeped in, though everything was done, just on warmer, the macaroni and cheese, the smoked turkey breast, even the miniature pizza squares for the children. She opened the refrigerator next and stared at her container of Caesar salad trying to decide whether to grate the cheese over it now, or wait until she was about to set it out. She knew that the cheese could wait, felt foolish for keeping her back to Johnson like this. "Anyhow, no, nobody else, really nobody since." She turned around then, could tell by the sad look that washed over Johnson's face that he understood that kind of loneliness.

"Well, do I have to step to that Negro? Is he doing all right by Sage?"

"Does what I let him do."

"Well, he better treat my girl right, that's all I got to say. You tell him your best buddy Johnson is back in town and he accepts no foolishness when it comes to his Kitt."

She nodded an embrace. Didn't run to him with her arms open and let her circle him in hers; her face did it though. And he acknowledged it with an embraceable nod of his own, and since things had gotten so pure between them, he almost asked her about Verdi. And Kitt braced herself because she could feel it coming, could see it welling up from his stomach that he held in now. And she was about to beat him to it, about to confess that yes, Verdi was on her way there, that his being there would be a shock to Verdi because she was emphatic that she didn't want to see him; she was ready to apologize to Johnson now because she felt even more strongly that having Johnson and Verdi meet like this was a mistake. But right then the doorbell rang and they both jumped, both relieved really, especially Kitt because she knew that it wasn't Verdi, expected Verdi to be at least a half hour late according to what she'd said earlier. And Kitt said, "All right now, a party's getting ready to start over here," and she rushed to get into the living room, with Johnson following behind her.

In groups they came. One mother bringing three of Sage's friends, Doreen and Nicole and Patrick, and another bringing Bretta and Lou; two sets of parents came with the attention-demanding Hawkins twins, then Leeanne, Kitt's next-door neighbor inched in, and the Tilleys from farther down the block, and two of her clients from the precinct came with somebody's child they'd borrowed for the afternoon just so that they could come and socialize with Kitt, maybe meet some of the single women who'd be there, and the three girls related to Penda were there, though they weren't different learners, Kitt had invited them because they were patient and caring with Sage, plus she knew that their mother wouldn't come, she was so polite with the distance she kept. And most everybody carried vibrantly wrapped boxes and Kitt started a tower of gifts atop the dining-room buffet, and Johnson helped her hang the coats, and pour the punch, and people were mingling and nibbling on roasted salted nuts and the crepe paper was hanging in streamers and tickling people's faces and it really was starting to feel like a party in there. Then Kitt wondered aloud where the heck Posie was, she was making Sage late for her own birthday celebration.

As if on cue Posie and Sage rushed in, Sage stood in the middle of the room and twirled around and around to show off her party dress, green and yellow like the crepe paper and balloons and other party ware. She made deep throaty laughing sounds and put her hands to her mouth so happy was she to see all of her friends. Posie almost did the same as Sage. Not actually twirling, but she did spin around once as if to show off her own brand of a party dress, waist-cinching, ruffles around the low-cut neckline. She turned from one corner of the room to the next smiling and batting her eyes and patting her chest lightly as if all these people were here to see her and she was very excited and flattered and careful to give them all a proper greeting.

Kitt and Johnson watched from the dining room, Kitt sucking her teeth and saying, see, told you Mama hasn't changed, still the little girl she was when you left here twenty years ago. And Johnson was about to burst he was so thrilled to lay eyes on Posie again, and he melted over the sight of Sage. "My God, Kitt, she's beautiful, Sage is such a beautiful little girl."

Kitt gushed. "God she is, isn't she? You know, I took one look at her when she was born, and I saw this wisdom in her eyes, and her name came to me in a flash. Sage."

Then Kitt called out to Sage and she barreled toward the sound of her mother's voice, almost knocked Johnson over to get to her, and Kitt braced herself and took her daughter's head against her womb, said, "Johnson, meet my slice of sunshine, my brilliant baby girl, Sage."

Johnson patted the top of Sage's head and she jerked back from her mother to look at him. Her directness as she stared at him, her lips pursed, her head tilted, her fists balled, made Johnson clear his throat and pat his feet back and forth and squirm. She extended her fist and Johnson made a quick move as if dodging a punch from this little girl. Kitt laughed, said, "She's trying to shake hands with you, Johnson. It takes a lot of effort for her to extend her fingers, I think she likes to reserve her fine motor skills for wrapping around her crayons."

"Oh, well, in that case." Johnson tried to shrug off his mild embarrassment. "Very pleased to make your acquaintance." He stooped to Sage's eye level and took her fist in his hands and began gently unfurling her fingers and then just held on to her wide-open hand.

"Miss Kitt," he said, "I'd like permission to give this little Miss Sage a kiss on the cheek."

He did and Sage smiled at the feel of his mustache against her cheek. Blue. That's what she thought she saw around him and now she was sure as he stood back up and tugged lightly on the barrette holding her cornrow in place. A blue that rose up like the inside of the biggest waves she'd seen last summer from the boardwalk at Wildwood that were also mixed with purple and black. She liked colors that moved and showed themselves from every side.

Johnson felt a tap on his shoulder as he continued to smile at Sage and marvel at the intensity in her stare. "Where's mine?" an Estée Lauder–scented voice hit his ear and his nose at the same time and there Posie was, a grown-up version—at least in looks—of the child who'd just stared at him so.

"Posie, baby," he said as he rushed to hug her and squeezed her so tightly until he could feel her giggling against him, until he realized when she didn't let go that she wasn't giggling, she was crying, and he rubbed her back in wide circles and held her some more and felt as if he wanted to cry too.

Kitt pulled Sage away, back into the living room where her friends were transfixed by *Beauty and the Beast* playing on television. And Johnson walked Posie in the opposite direction into the sunshine pouring off of the kitchen walls. "I'm sorry to be making such a spectacle out of myself," she said as she nudged back from Johnson and dabbed at the corners of her eyes and patted her chest. "But I prayed, I mean I prayed so hard for you, Johnson. Only people in my life I ever prayed as hard for were my chile and my grandbaby and my only niece." Johnson stiffened when she made reference to her niece. "And I'm not a regular churchgoer, but I do have a personal relationship with the Lord and He said, fast and pray, and I have done that on your behalf so many times and I'm just so overwhelmed with pride and joy to see you standing here, looking good, Johnson baby, you look sooo good."

"No, you look good, Posie," he said as he tried to keep the tremble from his voice, tried to keep the lumps accumulating in the corners of his eyes from liquefying and drizzling down his face.

"Complexion looks healthy, nice tone to it."

"Posie, you're the one with the flawless skin—"

"Hair got a rich luster means you're eating right." She reached up and rubbed her fingers along his neat fade of a haircut, then walked around to his back pretending not to notice the moistness around his eyes.

"God, Posie, so much I want to say to you. So many apologies I owe you for letting you down the way that I did."

She jabbed at his shoulders. "Nice muscle mass for a young man getting into middle age. You been working out too."

"I mean the disappointment in your face the last time I saw you when I was leaving Philly finally after I'd destroyed everything I ever cared about—I mean Kitt and I have at least communicated often and I feel as though I've really, you know, like our friendship is sound—"

"You been getting regular checkups, I hope. Especially your blood pressure, you know about black men and high blood pressure, and get your diabetes screening, and let's not even talk about your colon, you make sure you keep up with your health, you're getting to the age group that really takes its toll on a black man."

"Posie, please, let me apologize, I have to—need to do this for me."

"All you have to do for you is keep on doing what you been doing, 'cause it's working, baby."

"No—Posie, I have to say it—"

"It can wait, Johnson, it can wait."

"It can't. Now. I have to do this now." He took both of her hands in his and squeezed them to emphasize what he was saying. "I just have to allow the words to hit your ears. I swore to myself that as soon as I saw you, I didn't care how many years it took, that this is the first thing I had to do before we could even move any further."

"Okay, Johnson," she sighed, "if you insist on it."

"I apologize, Posie, if I caused you any discomfort, leaving the way I did, living the way I was, you know, strung out—"

"I accept it," she said as she pulled her hands from his and swiped at his sweater to the rhythm of her words, "but only on the condition that you accept my apology too."

"Your apology?"

"Yes, baby." She rolled the ends of his sweater up in neat folds over his wrists. "I overburdened you."

"What are you talking about, Posie?"

"With expectations," she said matter-of-factly as if he should have known that. "You couldn't have let me down if I hadn't first placed you on a pedestal that was too high for you to stand on all by yourself." She unrolled his sweater sleeves now and pushed them up in bunches instead. "And when I criticized you, actually I did a lot more than criticize you, I truly hated you for running off and leaving us the way you did so that it was months before we even knew whether you were alive or dead, when I criticized you for that it was because I judged you." She pulled the sleeves back to the way he had them in the first place and then stared directly at him. "Now look at me, who on this Earth am I equipped to judge, Johnson, who is any of us equipped to judge when you get right down to it. So I had to come to the realization that whether you let me down, or Kitt, or Verdi, or your mama, or your friends from school, whoever, all you did was the best that you could do for who you were during that time when you were doing it."

"Posie—I—" Johnson didn't know what to say really, so he just stammered around searching for something.

"Just hush and listen." She cut his nonwords off. "So all I'm saying is that I need to beg your pardon too. I propped you up so unfairly, and then I had the nerve to hate you when you misstepped and fell."

She reached up and pinched his cheek and Johnson's incredulous look just hung on his face, shocked at her level of grace and wisdom. No wonder he was able to love her in ways that he hadn't been able to even love his own mother. She enabled his feelings to have a levity not possible when a relationship is so steeped in guilt and anger and resentment. He leaned in and kissed her lightly on the cheek. "It's settled, then," he said, and for the first time in years felt as if it really was.

"Okay." She patted her chest and batted her eyes. "Now what had you started saying? You know, after I told you how good you looked, you were starting to tell me how good I looked and I cut you off, I didn't mean to cut you off. So go ahead, finish." She hit him playfully on his chest.

Johnson laughed so hard then, with all of him, the way he hadn't laughed in what felt like decades. He serenaded Posie with superlatives like magnificent, divine, and she feigned a demure "oh hush" stance and they walked arm in arm back into the dining room where the lights had been dimmed and the adults sipped wine or cider and naturally designated among them whose turn it was to be in the living room to supervise the children now watching *Sesame Street* videos, or beating drums on the carpet, or marching around the coffee table, or smearing themselves with jelly eggs.

And Kitt pulled Posie back into the kitchen to help her start getting food set up and in between slicing the ham and turkey and arranging them on her oval-shaped platter and separating them with sections of tangerine, and spooning up the potato salad in her gold-rimmed bowl lined with spinach leaves, and putting the macaroni in a chafing dish, the Caresser in her white Mikasa salad server, she said, "Mama, I'm scared, I think I did something terrible."

And as Posie handed Kitt the cheese grater, and went in the refrigerator for cheese, and recapped and re-covered all the containers once Kitt was done spooning up from them, she listened to the quivering in Kitt's voice as she told her that Verdi was on the way.

"What you mean on the way? On the way here? I thought you said she put up a powerful refusal over seeing Johnson."

"She did." Kitt's voice had a whine running through it. "She doesn't know that he'll be here, and Johnson doesn't know that she's coming. Neither of them know, Mama. You know, Verdi Mae and Johnson aren't expecting to see each other, not at all, Mama. I don't know what made me do such an indiscreet thing. And Verdi Mae was so adamant that she didn't want to see him, you know, I should have respected that. I have no right to play with their lives like that just because I think that they should be together. Shoot, damn shoot, damn," she said to the beat of the sound of the spoon that she tapped against the grater to loosen the slithers of cheese that hadn't fallen. "I need to just tell Johnson that maybe he should go, you know, he'll understand if I explain what I did and that Verdi really doesn't want to see him. You know, he'll leave for Verdi's sake."

Posie just stared at Kitt blankly at first finding it difficult to believe that her organized, calculating, must-know-the-outcome-before-she-makes-a-move daughter had actually gone and for once done something frivolous. "Well, what's the worst that could happen, Kitt?" she asked, trying to make her voice sound reassuring as she handed her the pepper mill, and not wanting to discourage what she saw as Kitt's attempt at throwing caution to the wind.

"Don't you see, Mama?" Kitt said as she turned the head on the mill and sprinkled black specks over the salad. "It's not fair to have them shock each other like that. I mean, suppose they shouldn't see each other. My stomach is jumping, Mama, and I'm afraid something bad's gonna happen because of what I've done."

"Well, maybe we shouldn't just, you know, put him out like that, baby," Posie said, hating the thought of watching Johnson's shoulders slump in disappointment. And even though she did trust Kitt's instincts, through it all, she knew that Kitt had a strong stomach, that her stomach rarely jumped for no reason, she trusted the power of true love more. "How about it if we tell Johnson that Verdi Mae is on her way here and we'll let him decide what to do. We'll be honest and say that she'd turned you down when you offered to arrange a meeting for them. And we'll tell him how much it's bothering you now. How about that? Because personally I think Verdi Mae will be thrilled to see Johnson looking good as he looks in there right now. Does that settle your stomach some?"

Kitt nodded and sighed and put the salad fork and spoon in their slots on the white Mikasa set and handed it to Posie. "This should go out first, I already have place mats set where the food should go, leave room in the center for the turkey and the ham, and tell Johnson we need to talk to him in the kitchen, Verdi's gonna be walking through that door any minute. You got to help me tell him, Mama, you got to."

There were two parties going on now as Posie emerged from the kitchen. The children's was happening in the living room under the glare of the television and the noise of balloons bursting, and clapping sounds as they tried to catch imaginary butterflies, and foot stomping as they marched in a parade organized by the girls from the church. And the adults' party was in the dining room where the living-room stereo speakers had been rerouted by the music-thirsty father of the Hawkins twins and the dining room ballooned with the sounds of soulful oldies and vintage jazz. Posie giggled when Kitt's client from the precinct grabbed the salad server from her and put it on the buffet and took her hand and started to bop. She almost forgot about needing to talk to Johnson and when she remembered she called out to him and he excused himself from the jovial conversation he'd been having with Leeanne from next door and Mrs. Tilley from down the street and the oldest of the Carson girls, Penda's relative, had just finished telling her to tell Penda that her favorite, though underachieved former student, Johnson, said hello. He was still laughing when he got to Posie and she told him that Kitt needed his help in the kitchen.

"Oh, so that's how it goes," he joked. "You come out of the kitchen to party and send me in there to work, un-huh."

"I'll be in there, directly," Posie said, doing a little spin in her hip-hugging dress. "As soon as I can tear myself away from this handsome young man, I will."

She winked at Johnson and Johnson said he'd be right in too as soon as he went up to the bathroom and washed his hands.

And Posie tore herself away from her dance partner and she and Kitt commenced to setting the food out and Johnson walked down the stairs from the bathroom on his way into the kitchen to help Posie and Kitt, and both parties were in full swing, the children enjoying themselves either in their own worlds, or those who could, engaged by the games the girls from church made up; the adults chatting, and flirting, and blushing, and patting their feet and enjoying intermittent bursts of laughter, and a cha-cha here and there, and now the titillating aroma of the food Posie and Kitt set down. And nobody even heard Verdi come in because the volume in both rooms was on high now, especially in the dining room where the music from the rerouted speakers sifted all the way to the front door. And Verdi walked inside from the enclosed porch and just stood there taking in the scene going on in Kitt's house thinking that she must have misunderstood Kitt, Kitt had emphasized that this gathering was to be small, so she just

[151]

stood and allowed her eyes to adjust to this unexpected crowd of people and nobody much noticed her at first, weighed down with bags where she'd bought twice more than what she'd intended once she got inside of that Imagineering store.

But suddenly Sage looked up from the card tricks the church girls were doing, prompted by a new hue that was coloring the air in the room. And she saw Verdi and she jumped up and barreled right for Verdi, squealing as she went, and that started a parade of children squealing and running to greet Verdi too. And then Johnson looked for the source of the commotion as he walked down the stairs, and he had a clear view to what was happening by the door, to who had just come in from the enclosed porch. And he hadn't felt so flush, so dizzy, so light-headed since his get-high days as he did right now looking down the stairs at Verdi, his Verdi, and he wanted to laugh and cry at the same time because she was so beautiful, so sweetly poised as the children gathered around her and pulled at her arms and bags and she laughed and said, "Wait, wait, let me get out of my jacket, I have enough surprises for everybody, be patient, children, please." And she looked around to see who could help peel some of the children away and Johnson stepped back up the stairs, one, two, almost to the top of the stairs from where he could look down on Verdi without her seeing him, he didn't want her to see him, not right now, not until he could tell his hands to be still because they were shaking now, because they just wanted to grab onto Verdi, just grab her and hold her and never let her go.

And the overly exuberant children half pulled, half pushed Verdi toward the dining room and she almost stumbled over the one or two in front of her as they clumsily made it to the buffet where the gifts were stacked. Except for Sage who hung back to look up at Johnson standing near the top of the stairs, so mesmerized was she by the way the color blue splashed all around him, turning itself inside out in huge waves that looked so beautiful to her.

And Kitt moved like lightning trying to get to Verdi as she stood in the dining room, trying to warn her that Johnson was here, my God, how could she have done this, she asked herself, how could she have maneuvered this situation so that these former lovers would meet unaware like this after twenty years?

But right now Verdi was being helped out of her jacket by her students' mothers who rarely got the opportunity to be out with their children's principal in a social setting. And they were taking full advantage as one folded Verdi's coat over her arm, and another relieved her of her bag, and another pulled up a chair and told her to sit as they went right into questions about their child's progress, and was such and such a teacher going to retire, and what about that unqualified aide who ran the extended day? And Verdi was eager to oblige since this was her first year in this position and she was still in prove-herself mode. And Kitt tried not to be rude as she said, "Oh, can y'all excuse me and my cousin for two minutes, please?"

And she pulled Verdi up out of the chair, away from her clingy audience, and Verdi kissed Kitt on the cheek, said, "Hey, cuz, you misled me big time, I didn't know you were throwing a birthday party for Sage and a cabaret for yourself."

"Did you see him?" is all Kitt said, breathless, perspiration forming as a glaze along her forehead and her cheeks.

"See who?" Verdi asked, feeling so light inside just being here with her cousin and her aunt and Sage and the other little ones from her school, even their parents. She was feeling so unburdened, so unfettered having escaped earlier from the shroud of Rowe's affection that had been too opaque, too tight and constricting for her today.

"Who, Kitty Kat?" she asked again. "Did I see who?"

They were standing under the molded archway between the living room and the dining room right next to the heavy cast-iron pole lamp with the cut-glass Tiffany-style shade. And at first Verdi thought it was the diffusion of light that made Kitt's face appear so scattered, as if she were midway between an apology and a moanful expression of pain but with a soft wiftiness about it that was so unlike Kitt. "What's wrong with you, Kitt?" she asked her again.

"I—I guess you didn't see—"

"Who? Who? Who?" Verdi asked, getting irritated, getting ready to look around for her auntie so she could explain what Kitt was talking about, or look around to see who the cause of Kitt's stupor was. And just as she was about to turn exasperated and scan the room, she heard the voice: "Me." That's all he said, but just the touch of that monosyllable against her ear and she more than heard it, she felt it as a jolt that went straight to heart and then as a burst of flames like spontaneous combustion that seems to happen out of nowhere, but only happens really because the elements are in place, ready: some kindling, oxidation, stillness over time, and someone opens a door and air rushes in and a massive fire lives again.

"Me, Verdi. She's talking about me, Verdi, baby, it's Johnson, it's me."

Eight

THERE WAS SPACE between them. This pair of lovers
who'd not gazed on each other for two decades. Kitt backed
away and threw up her hands conceding defeat or wanting
to shout hallelujah, she wasn't sure which. The Hawkins twins' father
had something soft and clear blaring through the stereo, Louis Armstrong singing, "You Go to My Head." And all around these two
was the laughter and frivolity of the two parties merging at the archway between the living and dining rooms. The children darted in and
out in neat circumferences and edged Johnson and Verdi closer in.
But they were too conscious of the space between them, the years,
the searing passion that had turned on them. It was as if the space had
its own form accumulating itself now from a heap on the floor, taking
on color. Blue: not Sage's blue that danced and showed itself in all

its variations. But a still sad blue as if symbolizing all the abbreviated trumpet notes that had sagged and then fallen at their feet.

Though they stood right next to the cast-iron pole lamp and the light filtered through the Tiffany-style shade and rained all over them, it felt dark in here under this crowded archway as Verdi and Johnson watched the space between them reverberating like a broken heart.

Until Johnson looked up. Thinking it silly to stand here in front of the only woman he really ever loved and stare at the floor like a pubescent boy at his first school dance, he looked up. And there was that face that had enchanted him all those years ago, that he'd dream about even now in dreams that were so real he'd wake swearing he'd just touched the mole on her cheek. The same doe eyes with that downward slant, the same brown-over-gold skin color, the same roundness to the cheeks, fleshiness to the lips, politeness to the nose. Her hair was cut short though, straightened and tapered at the sides. He didn't know why that surprised him, surely he couldn't have expected to see her still sporting that overgrown Afro he'd nudged her into wearing. What did surprise him was that she was so slim, thin actually, far too thin for a woman nearing forty and purporting contentment. She should have a roundness to the hips like Kitt, he thought, like Posie, like she had the day he met her. Surely it was in her genes. He felt himself growing agitated at Rowe, holding him responsible for her uncharacteristic smallness, damning him, damning himself too. But then Verdi looked up and the agitation dissipated. Just having the feel of her eyes on him after all these years and everything that wasn't good and honest and pure dissipated. He thought he could even forgive Rowe if it meant he could hold on to the feel of her eyes. And then he couldn't even meet her gaze anymore and was back looking at the blue space on the floor.

Verdi too. She looked up just long enough to glimpse his face, lean and brown, and though also absent the overgrown Afro, remarkably unchanged. Even the asymmetrical arch to his eyebrows that made him look as if he were always on the verge of a question, the slight hump to the bridge of his nose that used to make her giggle when she'd slide her finger from his eyes to his lips, his lips still thin and dark and soft looking. But he had a broadness about him now. Maybe it was the cable-knit sweater, but his chest looked so sturdy, so indestructible. And now she had to look away too, or risk being rushed with a cacophony of feeling that would have her swooning, her equilibrium so shot completely to hell as it was, have her running her hand along the broadness of his chest to find the spot where her head should go.

They both looked down and watched the space between them that did appear to be moving now and rising up from the floor like a smoky-blue cloud and then separating into two distinct forms that teased and gyrated and danced to the beat of Louis Armstrong's trumpet now. Their blues. Banishing their destructive past for this evening in the archway between Kitt's rooms that was brightly lit but felt sultry and smoky and dim to Johnson and Verdi as they watched their blues dancing like they wished that they could, until Johnson stretched his fingertips through the movable space between them, the years. And they touched fingers and then entire hands, palm against palm, and now they were dancing too.

Nine

KITT AND POSIE communicated across the dining-room table as they helped the children get settled into chairs, and tied napkins under their chins, and spooned up their plates. Kitt's loosened facial muscles said that she was so relieved that Verdi hadn't devastated Johnson by storming out after all; the confident tilt of Posie's head said see I told you, true love always, always wins. And now everyone crowded into the dining room as mothers and fathers and neighbors piled their plates high with food, and the children made instruments and weapons of their plastic utensils, and parents started to yell, stop that, put that down, and Verdi came into the dining room and lightened it a hundred watts she was glowing so. She did her special clap and wave that the children from her school understood and that always settled them down, and at least

Posie and Kitt were able to get pizza squares onto their plates. And now the party switched places as the children claimed the dining room, and the adults, grateful for the supervision if they had children here, and for the opportunity to pair off with a member of the opposite sex if they were here unattached, slipped unobtrusively into the living room.

Johnson still stood in the archway, leaning against the molded post, allowing it to prop him up because the whole substance of him had gone to mush. His palms were burning from where they'd just touched Verdi's palms, their lifelines facing, the bend in his fingers aching to curl around hers. He wanted to look down at his hands to see if they looked different, to see if they were red and flush or even on fire hot as they were. But he wanted more to look at Verdi as she walked around the dining-room table helping one child with her napkin, another break his pizza square in half. As long as he could see her he'd know for sure she wasn't some cruelly satisfying mirage. She kissed a red-faced boy on his cheek and right now he wanted to be that child, wanted to know again her lips against his face. He felt himself sinking as he watched her walk into the kitchen behind Posie because he didn't want to lose sight of her because if he lost sight of her he might have to wait twenty more years before their palms could touch again. He felt as if he wanted to cry even as he told himself that he was being ridiculous, acting like a little boy or worse a lunatic.

He straightened himself up and took up his weight again. He couldn't allow himself to just splatter like this in Kitt's house. He cleared his throat, began to search for someone he could laugh with from among the adults in the living room. Thought that he should get a plate of food first, put his hands to some good use, try to act casually, try not to let it show that he was on a launching pad headed for some heretofore uncharted emotional territories, spinning, weightless, and so filled up.

He was self-conscious as he crossed over into the dining room, the clickety-clack of the children's indistinguishable chatter mimicking his own inexpressible internal clatter as he walked to the buffet where Kitt was oozing melting lime sherbet from its carton into a punch bowl filled with 7UP and ice. She nudged him, poked her elbow into his side as she stirred the punch. "How you doing?" she asked.

How was he doing? he thought to himself. How did she think he was doing? There were no words to describe how he was doing. She might as well have asked Sage to explain to her how he was doing. He hunched his shoulders as he picked up a plate from the buffet, a napkin wrapped around a fork and a knife. "I'm—I'm, you know, I don't know," is all he said.

Kitt had her face tilted in a question mark, her mouth fixed to say something else, maybe apologize to him for manipulating circumstances so that he'd find himself shocked like this, shaken. She could see how shaken he was. But right then Sage began banging her fists on the table, then she pushed herself back from the table and jumped down, bounded across the room headed for the front door.

"Somebody must be coming," Kitt said as she handed the empty sherbet carton to Posie who'd just peeped her head in to see how the serving platters were holding up. "Can't imagine who it is, since everybody who's supposed to be here is already here."

Then Sage started spinning around and stomping her feet and pointing her fist toward the door.

"Obviously a stranger or she wouldn't be so agitated," Kitt said, concern splashing her forehead as she followed Sage into the other room and that started the parade of Sage's party mates as they all headed toward the front door. The children hampered Johnson from falling in line right behind Kitt though he tried to, had always had a peeve about a woman answering the door after dark if a man was in the house, probably from having felt the need to protect his mother after his father left.

Verdi walked in from the kitchen then with a pitcher filled with springwater floating lemon circles along the top. She edged past Johnson to get to the buffet to set the pitcher down and when she did allowed the entirety of her person to press against him. And surely he would have been otherwise so affected in this now empty dining room where her womanhood had meshed into its rightful place against him that he would have just grabbed her and taken her lips against his. But his street senses were too alerted by what was going on in the living room; whoever was at the front door had caused Kitt to react with a jolt that Johnson could see all the way from where he stood. And now it bothered him that they were taking too long to either come in or leave, and Kitt's tussles of locked hair pushing up from her yellow-and-green headband seemed hysterical as they flew from one direction to the other as Kitt moved her head from side to side talking to whoever it was.

Instinctively he counted the men in the room, told himself to settle down, as he reminded himself that there were at least three cops in there. "Yo, somebody get Kitt's back," he yelled in, and the men immediately pulled their attention away from their plates and their hounding ways and now from Sage who seemed to be in the middle of a convulsion she was jumping and spinning so out of control that it enticed some of her playmates to do the same. Verdi ran in the living room then to get to the children before they collided and hurt themselves, and the half-a-dozen men in the room had circled Kitt at the door, providing an impenetrable barrier should there be a need to block someone's entry into the living room, and something told Johnson to just stand where he was, to not join the others in the living room, and then he knew why as the barrier of men parted, and through this aperture in walked Rowe, right through the door on into Kitt's house.

Rowe. That goddamned motherfucking Rowe. How many years had he spent boiling over the thought of that pompous, conniving, lustful, old, old, motherfucking Rowe with his Verdi? His. And how many more times did the ambivalence of having to admit that Rowe had saved Verdi's life when he himself couldn't, when he himself had been responsible for her descent, when having to ingest that thought that he handed Verdi over to Rowe threatened to sever once and for all the tenuous grip he had on what was left of his reality, threatened to leave him a babbling imbecile just walking the streets dehumanized to be laughed at or pitied for the rest of his life?

He didn't even think about what to do as he watched Rowe go straight to Verdi who was on the floor now with Sage, rocking her, calming her down. And even though he felt the coals of a vengeful fire reignite in the pit of his stomach as Rowe leaned down and kissed Verdi on the cheek, he knew that sometimes the real strength of a man was exhibited in his ability to just walk away, the way he'd had to just walk away from Verdi twenty-some years ago when to stay in place would have meant the death of them both. He walked away now so that he wouldn't complicate Verdi's life tonight, so that Rowe wouldn't look up and see him standing there and assume that they'd planned some luscious rendezvous, especially since Verdi was so in-nocent, they both were tonight. So he walked away from the buffet in the dining room, right on through the kitchen, right past Posie who was running water in the sink, right into Kitt's therapy room, where he didn't even turn on the light, where he just stood and leaned against the mauve-colored wall and allowed the vanilla hanging in the air to calm him down.

. . .

VERDI DIDN'T stay long after that. She left before they opened the gifts, sang "Happy Birthday," cut the cake. Rowe's unexpected presence in Kitt's Sansom Street row house caused a disharmony in the air. Though he came in smiling, congenial, extending his hand to the men who'd been prepared to take him down on the first sign from Kitt, Sage's agitation didn't really dissipate, and the other children never completely resettled back into their dining-room spaces, which pulled the parents and neighbors from their free-forming flow in the living room. Plus Kitt's disconcertedness was all too showy. She started dropping things, losing her train of activity, she couldn't even remember names when she proceeded to introduce Rowe around.

So Verdi didn't, couldn't stay long. Just long enough to excuse herself from Rowe. "I need five minutes alone with Sage," she said as he nodded and stood stiffly in the middle of the room trying to act as if he belonged here, as if he'd been invited. And Sage clung tightly to Verdi's hand, whimpering, gasping after having cried so as they walked toward the kitchen. And Posie met them at the kitchen door and ushered them into the kitchen asking what had upset grand-mama's baby so. She pulled out a chair and took Sage on her lap and rocked her back and forth, the whole time looking at Verdi, talking to Verdi without benefit of words, using her eyes she let Verdi know that Johnson was just on the other side of the door, right in Kitt's therapy room. Posie better than anyone knew what it was like to be so fibrously in love when convention suggested otherwise. So she used her eyes to tell Verdi that she understood, really and truly un-derstood how badly she must want to go in there, but that she couldn't, not now. And Verdi just stood there staring at the door, and then ran her finger lightly across the vanilla-colored wood as if it was his chest she was touching. She turned around then and Posie's eyes were closed now as she rocked Sage back and forth and Sage had settled down as she stroked the ends of her grandmother's hair and enjoyed the feel of the rise and fall of her chest.

Posie opened her eyes as Verdi walked past and Verdi mouthed goodbye and blew her a kiss. Posie nodded, put a finger to her lips, and closed her eyes again.

Verdi wouldn't meet Kitt's gaze though as she got to the dining room. She went straight to the closet and grabbed her leather jacket. "I'll talk to you next week, cuz," she said more to the closet than to Kitt. She wasn't sure what she was feeling toward Kitt right now, gratitude, anger. How long had Kitt been planning this, this, shock that could have stopped her heart and killed her, that's how unsuspecting she'd been, how unprepared, and apparently so was Johnson. Angry, she thought, yeah, she was angry at Kitt because she'd truly set her up, just disregarded her wishes when she'd insisted that she couldn't see Johnson, just couldn't, she was still too bitter over the sight of his back the night he left her, too weak. Suppose Rowe had bounded in there ten minutes earlier, and what was he doing showing up there anyhow? She was about to transfer her agitation from Kitt onto Rowe, but right then she crossed the archway where she and Johnson had danced with their palms; she breathed in deeply as if that helped her to honor that space. She felt her anger draining away into an infatuated confusion.

Rowe stood at once when she entered the living room, and she cast around her goodbyes to the gathered, a college hoop game on the television had their attention now and even the children, exhausted from the outbursts precipitated by Sage, sat mostly uninvolved at their parents' feet. Rowe looked blandly around the room and waved to one or two people symbolically. "Have a good evening," he said, then opened the door onto the enclosed porch so that they could leave.

The air had changed outside, the sun had closed its lids for the day and left the night to take over with its cleared-eyed perfect vision. The earlier wind yielded to a chilly calm that was so intense it was startling. Verdi shivered as she looked up at the sky and tried to pick out the Big Dipper from the more than usual constellations offered up tonight as Rowe rushed to open the car door for her.

He stood in front of the door then and blocked her path, took her face in his hands and mashed his lips against hers. He lingered over the kiss and then pulled her in a close hug, confusing her.

"I'd better let you in before you catch a draft," he said, moving aside and helping her into the car.

He got into the car and just sat with his hands on the steering wheel. "I hope you don't think I was out of line coming over here like that," he said, staring at the wheel as if he were seeing it for the first time.

"I was just shocked," Verdi said. "That's why I reacted the way I did, you know jumped up when I realized that was you leaning over me and then that just got Sage all riled up again." She tried to sound as if she had nothing to explain about her behavior, but she explained it nonetheless. "I mean, I know how you feel about Kitt, that's why I got ready to leave as soon as you came in but I needed to spend some time with Sage, it's not good for her to stay in an agitated state. And as it was I hadn't even been there for very long, I mean I couldn't even tell you all the people who were there." She stopped. Looked right at him, at his profile that looked so studious and little boyish to her now as he sat there and stared at the steering wheel as if the wheel held the answer to some deep, complicated problem. "Why did you come, Rowe? What was that all about?"

The inside of the car was quiet save the keys tinkling as they hung from the ignition. He leaned back against the headrest. "I don't know what made me come, really, Verdi. I was asking myself that all the way up here. I just started thinking after you left how maybe I have been overly harsh and unfair in my treatment of your, you know, her."

"Kitt. You mean Kitt, right?"

"Yes." He breathed in deeply, audibly. "Kitt, your cousin, Kitt. Though I must say she doesn't take the prize on friendliness. She barely let me in, and only did after a barrage of questions about my motives. She even asked me if I was there trying to start something since she knows how I feel about her. And what got me is that I didn't challenge her, you know I was very, very polite. So no, I'm not sure, really, why I came, except that I hate it when you leave the house upset with me like you did today, and quite frankly I was worried about you trying to get home by yourself on public transportation. Look how dark it is around here."

"I would have, could have gotten home, Rowe," she said quietly. "I've been coming up here for twenty years and I've always gotten home."

He turned toward her then. His knee hit the keys and they jingled with a clarity and a rhythm that sounded like a musical instrument warming up. "And you'll keep coming home, won't you? Promise me you'll always come home." And even in the unlit car she could see the longing on his face, as if she were very, very sick and he was begging her not to die, as if he knew, but what could he know, she didn't even know.

"Rowe, what is it? What's wrong with you?" she asked, wanting to stretch across the armrest and burrow his head in her chest and take away the pleading in his face, or wanting to confess, the way she always ended up confessing to him from the time when she'd confessed to being strung out. But what would she confess now, that she'd just been shocked by the reappearance of her long-ago lover, that she'd been ambushed by the onslaught of twenty years' worth of feeling that had continued to percolate in all that time? That she would see him again, had to, even if just once to tell him that she couldn't see him again? How could she confess that? Better that she was dying. She folded her arms across her chest. She couldn't let herself soften toward Rowe right now, too risky, at least not until she had a chance to be with her thoughts. "Well, if you aren't going to tell me what's got you acting like this," she huffed, "can you at least get some heat going? It's freezing in here."

"Get some heat going?" he said, mild sarcasm running through his voice, angry at himself now for groveling like this, and at her for evoking this feeling in him that he was losing a grip on her hand, that her hand was sliding from his and she would fall if that happened. "For you? Anything for you," he went on, the sarcasm building in his voice like a train working up to its best speed. "It's all for you. Everything I do is for you. And you ask for so little too. Just get some heat going is all you want." He started the car and flicked the heat to high and a gush of cold air smacked her in the face.

She turned the vent away from her and raised her jacket collar up around her face and felt as if she wanted to cry. They turned off of Kitt's block and she looked out the window at the pockmarked block they cruised through now where the well-kept, freshly painted house struggled to keep its dignity next to an abandoned boarded-up shell. She started to comment to get a conversation going, but she really didn't want to hear his overly assured rhetoric about this neighborhood's decline being the fault of the people who live here. But on the other hand she didn't want to just sit in here and think about Johnson and try to process it all either. He might be able to hear her thoughts quiet as it was in here. And he was already picking up something. He was even driving faster than usual, so fast until he had to brake abruptly at the stop signs and red lights. Johnson had told her once that they purposely don't synchronize the traffic lights in poor black communities just to add to the frustration of the people so that the people are always stopping and waiting. Now she felt the jerkiness of the stop-and-go in her stomach and now too the reality of it all hit her like the blast of cold air just had and she put her hand to her mouth so that she wouldn't gasp out loud. "Um, Rowe, I'm feeling like I might be sick on my stomach," she said. "Could you slow down a little."

"Do I need to pull over?" he asked.

"No, it's just the jerking back and forth."

"I'll slow down then," he said, resignedly. "Simple request, simple action. Though I guess this means you aren't up for dinner, probably had too much unhealthy eating on your plate at your cousin's, maybe that's what's got your stomach upset." The sarcasm in his voice was yielding to concern.

"Actually I didn't have a chance to eat. The food had just been put out when you got there, we were just in the process of helping the children to eat when you got there."

"So then you are up for dinner?" he asked, a lifting to his voice.

"Sure, I mean, you've got to eat anyhow, sure," she said.

"Where do you want to go, want to go down to Penn's Landing, or what? Do you feel like some music? What do you feel like?"

"I don't know, whatever," she said, wanting really to just go home, just take a shower and plead a headache and curl up and pretend to fall asleep to the hum of the television while she really relived the evening, the way they'd touched palms, and Johnson, the way he just walked away to spare her, all of them, a scene. But she would go out to dinner with him, she would try to be pleasant, she told herself, not gushing, not over-the-top, but personable enough while she worked to submerge the guilt that was starting to flow a little higher than the rest of her crowded consortium of feelings. She would be nice. She owed him that much, she thought as he crept along now so that she barely felt the motion of the stop-and-go.

Verdi didn't know that Johnson was in trouble the fall of her junior year. Thought his weight had fallen off over the summer because his mother had moved to San Diego to try to lift her spirits with her other son. Thought he was moody because of the stress of working that UPS job and still trying to maintain otherwise. She wouldn't have known a track mark if he'd put a flashlight to his arm and traced it with his fingers, and as dark as he was it would have taken that. So she didn't have an inkling that he was up to a bag a week, sometimes more than that depending on whether he could shake the desire when it came down on him. And even when the fact of the matter was being shouted right over her head she still didn't know.

She and Johnson and Tower and Cheryl were playing pinocle this Saturday night, partners, she and Johnson against Tower and Cheryl. It was October and the air had already adopted a wintery bite but Johnson had the windows open in his low-rise dorm. And Tower got up and closed the window. And Johnson accused him of stalling on taking the bid. And Tower just sucked the air in through his teeth and passed. And Verdi passed and so did Cheryl and the weight was left on Johnson. So he named his trump and got back up and opened the window while everybody put down their meld, and Cheryl said, "Come on, Johnson, what's up with you and this infusion of cold air, you trying to give Verdi signals on what you got in your hand?"

Johnson pinched his nose as he sat back down to the game, said, "No, it's just hot as hell in here."

Tower looked at Johnson then, at his half-closed eyes and the perspiration outlining his forehead, his droopy mouth; he slapped his hand on the table, said, "I can't do this shit no more, either you got to move or I got to fucking move 'cause I can't do it."

And Cheryl studied her hand, rearranged her cards, braced herself.

And at first Verdi thought Tower was just playing around, talking trash as he was inclined to do especially during a card game.

But then Tower stood, kicked his chair against the wall, said, "Which one of us is it gonna be, man? Huh, 'cause you fucking around."

And now Verdi saw that Tower wasn't playing and said, "Tower, what's your problem?"

And Cheryl stood now, grabbed Verdi's arm. "Verdi, I think we should go, this a roommate thing and I don't think we need to be here."

Johnson just stared at the cards fanned out in his hand. Laughed a slow throaty laugh. "Go ahead, baby, Verdi, go back to the high-rise, I'll be there soon."

Tower was banging the table in front of Johnson. "After all your rousing speeches about not letting them fuck with your mind, not letting them give you a diminished view of yourself, not falling prey to their diabolical tactics, look at you, look at you, you had the motherfucking world in your hand and look at you, man. I hate you for doing this to yourself, man. Why'd you let 'em do it to you, man?"

"Tower, what are you talking about? What is wrong with you?" Verdi's voice screeched as she ran to where Tower was, to put herself between Tower and Johnson.

"Move, Verdi, this has nothing to do with you," Tower said as he put his hand around her arm, pushed her out of the way.

Johnson jumped up then. "I know you didn't just put your motherfucking hands on my lady," he said, stabbing his finger in Tower's chest.

Verdi was jumping up and down, yelling at them to stop, and Cheryl opened the door wide, pulled Verdi through the door, telling her come on, come on, this is between them, come on.

And when the door slammed shut sealing just Tower and Johnson in the small living room of that low-rise dorm, the chilling air wrapping them like a cyclone, Johnson dropped his hands to his sides and Tower started to cry. He grabbed Johnson by the chest of his sweatshirt. "Come on, man, fight, hit me, hit me, you motherfucker, aren't you the one always quoting 'Invictus,' dying, but fighting back, where's your motherfucking fight? Where's your fight, man? You let them rob you of your fight. Why you do that shit, why you let yourself get strung out, you junkie motherfucker, I hate you, man. I hate you."

Verdi was stretched out on her bed, Charity sitting cross-legged in the corner of the room, when Johnson got there. Verdi had just described the scene, Johnson and Tower about to go at it, best friends, like brothers. And Charity said, "You're so sweet and naive. I just love your spirit, don't you see it, you haven't seen it, it's the girl that's come between those friends."

"Girl? What are you talking about, Charity? What girl? Who?"

"Not a who, my confused friend," Charity said as she uncrossed her legs at the sound of a knock on the door. "Though I have known men to worship her."

And Verdi was about to ask her what she meant, but decided instead to answer the door because Charity could sometimes go on for an hour explaining something that Verdi would conclude was nonsense, and she assumed that would happen now, so she let Johnson in, and Charity said she was going to spend the night in the roof-top lounge with some of her friends, they were going to trip and hope for high winds so that they could feel the room shake.

Verdi looked at Johnson then, at his half-closed eyes and his face that was shallowing right in front of her and his stature even crooked and leaned over and she helped him through the door and asked him what was it, what? And what was happening between he and Tower? And had he taken some kind of downer pills as slow as he was moving. What? What? What was wrong?

And he told her that he just felt sick, that he just wanted to crash, could she please help him get to bed so that he could crash? He was whimpering and she undressed him down to his skin as if he were a six-foot infant and spoke soothing phrases and gave him a sponge bath because he looked so dusty to her, then she squeezed into the bed with him and couldn't understand why, but a brick came up in her chest and she started to cry.

Johnson woke the next morning mildly restored. He still felt dopey under his skull but at least his synapses were firing and returning a semblance of rationality to his thought. But now the feel of Verdi's naked body wrapped around his was both soothing and devastating. Soothing because her nearness was always a transcendent experience for him; devastating because of what Tower had said to him, about him losing his fight, giving up, becoming a junkie. A junkie. And now he was afraid that what he'd become had leaked from the inside and was now staining his exterior the way a leaky pen drips indigo blue clear through from the pocket in the lining to the beige breast front of a new linen suit. He rushed to cover the stain, to hide it under a handkerchief when he realized that Verdi was awake now; he smiled.

Her drowsy eyes came to focus on his face and made him feel warm and comforted in a delusional way, as if everything was the way it had begun with them, so honest and clean and unspoiled.

They were nestled under the blue-and-white covers and Verdi whispered, "Church?" And Johnson tightened, was afraid that the pillars might come crashing down if he had the nerve to step his lying, sinful, drug-addicted ass into a church right now.

"Why don't we, you know, lay low this morning, baby?" he said into her mouth as they faced each other wrapped up like a turban knot.

They agreed then that they wouldn't pry themselves from the softness of the sheets, of each other, to get up and go to church. And Johnson nestled again into his delusion. It had been a long week for both of them they agreed and they would just sleep in this smoky Sunday morning and turn the forced hot-air heat to high and open the window about a quarter of the way because they liked the sensation of the cold and hot air mixing at their heads. They would snuggle this morning, they agreed, and listen to the intermittent bursts of traffic down on Walnut Street along with the mellow sounds crackling like a slow-burning fire from the radio. Roberta Flack was singing "Our Ages or Our Hearts" and they watched the fog push through the window and settle in over the bedroom and take the edge off of things.

That's when Verdi quoted Rowe, something benign and meaningless about never being able to really catch up on sleep you've missed. But just the fact that she was quoting him at all turned Johnson's mood from the soft delusion that everything would be fine, to biting, prickly, and he lit in right then to insult Rowe, tried to cloak the insult, his sarcasm, his insecurities in a joke. Said, "Yeah well, that Negro looks like he don't lose no sleep with his corny argyle-vested ass. I know he's probably 'sleep by nine. Probably sleeps in starched pajamas too stiff as he is."

He laughed to hide his bitterness, but Verdi could see it all through the misty-colored air: his bitterness, his sarcasm, his insecurities dangling as a group from his smile that hung on his face like a weak crescent moon. She'd been feeling Johnson's insecurities a lot lately whenever he'd start in on Rowe. She wondered where it was coming from. Was beginning to fathom that Johnson was actually jealous of Rowe.

So she changed the subject from Rowe. Started talking about herself and Johnson as a couple instead. "I looove love love you, Johnson" she said as they faced each other on the twin-sized dorm bed, the covers pulled up over their chins so that their words were streams of heat bouncing between them. "All my love is just for you, no one, no one but you."

"Yeah right," he said, half-jokingly, wanting, needing to hear the confirmation of her love for him. "You can just tell me anything because you know you put a trick on my mind, you know you got me under your spell."

"Wrong. My auntie and cousin are always teasing me about how much in love I am."

He thought about Bug's orange vinyl couch when she said the part about her cousin and her auntie. Wondered if they'd seen through his weak promises by now that he would never touch that stuff again. Wondered if they'd tell Verdi and unspill her from his life. He cleared his throat and stiffened under the covers.

She circled her arms around to the small of his back when she felt him tighten like that. "Johnson, baby, please tell me what is it?" she asked as she breathed into his chest.

"I just feel like I'm losing you." He only said it so that when she told him it was over for real, he'd be able to point to this moment, and say, see I told you you would leave me. He thought this even as he struggled to get Bug's couch out of his mind because then he wouldn't have to think about the contents of the miniature wax-paper Baggie that he had hidden in the inner lining of his pea coat. But now he did think about it and his insides were responding to the thought with a jittering that he fought to keep at bay. So he blended the truth of how he did feel about Verdi with the lie of what he'd been doing, stirred them around in his words so only streaks of truth showed through. "You know, Verdi, even if you're getting ready to split on me, part of your mind, you know it's like it's not linked to my mind

[174]

anymore, like take for instance that joker, that mf-ing history Joe you always quoting, it's like he's serving up a little brainwashing along with the history lesson. You know. As if he's locked onto some part of you that I don't reach anymore. It's disturbing, baby. Just the thought is messing over me. I can't even think straight when that thought takes ahold of my mind."

"Johnson, how can you say that?" she asked in a voice markedly louder as she propped herself on her elbow. "Rowe is, I mean, he's you know, he's a damn professor is what he is."

"No, he's more than that," he said as he drew his finger along the outline of her chin. "He's got a prominence in your head that you don't even realize. That's what bothers me the most, how subtly he's trying to get a lock on your mind, my baby's mind. I'd rather die and go straight to hell than lose any part of my sweet, sweet, southern baby—" His words went low and crackled from the top of his throat so that he sounded as if he were moaning.

Verdi pressed herself against him, convinced now that Johnson was somehow ascribing to Rowe's grossly diminished view of him. That he was internalizing Rowe's opinions about all the ways that Johnson was unfit to be a student here, certainly not measuring up to be a suitable object of her affection. She wondered right now if Johnson was beginning to think less of himself as a result. Hadn't she studied the looking-glass theory in ed psych? And not just Rowe either, what about the other professors, the administrators, even his white class-mates, what about all the people with whom he interacted in a single day, how many of them made Johnson see a lesser image of himself, that he was less than them, less bright, less capable, less industrious, less honest, less clean, less worthy? When she thought about it now, even his walk seemed less deliberate on some days, it was either er-ratic, as if he were in a hurry but not quite sure where he was even headed, or reduced to a stride that was more the shuffle of the downtrodden, not the purposeful gait of her Johnson, the one who taught her things, put new dimensions on definitions she'd taken for granted. Right now it was as if she could feel Johnson's insecurities as a whir of circles in her own stomach. But not her too. She couldn't—wouldn't—allow Johnson to feel insecure about her love for him, her passion.

She pushed back down under the covers, her voice dropped to a whisper. "As God is my witness," she said. "Rowe, or no other man for that matter, has any part of me that's not already dedicated to you; even if you haven't gotten there yet, it's waiting for you, baby." She worked her hands then to draw him out, to consummate this moment, this declaration, so that there would be no doubt in his mind. His manhood was slow to rise though. Had been slow lately she'd noticed. So she worked her words right along with her hands. "Just a flash in my mind of our togetherness and a smile hints at even my most serious face," she said as she tickled the bulge in his neck. "You know, I have to shift in my seat, or if I'm standing I've got to squeeze my thighs together, fold my arms tightly in front of me so that the sudden erectness in my chest doesn't show. Look down, got to look down, baby, because if anyone looks in my eyes at that instant they might see what I'm seeing too."

She talked slowly and easily as their bodies entwined under the covers and they whispered sonnets to one another of everlasting adoration. And she was able to draw him out, finally. He throbbed against her and slid in and out and gurgled and pulsed and finally came in a stream that sputtered more than it gushed.

She was on her elbow again looking down at him as his breaths settled back to normal. He looked so tired to her right now, dusty and ashy the way he looked when he'd fallen through the door last night, as if even his virility was seeping away right before her eyes, and at the same time something about the way he lay there wasn't relaxed in a drained and satisfied way, but it seemed to her as though he wanted to jump out of his skin. She knew that part had nothing to do with Rowe. She wondered now if any of it had anything to do with Rowe. She asked him then if he was okay. "For all your talk about losing a part of me, it's like I can almost see you disappearing in chunky, definable segments," she said.

"What are you talking about, baby?" he asked softly, seriously, not wanting to lose her concern that had just swathed him and held him and made him feel reborn. His breaths quickened though at her question, and he started to cough.

"What am I talking about?" she asked as her voice cracked, suddenly, unable to carry the revelation that had made the brick come in her chest the night before and made her cry, that she now knew meant that she'd been closing her eyes to something, she didn't know for sure what, only that it must be significant. And now as she watched his chest heave in and out so that he seemed to be gasping, her memory was racing like a silver ball in a pinball machine, scoring, flashing lights and jingle bells, landing in the clown's mouth racking up points, hitting on image after image of Johnson over the past few months, always late, always exhausted, broke, broken, dragging, always dragging.

"What am I talking about?" she said again, louder, voice filling with irritation. "You tell me what I'm talking about. Something about you is not right, so you better tell me just what the hell am I talking about?"

"Verdi—"

"You been lying to me, Johnson." She cut him off as she sat all the way up in the bed. Now she was out of the bed, naked and unashamed standing up over him. "What is it, Johnson? Some other woman tying up all your energy? Is that why you have excuse after excuse over why you can't half get here?"

"Verdi—"

"Is that why you always broke though you supposedly working so much overtime?"

"Verdi—"

"Is that why you can't even come right, can't even fucking get hard?"

"Verdi—"

"Is that why you gonna throw up Rowe in my face, just to deflect attention away from you and whatever you're doing?"

"Verdi, Verdi, please, Verdi, you've got it wrong."

"Well, you better put it to right, then. If I've got it wrong, you'd better put the shit to right."

He swung his legs over and sat on the side of the bed and hung his head in his hands. He patted the space next to him, asking her, needing her to come sit beside him as he thought about what he should do. He knew what he wanted to do right now. More than anything he wanted to get to the contents of the skinny wax-paper Baggie in the lining pocket of his navy pea coat. His insides were jumping uncontrollably now at the thought. His naked body was cold and he hugged his arms across his chest and looked up at her and begged her to please come sit next to him. If he could have her warmth against him right now maybe he'd have a chance at talking his insides into being still, maybe he wouldn't convulse uncontrollably as he felt himself getting ready to do. "Please, Verdi, please." He begged. His words were soupy as he tried not to cry.

She just stood there. She was cold now too in her naked skin as the outside air was winning over the warmer gusts pushing up from the heater. She went to the window and slammed it shut, calling herself a fool as she did. "Why didn't I see it? Why didn't I see it?" she asked out loud, not sure what it was she hadn't seen so she just assumed it was another woman especially the way Johnson sat in a heap on the side of the bed as if he were in the process of collapsing even as his words streamed out and she wanted to cover her ears, hadn't Charity said something about a girl last night, she didn't want to hear it, because as long as she didn't hear it maybe it wasn't true. So she braced herself praying that it wasn't some woman she knew, maybe someone who smiled up in her face on a daily basis, maybe some tall, lithe, stunning beauty, maybe even a white girl, please God don't let it be a white girl, she thought as she listened for the spaces between his words, but his words had no spaces as they gushed forward, nor did they hold some woman's name, just Bug this, and Jones that. And what was he saying about Jones? And Bug told him how sweet it would be, and it was sweet—

"What?"

"It was so sweet."

"What tell me what?"

"The only thing sweeter has been you."

"Johnson, tell me what," she yelled. "What? Tell me what! Right now! Tell me what you're talking about!"

And he told her then what he'd been doing, how it had started out on Bug's couch just to be cordial sociable, to lift his mood. And before he knew it he was popping it under his skin once a month, then twice. Always turn-ons at first though, always free, he said. Until it became a regular thing, a three- even four-times-a-month ritual and he started paying Bug good money for nodding time on his couch. He wanted to stop, every time he'd done it lately he'd sworn to himself it was his last. But it was so sweet to him, the only thing with which to even compare this incalculable sweetness was their time together.

He was crying now, confessing to Verdi as if she wore a clergy's robe even though she was naked and cold as she came and sat down next to him. And now he was begging her to help him. "Help me, baby," he cried as if he were praying to a God who really could help him and since he didn't know how to invoke the name of a real God he just called Verdi's name over and over again and gave her the power to save him in that instant as their bare bodies shook against each other even as he broke out into a sweat.

But Verdi couldn't help him. Not even a little bit. It was unfair of him to ask; it was much too much of him to ask. She wasn't his God, as much as she studied her Bible, went to church, knelt down on the side of her bed before she went to sleep at night; as much as he admired her apparent goodness. She was just a confused college student out of her element since she'd been here, and since she had survived here, lulled into believing that she knew what she was doing, knew how to take the appropriate action when the man she loved sat next to her naked and convulsing saying that he had a jones, asking her to take it away. "Take it away, baby, please. Please take away this jones." And since she wasn't old enough or wise enough to understand that she could never save him, never could save anybody, that all she could do for him right now to really help him was offer to call student health, his adviser, his mother, the Pennsylvania Institute for the Mentally Ill. Then open her dorm-room door, ask him to leave her university apartment, to leave her entire world because she couldn't quell his cravings, nor should she, would she serve as their substitute. But she was only nineteen, only so smart. So unwise. So she did all she had the capacity to do at that moment, as her lips turned blue because she was so chilly even as Johnson leaked his sweat all over her, and he held her so closely until her chest was closing up and her breaths went thin and she started to cry and she thought the only way to help him, to save him was to understand him, understand what he was doing, had done. He could barely hear her when she said, "Show me, Johnson. Show me what you've gotten yourself into. Show me, Johnson. I want to do it too."

And had Johnson been more right-minded he would have denied her, even pushed and shoved her away if need be, he would have said no with a finality that she couldn't beat down like the way he said no when she'd beg to go with him when he went to buy their weed because he knew he couldn't keep her safe in some drug house. But he wasn't in his right mind, a fog still hovered over his brain from the day before yesterday's high and then having that high turn on him and make him sick when Tower confronted him. And now the itch was starting that was the surface of his skin warning him that it had to be soon, that this itch would spread from outside in to the next layer of his epidermis, down on through his muscles, that his brain would crawl like his skin was now if the liquid music wasn't soon to start, that even the very core of him would cry out needing relief. So it wasn't a decision he made with his right mind as he reached into the lining pocket of his pea coat and pulled out the wax-paper Baggie with the dull white contents, so beautiful that bag looked to him, more beautiful even than Verdi. Nor was it a decision he made with his heart, because right now he had no heart, was incapable of loving anything except the contents of that wax-paper bag.

He was skilled and clinical as they sat together on the beanbag pillow in the center of her bedroom floor and he told his insides to be still, his turn was coming up soon. And Roberta Flack's voice oozed from the radio and the forced hot air whirred through the vents. He didn't talk, didn't instruct Verdi the way he did when she'd first smoked joint, or sipped the head off of a beer, he didn't say you put this in the bottle cap, that in the spoon, he barely breathed as he traced his finger up and down Verdi's vein and let his thumb rest against the thickest one; the one that pulsed like a heartbeat. And then he tied the rubber tourniquet tightly just above her elbow, and he extended her arm and droplets of sweat shimmered on the vein highlighting it so that it was so easy to see even under the fog of the morning sky that hung over the room and watched in horror as Johnson pierced it in. All the way in. And Verdi squeezed her eyes shut and made a sucking sound as her rich healthy blood, O-positive, the kind the Red Cross begged for because of its versatility, her blood splashed around in the needle head furiously appalled and trapped.

And surely Hortense felt it at that instant as her breath caught at the top of her throat and made her cough and choke and spit into her lacy handkerchief even as she sat on the front pew and looked up as her husband began to pray; and Leroy felt it as a thud in the center of his chest that made him pause and clear his throat and then the words "Our Father" wouldn't even come. Kitt felt it as a squeezing in and out around her temples so that she started undoing the rollers in her hair. And Posie felt it as a shaking in her hands that made it impossible for her to smooth on her frosted lipstick right now. Even Rowe, sitting at his kitchen table unfolding his Sunday paper this morning, could barely see through his eyes to the print on the page though he boasted often about his perfect vision. They all felt what Verdi couldn't feel right now as she sang along with Roberta Flack that it was okay for Jesus to change her name. "Whew, shit, change it, Lord, ha, ha, ha, ha." Then she sang some more as her head bobbed around and the air in front of her turned thick and smooth as cream, she laughed that laugh that Posie had heard in Johnson that sounded like a death rattle. She didn't hear it as such though, didn't hear much of anything right now except pings of metal firing one after the other in an orgasm in her head that went on and on and on even as she nodded off into the milky blue.

Ten

VERDI CALLED KITT the first chance she got the day after Easter Sunday. She'd gone to a sunrise service, stayed and had breakfast in the lower auditorium, applauded the Sunday-schoolers through their Easter recitations. Rowe was at the gym by the time she got back in and Verdi had the house to herself so she yelled at Kitt and told her what an indiscreet thing that was that she'd done. And Kitt apologized over and over, said she died a thousand deaths when she went to the door and saw Rowe standing there, that as much as she loathed the man she didn't want to put her cousin in the position of having to explain something that she knew nothing about. "I was wrong, Verdi. I had no right to just disregard your stated wishes like that. Please tell me what I can do to make it up to you, please, cousin, please."

Verdi was quiet then, and Kitt seized on the moment and reminded her of the times she and Posie had tried to fix her up, ticked off the nicknames they'd given the Posie-and-Verdi-engineered blind dates gone afoul. "There was Nonie, who wore his pants too tight though there was no bulge where his thing should be so I assumed it was nonexistent; there was Toter who just wanted to smoke reefer, actually wanted me to stand and wait on our way into a movie while he ran into the bushes to do a bone; there was Tinker Bell who couldn't go five minutes without having to take a piss; and Woof Woof, whose tongue was always hanging out of his mouth like Lassie. Should I go on, cousin?"

Kitt listened for the heavy breathing from the other side of the phone that meant that Verdi was starting to laugh, she heard it and then she kept her stories going in order to hear the music of her cousin's hysteria, couldn't tolerate Verdi being upset with her.

And Verdi was hysterical, falling off the bed and dropping the phone she laughed so. And after they settled down and reason returned, Verdi asked Kitt to call Johnson for her, insisting that she didn't want to call him herself, she just wanted to see him, the next day if he could, at a public place, at the diner on Main Street in Manyunk at eight in the morning, if he can do it, cousin, you don't have to call me back, she said as she thanked Kitt and told her how much she loved her, and then looked at the clock and counted the hours until then.

A BREAKFAST meeting. That's what Verdi told her secretary to tell the assistant vice principal when she called her Monday morning. "Just saw it in my planner today though I've been staring at it for the past two weeks," she said, rushing to go over the morning's schedule so that she wouldn't have to be specific about the meeting, wouldn't have to say with whom, why, or what. She'd work out those details by the time she got to school, she told herself as she strained her voice to disguise that she was whispering, walking as far away as possible from the bathroom where the steady sizzle of the shower protected Rowe's ears from her deceit.

No sooner had she pressed the off button on the phone and tiptoed quickly through the house to the bedroom to place it securely back in its base, than there Rowe stood, dripping, rust-colored towel wrapped around his midsection.

He smiled and went to her and put his hands on her shoulders, she turned her head so that if he kissed her it would have to be on her cheek; she'd have to leave soon if she were going to hail a cab and make it over to Manyunk by eight. She hurried to her closet and rummaged through and suddenly everything seemed inappropriate. What was appropriate attire, she thought, for sneaking off to see a long-ago love even if it was just for breakfast at a public diner? She settled on her navy viscose suit, a starched white blouse though she disliked the formality of white against blue like that, but Rowe whistled as she slid her jacket over the blouse and said that she looked both sexy and administrative. His tone was very pleasant, his facial muscles very relaxed as he stretched his watchband onto his wrist and offered her the car for the day. "I think I'll walk in today," he said, smiling, tilting his head as if there were some easy-listening music playing in the distance that he wanted to hear.

She went to him and kissed his cheek, feeling suddenly sorry for him and said no thanks to his offer of the car, if the bus was coming she'd hop on it, she said, otherwise she'd hail a cab, she didn't want the hassle of having to park, but thank you, Rowe, she said as she just stood there and looked at him. "Thank you so much, for everything." She grabbed her purse from the ledge and was out of the door, trying to keep up with her emotions that were already walking through the diner door.

Verdi and Johnson couldn't look at each other for days after he shot her up that first time, after they nodded on and off that Sunday afternoon as reality swooped and lifted and circled like miniature planes doing their thing at an air show. And after Verdi stumbled down the hall to the shower to clean the vomit that had dried up by now in her hands where she'd tried to catch it even as that initial rush burst in her head like iron filings with no magnet to rein them in, and after Johnson cleaned up the remnants littering the usually orderly dorm-room floor: the bottle cap, the wax-paper Baggie that dulled in its emptiness, they went to bed for the night and tossed and turned and ended up sleeping finally back-to-back.

They woke Monday morning with heads full of ash and they were ashamed. As if they were suddenly keenly aware of their nakedness so that they rushed to cover themselves. Verdi poured herself into her books, Johnson, into BSL activities. They exchanged polite phone calls as each accepted the other's excuse for not being able to get together. And yet they missed each other in powerful gusts that swept them up, and finally landed them face-to-face again. They shooed away the awkwardness and hugged and laughed and kissed and pretended that nothing had gone awry.

But things had gone awry. Johnson had violated the code of every man who'd ever fancied himself a stuffer. He'd turned his lady on to it. He didn't know anybody who'd sunk so low, and he knew a lot of them now having spent so much time at Bug's. Married so-called professionals, hooked-up revolutionaries, neighborhood Jodies— even they protected the women they swooned from the sweet, beautiful knowledge of a mainlined heroin rush. So even though Verdi and Johnson tried to reclaim the way they'd been before that Sunday morning, they could never return to having not done it. And even though Johnson vowed never to do such a thing with Verdi again, he couldn't not do it. That seed he laid when he pierced her vein that Sunday morning had found most fertile ground with Verdi, curious young woman that she was, enthralled by prospects of living on the edge. Now it was an oak-sized desire that begged Johnson, just once more, please baby, we won't do it again after this, but please, let's do it just once more.

And they did once more. And Verdi started with her head held high; unable to tie her own arm to do it herself, she willingly gave her arm to Johnson, and after he hit her bulging vein her chin touched her chest and just hung there as she mumbled nothingness to herself. Johnson watched with envy because he was beyond that point, what he did now he did just to stay ordinary, just so that he wouldn't shit in his pants from his bowels breaking, or go into convulsions from the shakes, or gag and vomit from his stomach knotting. He did what he did just so that he could continue to be with Verdi, so that she wouldn't see what he'd become, what she herself was on the way to being.

And they played a game then of swearing to themselves that one more time and that would be the last time, and maybe two weeks later, she was begging Johnson again, and he couldn't resist her sultry persuasiveness and against his best intentions there he'd be tying the rubber too tightly around her arm again, and again, and again. And he was working as much overtime as he could, at least showing up and pretending to work, punching his time card so that he got paid, so that he could fund his habit that was now two to three times a week, and Verdi's habit that was quickly catching up. And they were missing classes and starting to fail exams, and Verdi just made it through the semester with a 2.0, but Johnson didn't and was put on academic probation and told that if he didn't have a dramatic upturn, he'd be asked to leave. And she made herself scarce when it came to Posie and Kitt, keeping her contact with them to her normal periods, though normal had become relative in a dramatic way and Kitt told her she looked like shit, what was wrong? "Impacted wisdom teeth," Verdi lied. "Can't eat, can't sleep, getting them all pulled when I go home for summer break." And Posie and Kitt looked at each other, denied the sinking that happened in their chests, accepted the toothache story. This was Verdi, their Verdi, not even Johnson who they loved dearly but whose shortcomings were at least acceptable. Impacted wisdom teeth, of course.

She concocted a story for her parents about spring break, said she'd been invited to spend the week with Cheryl's cousin at Cheyney, please, please, could she go? And her father relented; though she was at the university, he still had a soft spot for black colleges. And Johnson and Verdi measured that week not in days, but in bags, and they proceeded to unpeel themselves from all the relationships and finally at the close of the semester, when Johnson didn't graduate, and Verdi was put on academic probation, they peeled away from each other too.

Verdi was hot and cold in this dorm room, it was the end of April, Penn Relay Weekend, and she could hear the sororities and fraternities chanting and stepping down on the concrete of the super block. Charity was done with her course work for the semester and was going to California, at least Verdi thought that's what she said that morning when she'd floated into her room like a fog, denim duffel bag on her arm, and kissed Verdi and told her that she loved her and that she had good Karma and would soon be free of that gorilla on her back.

It was only six months after she'd begun her descent into hell and she was rocking on the bed, midway between the chills and fever she'd been suffering through for the past forty-eight hours. The flu.

She should go to student health, she thought, but she couldn't stand up long enough to try to get dressed without the room going into a spin. She hadn't even had a cigarette the past day and a half. They had smoked joint and drunk cheap wine the night before, the basic high Johnson called it. And though she'd begged him for some stuff, he said that Bug was out of town, that you never know what you're getting when you changed suppliers so he would wait for Bug.

And she had talked to him earlier, he was on the way, he'd said, and yes he had her stuff. And now she tried to sit up praying that he'd be there any minute. Her refuge in a time of need, she thought with a weak smile. Then erased the thought thinking it blasphemous to elevate him so. But he had been there with her seemingly around the clock the past two days since she'd been sick. Brought her a jar of homemade soup from Father Divine's on Thirty-sixth Street, though she hadn't kept it down five minutes, the sheer gesture, the almost sheepish expression that took over his face as he'd spoon-fed it to her, touched that spot in her that only he could touch that radiated a shrillness that was so intense that she wanted to laugh and cry at the same time, because now that the other substance that they poured into their arms, and even in the veins running between their legs, was touching that spot that had been reserved for Johnson, and now that made her cry.

She had to go to the bathroom. Wished she could use the trash can that was catching the intermittent contents of her stomach because the bathroom seemed an impossibly long walk up the hallway. "Oh shit," she said out loud as she tried to sit up again and the sickly-smelling air in the room made a whirlwind around her head. She turned on her stomach and put one foot on the floor. Moose had told her once during one of their all-night get-high sessions that if she ever drank too much and the room was spinning, just put one foot on the floor and everything would settle back to its rightful place. She tried it now though this room spinning hadn't been induced from too much drink, but the turning air did seem to back up some from her head, and she slanted her body to try to sneak and sit up, if she did it slowly, gradually, maybe her head wouldn't notice, she reasoned. And it seemed to be working until she sat all the way up and her head was not to be fooled and the cyclone kicked up with such intensity that she fell back against the pillow too weak to even sleep.

When she came to, it was night again. Johnson hadn't been there. She could tell because the contents of the trash can streamed into her awareness before she was fully awake. And the first thing he did the past two days after he entered her room with the key she'd given him months ago was to touch her forehead and lightly kiss her lips and then whisk the trash can away from the side of her bed and return it a few minutes later smelling of the pine disinfectant that they used to clean the bathroom. But only foulness emanated from that trash can now and she pushed it from under her nose and turned to face the wall and tried to go to sleep again but her back was cold and she burrowed farther under her blue-and-white-flowered bedspread and she couldn't seem to warm her back with the spread until she realized that it was not just cold but wet and that she had peed on herself while she'd slept.

She realized then that this wasn't just the flu as a sensation started coursing through her muscles that had the effect of a dentist's drill and she had to move around, told the dizziness to be damned because she had to sit up, because, because, "Lord have mercy, Jesus," she said out loud, this is what she'd heard horror stories about, because this is how you felt when your jones was coming down. She stood up and shrieked and jumped up and down in the middle of the floor. She'd sworn to herself this would never happen to her, how could it happen to her, wasn't her daddy a preacher, and wasn't she from a fine home, a well-raised southern girl? Sweet. Isn't that what everybody said about her that she was such a sweet person? And didn't she go to church and even tutor in the after-school program? And hadn't she had such devoted parents? College-educated daddy, politically connected. The best. She'd had the best parents. "Mommy, Daddy," she called into the foul-smelling air in that little girl's voice that would bring her parents tearing into her bedroom in the middle of the night to chase away the witches only she could see. She called again, as if her calling could make them assemble themselves right then in her university dorm to give her relief from this powerful flu. Flu. No flu, because there it was again, the sensation of wanting to spin herself in a ball to stop the dentist drills in her head. This wasn't the flu. This was what wasn't supposed to happen to people like her, not her. My God, she screamed, this can't be happening to me, not to me. No Lord no, please stop this from happening to me. And now the person who could stop it, to whom she'd given her last money, wasn't here, wasn't going to show, the first time she'd given him money for it and he had ripped her the fuck off.

She thought about what she could do, concentrated on her goal right now which was just to get high, she'd get help after this, she told herself, but right now she had to get high. Who could she call, Kitt? She couldn't call Kitt. Couldn't beg Kitt for money and not tell her why. She'd been lying the past six months to Kitt and Posie. When they said they were worried about Johnson, she lied and said she was too. When they told her he needed help, she told them he'd gotten help. And he only went over there when he could walk straight and not go into a nod which meant that he wasn't over there every day anymore and she told them he was working very hard. So she couldn't call Kitt—but she could call Rowe.

Of course, Rowe. She could say she needed a prescription filled, that she was a little short of cash until the banks opened on Monday, could he help her out please? She could meet him for the money.

She could run out to that car in the middle of the super block that sold any kind of drug imaginable that Johnson told her to avoid that nonetheless saw a steady stream of action, all kinds of students, red and yellow black and white, that car's so precious to their sight, she'd sung once when she was high and bastardizing songs that had once meant so much to her.

That's what she'd do, what she'd have to do just to get through this night. Then she could think tomorrow, she could solve it all tomorrow. But right then the phone rang, and it was Johnson. And just hearing his voice in her ear and associating his voice with her stuff and she couldn't contain her need for it and started to cry and beg. "Johnson, baby, Johnson, I'm sick. Please come to me, baby, please bring me my shit."

"Verdi, Verdi, Verdi I—I love you so much."

"What in the fuck are you talking about, get here, right here, right now, get here with my motherfucking shit."

"Verdi, I—I can't."

"What you mean can't!"

"You want it, baby, you got to come to me, this time I can't get there, you got to come to me."

"Johnson, please, please, I'm sick baby, please."

"Got-to-come-to-me."

He was sobbing in the phone and Verdi asked where? Where was he, she was on the way.

On the west side of College Hall, he told her. Adding, "Hurry up because I got it and it's so, so good." Even as he sobbed into the phone.

Verdi pulled on jeans and a sweatshirt over her pee-stained bed-clothes, didn't think about her hair, or unbrushed teeth, just pushed through the relay assemblages that were just crawling through the campus, like roaches she thought, she just wanted to step on them to move them out of her way because they were separating her from her goal, her target, help me Jesus, she prayed as she ran across campus this April night to try to quell her jones. By the time she got to the west side of College Hall she thought her lungs would explode, and her head, and the pit of her stomach because they were all spinning now and then she spotted Johnson and he was running too. But he wasn't running toward her waving the treat he had for her in the wax-paper bag. He was running away from her. All she could see was his back in the clarity of the light beams gushing from the spotlight on the side of the building.

"Johnson!" she called to his back. "Johnson, don't do this to me, you motherfucker, I hate you!" That's all she could do, she couldn't run anymore, couldn't catch him, she was too weak, too defeated, too strung out, too sick. She started vomiting out there, and now her bowels were breaking and she busted into College Hall, into the bathroom, the men's room, and collapsed right there at the urinal's base.

Eleven

VERDI'S CHEST CLOSED at the thought of sharing a meal with Johnson after twenty years. Her breath caught at the top of her throat as she pulled open the double glass doors of the diner. She breathed through her mouth once she smelled the bacon grease that hung in the air. She wasn't hungry; the thought of chewing and swallowing right now sent her stomach in a swirl as she looked around for Johnson and was blinded momentarily by the sun glinting right into her eyes as it bounced off the old-fashioned chrome-trimmed counter and stools. He wasn't at the counter she was sure as she blinked down the row of on-their-way-to-work types gulping coffee and taking in mouthfuls of scrambled eggs.

"You must be here for that good-looking brother I seated in the back," a rounded tight-jeans-wearing hostess said as she picked up a laminated menu and motioned for Verdi to follow her. "You sure kept that fine thing waiting long enough, my my, my, my, my."

Verdi wanted to tell her to stuff her commentary where the light doesn't hit, but figured the light probably hit everywhere with this one who was making circles in the air around her as she switched her butt from side to side. She could only imagine how she must have exaggerated that walk for Johnson. Wondered if Johnson licked his lips as he followed too closely behind her, wondered if he liked this Coca-Cola-bottle-shaped woman, wondered what kind of women he'd been with over the years. Then she caught sight of him as they neared his booth and the swirl in her stomach quickened as she focused on him sitting there, swathed in sunlight, sipping from a cup of coffee, looking so calm and self-assured. She tried to settle herself down even as she was bombarded with all the reasons why she'd refused to see him over the years beginning with her loyalty to Rowe and ending with the way he'd turned his back on her, just walked out of her life and left her while she was screaming out his name. She shouldn't be here she told herself; should be at work with her teachers and especially her students who needed her. Johnson didn't need her, maybe he needed someone like the woman fanning in and out in front of her, someone to lay back and spread open her floppy thighs whenever he got the urge, probably how he spent his free time in all the cities he slid in and out of. He didn't even think enough of her right now to be sitting in an anticipatory posture maybe on the edge of his seat, or even standing, shifting back and forth unable to box in his excitement like she'd been unable to box in hers the whole cab ride over and ended up getting out of the cab a block away just so that she could walk off all the mild electric shocks passing through her stomach at the thought of seeing him. He'd probably been distracted by this waitress shaking her fat ass all in his face. She stopped herself, couldn't believe that she had allowed her thoughts to board a runaway train like this and that on top of all the conflicting emotions she was actually experiencing a streak of jealousy trekking up her spine making her warm now, and suddenly exhausted, as if she couldn't even hold her own weight. She never got jealous over Rowe.

They were at the last booth now, and Verdi was standing in the sunlight panning through the wall-to-wall windows and the hostess was calling Johnson "handsome" and resting her palm on his back as she told him that his breakfast mate had finally arrived.

Johnson's cup made a dull smashing sound as he missed the saucer he set it down so quickly. He was up in a flash, taking Verdi in a hug. He squeezed her tightly against his chest and she relaxed her face against his blazer that smelled of dry-cleaning fluid and then felt a fire starting deep, deep inside of her the way it had Saturday at Kitt's but then a shyness descended over her and she pushed him away, allowed the morning sun to pass between them. "I'm late, I know," she said, looking down at his half-empty cup. He started helping her out of her trench coat and she was sorry now that she'd worn the viscose suit that made her look padded and ripe. Ripe for what? she thought.

"Don't worry about being late, Verdi Mae," he said as he hung her coat on the hook protruding from the side of the booth. "I mean I'm late too. About twenty years late—" He stopped himself then, almost wanted to apologize for saying that. Hadn't wanted to start this encounter bombarding her with come-ons. Thought about what he could say that wouldn't sound like a come-on; surely couldn't compliment her on how gorgeous she looked right now, her face so open, so filled up, her entire person brimming with the essence of her womanhood as she slid into the leatherette booth that was a wispy blue color like the air in here. He knew if he told her how good she looked it would be impossible to keep the physical manifestations of his desire for her from swathing his face like the sun was now.

He was facing her in the booth now. He cleared his throat, as she told the hostess-now-waitress that she'd just start with orange juice for now. He was about to say how glad he'd been to see her Saturday. Settled on, "Thank you, Verdi, for inviting me out to breakfast."

She blushed through her cheeks and then coughed a nervous cough and then looked away, outside into the sun-soaked parking lot. They both did now as they inhaled the bacon-scented air that had turned awkward and still. They squinted through the window as if each was trying to figure something out, as if suddenly they realized that they had twenty years' worth of strangeness between them.

The hostess-now-waitress was back with Verdi's juice. Said to Johnson, "You want a nice, warm head on your coffee, baby?"

Johnson smiled at her in spite of himself, said, "Uh, yes, thank you, thank you very much." She poured the coffee and the steam rising up between them provided a momentary buffer to their awkwardness and gave them something else to focus on as Johnson waved his hand back and forth over the cup and asked Verdi what could she recommend.

"Recommend?" she asked.

"Yeah, from the menu, you've been here before, right?" He wished now that Kitt had arranged this meeting like she'd arranged the one Saturday. Kitt was obviously better at getting them together than they were themselves.

"Oh sure, I mean it's standard breakfast fare, the omelettes are decent enough," she said as she scanned the menu. "Though I'm not really in a grits-and-eggs kind of mood this morning."

"What kind of mood are you in?" he asked, looking right at her now, at her perfectly shaped face made even more so by the cut of her hair that framed her face and pointed in right at the space where her cheekbones jutted. He wanted to suggest that they head for his leased apartment that was only five minutes from here. The sight of her mouth with its pouty fullness made him want to be nowhere else right now but in that apartment, taking his time with her forever. But he didn't want to disrespect her by suggesting it. Already he'd noticed her button her blouse along the top. "Never mind, you don't have to tell me what kind of mood you're in," he said quickly, before she could.

She caught the erection that came up in his eyes then. How well she knew that look. That effusive roundness that said that if he couldn't have her right then he'd explode. In her beginnings with Rowe after Johnson had left Philly, left her, she'd imagine that look even while Rowe moved against her and panted out her name. "No big deal, I'll answer," she said, wanting to set him straight if he had any ideas. "I'm in a rushed mood because I have to be at my school by ten and it's already—" She started to pull back the oversized stark white cuff of her blouse to get to her watch.

"It's eight forty-five," he said, without looking down.

"And I'm on public trans—"

"I've got a rental, that maroon Grand Am right out there," he said, nodding toward the parking lot.

"And that helps me how?" she asked, a discernible irritation rising in her voice as the waitress stood over them again with her check pad in her hand.

"I mean however you want it to help you, Verdi," he said, smiling up the waitress again, motioning her to give them a few more minutes. "I mean I can give you a ride to your school, my schedule is yours all morning, I have a lunch meeting with some black clergy at the AME Plaza, but until then, I'll be your chauffeur, or anything else you want me to be." He reached for her hands and covered them with both of his. He went to mush at the feel of her hands inside of his.

She tugged to get her hands back, then looked around the diner.

That's all she'd need was for someone she knew to see her here like this, to tell Rowe that she was sitting in a sunny corner holding hands with some man over coffee and juice. She felt sorry for Rowe right now; he'd been so good to her really. She stopped herself, plucked her thoughts off that runaway train again, it wasn't as if she were packing her bags and leaving Rowe. She hadn't seen Johnson in twenty years; he was certainly no one to be thinking about leaving Rowe for.

Johnson yielded her hands and sat back against the booth and sighed. "I'm sorry, Verdi, if that was inappropriate," he said. "I guess I just don't know what the rules are with us."

"We don't have any rules, how can we have any rules? You're just back after twenty years," she said.

He held his hands up as if in surrender, not responding that he had been back in the past twenty years, several times he'd been back but she was always so fervent in her refusal to see him. And then when she did see him Saturday, albeit unplanned, she seemed as if she felt something. And now she wouldn't even allow him to touch her hands. He squeezed himself against the seat because now the coffee was running through him and he had to go to the bathroom, also had to check his voice mail. But he was afraid to get up, afraid that when he came back she would be gone, the way she'd disappear when he'd dream about her, right before he was about to touch her a cloud of blue smoke or some other dream cliché would envelop her and he'd wake crying the way someone cries after dreaming about the dead.

The controls for the diner's jukebox sat low on the table seventies-style and he twirled the red button absentmindedly at first, while he waited for her to study the menu as if she were reading the Bible. He sent the metal-plated tabs listing the music offerings flapping. Then he started to focus in on the titles and he couldn't believe it when he saw it. "You Go to My Head," the Louis Armstrong version. The same version they'd touched palms to at Kitt's. Damn, times like this made him wonder how he could have spent so much of his life doubting a God. He slid a dollar in through the receptacle and double-punched so that the song would play twice, and now he really couldn't hold his water anymore and the hostess-now-waitress was back, writing down Verdi's order of English muffin and fresh fruit and then winking at him when he said that he'd have scrambled eggs and toast and she asked him if he'd like those hard or soft.

He smiled at the waitress again, more out of politeness than any affirmation of an attraction, as he stood and excused himself to Verdi, said he was going to the men's room, and then looked at Verdi with a pleading in his eye begging her as much as one could beg absent words that she please just be there when he returned.

Verdi looked at him in his entirety for the first time as he stood and leaned in her direction. Saturday she'd seen only pieces of him, his face, then his hands, as they touched palms under Kitt's archway, then not at all as he disappeared into Kitt's therapy room, only feeling his presence through the other side of the door. But now she looked at him all at once and was struck by how professionally groomed he was in his neat fade of a haircut that brought out the crinkles in his hair, his navy blazer and taupe-colored pants and a tie that blended the two, mild brown complexion unhampered by creases or scars standing there commanding his space so well in the graciousness of the window light, a hint of desire still rising in his asymmetrical eyes, and a vulnerability now too. And now she was watching his back as he walked away, and the sight of his back moving quickly, an edginess about it, and she couldn't stop herself from remembering the sight of his back when he first left Philly, left her, and she was chasing him, calling behind him, a gorilla jones racking her back and forth threatening to pitch the life out of her the way the life is pitched out of a violently shaken infant. And he'd kept walking that Saturday night, the floodlight on the side of College Hall illuminating his back as he squished new grass under his feet and sent up a cloud of dirt around him he moved so quickly. "Johnson, you motherfucker," she'd shouted at him, "how can you leave me like this with my shit, give it to me, give me my shit, I gave you my last money for my shit."

She tightened inside when she thought about it now. She sipped at her orange juice that was fresh-squeezed with ice chips and leaving bits of pulp between her teeth. She looked for a cord to a shade she could pull to block out some of this sun gusting in this diner in huge billows more like rough waves than plates of sunshine.

The diner had filled up quickly in the past few minutes and Verdi didn't see another empty, shadier booth she could move to. She motioned for their hostess-now-waitress who was taking an order at a table next to their booth. "WhatcanIgetya?" she asked after she took her time sashaying to where Verdi was.

"Some drapes for this sun would be good, or another table," Verdi replied, trying to ignore the smirk on the woman's face.

"Sorry, girlfriend, we're to capacity. Your man-friend asked for a booth in the back so I seated y'all here, you know what I mean?" She swiped a minuscule crumb off of the table into her cupped hand. "Only thing I can suggest if you having a reaction to the light is that there's a bar next door, nice and black in there, probably suit your type." This last part she said under her breath as she bounced her hips in her walk away.

Verdi didn't know why the simpleminded comment made a lump come up in her throat as she angled herself to a slant away from the window and decided that they'd just leave when Johnson got back. Nor did she know why her memory was going so fluid on her now. She hadn't thought about the particulars of that night for years, and even when she did think about it, she'd always freeze that scene at the point when she was calling to Johnson's back, and then skip ahead in a fast forward to when she woke up at Rowe and Penda's house. Even during years of weekly fifty-minute drug-therapy sessions at the Philadelphia Psychiatric Center she'd end her story with calling out to Johnson's back and then leaping ahead to the point when she'd drifted into consciousness and there was Penda, spooning her up clear broth, encouraging her to put something warm in her stomach to help her get rid of the chills. She had to talk that part out with her therapist and with Rowe every chance she got because of the weight of the magnanimously sized guilt that threatened to crush her over how she'd betrayed Penda.

But the other part—right after Johnson kept walking and she'd staggered into College Hall—she'd kept frozen because it was simpler for her that way, cleanly preserved, because then she could hate Johnson for leaving her, and love Rowe for saving her. Black and white, no variations of gray to fuck with her.

But right now, she didn't know why, maybe it was the sight of Johnson's back again after all these years, maybe it was the pushy sunlight, but the fullness of the memory of that night was melting right in front of her as she ran her fingers up and down the chilly exterior of her orange-juice glass.

She saw herself, how low she'd sunk the night Johnson left. So unkempt, unwashed, uncombed, unrefined, unraised, unschooled, unchurched, so unclean. A nearly dead forest spawned weeds in her mouth from vomiting up so much foam and bile and not rinsing her mouth out afterward. And when she hadn't been able to get Johnson to turn around with her voice, she at least knew enough not to try and chase him down, knew her diminished body surely couldn't accomplish what her words had been unable to do. So she staggered into College Hall to get to a bathroom to piss or shit or vomit, or bang her head repeatedly against the porcelain until her brain was swimming in blood because at least that would be a relief. And as she passed out retching over the urinal, unaware, or not really caring that she had stumbled into the men's room, she heard someone calling her name, and in her paradoxical stupor-manic state she thought it must be Johnson calling her, who else knew she was in here to be calling her. "Johnson," she said over again and over again, "you came back for me, baby, I knew you wouldn't leave me like this." She was twitching on the bathroom floor, folded up from stomach cramps, fading in and out as she waited for Johnson to come on in and shoot her up.

The droplets of water draining off the side of her orange-juice glass made a circle on the Formica table. She lifted the glass and put it down over and over making a series of linking circles. She could see it all with such startling clarity now: Rowe busting through the men's-room door frantically yelling out her name, stooping down to lift her face away from the urinal, tenderly wiping away the vomit caked around her mouth with his argyle vest. He held her and rocked her and told her that she was going to be okay, he was with her, would stay with her, and she was going to be okay.

She was perspiring now and she put the orange-juice glass to her cheek to cool her face. The hard coldness of the glass shocked her face and now there was water accumulating in the corners of her eyes as the sun seemed to be coughing now and covering the booth with its stark yellow phlegm. Verdi made a visor of her hands as she sat there waiting for Johnson to get back to the table. She rewound that scene to the point when Rowe busted into the men's room yelling, "Verdi! Verdi! Are you in here?" Over and over she replayed that scene until she could accept that night for how it really happened. It was a Saturday night after all, and though it was common campus knowledge that Rowe kept office hours on Saturday nights, she'd never ventured into any university classroom building on a Saturday night that didn't have a party attached to it.

Nor for that matter did she know any other student who did. Especially not on Relay Weekend. Yet Rowe knew to call her name as he ran down the hall to get to her. Before he opened that men's-room door, he knew she'd be there, knew what condition she'd be in. Knew, knew, he knew. "Lord Have Mercy," she said out loud. "Rowe already knew."

Never let on that he knew, how he knew, never let on that it was Johnson who tipped him off. Had to be Johnson, no one else but Johnson. My God, she thought as the memory went completely to water and tumbled down her face and she covered her face with hands. Why else would Johnson have told her to meet him at College Hall. "If you want the bag, you got to meet me, Verdi Mae," he'd said through the phone right into her ear.

"I can't get there," she'd protested. "I'm sick, Johnson, baby, please don't make me come out, please baby I gave you my last money, please come to me, baby, we can get high, we can get down, baby, bring it on to me."

He hadn't budged; she'd never known a time when her begging him hadn't made him budge; she could budge him off of everything; make him do anything when she begged.

"You got to go through to get to it," he said in her ear. "This time, baby, you got to come to me."

She covered her face completely with her hands now and her breaths against her face were moist and shallow and shocked. Johnson had drawn her out that night with no intention of getting her high. Just the opposite, he'd meticulously plotted her fall, so carefully laid the pillows to buffet her crashing descent by making sure that she landed into Rowe's open, willing arms. Rowe! As much as Johnson hated Rowe, hated his demeanor, his politics, his speech, the way he dressed, the way he walked, his laugh even, especially hated the attention he turned on Verdi every chance he got, Johnson had bowed out, left, shown her his back, incurred her most fervent wrath in order that she might be cared for by Rowe.

She felt objectified right now, as if she'd been a stuffed doll to be handed off between them, as if Johnson had said, Here, Rowe, she fell in the mud and got dirty, why don't you take her over from here and clean her up? She was trying not to sob out loud as she pressed her hands tighter against her face, her emotions had gone to gray now with no clear demarcations of love or hate or gratitude or shame.

Johnson was back at the booth standing over Verdi. The sunlight was still overflowing in the booth and at first he thought that's why she was sitting there with her face in her hands. Then she made a sound from the back of her throat and another one and he recognized the sounds as unfulfilled sobs. He crowded into the booth next to her and put velvet to his voice and called her name, and took her head against his chest as she sobbed openly into his chest. He rubbed his hand up and down the back of her viscose suit and said a silent thank-you to Louis Armstrong and his trumpet for softening her up so. Though she hadn't heard any of the selection that was just beginning to play for the second time. Not the blaring, melodic trumpet, nor Louis singing the part about a sweet Merlot, she'd heard only this as she sat there melting in the luminous booth in the back: Rowe calling out her name from the other side of that bathroom door over and over again.

When she could dry her voice out enough to speak she pushed away from Johnson, she was facing him in the booth her back to the sun now. "You set it up, didn't you?" she asked, her voice holding on to a plaintive whine.

"Set what up?" he asked, squinting as the hostess-turned-waitress put down their breakfast without comment, and with deliberate attempts at being nonintrusive, and Johnson made a mental note to leave her a healthy tip as he focused in completely on Verdi.

"What, Verdi, what?" he asked again as she dabbed at her nose with a napkin.

"When you left, when you left campus, left Philly, left me."

He dropped the muscles that were holding his face in a congenial tilt. Knew that they'd have to go through this, shovel through layers of rocky mantle to get to here, this part of their lives so buried, but still so affecting, like a piece of uranium that only a Geiger counter can find that's still disrupting the earth for miles and miles around.

"Verdi—I—I, you know what condition I was in, how strung out I was. You know I had to leave or it would have meant an ugly death for both of us." He lowered his voice as a stream of on-their-way-to-work types was seated at the booth in front of theirs.

"You could have taken me with you, I was strung out too." Her voice was still wet, her tone was more declarative than accusatory.

"How? I didn't even know where I was going, how I was going to live. At least there was hope for you, you know, a support system already in place. You, at least, could make it."

"But you decided how?"

"Huh?"

"How I should make it, how I should live?"

"Verdi, I—"

"You decided Rowe should be how I would make it."

"Verdi—Verdi—mnh."

"You did, didn't you? Set me up so Rowe would find me then just turned your back on me as if you were giving me your ass to kiss."

He locked on Verdi's eyes. Her eye shadow was smudged and specks of pink glistened on her nose. He tried to discover the correct words for the telling of it, in all these years he hadn't been able to come up with the words, would lapse into a vat of sensations of having felt so gutted when he realized the course of events that would have to occur, as if his insides had been slowly and torturously pulled from him and then hung on a line like stained laundry flapping in the sun. He couldn't find the words now, as he started rolling his hands in front of him trying to evoke the words.

"I didn't know the man was gonna leave his wife, goddamn," he said, diving right in, not even trying to find a logical starting point. "Even though had I known, I still may have done what I did anyhow. I mean, really, Verdi, we both know he was your only hope at that point."

Verdi didn't say anything, she barely breathed as she watched his face fade further into twenty years ago with each word he spoke.

"I knew he could pull strings to make sure that the university didn't boot you," he continued. "I knew he would make sure you got the, you know, the appropriate care like doctors and psychologists, I figured he'd, you know, enlist his wife in your recovery and that she'd be sympathetic, a sociologist and all. You know, I even—even," he coughed and sipped from Verdi's orange juice, "I guess I knew he had a thing for you, the way he was so attentive, I'd even catch him looking at you and it was disgustingly obvious how badly he wanted you. I suppose I could have gone to Kitt and Posie, but I mean, I wanted to save them that devastation if it was at all possible, you know they were so proud of you, they had you on such a pedestal, I mean deservedly so, you know, you were just so much their heart. I mean, what can I say, and honestly I didn't want to lose them either. You know. I knew someday they would forgive me for fucking my life up. But yours? They would hate me forever for fucking up your life. I was afraid to tell them, I was a coward. I was all in. I couldn't help you, I couldn't help my damned self. I was broke, had punched out of school, owed everybody who used to care about me, I mean I was gonna have to revert to stealing just to maintain, you know, shoplifting, or breaking and entering. Either that or commence to bleeding you. Had I stayed it would have only been a matter of time before I had you tapping into your trust fund, or wherever your daddy had your nest egg secured. So I took your money that Saturday night, you know in all the times we'd gotten high, that was the first time I ever took any real money from you. So I copped enough for both of us and then I shot enough for both of us too. I pumped yours and mine into my arm that night. You know, I was hoping it would just take me on out, you know, just OD. At that point I was better off dead anyhow. And had I gone up to Bug's I could have OD'd. Would have pulled it off cleanly, but I was jonesing, didn't want to take the fifteen minutes to go into West Philly so I copped from the car that used to sit in the middle of the super block. And the motherfuckers lightweighted me and I barely got, you know, got on, less more died. And when I started coming out of it, I knew I had only a small window of time when my thinking could approach a normalcy, you know before I'd need to get high again and all of my life force would be focused on copping again. I knew Rowe would be in his office probably grooving off of his argyle vest and telling himself how wonderful he was. So I called you, you know, I, what can I say, I baited you. Then I beelined to College Hall to his office, I just opened his door without knocking and slid on in. And I suppose I didn't have the appearance of a choirboy right about then because he looked at me with a terror in his eyes, as if I had come in there to rob him, and honestly, Verdi, at that point I vacillated, I swear I was considering just knocking him over his head with his cast-iron desk lamp and taking his watch and any cash he had, his desk set could have gone toward a bag, honestly. Verdi, had I gone in there maybe an hour later when the jones was telling me what to do I would have hurt him, I hated him with such a passion anyhow, especially after he looked at me as if he expected it anyhow.

"But I didn't, I guess somebody must have been praying for me, you know maybe Posie and Kitt, maybe my mother if she knew how, or maybe somebody was praying for Rowe because I do believe his life was spared that night, it would have been easy—you know, but like I said I didn't do anything to him. He asked me what did I want barging in there like that, he stood up slowly as he asked it, looking from my face to my hands. And I asked him if he could spare ten dollars. Hell, I was a drug addict, at that point I had no shame, at least I figured I could get one more bag before I hitchhiked away from Philly. And his response was what I expected. Told me to leave, said I was a disgrace to my family and community and the school, it was my ilk that made it hard for legitimately talented black students to get in because the admissions people could point to the stats crowded with black people like me. I wanted to tell him that white boys get strung out too, that nobody makes a proclamation that no more white boys can be admitted into the university because some of them dib and dabble in drugs. You know, I think I did say something to him like a white boy at least being free enough to get high without strapping his whole race on his arm with him. And of course that enraged him and he told me to get out again, to go pervert scholarly thought about race with some other professor. And I asked him again for the ten dollars. And he sat back down and opened his book, apparently I was no longer a threat to him and he asked why should he give me a tarnished penny, and I said that if he wanted to save the life of his prized female student he should give it up. And then he came at me with his short-assed self, I'm telling you, Verdi, his life was truly spared that night because I would have taken a man down twice his size for coming at me like that, you know all the hate I had toward him, but I let him come at me, at that point it was for you, it was all for you. And he reached up and grabbed me by my collar and started shaking me, asked me what was I talking about, what had I done to you, if I wanted to live, you know shit like that. And I think I even started crying when I told him your condition, I think—I know I was begging him, you know asking him to help you stay in school, get you some help, that as long as I was on the scene that wouldn't happen, but I was leaving, I was going to stay away once I left, so please, please get you some help. And he asked where you were, and I told him you were supposed to meet me right outside, that you would be there any minute, and then he was pacing up and down his office, I guess figuring out what he should do, and I still asked him for the ten dollars and he picked up the unabridged *Webster's* off of the pedestal stand and hurled it right for my face, thank God it was so heavy and his aim was off, and I bolted then but I was just a little too late because you saw me, and you were calling me, and I wanted to turn around, God knows I did, but I knew I surely couldn't turn around, couldn't have your eyes on my face, I never could deny you anything once you put your eyes on my face, that's been as addicting to me as heroin. The feel of your eyes."

He sipped some more of Verdi's juice when he was finished. His voice had felt so raw coming out of him like that, propelled out actually by his entire being it seemed because all of him was drained right now. He exhaled loudly and then slumped against the booth back. He didn't look at Verdi now, hadn't looked at her the whole time he talked, just stared straight ahead as if seeing the whole scene click before him like 3-D images through a viewfinder. But even though his words had stopped, the images continued on in front of him. He watched himself that night thumbing a ride to the turnpike, and another one to Harrisburg but the big rig driver forced him out in Reading because he started gagging and going into the shakes, and ended up a scrambled heap on the side of the road inhaling his own stench and begging for the ground to open up, begging to be accepted into the barb-wired gates of hell, because surely that couldn't be worse than this.

Verdi had her hand on his wrist and she shook him gently. She knew all too well how consuming it was to travel to there, could stay locked up back there for hours at a stretch if she allowed herself, which is why she avoided it, so terrified that maybe one day the hell of it all wouldn't resound as clearly and she might allow a molecule of temptation to be laid.

"Let's go, Johnson," she said gently, strands of compassion, of tenderness toward him mixing in and then overpowering her plethora of feelings the way that a pinch of thyme takes over a stew. "Cheniqua's over there stashing on us and I do believe she's gonna bounce us out of here with her bare hands in a minute."

Johnson straightened himself up and blinked away the scene clicking noisily in front of him; he'd just reached the part of his dip into hell where he'd spun himself into a hysterical ball on a naked cot in the corner of some county-run shelter for indigents. But now, suddenly, he was looking into Verdi's face again. He almost said something like damn, Verdi Mae, I've just gone from hell to heaven in a blink of an eye; he didn't say it though, thought it too trite a thing to say, just allowed the unclothed truth of it to drip steadily and spread through him like olive oil, helping him to come unhinged after the memories he'd just experienced that would have otherwise left him so caged and internally bound.

He reached into his pocket and pressed a twenty-dollar bill on the guest check next to their untouched food and then handed it to the hostess-now-waitress. "No change back," he said.

The waitress grinned and squeezed his arm and apologized for the overbearing sunlight, said she wished he'd tried just a taste of the food. "Meals here are so good, sweetness, I know you would have devoured the whole plate after the first touch of it soaked into the tip your tongue," she said.

He told her he was positive she'd be serving up someone with the appropriate appetite before the morning was done as he slid from the booth and extended his hand to help Verdi out. He put Verdi's trench coat on her shoulders and tried to keep himself contained, from just spilling out all over this diner floor as they moved toward the chrome-backed double glass doors, and it sank in that they were headed for the maroon Grand Am, headed to his leased apartment that was just five minutes away.

Twelve

VERDI ENDED UP taking the whole day off. Called her school and said she thought that she had a sinus infection, slight fever, bad headache behind her eyes, very bad, so bad she was going straight to her HMO to get a prescription for antibiotics and then right home to bed. And she really did have a headache. Watching Johnson's face fold in on itself the way it had as he convinced her that he'd not left her, that actually he'd left *for* her. Then trying to find her own words on the ride over and an hour beyond that as they sat in the maroon Grand Am in the darkened underground parking lot to Johnson's building, and Verdi almost whispered she talked so softly when Johnson stammered that he'd hoped it had not been too much like hell as the fog lifted for her while she was coming out of her addiction.

"It wasn't *like* hell," she said on an extended breath that was raspy, as she stuck her hands into her trench-coat pocket. "It *was* hell, it was as if I was crawling on my belly. No one but the devil himself should go through what I went through coming out of it."

Then she stopped herself. His jaw was clenched and she could see the hard line of it even in this darkened car, could tell that he was trying not to cry and the sight of him sitting there, hand squeezing the vinyl-topped gearshift, looking so turned inside out as if she could see all the hurt he was trying to keep contained, the contusions left after years of blunt trauma, and she wanted to jump out of herself and become stronger than him, to protect him for once. She tried, opened her arms ready to take his head against her shoulder but he put his hands up in front of him.

"You can't take this from me, Verdi Mae, I need to feel it," he said. "Me. It's a consequence and I own it, will not let it become yours." His words were suddenly acute, as if they brandished knives and then he fell silent, and threatened to crack his molars he clenched his jaws so tightly, and held his eyes wide open so that dry air in the maroon Grand Am would absorb the moisture accumulating in his tear ducts.

She insisted that he not hold himself responsible for stringing her out, that she was so wildly curious back then she would have tried it in some other venue eventually, she believed that. He reminded her though that ultimately it was him who tied her arm and shot her up.

They were quiet for a time until Verdi found his hand and squeezed it as she asked him how he'd turned away from it. Johnson chronicled his introduction to the Twelve Steps after he was arrested for vagrancy and sentenced to a rehab in Williamsport; then Verdi described her weekly therapy sessions, no one really ever knew how she'd bottomed out except for Rowe and Penda, she said, lowering her head, her voice the way she always did when she referred to Penda as she told him how Rowe and Penda had kept her with them during all of that November, even fashioned a story to her parents and to Posie and Kitt about a Thanksgiving retreat they were sponsoring at their home for some of the semester's special students. "Rowe did make some calls on my behalf to a few of my professors and Penda, Penda was just a godsend," she said as she went on to tell Johnson that the weightiest consequence that she owned was the look on Penda's face when Penda caught Rowe's too-affectionate expression toward her as the three sat down to dinner one night.

They were quiet again as they sat in the car of the darkened underground parking lot. They breathed the recycled air and tasted each other's sighs that were comforting because both were weighted with the same kinds of sadness and regrets—their consequences as they called them. And soon the windows started to fog up though the gray against the car window actually made the car seem lighter and they pulled themselves from their settling breaths that had also acted as a sealant and Johnson said that they could just sit in the car the rest of the morning or they could go up to his apartment though whichever she decided was fine with him because his apartment wasn't much larger than the inside of this car.

She opted to go inside and a sudden lightness descended upon them as they stepped into Johnson's spruced-up temporary living quarters— the management had finally responded to his demands for a decent cleaning service. It changed their moods and they spent the rest of the morning in incessant, friendly conversation moving beyond what had been so tattered, so devil-inspired about their pasts.

Verdi said that the minuscule one-bedroom efficiency reminded her of the high-rise apartment dorms at the university and their conversation went rollicking after that as they called up scene after scene of how life was once, concentrated in those early college years like air in latex balloons, captured and formed and in need of anchors so that they wouldn't float away. They ticked off the current doings of Tower and Moose and Cheryl and the rest of their classmates. This one had been featured in *Black Enterprise,* that one in *Jet,* alas that one in the *National Enquirer.* They whispered about those who died, the suicide, the car crash, the violent encounter with police. They drank water from the tap, and munched on grapes and unsalted pretzels and sour cream and onion dip. They found the oldies station on the radio. They faced each other on the tweed couch, Verdi with her feet tucked under her thighs, Johnson with his ankle over his knee; she was out of the jacket to her viscose suit, Johnson had undone his tie. They felt in perfect harmony with each other right now, with the universe it seemed, as if they could go anywhere from here, as if they were on a launching pad strapped into each other's presence, and the sun or the moon or Alpha Centauri could be as easy to access as Fifty-second Street from the el.

But reality drifted in around noon and Johnson said he had to go to his meeting, the black clergy were not a group to be standing up, he said. And Verdi said she should leave now too. That actually she was feeling a little under the weather so she'd go home and get good and rested for her workday tomorrow. He grabbed her hand then. The first time they touched since they'd stepped inside his apartment. "Please stay; I'll be an hour and a half at the longest," he said.

"No, I really should go," she said in a voice that was also dripping with "persuade me."

"I know it's undignified to beg," he said as he held on to her hand, "but I'm begging you, please, I'm enjoying your company so, I just want to spend the afternoon with you, Verdi Mae, please."

She was persuaded then. She relaxed her hand in his and there was so much happening in the air between them that he almost said the hell with the meeting, but then Verdi pulled at her hand and told him to go, go right then and take care of his business, and bring her back a doggie bag because her appetite had gone into high gear.

She went outside while he was gone and bought fresh flowers, made a centerpiece bouquet for his two-seater dining-room table out of an oversized blue-and-white "Welcome to Philadelphia" mug.

She repositioned herself back on the couch and went through her case and pulled out some literature on speech pathology to help her with teaching aids for Sage. Immersed herself in the medical histories of children who seemingly out of the blue began to speak, leaving the professional therapists scratching their heads over why. She'd fantasized for several years now about what it would be like if Sage ever spoke her first real words. Maybe it would be around Kitt's table during one of those meals that made the eyes drool as platter after platter was set in the center of the table. Then after grace was said, maybe they'd be in the process of passing around steaming, browned dinner rolls glazed with nonfat oleo, and Sage would blurt out, "My name is Sage," and they would all jump up and down and shout hallelujah. She smiled to herself sitting there on Johnson's couch, and since she was already in fantasizing mode and she was seeing fine detail like the strands of gray starting to come up in Kitt's locks, it wasn't such a stretch that she'd see Johnson's face too, ecstatic, understanding in ways that Rowe never could her tremendous affection for Sage and all that it would mean for her to hear Sage talk. And now that she had gone on and seen Johnson's face, her fantasy floated off like a dinghy leaving the main ship, left Sage and Posie and Kitt and anybody else privileged to have a seat at Kitt's table and it was just Verdi and Johnson, unspoiled the way they once were when only promise filled the air between them: no cheap wine to distort their thinking, no good weed to put them in a drug-using bent, no drug dealer named Bug for Johnson to acquiesce to, no Rowe to save her, no Penda for her to betray; she was sinking into the fantasy, she and

Johnson like naked cherubs their goodness so prevalent, and then Johnson walked back in through the door for real, saying he was done with the black clergy sooner than he'd expected, that the dry chicken wasn't worth wrapping and bringing back, that he'd stopped at Larry's Sandwich Shop and picked up a turkey hoagie and a chicken cheese steak for them to share. Said that's one of the things he missed most about here, that he couldn't get in all the cities he'd traversed, a real Philly hoagie or cheese steak.

And the sight of him with those long sandwich bags, the aroma of fried onions and ketchup in the small temporarily furnished efficiency that could be her one-bedroom apartment in the high-rise dorm, and she felt innocent all over again. She bounded from the couch like a little girl, and rubbed her hands together as he put the bags on the counter. She giggled and kissed him on the cheek; he countered with a smooch on her forehead; she went for his other cheek; he, for her chin; and then it was nose for nose, until finally she and Johnson were almost lip to lip, mouths parted, tips of tongues revealed, their memories swirling all around them like a lasso, roping them in closer and closer, as the sandwiches were patient on the counter staining beautiful circles of grease through the brown paper bag.

His mouth was against hers and they stopped talking with words, and even though Verdi wasn't ready to relinquish this sense of innocence that had covered her while she'd waited for Johnson to return, every fiber of her had already yielded to the minty smell of his breath riding up her nose, and she tried now to draw some speck of self-control that was embedded so deeply it had never kicked in before, too embedded because it certainly didn't kick in now.

They talked with moans and sighs then as he walked her into the bedroom sweeping her face with his thumbs, kissing her pouty mouth, holding her breasts in the palms of his hands. He could feel her breasts throbbing against his palms like he was throbbing too. And he leaned down and kissed her breasts right through her stark white cotton blouse, he even tolerated the taste of the fabric against his tongue feeling her breasts pulsing and begging for his mouth like that. And she arched herself and moved against him in circles and felt his manhood thickening and finding her pinnacle and was sure she was going to come in a rush standing right in the middle of his bedroom floor. She yanked his shirt from his pants and unzipped his pants and he undid the buttons on her blouse, they pulled at each other until they were both bare and he just kept saying her name over and over. "Verdi, I can't believe—finally—you, I'm finally with you," he said. And they caressed and tasted and prodded and squeezed and they were slippery with perspiration and naked and cold and hot at the same time, and open, so wide open they both were, so expandable. They fell onto the bed and thrust and cried out and tried to fill each other up, tried to cross the gulf their twenty years apart had left. And then it was as if they'd never been apart, when their confluence erupted and rained over them and shimmered like the rivers of sweat traipsing down their legs.

They were silent afterward. She turned shy and stiffened even as he tried to snuggle her against his chest. He wrapped his arms around her and played with the clasp on her gold chain. Walked his fingers up and down her spine. Tried to be congruent, tried to match her breath for breath but her breaths wouldn't settle into a predictable rhythm. He felt a steady stream of moisture leaking down his chest rushing to find the hollow his navel made, thought at first it was their perspiration mixing and overflowing down his chest, realized then that she was crying. He squeezed her head tighter against his chest, rubbed her back in gentle sweeps, pulled the covers up because she was shaking against him now. He didn't know what to say, had been so absorbed in the beauty of what had just happened between them he'd forgotten she had such complicated issues, had forgotten about

Rowe. Or had he? Maybe he had just purged himself of the twenty years' worth of vengeful feelings he had toward Rowe. Stopped himself. Told himself it was all for Verdi, not against Rowe, told himself he wouldn't taint what had just happened between them by adding some dark ulterior motive of his getting back at Rowe as if some sense of vindication increased the pleasure of it all. The hell with Rowe. He wanted to say that. Couldn't. Too insensitive a thing to say. He'd just rub her back and keep her warm until she was ready to talk.

But she wasn't ready to talk. Couldn't believe what she'd just done, lain down with Johnson the first time they were alone together in twenty years. Got the picture then of two dogs jaunting through a park, and then stopping right in the open to mount and hump, then continuing on through the park as if nothing had happened. She pushed herself deeper under the covers. She'd have to act as if nothing happened when she got home later today though she knew that the glittering remnants of Johnson's essence would still be flickering on and off like lightning bugs at dusk, would have to look at Rowe and pretend that the earth hadn't shifted for her just now. My God, Rowe. She'd actually been unfaithful to Rowe. And he'd been so good to her, had been her savior. He deserved better. Much better than the liar and cheater she was. All over again, she was ashamed right now, because here it was happening all over again.

She was sobbing into his chest and he couldn't stand it anymore. Sat up, lifted her face from his chest. "Verdi, baby, talk to me. Maybe I can help you sort it out, baby, please, you're breaking my heart here."

"You can't help me with this, Johnson." She cried as she talked. "You wouldn't understand what all he gave up for me. He had a good marriage, he was content, and he gave it all up, his wife, his contentment just to be with me, to make sure I didn't use."

"He wanted to, Verdi. Nobody asked him to leave his wife, did you? I mean maybe I'm wrong but I'm sure he made the first move, or did he?"

"I told you you couldn't help me." She sniffed and tried to dry out her voice.

"I'm sorry, baby," he said as he squeezed her to him again. "You don't have to talk. Just lay here and let me hold you, I been waiting for this for two decades, please just let me hold you for a little while."

She was seeing that roast beef all over again. The one Penda had cooked for the dinner she'd prepared in celebration of the offer she'd just received from the university for tenure. Verdi had been back in her apartment at the dorm for the past two months mostly alone because Charity had taken the semester off to live on a farm in northern California, and her relationship with Cheryl had been strained beyond repair with all the lying she'd had to do to maintain her habit. Still in all that time she had not used any aberrant substance, hadn't even taken a sip of wine. And Rowe insisted that Verdi join them for dinner, that they could also celebrate Verdi's keeping herself so clean, her comeback.

And Verdi and Penda were in the kitchen and Penda was trying out a brown-'n-bag for the beef, the first time she'd used one, she said, and Verdi giggled, maybe a little inappropriately, she was still shy sometimes around Penda having come to her senses in their guest bedroom the way that she had. And when she finished giggling she said she couldn't imagine herself roasting a beef with or without the bag.

And Penda stood up from her lean over the oven where she was poking holes in the bag to let the hot air escape; she looked directly at Verdi then, said, "Well, maybe you should try to imagine it, Verdi.

Then you can decide whether or not it's something you'd like to try to do before actually going through with it. I'm sure you never imagined yourself addicted to heroin. Maybe if you'd seen yourself there in your mind's eye, shuddered over the consequences, maybe you could have spared yourself a torturous year."

Verdi went to wood then, felt as if splinters were peeling from her face. Penda had never been so strident with her, and Verdi understood, knew Penda was right. She'd certainly never imagined herself with Rowe, never foresaw his coming over day after day to check up on her after she went back to her dorm, being so sweet, so gentle, hugging her so close when he got up to leave, so close that she could feel his hardness against her when he told her to take care, be strong, he'd see her the next day. Never imagined that she'd actually look forward to his knock on the door, their secret code he called it, already setting her up for the undercover slant things would take on. As God was her witness she'd certainly never imagined herself responding to him the way she did that night when he sustained the hug, sought out her mouth, parted her lips. Begged her to let him help her forget about Johnson. And she opened herself, her arms, her legs so easily, so willingly, allowing him to move against her, to push inside of her as he whispered that this would do it, God, yes, this would help her to forget about Johnson, she needed to forget about him, he would do whatever it took for her to forget about him, to save her, whatever it took. It was all for her, he moaned, yes, yes, ooh, so young and soft, my God, as he spread her out on that dorm-sized bed, took his time until they both exploded in waves and she surprised herself with the force of the gushing that happened when she came.

She'd not imagined any of it beforehand, like she hadn't imagined the electricity when they were together, he was so much older, so patient; an experience, a confidence to his touch, and she found herself encouraging his visits after that. Found that she needed his visits because at times she was just so afraid of facing the day, what if she wasn't strong enough: she was reading her Bible and praying, was going to the psychotherapy sessions, and was still afraid. And Rowe was so capable in her mind, so strong, and she just needed to borrow some of his strength to get her through until she could make it on her own. He was a distraction for her so that she wouldn't use, so that she wouldn't be ravaged again with the physical withdrawal and that hell, so that she could remember less and less of her time with Johnson. And she no way had imagined that just the night before Rowe would tell her that he was falling in love with her, that he had to tell Penda, that he at least owed Penda his honesty, and Verdi begged him not to, said she wasn't well enough for that yet, could they just pretend around Penda for a little while longer, please just until she was stronger. She hadn't imagined it beforehand though, not any of it.

So she just stood there turning to sawdust as Penda split the brown-'n-bag, and slid her carving knife from the wooden knife block and started hacking into the beef, serrating huge chunks. And the beef gushed out its juices all reddish brown and succulent looking and at first Verdi was confused as to why Penda would disfigure the roast like that, and now Penda was cutting at a ferocious pace and right then Rowe walked in sipping brandy from his globe-shaped glass and looked at Verdi and smiled a soft smile that made his face light up as if he were a high-school senior watching his prom date come down the steps, and it almost seemed as if he'd forgotten where he was, looking at her the way he was, as if they were in her dorm room and he was on his way to kiss her fleshy mouth, and she furrowed her brow to get his attention to tell him to snap out of it, but Penda saw his face, not that she needed to see his face for confirmation, she'd already confirmed it as far as Verdi was concerned, and she started hurling the slabs of beef across the room, aiming for Rowe's face, landing the luscious meat on his face, telling him to wipe that god-dammed perverted smile off his face.

And Rowe left Penda that night, left his home, moved into temporary quarters. And Verdi left too, went back home to Atlanta, took the rest of the semester off to be with her parents. And they were horrified at how she'd gone down, hardly accepted her explanation that it was a bad bad virus, sent her to the family physician who'd been treating her since she was born; he took one look at her and asked when had she last used, she begged him not to tell, persuaded him that she was twenty-one after all, that there were confidentiality issues, that the drug use was now a closed chapter in her life, and to her fortune her blood work showed no traces of heroin, though it did show that she'd contracted mono, her parents knew only about the mono.

And she promised herself that if God could see it to forgive her for betraying Penda the way that she had, for causing Rowe to leave his wife, for lying to her parents, to Posie and Kitt, promised herself that she'd try to live the rest of her life above deceit, that she'd go into a profession that was of service to someone else, decided then to work with children who had special needs.

Thirteen

J OHNSON HELD VERDI for more than a little while. Held her until the sun turned orange then red then gave into the dusk and night fell over Johnson's City Avenue efficiency apartment. Verdi jumped up then, felt like Cinderella at midnight's approach as she took a quick shower and let Johnson drive her within a short cab ride of her house.

Rowe was late getting home himself. Had stopped at a travel agent to pick up brochures, was going to surprise Verdi, tell her to pick a spot on the globe, name the time and they'd go. He could cancel classes if her desire was for an immediate getaway. His certainly was, suddenly. He wanted to take her away someplace far. Would take her away tomorrow if she gave the word. Brazil, or the Caribbean, some-place swampy hot where they could taste each other's sweat; he had a small shopping bag filled with glossily colored possibilities. But the emptiness of the house smacked him in the face as soon as he turned the key in the ornate wood-and-stained-glass door. He felt his stomach tighten, she hadn't mentioned being late. He hit the answering machine, heard her voice lilt through the kitchen. "Hey, babes, stopping to get my ragged perm touched up, not my scheduled appointment so they're treating me as a walk-in, hope they don't keep me in there all night. See you later in the P.M."

He started himself a light dinner and listened to the tape again after that, and again. Didn't know what he was listening for as he stirred around broccoli and bowtie pasta in tomato paste. Didn't want to admit that he was listening for a slurred voice. Wished he'd been home to answer the phone, could have at least insisted on picking her up so she wouldn't be out alone on public trans. He felt unsettled as he allowed the blandness of the pasta to linger on his tongue, felt an ominous something lurking, felt it as dark wavy lines dancing just along the edges of his peripheral vision. He dumped the meal after only a few forkfuls. Took off his glasses to see whether he needed to tighten the arms. Looked around again because it was still there, went to the window and closed the white wooden blinds.

He went upstairs after that, poured the bag filled with brochures onto the bed, spread them out in a variety of fans covering the comforter. Stretched himself out on the chaise and felt his stomach sink in discernible degrees the longer it was taking to hear her key turn in the door. Was just about to call the shop when he did hear it.

Clicked on the megawatted chandelier and met her downstairs in the foyer and was struck by her smile, too broad a smile, and were those traces of red showing up under the brownness of her skin? His palms were sweaty and his stomach was grinding all the way to his groin. "I was just beginning to worry," he said as he he went to her and took her face against his chest. Ran his fingers through her hair. Loved her hair short and straight, could feel it crinkling near her scalp though. He pressed his nose into her hair, missed the aroma of the perfumed spray they used to mask the harsh scent of the chemical straightener.

She tugged away and let her briefcase drop from her hand to hit the floor with a thud. "That shop was sooo packed," she said as she went to the closet and hung her trench coat. She started humming then. It was either hum or cry with all the contraries rising up in her right now so that she was at once weighted down and buoyant, mournful and giddy, whorish and innocent. Didn't know whether to sing right now, or moan. Was on a seesaw. Knew only that she had to plaster a semblance of normalcy on her face, especially when she caught his face as she walked past the hallway mirror, face looked so boyish and desperate, as if he were watching his favorite ball roll into a busy intersection and he was trying to decide whether to chase it. Now it was guilt that overrode all the other paradoxes swinging like a jagged-ball pendulum inside of her. She went to him then and circled her hands around him. "I'm so tired, babes, I'm going to take a nice hot shower and then I want to hear all about your day." She swallowed hard. Was that the best she could do? she asked herself, even as she felt his nose rifling through to the crinkles in her hair.

He did ask it. Shocked the shit out of her because he used those very words. "Is that the best you can do, Verdi? Getting your hair done?"

"What are you talking about?" she said as she pulled away from him and started walking toward the stairs. She just wanted to get in the shower. Though she'd showered already at Johnson's she was feeling gritty all over again, feeling as if Rowe could see Johnson's mouth prints straight through her blouse, as if her breasts were exposed right now still dripping Johnson's saliva.

"Un-unh. Come back down here," he said with a crackling authority. He caught up with her then midway up the stairs. Grabbed her elbow. "Why you lying to me, Verdi, huh, where have you been, what in the hell have you been doing?" He was breathing hard, had her pinned now between him and the banister. Had himself braced for what she might say, had his stomach sucked in, his shoulders squared, even pulled himself in at his bowel, feeling he might actually shit on himself if she blurted out that she'd started using again.

"What's wrong with you? Are you crazy? Get off of me," she screeched, allowing an anger to rise up in her because at least it felt better than the guilt. "Why would I have to lie? What do you think I've been doing, it's your deranged mind that's conjured up some fantastic scenario."

He loosened his grip on her arm. Felt somewhat deranged, actually. Didn't know why he was suddenly so overtly preoccupied with her shooting drugs again. It had been twenty years after all; she certainly couldn't be thinking about going down that drain again after twenty years.

"Look, Verdi," he said, trying to get his breathing under control, "you come in here after nine, looking all flustered, you say you been getting your hair done, hair looks like it did when you left out of here this morning."

"I was gonna say I didn't get my hair done, that I'd still be there waiting right now. You didn't even give me a chance, just rushed me with accusations is all you did."

He was staring at her trying to decide whether or not to believe her, felt embarrassed now too at his possible overreaction.

Verdi saw the embarrassment. "You want to call?" she said as she pushed past him back down the steps and grabbed the cordless from the console in the hall. "Call. Ask for Jeff. Here, call." She threw the phone at him. Tore off her jacket and pulled at the cuff on her stark white blouse, rolled her sleeve up. "You want to check my arm like you did the other week." Almost hit him in the face with her arm. "Look at it good, Rowe. I don't want to have to go through this shit every time I'm a little late getting home. You weren't here when I called you, suppose I accused you of doing some aberrant thing."

"I didn't accuse you of anything, Verdi. I just asked you where you were."

She turned her back on him. Started up the steps again. Stomped up the steps. She was shaking by the time she got into the bedroom. Went straight to the bathroom, closed the door, wished the door had a lock on it as she ran the shower as hot as she could stand it, let the water singe her skin to punish herself, absolve herself of the guilt of what she'd done, had almost convinced herself she was telling the truth. She took a long shower and said her prayers and asked for forgiveness even as images of her and Johnson's togetherness rose up in the steam and condensed against the tempered glass of the shower door. She couldn't do this again, wasn't cut out to have an illicit affair at this point in her life. She'd either go crazy or have a heart attack trying to do this. She lotioned herself down then and wrapped up in her white chenille robe. She'd apologize for the outburst. Whatever he wanted she'd do tonight.

HE WAS stretched across the chaise when she came out of the bathroom. Had gathered the travel brochures from the bed and thrown them back in the shopping bag and was now leaned back, the hum of a tennis tournament radiating from the television. She sat on the end of the chaise and took his feet in her lap. Pressed her thumbs against his soles. He looked at her and smiled a settled smile.

"Okay, so I worry about you," he said. "I love you too goddamned much and I just want to keep you safe, forgive me for caring, please."

She struggled not to look away, managed to hold his smile, then did look away, up at the flowered border dripping from the rim of the ceiling; she shook her head, that was Johnson's ceiling she was seeing, her ceiling was rimmed with a cedar molding. Rowe sat up then. "What? What is it?" he asked.

The thump of her heartbeat rushed in her ears and she grappled for something to say. Told him then about her vice principal's treachery. "It's just eating at me," she said. "I didn't want to admit it to you, but you were so right about her." She knew that would satisfy him, give an explanation for her strangeness if she was in fact being strange. Plus he'd enjoy having it confirmed that he'd accurately predicted how things would play out.

"I told you you should have gotten rid of her sneaky ass, Verdi, didn't I tell you? There are ways, legitimate ways, manuals filled with ways to give the victors the spoils."

She told him then how wise he was. "I just thought I could bring her around, you know what I mean, Rowe, I was trying to be gracious, you know, not stooping to her level."

"That's because you're sweet," he said, "come 'ere." He reached for her to prop her up next to him. "And a lot of people out here have no conscience, they'll lie and cheat all they have to to get their way."

Her stomach tightened when he said that and she couldn't find a position where his shoulder wasn't pushing into her face. She sat up then. Asked him if he wanted a bowl of frozen yogurt. Anything so that she didn't have to be so close to him right now, afraid he might pick up her lies through the pores of her skin.

"Frozen yogurt sounds good, actually," he said as he patted her butt, "and don't worry about that lying Shannon bitch, we'll figure out what to do about her."

She rushed from the bedroom, dialed Johnson's number when she got down to the kitchen. "I was just thinking about you," he said, and she pictured his smile.

She whispered into the phone. Made her words come fast and with an urgency. "I can't do this, I'm rusting inside. I can't be with you anymore." She mashed the button to turn off the phone. Held the phone to her cheek, then went to the freezer for the yogurt.

ROWE TOLD Verdi that she should float a rumor at school that she was leaving, that would catch the vice principal off guard, cause her to ease up some of her instigating, might even make her willingly look for another position too since the principal slot would appear less desirable to the woman with Verdi so willing to abandon it. "It's not about the position," Rowe kept reiterating, "it's about you being in the position, she only wants it because *you* occupy it. She's made it personal, you got to go a little dirty here."

And Verdi thought that's what she'd do, but when she got to school and planted herself at the front door so that she could smile and hold the gaze of each of her children and she caught the folded red construction paper pinned to Sage's Elmo raincoat she swooned a little, she knew it was about Johnson. And when the aide whom Rowe suggested she use as the mouthpiece joined Verdi at the door to help with the more physically challenged children, Verdi just said good morning, pulled Sage from the line and unpinned the note, and snuck in a kiss on the cheek and returned her to the children. Slipped the note in her pocket where it burned a hole she wanted to read it so badly. But this aide was infectiously nosy, had large eyes to match her mouth, and would have had no problem reading Kitt's oversized scrawl. So she continued with her ritual she'd been criticized for of greeting the children as they entered each morning—the group of dissident teachers said that Verdi was disrupting the bonding that the children needed to have with them, not her. Verdi stood her ground, and her spot here at the front door, and also greeted teachers now as they came to collect their children from what Verdi had named the Gathering Room. She opted out of starting the rumor today, even as Shannon came down the hall, telling Verdi that Room 2 had called out sick, that she'd left the message on the answering machine, her voice rose when she said that their previous principal didn't allow such looseness, that she manned the phones instead of standing at the door and it cut down on absenteeism if someone knew they had to explain it to the boss, not an answering machine. Also reminded Verdi that staffing plans were due to the headmaster that day, that she'd thought they'd complete them yesterday but when Verdi didn't show up— Verdi cut her off, was calm though, at least pretended to be, said she'd cover Room 2 until the sub arrived, they would get right to the plans after that, though she wanted to do as Kitt had advised and tell her to get the fuck out of her face, even as the aide's eyes further bulged, itching, Verdi knew, for a confrontation.

And once her time was up with the class—just four children in this class, mildly to moderately autistic though she had been able to keep all four simultaneously engaged for up to three-minute stretches, enough time to practice D sounds—she'd had to rush to her office to get on the staffing plans, had to have her secretary in and out getting her data, also to her chagrin, Shannon. So it was the end of the day before she could empty her office, sit back, squeeze her temples, wonder out loud if she was in over her head with this job, and finally pull Kitt's note from her jacket pocket.

"Okay, I shouldn't have put you two together," Kitt began. "So my penance is that now I'm the go-between, I'm not, I'm out of it after this. He said call him, following is his day number. He said he's begging. Love you, cousin. Peace Out."

Verdi was disappointed in herself that her resolve hadn't lasted eighteen hours as she dialed the number in Kitt's note, committed the number to memory as she tore the note into shreds, dumped it in her trash can, and spilled her leftover coffee into her trash can to cover her tracks. Was further disappointed in herself when she felt a tinge of jealousy at the sweet, young, sultry voice answering Johnson's office phone, saying may I tell him who's calling, with a certain authority. But then she heard his voice pushing in her ear, and her disappointment in herself transmuted into a mammoth desire to be with him again, even as Rowe's face flashed across her mind all excited at being involved in the shaping of her office politics. She blinked hard to get rid of Rowe's face, was seesawing again as Johnson asked her if they could meet just for a cup of coffee, she could name the time and place, didn't mean to pressure her, he said, but he couldn't just let things end with her phone call last night. And she told him that she couldn't today, or tomorrow, or the next day—

"Verdi, please," he said, "just for coffee."

She sighed into the phone, felt herself swooning. "Friday. There's a Mexican restaurant off of Thirty-sixth Street, meet me there at four-fifteen, but I won't have long to spend." She tried to slow her breathing as she hung up the phone and smoothed her fingers through her hair, and thought about what excuse she'd give to Rowe for coming home late on Friday.

THERE WERE intermittent silky strands of rain falling by the time Johnson got to his car and reminded himself how to get to Thirty-sixth Street from downtown. Charee had helped when she'd given him directions to her house for this weekend. Only his second week here and already he'd been hit on. One of the teachers assigned to one of the teams he was charged with leading, this one was gathering case histories on the boys who would serve as prototypes. Pretty woman. Soft. Said she was having a few friends over this coming Saturday. Nothing lavish, just an intimate evening with two other couples she knew. Would he like to come and keep her from being the fifth wheel? She'd laughed. He'd tenuously accepted at first, then after Verdi called he declined, said plans that hadn't been confirmed had just been confirmed. She apologized for crossing the line if she in fact had, said that she'd assumed he wasn't involved with anyone since he'd just arrived, that he was so approachable and warm and that she'd actually felt herself liking him after only one week of their working together. He smiled then and told her he'd grown up here, still knew people here, that he was and he wasn't involved, that it was both simple and complicated but that please she shouldn't mis-interpret his unavailability this one time as his being permanently unavailable. She told him to call if he changed his mind even if it was as late as Saturday. That her friends would probably leave by eleven and even if he wanted to drop by after that, just give her a call, no pressure, no expectations, she'd emphasized.

He spotted the restaurant now and started hunting for a place to park as he thought about how there had been a Charee in every city he'd ever lived. Smart, confident, principled, beautiful women, un-attached for whatever reason; women he respected, politically astute, easy to laugh with, or slow drag; women with whom he could have settled into a sensuous monogamy, so unencumbered with excess emotional baggage they mostly were. So unlike Verdi in that regard. He'd actually almost married one in Chicago; lived with another for two years in Cincinnati; spent eighteen months with one in Detroit. All of them though ultimately sounded the same plaintive note, that there was a too-huge chunk of him that he held back, what was it, they all begged, they couldn't go on with him without knowing what it was. So he'd allowed them not to go on with him, better than trying to explain about his darker past, how he hadn't reconciled his greatest transgression, that he'd slipped and fallen in love with a sweet pretty southern miss named Verdi Mae, that he'd allowed her to be pulled, deeper, too deep, until it was so easy, so unintended that he strung her out, and then baited her, left her to be captured, ensnared by the wolf in professor's clothing.

The street felt swampy from the light rain by the time he stepped out of the car. Only April and already in the eighties. He walked slowly, allowing the steaming pellets of water to sizzle against his head and run down his face as if they were so many ladies' fingers. Now he felt his manhood edging him on to go ahead and let things develop with Charee. Told himself to settle down.

He knew what the pattern would be with Charee: soft yellow lighting, mild potpourri scent to the room, a plush velvet couch under a framed Varnette Honeywood, signed first editions by contemporary authors stacked up on the mahogany-and-glass coffee table, Waterford crystal flutes holding champagne for her, sparkling water for him, spinach-filled phylo-type hors d'oeuvres, mood music, light conversation, a smile, a laugh, a finger against an arm for emphasis, a prelude to his genuine display of affection, their eventual attachment for one another, the push by her for a commitment, his yearnings for the same, then the prolapse, the dropping out of place of his emotions because of his unresolved guilt over how he'd brought Verdi down, as if he didn't deserve to be fulfilled in a relationship until he'd made sure that Verdi was too.

He was opening the door on the Mexican place, practically empty at this predinner hour, so his eyes went right to her sitting under the green and red and yellow mural of a cockatoo. He got a surge then that was not just his manhood responding to her as she picked up his face from across the room, and her fleshy mouth pulled back in a smile, and her downwardly slanted eyes lowered even more, as if she was suddenly shy, it was all of him responding to her, his intellect, his intuition, his skin, his hands, his heart, ooh, his heart. "Be still, my heart," he whispered in her ear as she stood to greet him and he kissed her lightly on her cheek.

He asked her how was her job going and she told him about getting the four autistic children to say a collective D the other day. "I miss the classroom," she said. "Can't admit it because I'm told that's a nonmanagerial stance, but God knows, I miss the extended one-on-one with those children."

She asked him then about his project and he excitedly described the nonprofit he was raising funds for. "Teenage boys at risk, Verdi. Such an emotional tug this project has as I'm studying the population to be served, you know, these boys who are at the pivot of making it or not, you know, I keep seeing myself, keep seeing my mother in their family histories. So I'm looking in every nook and cranny, pulling lists like you wouldn't believe, I plan on surpassing the targets for this one, baby."

And they talked like that for three hours that flew like fifteen minutes. They sipped virgin margaritas and nibbled on tortilla chips and salsa, unaware that the place was crowded now, that the dinner hour was in full swing, that nightfall was raining in through the window. And when they did realize it, Verdi let out a small gasp, and Johnson apologized, said he hoped he wasn't causing problems for her. And she said no, none that she couldn't handle, that she was feeling overwhelmed when she called him the other night, that she was vacillating though.

"So vacillate toward me," he said, and she waited for him to laugh, but he didn't laugh. Looked right at her, put his finger to her chin so that she couldn't look away.

She melted then, couldn't do anything but melt as she took in the seriousness of his asymmetrical eyes, circles of heat moving through her now, reducing her to a clump of wax needing the press of his hands to shape her, form her, so malleable she'd become. Couldn't do anything but acquiesce when he said, "Come home with me, Verdi Mae, stay as long as you want to, as long as you can. Come on home with me, baby. Please."

Fourteen

THIS TIME VERDI told Rowe that she'd gone to Kitt's. That Sage seemed close to a breakthrough and she wanted to spend the evening working with her. Rowe's mouth went to paste when he listened to Verdi's voice float through the answering machine; her voice so wavy, so excited. He just stood there in the kitchen with his hands in his pockets thinking about what to do. Felt a tug to be happy for her that she was somehow involved in a life's calling, what if she were actually responsible for the child finally talking, how much that would alter her view of herself that had been so diminished when she was drug-devastated twenty years ago, her sense of self had never really risen again to the level of confidence she'd once had; she wouldn't be letting her vice principal give her shit if her confidence was where it needed to be, he thought. But also with the tug to be happy for her came a pull in the opposite direction, a jealous anger that this potential opportunity for her fulfillment wasn't because of him. Then the thought that had been working its way under his skin for a couple of weeks now—since that evening when he'd been compelled to step foot in her cousin's house—that he'd been a large contributor to her diminished sense of self, always giving her instruction, snatching from her the opportunity to make her own mistakes. That thought had grown under his skin now over the past days like a family of mites, burrowing, nesting, laying eggs, feeding almost imperceptibly at first until the rash, the irritation, the compulsion to scratch to give himself relief, especially now standing alone in the kitchen, leaning on the center island's unyielding granite surface because now the thought pulled the wind from his lungs—that he was losing her, her amenability, her attention was slipping from his pull the way that a worn magnet loses its hold on a nail. There was a defiance about her now. He'd seen it in her eyes when he'd pinned her against the banister the other night demanding to know where she'd been. But what was he losing her to? A recurrence of her addiction? Another man? Herself? He now wished that they'd gotten married after all. Even though he'd always wanted to, but Penda would have dragged the divorce out, and Verdi pleaded with him that she couldn't handle the exposure of the divorce proceedings, too much about her would be revealed and hurt her family. She'd cry whenever he broached the subject of marriage, and he'd agreed and relented, and their current arrangement of living as if they were married had been comfortable and fulfilling. But suddenly standing here feeling her fingers slip away from his clutching grasp, he needed the completeness of a total commitment, suddenly he needed for her to be his wife.

VERDI WAS still tingling when she got home, still holding on to that silky feeling wherever Johnson's touch had been that even went beyond the physical palpations, where he'd touched her just by the way he listened without a threatened look tightening his face, so noncritically he listened, not rushing in to say that she should feel, think, act, do, this that or the other. The only person who'd ever even come close to listening to her in such an openhearted way had been her aunt Posie. And she thought she'd reciprocated. Even when he described how he'd called his father right before he left Philly, told him he just called to say good-bye and to thank him for everything, that he'd turned into a lying, cheating, common junkie, a stuffer, and he just wanted to thank his father for helping him to become that. She didn't stop him when he described the feeling of staring into his father's casket years later, even as his voice cracked, she didn't say, okay, Johnson, don't torture yourself, she just squeezed his hand and let him talk. So she was just dripping with the feel of Johnson as she took a deep breath and walked into the tight air of the too-large bedroom that she shared with Rowe. And the last thing she wanted to see right now was the back of Rowe's head leaning against the velvet chaise, and now his face as he came toward her smiling and she felt a dropping inside the closer he came.

"Hi, Verdi, sweetheart," he said as he pulled her against his chest. "Lonely evening without you, but was it worth it?"

"Huh?" she said, trying to pull herself away.

"Was it worth me being here all evening watching one nonsensical pay-per-view movie after the other, huh? Did she talk? Did your cousin's daughter talk?"

"Mnh, not yet," Verdi said as she managed to disengage herself from the tangle of his arms. She walked toward her closet and kicked her shoes from her feet, her back to him. "But I do think it's going to happen soon, you know, I just have to be very consistent from now on, you know, I'll probably be spending more evenings with her, most likely it will happen outside of school, outside of an overt learning situation, you know, in a more natural setting, so I'll probably spend at least an evening or two out of the week with her."

"God, Verdi, she's so lucky to have you." He went to her and turned her to face him. "So am I. I'm the luckiest of all to have you." He leaned in to kiss her. "I need to you ask you something, Verdi," he said as his breath was hot against her face.

Verdi sighed and turned her head so that he couldn't kiss her, and that made Rowe drop his hands as if the silk blouse she was wearing had just scorched his hands.

"Oh, forget it then," he said blandly, feeling her turning away like that as if she'd just stomped on his fingers, feeling that kind of throbbing right in his chest. He walked to the armoire and clicked the television off.

"No, don't forget it, what were you going to say?" she asked, agitated, as she took off her blouse, held it up, and saw Johnson's hands on the blouse the way they'd been just an hour ago.

"Just fuck it," he said, and then he went silent as he sat on the green velvet chaise and tightened his arms across his chest.

"Well yeah, then fuck it," she said as she tossed the blouse into the dry-cleaning bin. Her voice screeched and she almost shouted at him and this sudden rise in her directed at Rowe when he hadn't even done anything was new for her. It frightened them both as Verdi looked at the blouse crumpled in the bin the way her emotions were crumpled right now. "I just don't understand what's gotten into you," she said, crying now.

And before she could finish her sentence Rowe had her in his arms, had her face pressed against his chest, apologizing, telling her he didn't know what had gotten into him either, just that he adored her more now than he ever did, and he wanted for them to get married, that's all. He just wanted for them to spend the rest of their lives as legitimate husband and wife, not just pretending at it. That's all he started to say, he soothed her.

He mashed his chin into the space between her bare shoulder and her face and she could feel him throbbing against her, and she wanted to push him away except now she was so confused with so many emotions swirling that she couldn't even ferret out and give names to, so she let him find her mouth this time, and she kissed him back out of pity and guilt and anger and affection and gratitude so that it was a forceful kiss and now she could feel him trembling against her.

"So what do you say? I'll talk to Penda, she's moved on by now, we'll just do it, a small ceremony at city hall, you know, maybe your cousin can be your maid, or whatever they call them these days." He swayed against her and she was really sobbing now, and he took that to mean yes, and he kissed her some more and stroked her bare back and got himself aroused against her and then they took some time and swallowed each other's saliva and Verdi cried all the while because her feelings were so conflicted, so variant, all trying to bubble to the top simultaneously. And Rowe took solace in that as he nibbled at her neck and moaned and breathed out her name, if he could still evoke these free-flowing tears then surely her passions must still rush for him.

He was humming the theme song from *Beauty and the Beast* afterward, when they were dressed again and Rowe suggested they go out and find something light to eat, maybe listen to some jazz. And she knew that was for her because he wasn't a huge jazz fan, and she figured that's the least she could do for him this evening, even as she thought about them getting married and kept coming back to the look on Johnson's face when he described how he felt when his father died.

Fifteen

ERDI WENT ON like that for the next month. Vacillating between Johnson and Rowe. Wanting to be with Johnson all of the time, lying consistently so that she could. Doing whatever Rowe asked when she was with him because she was so cut up with guilt that she'd only see herself in pieces when she was with Rowe, as if she couldn't stand the sight of her whole self. Even agreed to marry Rowe out of the inability to see herself as a whole person.

When she was with Johnson though, or getting ready to be with Johnson, she was buoyant. He'd been saying to her that they should take it a day at a time. That they would neither fret over yesterday, nor worry about tomorrow, that the space of time shaping the day they were in together is all they'd concentrate on, revel in.

And she'd grasped onto that concept, ingested it. Found that her job even felt less burdensome when she could keep it in the perspective of one day, even found herself thinking more and more about going back to the classroom, come September.

And so she was buoyant this Friday evening ushering in the month of May as she sat under the potted tree on Kitt's porch sharing the long glider swing with Kitt and her aunt Posie. They'd just finished another one of Kitt's scrumptious meals, tonight it was grilled salmon and roasted peppers and scallions and brown rice with a dill-and-lemon sauce. And now they let their food digest and watched the sun's head slip under the covers as the day declined into a purple-tinged sky. It was comfortably warm out here to Verdi as she predicted a hot summer with the temperatures climbing so and this was just the early part of May. Posie agreed, said she'd been breaking out into sweats all afternoon into this evening, her hair wasn't even holding on to its press she'd been perspiring so.

"Had to just pull it back in this little old tattered roll, didn't feel like putting a hot comb to it, too tired this evening, arms even stiff," she said.

Verdi sat up to look at Posie, was dazzled again by her aunt's beauty even as she approached sixty. The hair pulled back made the skin on her face even tighter than it was, made the hollows that etched out her cheekbones even more dramatic, completely uncurtained the view to her eyes with their downward slant that lent a provocative mix of innocent and temptress. Even the perspiration had settled to give a perfect sheen to her brown-over-gold complexion. "Oh Auntie, you're still the most beautiful woman I know," Verdi said as she reached beyond Kitt to squeeze Posie's hands folded quietly in her lap. "Plus I actually like your hair off your face like that; I just hope that I can age as well as you."

She leaned back again against the swing and let her head rest on

Kitt's shoulder. Her aunt started humming some old-time love song and Sage was sprawled across the vinyl-tiled porch floor rolling her fat crayons up and down oversized construction paper. And Verdi felt so complete, so engaged in the rhythm of her life right now as if she were the last piece to a jigsaw puzzle and had just been snapped into her rightful place so that she was no longer one of a thousand irregularly shaped curious pieces, but now her edges blended with the totality of the completed puzzle's scene around her and redefined her as part of a greater, more glorious whole.

She and Johnson met here at Kitt's often before their evenings together so that she could at least tell Rowe a half-truth when she said she was going to work with Sage. And they were very respectful when they were here, only their hands touched maybe across the table if one was saying something that needed to be emphasized with a squeezing of the fingers, or their cheeks when they hugged politely, and of course their eyes and their intellects, but in such clean and honest ways when they were here that she never even felt the need to look away or down out of guilt or nervousness.

And even Rowe had calmed down remarkably at least in Verdi's view. Accepted her spending so much time over here as something she needed to do that even added to her sense of completeness when she got here.

She'd tried to explain it all to Kitt, this calmness, this feeling of completeness. Still trying with her head on Kitt's shoulder to the swing's gentle to and fro as Kitt worried out loud about Verdi being in over her head trying to play both sides up the middle between Johnson and Rowe. "Just relax, Kitt," Verdi said, waving her hand, "you know, everything is everything."

"Everything is everything? You hear this flower child, Mama," Kitt said, sitting in the middle of the swing between her mother and Verdi. "Let me remind you, Verdi Mae, that you and Johnson have both spent one Sunday, two Saturday afternoons, two Tuesdays, and every Wednesday evening at my house the past month. And you're back again this Friday evening and Johnson's on the way, and you telling me to relax? What if Rowe decides to show up over here again? Huh? 'Cause I'm not cloaking anybody I don't care how much I love you."

"He won't show up here," Verdi said, smiling with confidence. "He was just feeling insecure that night of Sage's party, but he won't, wouldn't just pop over here unannounced."

Kitt was not so easily dissuaded. Though she enjoyed the sight of Verdi and Johnson at her table she felt so responsible, that by putting them together as she had, she'd turned Verdi into a common cheat. And even though in the final outcome, she'd always wanted to see Verdi end up with Johnson, she didn't want it to be like this, not starting off as a lurid affair, especially not starting off as a result of her hand stirring in the bowl that got the mix of ingredients blending the way that it was.

Verdi smiled again glowingly and pointed out the remarkable wash of colors Sage had created against the construction paper and then went on to tell Kitt how much more precise Sage's tongue movements were becoming during their speech-therapy sessions.

"You hear her trying to change the subject, Mama," Kitt said to Posie as Posie sat back enjoying the sky and controlling the motion of the swing.

Posie didn't answer, just kept her lilting hum going to the rhythm of the swing.

"I mean, honestly," Kitt directed herself at Verdi again, "I can't even fathom how we've changed sides on this; don't get me wrong, I still think Rowe is a pompous, arrogant, overly literate drone, but, Verdi, you really got to think carefully about what you're doing. Make sure you're not the one who gets hurt in all of this."

Verdi was so breezy right now, flitting on air it seemed as she continued to laugh away Kitt's concern. Said that from the time they were little girls that Kitt never could trust her to make the right decisions.

"Yeah, well tell me this, Verdi Mae, does Rowe know that Johnson is over here every time that you are? Does he even know that Johnson's back in town? I mean where did you tell him you were going this evening."

"Told him I was coming here, then going to get my relaxer perm touched up and my ends clipped, and then to the gym," Verdi said, resisting the impulse to giggle.

Kitt sucked the air in through her teeth. "See what I mean. Now, that's dumb, just plain dumb, Verdi Mae."

"You do have quite a bit of new growth, darling," Posie said almost absentmindedly, still looking at the sky. "And all of Kitt's good cooking is putting a curve back in your hips."

"Auntie Posie," Verdi blurted, laughing, "I can't believe you telling me that I'm getting fat, it's these khaki pants, Auntie. And as for my hair, since you telling me it's looking bad, that's 'cause I just washed it and blew it dry before I left to come here—"

"What she's trying to tell you," Kitt said, jabbing at Verdi's thigh as she spoke, "that if you gonna maintain untruths with your man, you at least need to cover your tracks. How much sense does that make, telling somebody you're going to get your perm touched up and then coming back looking the same way you went out? Huh? Rowe may be many things, but trust me, baby, he's not at all unobservant."

Verdi nudged Kitt as she rubbed her hands through her hair. "That reminds me, cousin—"

"Don't even be calling me cousin," Kitt said. "You only call me cousin when you want something, and I know you're getting ready to ask me to clip your ragged ends."

Sage reached behind her to hand her mother her dull-edged children's scissors, and Kitt's mouth fell open the way it always did when Sage revealed this gift for being in her own world and still so attentive to what was going on around her. And Verdi stooped on the vinyl porch floor to Sage's level and put Sage's hands to her jaw so that she could feel Verdi's facial muscles as she said scissors, over and over, "scissors."

And Kitt got up to get her clipping shears, said, "Mama, you want some water," as she noticed sweat accumulating on Posie's face again and took her mother's temperature with the back of her hand against her forehead, and Posie told Kitt that yes a little cold water would be good and Kitt was right back in a flash with Posie's water plus the scissors and a towel, a wide-toothed comb, and leave-in conditioner for Verdi's hair.

"Come here, girl," Kitt said, mocking sternness, and Verdi scooted giggling across the vinyl-tiled porch floor and leaned against Kitt's legs as Kitt spread the towel over her shoulders and commenced to parting her hair with her wide-toothed comb and massaging conditioner in her hair.

"Awl goodness, cousin, you putting me in heaven," Verdi said as she rolled her head around to the motion of Kitt's fingers pulsing through her scalp.

"Actually, I don't think so," Kitt said as a seriousness overtook her tone. "I think it's Johnson's presence here that's got your face in the clouds and you can't even admit it, that's what bothers me. And somebody's bound to get hurt, and I just don't want it to be you, really, I don't want it to be Johnson either, and if truth be told as much as I can't stand his arrogant self, I felt kind of sorry for Rowe that Saturday night at Sage's birthday party standing in the middle of the floor looking all pitiful." She felt Verdi's back stiffen against her legs when she said that, and a dread that she had been picturing as a storm cloud all day resettled in her stomach again the way it had been dropping and dissipating all day. It felt darker and heavier now and she got quiet as she measured portions of Verdi's hair between her fingers and snipped the ends off and then started on a new section. There was no way this could end well. The least painful would be if Johnson left soon to go tackle his next fund-raising project in some other city; the most devastating would be if the fire were really turned up between Johnson and Verdi and she left Rowe. Messy, she thought. Thinking about how horrific it was when Verdi had first admitted to being in love with Rowe, that it had just happened, she'd cried to her and Posie, that she hadn't meant for it to happen, but they were hopelessly in love and couldn't live without each other. And Verdi was so frail back then, some horrible case of mono, according to Rowe, and she had lost all the weight she'd come here with along with the glimmer in her eye that said I'm waiting to be delighted. And it was like stolen moments for her and Posie to have a little time with Verdi because Rowe was so overly protective, dropping her off, picking her up, and when they did have an hour with her the best they could do was prop her between them and rub her back and listen to her cry about how sorry she was over betraying Penda. And then Rowe would show up after too little time and say that he was there to pick her up, that she had antibiotics she had to take, that she needed her rest. And each time she would come Kitt would beg her to pack her bags and come live with them, that they could nurse her back to health as well as Rowe, but he seemed to have a hold on her and Kitt started asking where was he from anyhow because it was as if he

[2 4 9]

had put some juju on her the way she insisted how badly she needed him, that without him she would die. But over time she started coming back to herself, her eyes reclaimed their waiting-to-be-fascinated brightness. And once she started working with special children a fulfillment settled over her, and they didn't even have to suffer through interacting with Rowe because Verdi seemed to be coming and going as she pleased. So it was just the messiness of breaking up that Kitt dreaded and suspected was imminent—try as she might Verdi couldn't convince her that she wasn't mired deeply in love with Johnson—and the emotional strain on her cousin whom she still viewed as needing her protection, and the memory of the hollowness that had taken over her eyes when she'd moved in with Rowe because she'd gotten into a situation too big for her and it had taken its toll on her physical health, made Kitt worry all the more. She didn't say any of this, just efficiently moved through section after section of Verdi's hair and listened to her mother's light hums and the rolling and stamping of Sage's crayons against the construction paper.

When she had evened Verdi's hair in a half-moon around her face and trimmed the edges at the nape of her neck and even chiseled points where her cheekbones began, she knew she was still participating in Verdi's charade, a charade she'd started, tried to convince herself that it would all work out as Verdi was insisting, that Johnson would leave and everybody would be happy ever after, even as the storm cloud in her stomach coalesced and thickened and felt like a rock. "That hair's looking much better," Kitt said as she smoothed her fingers through it and then took the towel from Verdi's shoulders and gently swiped flecks of hair from her face. "Be glad you're keeping it so short, much easier to maintain, or try to convince somebody you're maintaining it anyhow."

"Thank you, cousin," Verdi said as she stood and stretched and then leaned down to give Kitt a smooch on the cheek.

Right then Johnson stepped through the opened door to the enclosed porch and was stopped by the sight of Verdi's behind as he walked onto the porch. He squeezed Posie's neck, and winked at Kitt, and put his finger to his mouth when he looked at Sage who was blowing spit bubbles as she glanced up from her coloring and tried to sound out an S. Then he went straight to Verdi's back and poked her in the sides and she screamed then collapsed against him and they both landed laughing on the porch floor. And they were all hiccuping they haha'd so except for Posie who though she was humored by the scene going on in front of her didn't want to get another one of those god-awful piercing stabs that had been moving from her back to her chest.

Then Hawkins from down the street walked onto the porch with news about the upcoming primary election. Told Kitt that Jeff, the candidate they were supporting for committeeman, needed help in understanding how street money worked because the ward leader wasn't even trying to explain. And Kitt said that she was going to have to give the ward leader a call anyhow because she wasn't crazy about a couple of the judges he was endorsing up for retention, and they got on the subject of local politics then, and Johnson knew some of the names from his coalition building, so they got a gossip session going about who was sincere and who wasn't when it came to the plight of the neighborhoods.

Then Kitt added emphatically that if Jeff was elected committeeman she was sure he'd help them do battle with the situation on Ludlow Street just a block and a half away. "They sell everything on that corner, don't even have to get out of the car either, hear tell all you have to do is stick your finger out of the window and they push whatever you want through the window. The regulars even know the signals, certain fingers mean crack, others joint, others heroin, tell me they even give you a bag filled with a syringe and anything else you ever thought you needed to get high."

Verdi flinched when Kitt said the part about the syringe. She was sitting next to Johnson on the porch floor, their arms just barely touching and their hips. She tried to keep her body loose and soft so that Johnson wouldn't sense her stiffening, why was she stiffening anyhow? she thought. It's not like Kitt even knew really what a stuffer she'd been. Even when she'd tried to tell her Kitt had turned her ears to metal and wouldn't even let such a notion penetrate. So no need to feel embarrassed as they denigrated those who were swishing the neighborhood closer and closer to the drain. Hawkins said they were going to start taking down license numbers. "Most of the clientele is made up of suburban white boys, anyhow," he said. "Shit, let them open a drive-through cop spot on their own corners, see how long that would be tolerated."

Verdi agreed, her voice squeaking, and Johnson turned to look at her and she turned her face in the opposite direction because she didn't know what was coming over her to suddenly make her heartbeat step up.

Then Penda's relative from farther down the street stopped by with Stella Dora lily cuttings she'd just separated from her garden, and Kitt said they'd work perfectly in the corner lot because they could follow the irises and keep the progression of color going.

They settled in for Friday-evening banter as the swish of roller skates floated up from the street and a jump rope smacked the pavement to the rhythm of little girls' rhymes, then the jingle of the water-ice truck mixed in with these Friday evening sounds on this insular block that had even managed to garner a cop on foot patrol. And though they'd occasionally hear gunshots reverberating from a couple blocks away the dregs knew to avoid this diamond of a block, the way that the enemy reconnaissance know to wave the troops back when they sense the fortification is solid.

"My gosh, summer must be around the corner if that's the water-ice truck I hear," Kitt said.

Then Johnson said water ice was another thing he missed about Philly.

And Kitt said, "Johnson, every time I turn around I'm hearing something else you missed about Philly, why don't you just admit that you missed everything about Philly."

And Verdi blushed, and Johnson and Hawkins walked off the porch laughing, swinging Sage between them out to the truck to buy everybody a round of water ice. And they licked and slurped and enjoyed the cold sweetness in their mouths as they talked about what the overly white Phillies weren't going to do this season, and Posie wasn't hearing any of this, was too absorbed in other sounds trying to swallow a bit of water ice, grape. Tried to let its cold wetness navigate down her throat to coat the inside of her crowded chest where the intermittent stabs in her back had radiated now and stuck. She knew she should clear her throat, clutch her chest, wave her hands around, make some overt gesture to call attention to herself.

The volume was way up on Kitt's porch now as their conversations bounced from point to point like lightning bugs. And at first nobody even noticed that Posie's grape-flavored water ice was sitting in her lap, staining a purple puddle in the middle of her brightly flowered dress until Sage jumped up and made grunting sounds and bounded for her grandmother, followed by Kitt, hollering, "Mama! My God, Mama, what's wrong? Help! Help her! Mama, please what's wrong!"

Then Verdi, "Auntie! Auntie! Oh no, my auntie Posie. Oh Jesus. Does she need her oxygen, where's her tank, Kitt? Kitt, where's her tank?"

And Johnson cradled Posie's head and found a pulse in her neck, and Hawkins went to dial 911, and now it was the baleful whine of sirens interrupting the glimmering sounds that had been so perfect on this block this Friday evening under the purple-tinged sky that was now more navy with a hint of a crescent moon starting to turn its light on.

Sixteen

THIS FRIDAY EVENING in May and Rowe was headed home thinking how happy he should be. He'd just given his last lecture of the semester, had stopped by the travel agent and picked up more brochures this time for their honeymoon so more exotic than even the first batch. Maybe they could nestle the night away looking at the pictures and reading the delicious propaganda and narrowing down how they'd spend their first vacation as a married couple. He'd had to rein in his attempts at spontaneity though when Penda said she had to think about the divorce, she had to think about the loss of retirement benefits and their other joint holdings. He'd be patient. Knew Penda wasn't someone he could rush. What was the urgency anyhow? he asked himself as he walked up the steps to their room burdened down with a widemouthed urn stuffed with two dozen startling red roses. He felt the urgency though. Felt it as a flash of a shadow just outside of his peripheral vision that would sometimes make him turn his head to catch whatever it was that lurked around him, around them now, and wouldn't allow him to settle down and enjoy their life the way Verdi seemed to be enjoying it.

And she really did seem to be happier than he'd remembered, moodier now too, he reasoned, from the pressures of her new job, but when she smiled lately it was a startling gushing smile that disturbed him because it was tinged with a familiarity that he couldn't pinpoint. He felt himself stirring as he thought this, and put the urn in the center of the kitchen table and momentarily admired the roses' velvety perfection.

He wasn't happy. Headed to sixty with more successes than failures, secure relationship with a pretty, smart principal at a special-needs school who could undress at night and turn into his fantasy. Never wanted children and was never burdened with them, enjoyed academia and scholarly thought and was paid well to indulge his tastes in both. Sought-after lecturer, fairly well published by a modest university press. Good life, exceptionally good life. And he wasn't happy.

He tried to remember when he'd ever been happy really. Had to go back years, maybe when he and Verdi first kissed, because up until then life had been so burdensome, once he'd escaped the abject poverty of his past, he was always onstage it seemed, needing to be precise and calculating, writing the appropriate papers, getting noticed at the proper places, keeping his past away from his present. But when he'd first moved inside of Verdi that night in her high-rise dormitory he'd experienced a jolt of what he thought happy must be, a sensation of wanting to giggle, or click his heels together, put his hands in soft unformed clay. He'd made love to Verdi in his imagination many times before he did it in reality. But he'd felt such guilt over the fantasy that he'd go out of his way to do something special for Penda, buy her a pair of those gaudy southwestern-style earrings she insisted on wearing with the matching chokers, some hand-beaded monstrosity as he thought when he'd made such purchases from what he considered a low-life street vendor. But when he touched Verdi for real, the irony was that he felt no guilt. Felt instead a levity, an undoing of the pressure he'd been so accustomed to. He'd never figured out whether it was her youth, or the way she looked up to him, or seemed to need him especially then when she was most vulnerable, all he knew for certain was that once he kissed her, and her mouth parted without resistance welcoming him, he knew he'd had to have her, have that jolt that struck at the pleasure center in his brain over and over again.

He didn't know why he was thinking about all of this Friday evening as he walked into the bedroom to change, sitting on the cream-colored bedspread and undoing his shoes. Probably because Verdi wasn't here to open the door for him, his dram of brandy already poured, some light dinner started. But this evening she'd gone to work with her cousin's child, then to get her hair done, and then to the gym. He'd resisted calling the shop to confirm her appointment the way he'd done from time to time over the years. He couldn't figure that out either except to attribute it to how he'd embarrassed himself going over to her cousin's last month. It had been at least ten years since he'd gone over there, and then only because Verdi begged him to share with them in maybe a Thanksgiving dinner, and Kitt would insult him the entire time, introduce him to the neighbors sitting around the table as the big-shot, Republican professor at the university. He reached deep inside for some self-control right now so that he wouldn't call the shop.

He decided to distract himself by stirring something up so that they could eat when she got in; she was usually famished after her workout.

Her closet door was open and he stared into it absentmindedly as he slid his shoes from his feet. Maybe he'd boil some tricolored, vegetable pasta and open a can of tomato paste. He pushed his feet into his slippers and walked out into the dining room and poured himself a dram of brandy and let a drop of it singe against his tongue as he headed into the kitchen to survey what ingredients he had to work with for a meal.

He started a pot of water boiling for the pasta and pulled down a can of sockeye salmon. He hit the remote that controlled the miniature television on the kitchen counter and the opening sounds of the nightly news filled the room. The lid to the tomato paste was stubborn and the can opener kept popping out of the groove and he ended up trying to lift the jagged edge with his finger. His finger got caught just inside of the can opener and when he pulled it out he thought at first that it was just covered with tomato paste but then the sensation of ripped flesh registered in his brain and he realized he was bleeding and he stuck his finger first in the brandy and then in his mouth suppressing the need to cry out. That's when the phone rang and he hit the speaker button and Penda'a husky voice flooded out Peter Jennings.

"Penda, I hope you're giving me good news," he said as soon as he heard her say hello. His words distorted from his finger still in his mouth. He pictured her oversized fish earrings dangling from her lobes.

"Well, as a matter of fact, yes, I've decided," she said, her voice taking over the kitchen so that he hit the down arrow on the volume to the speakerphone. "I'm granting you a divorce, free and clear, all I'm asking is that you give up the title to that property, that's all, I won't even lay claim to your retirement benefits."

Her words caused a burst of excitement to rise up in him as he stood there sucking on his finger as if it were a red-and-white peppermint stick.

"Penda, are you sure? You won't let proceedings get started and then call a stop to it?" he asked, now hitting the up arrow on the phone to make sure he'd hear her response.

"I said, I'm agreeing to what you've wanted all along, legal disentanglement from me. I just want that property, and then I'm leaving the area, maybe for good."

"Wait a minute, I hope this isn't about you going up to Portland to live in some commune with some two-bit, washed-out hippie." He couldn't restrain himself though he knew it was none of his business, there was always something so natural and ordinary and stable about Penda living so close.

"I thought I told you that you don't control me, ever, married or not, so I don't give a shit what you think, you go try to control Verdi. Which reminds me, why I really called, because believe it or not, I didn't call you to tell you about the divorce, I was going to surprise you and just have the papers served on your sixtieth birthday." She laughed her husky laugh. "Just that hearing your voice and I couldn't resist telling you about the divorce myself. Anyhow I really wanted to find out what happened to Verdi's family over there on Sansom Street?"

"What are you talking about, Penda?"

"You know my niece and her three girls moved over there, lovely block, I must say—"

"Yeah, what about Verdi's family?" he cut her off.

"Say excuse me, Rowe."

"Penda, please."

"Look, you are going to respect me."

"Excuse me, Penda, now please, what were you saying?"

"I just spoke to my niece and she said something happened in that house, an ambulance took somebody out this evening, not long ago. Justine thinks it was the aunt. Knows it wasn't Verdi though because she saw her rushing half-hysterically into somebody's car and taking off behind the ambulance."

"Whose car?" Rowe's voice was tight as he exchanged the speakerphone for the cordless attachment and took measured steps into the bedroom, hardly breathing. He'd realized now that he'd seen them when he sat on the bed and looked into her closet, didn't want his brain to register that he'd seen them there. He was in her closet now, looking at the floor where there should be a bare space, where her gym sneakers sat boldly laughing at him right in his face.

"Sad. I do remember how close they all were," Penda went on. "And I also remember the aunt actually coming down to visit with me after that whole fiasco of you moving out to say how sorry she was about the way things had turned out with you and Verdi, but that Verdi was a good girl and she hoped I could find peace with the situation as she and her daughter were trying to do because it was all so disturbing to them too. I must say I'll never forget that. That took a special breed of class."

Rowe wasn't hearing any of this, just stood there in Verdi's closet while her sneakers mocked him. "Penda, please. I asked you about the car, whose car, Penda, I'm being polite, please tell me whose motherfucking car?"

"Rowe, calm down. Why are you losing control like this? I mean can't the poor woman get in a car with someone and you not know who it is?"

"Penda, please." Now he was begging, feeling as if his scalp was going to choke the neurons right from his brain, that's how tight it was right now.

"You really need to get a grip, I guess you must be beside yourself since Johnson's back in town."

"What did you say?"

She realized then that he was hearing this news for the very first time. She got quiet then. They both did as they listened to each other's hard breaths. And though this could have been Penda's finest moment of revenge, she could have let go a series of racking, convulsive laughs like the evil witch who'd just cast a spell, she didn't. She just fell silent and Rowe even detected a bit of pity in the silence now.

"I'm sorry, Rowe. Honestly. I thought you knew." But then she was talking to dead air because he'd hurled the phone across the room, and now he punched into the air, cursing Johnson, Verdi, Kitt, Penda, his depraved sisters, his dead mother; he ran into the kitchen, flung the pot of half-boiled pasta across the room, crashed over the wide-mouthed urn with the two dozen startling red roses, just stood then and watched the waters mixing, the pasta's, the roses', and listened to the beep beep beep of the phone off the hook.

He grabbed his keys. Moved through the house like a derailing train knocking over chairs, books, pictures off the shelves. No wonder she'd been so happy, so moody. She'd been fucking around, with Johnson. With. Johnson. He was out the front door. He'd find him. Find her. How dare they do this to him? He understood now the rage that could propel a man to commit murder with his bare fucking hands. Let that rage take him over as he ran to get to his car.

Seventeen

OSIE WOULD LIVE at least through the night. They didn't know how badly her heart had been damaged, whether she'd also suffered a stroke, but she was on a ventilator now, she was medicated, reasonably comfortable, for right now, she would live. And they were beginning to disassemble themselves from the waiting room, the faithfuls from Sansom Street who'd jumped in their cars and followed the ambulance down here to Mercy to give Kitt emotional support—though if Posie had been given a choice she would have insisted on the University Hospital, she so swore by the University Hospital, called it her hospital the way people claimed churches. So Kitt's neighbors sighed out, "Thank you, Lord," and squeezed Kitt's shoulder, and reassured her that they were there for her, whatever she needed, don't hesitate. And finally Hawkins said good night, as did Leanne from next door, and Kitt waved them away expressing her gratitude for their kindness, said that she wasn't going anywhere though, that she'd secured Sage with the Whitney girls down the street, and she was just calling this waiting room her home until her mother was completely out of the woods. And Verdi said she'd share a couch in the waiting room too; she'd already called her parents and they were taking the first flight they could get booked on, a night owl; Hortense had already called back with her efficient self and said that they'd rent a car at the airport and be rolling into the parking lot by one o'clock in the morning. So Verdi insisted she'd hang out there too, but she hadn't been able to get through to Rowe, hadn't told him about her auntie, that her parents were on the way, that they would spend the night with them. The phone was off the hook and it was almost ten and she was sure he must be out of his skull with worry. She needed to go home, she said, but she'd be back in time to greet her parents, she'd borrow Rowe's car and be right back. And now it was just Verdi and Johnson and Kitt.

The lightly paneled walls in this waiting room gave off the scent of oil soap, and the fluorescent ceiling lights diffused a buzzing sound that streamed down with the lights, and the three were silent with their heads lowered: Kitt with her eyes closed no doubt praying for her mother's total recovery, and if not that then at least for Peace that surpasses all understanding; Johnson's and Verdi's eyes were on each other as they raised their heads slightly and now Johnson looked at Verdi with his eyebrow cocked.

Johnson used to look at Verdi like that often during the years when they were so totally fused. Strategically, that one eyebrow with the deep furrow would shoot up higher than the other if they were maybe in a packed room, a party, a lecture, and suddenly her appetite for him would become engorged, her feeling of emptiness so expandable and he'd look at her with that eyebrow darted and she'd know he was feeling exactly as she was, and they'd do signals with their bodies motioning toward the exit and then fade into the crowd and then out of the room, giggling and silly until they could get on the other side of the closed door and a seriousness would charge the air between them as they'd proceed to shift and grind and fill each other up. And after they'd started popping the syringe under their skin, and Johnson would walk into a place where Verdi was, he'd raise his eyebrow that same way to let her know that he'd just copped their stuff, that it was on, all the way live, so say your good-byes and let's go do it, Verdi Mae, is what that eyebrow would say. And just for a flash as she looked at him in this waiting room, looked at the upside-down U his eyebrow made, her brain was confused, understandably so considering the onslaught of impulses her brain had had to ferret out and redirect to new emotional levels when she thought that her aunt was dead. And in her confusion she didn't recognize the eyebrow as Johnson simply asking, well, are you ready, Verdi? Should I be the one to drive you home or what? But instead she misread his face as an invitation, an enticement to tie up their arms, to just dibble and dabble, just hit it and go into a nod one more time just to see if it would still be as sweet as it once was. And when her brain straightened out the confusion, it only took a millisecond really, she gasped because in that instant of misunderstanding that felt like an eternity to her, she hadn't recoiled in horror, neither had she felt the need to vomit, nor fall to her knees and call on Jesus to lead her not into temptation. She'd felt instead a dot of desire to pop her vein, felt it as a heat in the recesses of her being, maybe a speck of glowing charcoal that had disguised itself all these years as immutable ash but that still held the memory of how lavishly the fire burned right there during the days when she tasted hell.

She just stood in the middle of the waiting room, her hand against her throat unable to cough or gag or breathe, so stunned was she by how favorably she'd reacted to the misinterpretation of what Johnson's out-of-sync eyebrow meant. She could hear Johnson's voice coming from some remote place, as if she'd already been swallowed up by that dot of desire that had gone monstrous, dragonlike.

"Are you, okay? Verdi? Verdi? What's wrong?" Johnson said, his voice going right in her ear now as he shook her gently.

"I'm fine," she said finally, swallowing hard to unclog her ears that seemed to be reacting to a sudden change in altitude, trying to take all of Johnson's voice inside of her. "I'm going to go down out front and hail a cab and run home, and I'll be right back," she said.

"Cabs in short supply out there this time of night, girl," Kitt said, her tone heavy, her eyes darkening toward Verdi, somewhat, shaded with resentment that she'd sat on the porch gearing all of her attention to what might happen to Verdi and Johnson and Rowe when that storm cloud settling in her stomach was really meant for her to direct her attention toward her mother. "You not at the University Hospital, you in West Philly at Mercy, I don't know what makes you think you can just wave your little old hand and a cab's gonna appear." Kitt's voice was shaking and she was struggling with this new sensation of being totally alone once Verdi and Johnson left the waiting room, of being needy.

"Come on now, Verdi, don't be ridiculous, you know I'll take you," Johnson offered in a rush. "Please, Verdi, let me take you."

"No, no," she insisted, still swallowing, still patting her chest.

"Verdi Mae, let the man take you!" Kitt said, snapping it out like a Doberman taking off somebody's hand. "You claim it's not a problem, Johnson being around you so goddamned much. So let him take you the hell home, let him stand in the middle of your living room while you reintroduce him to Rowe. Stop being so coy acting for once in your life; be a woman." She didn't know where that came from nor did anybody else as a hush took over the waiting room then Verdi started to cry.

Johnson took Verdi in his arms. "Shh, it's okay," he said.

"She doesn't have to be so mean to me," Verdi cried into the hollow between Johnson's shoulder and his neck.

"Kitt's upset, Verdi, I mean, um, it is her mother."

"It is, it is," Verdi sobbed. "I know it is. I'm being so selfish, Kitt, I'm sorry. Please. I'm sorry."

Kitt didn't respond. Just held her face like stone and folded her arms tightly across her chest and shrugged her shoulders. There were too many sensations climbing in her now, each trying to outclaw the other: terror that her mother might die, gratitude that so far she hadn't, envy that Verdi always got everything she needed, always; she couldn't also allow this sensation of feeling needy, alone, to further complicate the range of feelings.

Verdi and Johnson were on their way out of the lounge door, and Verdi was sniffling and sounding like the little girl Kitt would always rush to protect, and now Verdi's childlike sounds were tugging at Kitt too and making her feel guilty and now she felt the urge to at least accept Verdi's apology because given what had just happened to her mother there was no predicting when would be the last time she'd hear the voices of the few people she truly loved. "I forgive you." She sniped it out but at least she said it. And it was enough for Verdi who untangled herself from Johnson and ran to her cousin and now they both cried, hugged up in each other's arms.

Eighteen

THE MAROON GRAND AM was familiar to Johnson now as he slid in behind the wheel. He could adjust the radio without looking, sprinkle the windshield with cleaning fluid minus all the fumbling for the controls, the sideview mirrors were set to his liking; it was as if this was his car as much as he'd driven it since he'd been in Philadelphia. Though certainly not a car he would have selected himself had he gone into a dealership and stood in the middle of a showroom and watched the salesmen in their too-tight suits rush him because everyone knew how easy it was to exploit a black man buying a new car, the Grand Am had a nonpretentious homeyness about it, almost as if it should be his, with a four-year note attached, not the short-term monthly rental fee.

Verdi should be his too, he confirmed to himself all over again as he glanced at her snapping her seat belt into the silver clasp. She should be more than these borrowed hours he was allotted with her where if they were in public he couldn't even hold her though sometimes the desire to take her head against his chest was so intense that his shoulders ached. And now it was more than his shoulders that were aching, it was all of him because his time in Philadelphia was just about up. The season for their togetherness was slipping through his fingers though he'd cupped his hands, tried to hold on to their contents, their time, but what hadn't oozed out through the spaces between his fingers was quickly evaporating; seeping, or drying up, either way his hands were almost empty of this, their season, and he hadn't even been with her in a way where he could take his time, fully express the mountain that had sprouted over his heart because his heart alone couldn't hold how he felt, hadn't been with her purely and honestly without the complications and the guilt that her ties to Rowe kept in the air between them.

They had only driven a few blocks and he could tell by the rhythmic spaces in her breathing that she was falling asleep. "Watch your neck, baby," he whispered as her head dropped forward and then she sat up with a jolt. "Put the seat back, go ahead and relax before you give yourself whiplash."

She reclined the seat and nestled against the fabric upholstery and went into a quiet snore, and Johnson was impatient for the light to change so that he could just drop her off at her house, or at least at the corner of her house. He tightened his hand around the steering wheel at the thought of having to drop her off to Rowe, couldn't get around that it seemed, from twenty years ago until now he was still dropping her off at Rowe's feet.

He looked over at Verdi sleeping so soundly now. He relaxed his hand on the steering wheel as right then, instead of keeping straight on Chestnut Street just ten more blocks to turn to go where he'd drop Verdi off on the other corner so that Rowe wouldn't see that he, Johnson, was the driver of the car, he turned instead, turned on red and went north, went directly to City Avenue, to the modest leased apartment with the slightly tattered tweeded couch that was his for only one more week.

He just sat in the car once he pulled into the blackened parking lot in the space that had become familiar to him too. He listened to Verdi's sleeping breaths and thought about what he should do if she woke and tried to claw his eyes out for being so audacious as to bring her here. He guessed that wouldn't happen though. Verdi had always been so easily led down paths she knew were wrong, that had always excited him about her; he'd loved her for that, and now he was acknowledging for the first time, he'd hated her too, hated her for not holding on to her right mind, for not resisting more, for not tying a rope to a tree and then hurling him the other end so that he could have climbed out of the cesspool he'd made of his life; he did hate her for that, for being so weak.

He remembered Posie's words then when she'd apologized to him for putting him on a pedestal and then hating him for falling from a place where he had no business being anyhow. It was as if he could hear Posie in this car, in his ear, telling him that he owed Verdi such an apology too.

And now that he'd thought of Posie in that context he allowed himself to feel the terror he'd put a cap on while he was trying to be strong for Verdi and Kitt. Damn. Posie. "Please don't die," he said out loud. He was rushed with an onslaught almost as if it was his own mother for whom he'd returned too late to say good-bye. He gritted his teeth to hold it back, but he couldn't hold it back and he let go a cracked sob, and then another one and he covered his face in his hands and it was that sound that startled Verdi awake as she sat up and looked around confounded, trying to see where the hell they were.

"Johnson, Johnson, what is it?" she asked frantically as she squinted through the darkness and found his arm and shook it. "Is it my auntie? Tell me, Johnson, what's wrong?"

He didn't answer, stretched across the bucket seat and found her mouth instead, could taste his own salty tears running into her mouth as he covered her lips with his own, she didn't resist, pushed back with her mouth, until he couldn't stand it anymore and said, "Come on, baby, come on, let's go inside."

THEY WERE out of breath by the time they practically burst through his apartment door. And once the door slammed shut and sealed them in the tiny living room an unfamiliarity descended as if they were about to become entwined for the first time. They stood facing each other; Verdi looked at her fingers, curled and laced her fingers. "Maybe I shouldn't be here," she stammered, "it's so late and Rowe doesn't even know—"

"Maybe you shouldn't be anywhere else but here," Johnson replied as he interrupted her and moved in closer.

"But, um, but I need to, I mean, what about, um, Rowe—"

"Fuck Rowe."

"But you don't understand—"

"I understand that my project here is just about done, I've done the foundation work, Troubled Waters is a real entity now, you know a grant writer comes in after me. I have no other reason to stay here now unless you give me one."

"No! Done! My God, why you just springing this on me, how much longer?"

"I can milk it for another week, but essentially I'm finished."

"One more week? You don't mean you're leaving town in one week."

He had her face in his hands. Such a panicked look to her face. Such a small, helpless face. "I'm—I'm just floored, it seemed as if you'd be here, you know, at least through the summer, I mean where next, oh God, don't let it be someplace all far. Awl. One week? No! Shit!"

He kissed her face as she spoke. Her face was so pliable as it just yielded to the press of his lips. How could he have ever expected her to save him? So unfair, even hostile of him to have hoped for that, she was just a girl, not even ripe in her womanhood, just a bud on a branch, an embryo, not even born, and he had hoped for her to save him. "I'm sorry," he said as he kissed her lowered eyelids.

"Well, don't be sorry, just don't leave."

"It's not the leaving I'm sorry about, Verdi, not the leaving this time anyhow. I'm sorry because I put you where you never belonged, then I hated you for not holding your position, for not stopping me, for giving in to me, I'm sorry, I'm so, so sorry. You never belonged there."

"Where do I belong?" she asked him and the air surrounding him as her eyes looked beyond him into the dark living room, thinking that's how the days ahead of her would be, dark and formless like the living-room air if he were no longer here, no longer this close.

"Right here, baby, At least now, tonight, this moment, you belong right here."

They stopped talking then. They tore at each other and pushed and squeezed and panted and gasped. They were rough and fervent and clawing and biting, and Johnson tried to slow it down, to go at it at a milder pace, but Verdi pressed her heels into his back, she so wanted—needed—for it to be ferocious right now; tenderness could come later, right now she just wanted Johnson to fill her up, fibrously, she could even let him go, retreat back to her safely packaged life with Rowe, she could spend a million more nights with Rowe if right now Johnson could fill her up, if he could be the one to take away, take away, please could he take away that dot of desire that started burning when she'd misread his eyebrow, could he? Could he take it away? "Please, please," she started begging him and the sound of her voice like that made him come in a rush, and she did too, and in that instant as her center burst and spewed glitter that caused reverberating tingles wherever it landed she thought that she had actually hit her vein, that she was getting off not on Johnson, but from that poison that she'd once enjoyed in her vein. "Oh my God," she cried as she clung to him, not allowing him to move. "Please God, no, no, no, no. Please God don't let me want it again, Lord. Not like that. Never again. Please. Lord. No."

Johnson didn't understand, thought she was talking about him, being with him, thought she was begging the Lord to take away her desire for what they were doing right now, not what they used to do when they'd plunged needles into their arms and thighs. And since he misunderstood her he told her to go ahead want it. "It's okay, Verdi," he moaned in her ear. "You can want it, want it, go ahead and want it, baby, I want it too, all the time, I want it so bad I want you to leave your old man, I want you to come with me, if you want it, you'll come with me, will you, Verdi? Do you want it that badly? Huh, how badly? I love you, Verdi Mae, so much, so much." He was still inside of her and she was still holding on, squeezing him so tightly, and he started to kiss her face as he asked her, begged her to leave with him. And his professions of love and her squeezing him like that were making him throb all over again inside of her and he started moving again too. "Will you? Will you leave with me? We can even stay right here in Philly, but you got to leave him to be with me. Awl, Verdi, baby, please, please, please leave him, please be with me."

"I can't," is all she said, all she could say, certainly couldn't explain it, couldn't tell on herself that after all these years she wanted to get high again. Couldn't make him understand that it was Rowe who had protected her from that, and who else but Rowe would protect her, especially now, especially after feeling an enticement for it just now.

"I can't. I can't. I just can't. You don't understand. I just can't."

Johnson went limp then. Pulled himself from her and sat on the side of the bed with his back to her.

"You love him?"

"It's bigger than just a question of love."

"What is it, a question of debt?"

"He has kept me safe."

"What are you, a lamb, you're a grown woman, Verdi, you're forty fucking years old, you make your own way, been making your own way, what? Is he the one telling you that you can't make it without him, if so that's shit, Verdi, pure bullshit. He hasn't kept you safe, he's just kept you. Period."

"You wouldn't understand, I mean you left, you got yourself together on your own, Rowe did it for me. Sometimes I think that it was his presence more than anything else that's kept me from wanting to get high."

"His presence kept you from wanting to get high? Whew!" he said, sarcasm making rings around his words. "That's some heavy shit. Who the hell am I to compete with that. Damn. Yeah, you're right, you better stay with him, I damn sure can't promise you that I can control your desires. I know I don't have that kind of power, wouldn't want that kind of power over another human being, a pet maybe, a fucking collie, not another person though. Damn, the power to control someone else's desires. Mnh. He's a bad motherfucker. Scary too. Mnh. That's some scary shit."

He didn't say the rest of what he'd been thinking. That if Rowe's presence took away the urges for her, then maybe his, Johnson's, presence was inciting it. He was even remembering now how fidgety she'd gotten on the porch when they were talking about the drug corner, had thought then he'd have to ask her about that, but then the thing happened with Posie and it was pushed completely from his mind. He didn't mention it now. She might admit to it, might entice him into thinking that he could save her, that kind of scenario would have them both nodding again. He would leave sooner than later. It was better for them both if he did. "You should get up so I can drop you wherever you need to go," he said, his words feeling like wood coming out of him. "To the hospital, to him, wherever."

Nineteen

HORTENSE RUSHED INTO the hospital waiting room and the quiet of the room dissolved into Kitt's and Hortense's squeals and then sobs.

"Oh my baby, my poor, poor niece," from Hortense as she held Kitt closely then at arm's length so she could look her over.

"Auntie, I'm so glad to see you, God knows I am," Kitt said, melting at the sight of this woman who could be her own mother, just a more prosperous version: same face with those downwardly slanted eyes and those healthy lips and those cheekbones that competed with the eyes and lips to be that face's dramatic high point, though Kitt noticed now that her mother's face had a softness about it that Hortense's did not. "Verdi just left to go home, but she'll be back directly—"

Hortense cut her off then, said, "I'll see Verdi Mae when I see her, right now it's Miss Kitt who needs tending to, and that's just what I came here to do. Now, your uncle Leroy's parking the car, in the meantime, tell your auntie what exactly did they say about your mama?"

"Auntie, I'm so scared, they don't exactly know how damaged her heart is, they think she may have suffered a stroke as well, if my mama doesn't make it—"

"Now hush, just hush, we not even gonna think like that." Hortense smoothed down Kitt's locks as she spoke. "My sister is a strong, strong woman, I can't wait to tell her so myself, she's a full half of me after all, my twin, my twin and I just shut her out like I did all these years." Hortense had stopped looking at Kitt, was now looking beyond Kitt to the plaque on the wall that said which hospital charity had furnished the room, not seeing that either, eyes going unfocused and cloudy. "You know, you always think you're gonna have tomorrow to make things right with people, even when you've wanted to do it a thousand times, how many times have I told myself today is the day I'm going to pick up the phone and tell my sister how silly we're being, that I miss her in my life, you know, and then some days you even pick up the phone, and then you say Lord have mercy, I can't do it today, but tomorrow—"

Now Hortense was raining tears and Kitt was hugging her aunt, until Hortense straightened herself up, said, "Look at me, how foolish and selfish of me, I'm supposed to be here consoling you, and I'm all worked up over my own inadequacies, Aunt Hortense is sorry, darling. Come on." She rubbed her hands up and down Kitt's arms as she spoke. "Lead me to a ladies' room, and we're going to tame down that soft beautiful hair of yours, yes it is, even beautiful in those dreadlocks and that's saying something believe me. And we're going to repair our faces and find some tea and you going to spend a few minutes telling me what that angel-face Sage is up to these days, something to lighten our spirits a bit, and then once we've gotten ourselves good and composed, we're going to go in to see your mama with our composure intact, and our calmness shall spread all the way to her heart, yes it will, now, and ease her heartbeat right into its natural rhythms, come on now, Kitt, darling, we can't be of any good to another soul if we are not first good to ourselves."

Kitt took her aunt's hand, gold and platinum wrapping around four of her five fingers. She looked at Hortense fully with her meticulously coiffed silver-highlighted hair tapered at the nape of her neck, her perfectly arched eyebrows, her diamond-studded earrings, her spa-pampered skin, her richly threaded linen pants suit. She wished that her own mother had been blessed with such a soft life, had always assumed that Posie never got the man, the money, the trimmings, because somehow she hadn't measured up, that it was an issue of intelligence, of worth. But how much her aunt sounded just like Posie right then, not just the tone of her voice that was smooth as chocolate, or the way she breathed with her words that made her voice rise and fall like a hymn, but the actual words she spoke, the common sense behind them is what struck Kitt right then. How wise Posie had always been, and how much Kitt now realized she'd diminished her mother's wisdom, because, because why? she asked herself as she and Hortense walked hand in hand from the waiting room, because her mother hadn't been Hortense, because Kitt spent her life angry at Posie because she always thought she'd been born to the wrong twin. Now she felt pangs that started in her stomach and rose up into her chest. Now she wanted to see her mother before they repaired their faces or sipped hospital Tetley tea. They had turned the corner at the end of the long hallway and Kitt told Hortense to go on, she'd meet her in the ladies' room, that she'd left her purse back in the chair by her mother's bed.

KITT WALKED on tiptoe as she edged into her mother's room hardly rustling the air around her, something about the in-and-out sound of that ventilator commanded absolute quiet in Kitt's mind, almost reverence since the machine was taking breaths on her mother's behalf. The curtain was pulled halfway around the bed and Kitt could see someone standing at the head of the bed, at first assumed that it was a doctor or a nurse except that she could see cuffed dress pants, nice leather shoes, knew that any intern on duty this time of night wouldn't be dressed so. She remembered then that Verdi's father, her uncle Leroy, had come with Hortense, and she was just about to step all the way into the curtained area when she heard him whispering, thought he was praying, so she stilled herself even more out of respect for a prayer issuing forth and listened to his voice and to the machine doing her mother's proxy breathing. She realized then that he wasn't praying, that he was talking to Posie, his voice soupy and low as if he were crying, or on the verge of crying; she cocked her ear, held her breath as his words seeped through the thin curtain. "Posie, get better, sweet sweet Posie," he kept saying over and over again. "My first love, my sweet sweet Posie, my very first love. Mnh."

Kitt had to cover her mouth so that she wouldn't gasp out loud even as she reversed her steps to the doorway as quietly as she'd come in. It wasn't just Leroy's words, his profession of love for her mother that caught her breath right then, it was the sight of the outline of Leroy's back shadowing against the thin yellow curtain. She knew the backs of men after all, had been studying their construction, their anatomy most of her adult life, had been so affected by the sight of that one back in her childhood that her mother had cried more for than all the others combined, so much that Kitt had cried too and felt that one's walking-away as her own personal loss. Recognized that back now in silhouette form against the curtain: the short neck, the wide, rounded shoulders that tilted higher on the right so that the back appeared to be in a lean and caused a pronounced lopsided jutting of the shoulder blades. No mistaking it. It was him, Uncle Leroy.

Now she'd have to strap this also onto the accumulating baggage of wrongs she'd have to make right, that she'd never fully believed her mother when she insisted that Leroy had loved her first, that her twin sister had connived him away, that he'd tried to come back to her, Posie, even after he and Hortense had been married for several years, that Posie hadn't let him get any farther than the front porch, tore her heart out of her chest to do it, but he had a wife and a daughter that were legitimate, not only that his wife was her twin sister and she would never allow herself to be in a place to come between that.

Kitt stepped all the way out into the hallway now, she could no longer control her sobbing as she moved up the hall, past the lounge, the nurses' station, on toward the ladies' room where Hortense was. She could feel a thick line of resentment moving through her for her aunt, even for Verdi. Posie had after all been robbed of a more privileged life, and so had she, Kitt; what if she'd been afforded private schools, cotillion dances, college.

She pushed open the door on the ladies' room, Hortense had repaired her face and was about to brush her hair. Kitt just stood there looking at Hortense's perfectly remade face, tussling with herself because as much as she wanted to hate her aunt right now, she stopped herself—resentment is nothing but compassion that took a wrong turn, her mother often said—she could almost hear her mother's voice in her ear saying those words. She relented then, allowed a compassion for her aunt to course through her instead, cognizant of how startlingly swift epiphanies can happen for a daughter when she watches her mother teetering on the line between life and death. At least her mother had experienced expansive gusts of passion through-out her life, had been truly loved over and over with the kind of fervor men are willing to die for. Started laughing and crying simul-taneously as she pictured how her mother's funeral would be, church packed to the rafters with a bunch of grown men bawling out loud. Wondered how many men would cry over her aunt. Wondered if there would even be one, her lip liner was applied with precision, but would there even be one?

Hortense looked at Kitt bursting with emotion, crying and hic-cupping, and was she laughing too. "Lord have mercy," Hortense put her hands to her chest, "Is she—is she?"

"No, no, I just, I just love her so—"

"Poor darling, poor poor darling, hysteria has taken over you, hasn't it now?" Hortense said as she lifted her brush toward Kitt's hair, and then realizing again that Kitt had a head full of locks, stopped and sighed and said, "Oh, what the hell, indulge your aunt Hortense while I pretend that you're that little darling that used to spend sum-mers with me and I couldn't wait until bedtime so I could brush that hair that was soft and thick like your mother's hair and I would pre-tend back then that's what I was doing, brushing my twin sister's hair."

And even though Kitt's hair was locked, and she wasn't accustomed to putting a brush to it, she watched through the mirror as Hortense closed her eyes and stroked the brush against her hair, and she prayed that the compassion would stay the right course, that it wouldn't take a wrong turn into resentment, because a resentment this large could eat her alive. Decided then that she was calling Bruce, accepting his invitation to massage her back for a change.

VERDI WAS back in the hospital waiting room, had had Johnson drop her back here instead of taking her home. She'd already connected with her daddy and was sitting under his arm both of them dozing by the time Hortense and Kitt returned from having their tea and from crying, and praying, and whispering words of endearment to Posie as they'd lingered at her bedside. Hortense was overcome at the sight of her sister like that and it was the sound of her mother's sobs that woke Verdi and Leroy and they both jumped up to help Hortense and Kitt to the couch. Leroy and Kitt hugged each other politely. Verdi and her mother greeted each other profusely, Hortense reminding Verdi that it had been a full seven months since she'd seen her last, and then it was only because she'd come north for a sorority function.

Leroy interrupted her. Cleared his throat and asked Kitt what was her mother's prognosis? And Hortense held her breath as she watched Leroy's face go transparent while he listened to Kitt's words. Hoped that nobody else could see it as plainly as she could see it, his concern for his wife's sister, his daughter's aunt, mingling with that unmistakable weak-eyed, slack-jawed, nose-opened look of a man with his passions revived. She was bursting with irritation as she watched him allowing his emotions to seep all over his face like that. Told him then that he looked absolutely ghastly, that that flight had taken everything out of him, that he should leave now and get some rest, that she would stay in the hospital room with Kitt for the night. "Go on now, Leroy, go. Take Verdi Mae on home and let her and Rowe put you up for the night. We stay with the Reverend and Mrs. Bright tomorrow night anyhow to go to their early service with them Sunday morning, so you go, y'all get some rest now. Verdi Mae, you come on by and relieve me in the morning. But right now go, go on, just go."

Twenty

ROWE DIDN'T KNOW for how long he'd even been standing at the bedroom window when he saw Verdi get out of the passenger side of the black Taurus. Knew only that after he'd left in a rage and tried to find them at the University Hospital, and then went to Kitt's where no one was home, and rode around Kelly Drive twice to allow the river and the sight of the lit boathouses to calm him down, and then realized that she was probably at Misericordia but got there and the guard called up to the waiting room but it was empty, and he'd come to his senses and come back home and finally tired himself out putting the house back together, he'd ended up at this window. He'd relived his entire life with Verdi standing at this window, especially the past six weeks. His twenty-twenty hindsight allowed him now to pinpoint with precision each time she'd been out with Johnson, each lie she'd told, even what she'd been wearing, the smell of her perfume.

He'd gone from calling her low-down dirty-bitch whore, to my baby Verdi, why did you pounce on my heart like this, to cursing her again as he stood at this window. He'd cried, cried out, kicked the window seat, tore his shirt when he punched repeatedly at the air. And now his heart was pounding at the thought that Johnson actually had the balls to drop her off in front of her house like this. Wished that he kept a gun in the house, but then he saw the door on the driver's side open, saw Leroy getting out of the car. He hadn't figured on Leroy. Probably the only person she could walk through the door with right now and avoid an encounter with his wrath was Leroy, and here he was. He cursed her luck. That's all it could be, luck. She certainly wasn't that calculating to come home this time of morning with one of the people he most respected. He was sure Verdi didn't even know that he, Rowe, knew Johnson was back in town, wondered if she'd even thought that far ahead to him finding out.

He was down the stairs with the door opened by the time Verdi and her father were on the porch. He took Leroy's bag, expressing surprise but delight to see him as Verdi went right in with the description of what had happened to her aunt, and what was wrong with the phone, she'd been trying to reach him all night, he must have been worried sick about her.

He said that yes, yes he was, he'd even tried to reach her at Kitt's house, was actually relieved when he hadn't gotten an answer there, couldn't have tolerated it if even they hadn't known where she was. Then he expressed concern for Posie and Kitt, asked Verdi what did she want to do, did she want to go back to the hospital, he'd take her if she wanted to go.

Verdi said that she was so tired, that she could barely stand up, that her stomach was upset, even felt like she was going to be sick right there, and Rowe just stared at her with a mix of hurt and disdain and longing and Verdi's breath caught in her chest because she couldn't read the look.

Leroy cleared his throat then, said that he just wanted to fall into a bed, maybe preceded by a corner of that good brandy Rowe drank if Rowe was amenable to joining him. And Rowe excused himself over his lack of manners, went to pour himself and Leroy a drink while Verdi showed her father where he'd sleep.

VERDI HAD already taken a steaming shower by the time Rowe came up into the bedroom, had rid herself of Johnson's scent, felt less guilty when she was clean. Was so grateful to her father for holding Rowe downstairs like that, when she'd remarked on the way over from the hospital how exhausted she was, that Rowe would have an hour's worth of questions about what happened, where was she when she found out, her father had cut her off. Said, screw him. You don't owe him any explanations, your aunt almost died tonight, period. That fact preempts any questions he might have. So she had already decided that she wasn't even entertaining questions tonight, was in her pajama bottoms and was just buttoning the top when he walked across the expansive room.

He hit the switch on the wall to turn off the ceiling lamp and the room went dim, illuminated only by the miniature touch lamp on the nightstand next to where Verdi stood. Verdi still couldn't read his face as he walked toward her, and she'd become used to doing that the past six weeks, picking apart his face for signs that he knew. But there was something in the air now that was different from all the other times she'd come home after being with Johnson, the air was heavy and close to her skin and now Rowe's steps were deliberate and his breaths were sharp as he got right up on her.

"You know you worried the shit out of me, I saw your gym sneakers in the closet and I wondered why did you lie to me about where you were going?"

She didn't say anything. Just backed up until the heels of her bare feet were pressing against the woodwork, tried again to pick up his face in this dim light, but now his face was too close as he leaned in and mashed his lips against hers and tried to open her mouth with his tongue.

"Rowe, what are you doing?" She squirmed and tried to push him away, relieved though that he hadn't hit her, even though he'd never hit her, she told herself now, and her father was right in the house, he certainly wouldn't put his hands to her with her father here.

He had her face in his hands. "What's wrong, you don't like my kisses anymore?" he asked as he drew his tongue along her forehead.

"Rowe, please, I'm exhausted, and Daddy's here."

"Daddy's all the way on the first floor on the other side of the house, Verdi Mae, we could be setting off fireworks and he wouldn't hear a thing."

She felt the air in the room tighten around her then, as if the air were a snake that had been circling her all the while and she just now realized that she was wrapped under the rough and smooth scales of its cold-blooded skin. Rowe never called her Verdi Mae, felt the added Mae drained all the sophistication from her name, would even grunt when he heard other people address her so. He knew. She was certain. She felt the air leaving her lungs at the thought. Finally it had to come to this. In retrospect she was surprised that it had taken so long, that she'd had six whole weeks snuggled temporarily in the hollow of Johnson's life where the original print of her frame still was. Had deferred all thoughts of this moment that she knew was imminent once she and Johnson touched palms in Kitt's living room.

Rowe was nibbling at her neck, unbuttoning her pajama top, had her breasts in his hands, fondling them so gently, barely touching them, and it was the barely touching that made her want to cry for Rowe, she'd really not wanted to hurt him, and now she did cry pressed up against this wall, her bare heels pulling splinters from the woodwork.

"Rowe, Rowe—"

"Shh," he whispered into her chest, "I'm trying to create a mood here, Verdi Mae, I want to be able to fuck you as well as Johnson fucks you."

"Oh my God, Rowe—"

He had her breasts in his hands, kissed one then the other. "Is this what he does to get you stirred up, huh? Does he kiss your breasts like this, huh?"

"I'm sorry—so sor—"

"No need to be sorry, Verdi, really. Just tell me what he does, it's got to be magnificent to make you run around on me, huh?"

He had his face buried in her chest, and she could feel moisture leaking down her chest, thought at first that he stabbed her and it was her blood, realized then that he was crying in her chest. "Rowe, I didn't mean for—"

"Does he bite you, huh? Pinch your fat ass, huh? I just want to make you feel as good as he does. Does he still shoot you up, huh? Does he pop your vein, get you flying high? How's that feel, bet that's even more supreme than when he's ramming you. Is that like heaven, huh, Verdi? Is that what you want? You want heaven? Take off your bottoms we can do it right now, we'll just follow those dark lines on the insides of your thighs, I got it all here for you. I copped. Isn't that what you druggies call it, copping. I went out to find you, when I couldn't find you I copped for you instead." He leaned one hand against the wall just above her head, reached down into the nightstand drawer with his other hand, pulled out a plastic bag. "Right here, the substance and the works, all I had to do was stick

[2 8 6]

my finger out of the car window, hand them a twenty-dollar bill." He held the plastic bag over the top of the miniature touch lamp. "See, see. I just wanted you to be the best person you could be, and now I see that this is all you really are. I'll help you be that too, that's how much I love you, Verdi. So much, too much, this is too much fucking love."

He backed up from her, tossed the bag on the bed. Then just stood there looking at her, watching her face turn horrified as she peered through the dimness to make out the bag. A piece of him wanted for her to salivate over it, to yield to nonrestraint and tear open the bag and go into a frenzy and shoot herself up. He'd bought it just to shock her, to insult her, but a piece of him really wanted her strung out again, dependent, a piece of him was ready to save her all over again. Now he was horrified as he acknowledged that piece of him, what ugliness, this wasn't love that would drag him to this length, this was some perversion, some mutation, something in the water that had caused his desires to be reborn with two heads, flippers for hands, a missing soul. That he wanted, needed for her to do that bag right now was more than he could stand about himself. He choked back a sob. Held his hands up as if in surrender. "Too much love, Verdi. Too much. Too much." He backed away, backing out of the room. Watching her put her hand to her horrified mouth to catch the vomit gurgling from her mouth, she was sliding down the wall as he left, as if he were taking his strength with him, draining it right through the pores of her skin, she slid down the wall until she was stooping against the fringes of the hand-knotted rug, she sat, then folded herself in a heap on the floor. He was leaving her as he'd found her, curled up in a ball inhaling her puke, the way he should have left her the first time, should have forced her to find her own strength, she was young then, resourceful, smart, she could have made a way for herself. But what about his strength, that's when he was most strong, when he felt most alive, engaged, when his own life had heightened meaning: when he was saving her. He realized that now too as he kept on walking, walked right on out of the bedroom, down the steps, out the front door.

It felt to Verdi as if the whole world shook in the instant when he closed the door on the house, their house, where he'd kept her so cocooned the past twenty years, so warm, so caged, but with lambs-wool covering the barbwires so that all she felt was softness. She curled herself up tighter in a ball, she was dizzy and warm, and weak, and so very tired. The knotted rug fringes pressed against her thighs and the smell of her vomit came and went with her breaths and she was too overwrought to lift herself up, to drag herself into bed, too emotionally exhausted, destitute, with her world spinning out of control right before her eyes. So she pressed her eyes shut, fell asleep like that, the vomit going from sour to sweet as she drifted off, dreaming about the contents of that plastic bag.

THE PHONE ringing in Verdi's ear hadn't nudged her awake, nor had the sunlight smacking her in her face, but finally her father's voice did coming from the other side of her bedroom door. "Verdi, Verdi," he called, and mixed in with light taps against the door.

"Mnh, Daddy, just a minute, Daddy, I'm just on my way into the shower." She jumped up, looked at her hands, smelled the putrid remnants of what had been her stomach's contents. "Give me five minutes, Daddy." She tried to control the shaking in her voice, tried not to start crying all over again.

"Just tell me where you keep your coffee filters," he said through the door. "And call down to the hospital and ask for the fourth-floor lounge, Kitt and your mother are waiting to hear from you. Report on Posie is much better this morning."

She didn't answer him at first. Couldn't. She was looking at that plastic bag, picked it up, traced the outline of the needle glistening in the sunlight.

"Verdi? The filters?"

She jumped then, almost screamed. Pushed the bag back into the nightstand drawer. "Far right cabinet. Thank God about Aunt Posie. Make a big pot, Daddy. I'll be right down." She tore off the vomit-stained pajamas and went into her bathroom and let the water run hot, though she should have let it run cool, because now she was burning-up mad, how dare that fucking Rowe wave that dope in front of her face like that. How dare he.

LEROY HAD already poured Verdi's coffee, had sliced up strawberries, toasted raison-cinnamon bread, had set two place mats on the center island. Verdi kissed his cheek. Said you such a good daddy. Then she started to cry.

"Verdi," he said as he pulled out a counter stool and helped her to sit, and handed her a napkin, and patted her back as she blew her nose. "I heard him leave. I didn't hear him come back in. I don't know the specifics, and I'm not your mother so I won't try to pry them out of you. All I have to say is shit on him. He was too old for you back then; he's too old for you now; you never were the broken-legged sparrow he made you out to be. Shit on him."

THEY LEFT for the hospital then and Verdi's father took the long way around. Asked her if she minded riding down to Ninth Street so that he could take Kitt a bag of fresh sweet peaches, filled the ride with stories of Verdi's childhood, choosing scenes that highlighted her strengths, her intelligence, her independence, a gifted preacher after all, he was adept at fashioning stories to soothe a broken heart. Verdi laughed and cried and was mesmerized when her father pretended to be lost as they maneuvered through North Philly and he told the story of a man who had to choose between two roads, one a slick superhighway, sure to get the man to his destination with unparalleled swiftness, with nary a pothole, and unchanging scenes from tollgate to toll; and another road, undeveloped, bumpy, craggy, sure to cause flats, transmission problems because of the topography, but what topography, the streams, the one-lane wooden bridges, the woods, the beautiful woods, Verdi, that blaze in the fall, and open up to expansive meadows and lakes that freeze over and shimmer in December, and explode with the chatter of migratory birds come spring, and the destination is not assured on this road, but what a journey, a tenuous, remarkable, dangerous, sweet, sweet journey. By the time he was finished and they pulled up into the curve of the hospital parking lot, Verdi was certain he was talking about Johnson and Rowe, except that she looked at his face as she reached around to retrieve the peaches from the back, knew then he was talking about himself.

"But, Daddy, sometimes a man should take that highway, especially if it means that his swift destination will allow him to do service for hundreds and hundreds of broken-down hearts."

He clamped his mouth then and forced a smile, said, "Tell your mother I'll be back for her in a while."

Twenty-one

VERDI LEFT KITT and her mother keeping their vigil over Posie's bed and went to retrieve her slice-of-sunshine Sage from the Whittackers, Kitt's down-the-street neighbor. Verdi was keeping Sage with her for the night. Glad. Forced her to compartmentalize, to pack her sorrows in a separate case than the one she'd use for Sage. Forced her to become more other-directed, to think about what she'd feed her, the books she'd need, the videos, barrettes, socks, sneakers. A dress in case they'd go to church the next morning, undershirts because it wasn't June yet, bananas for her cereal, cold cream for her knees, post earrings, Mr. Snuffleuglious doll. Construction paper, children's scissors, barrel-shaped Crayola crayons. Was all organized, back to the efficient self that was a school principal: the one who lined the children up, hung the star papers on the bulletin board, hid behind a pretended tough-ness when her vice principal crossed her path.

And now she was finished gathering all that Sage would need for the night, was about to leave Kitt's house, to go down the street and be uplifted by the sight of Sage's smile. But there was the telephone sitting on the end table almost to the door. And the sorrow-filled case started leaking, threatening to soil Sage's anklet socks. And Verdi sighed, and picked up the phone and dialed Johnson's number yet again, like she had before she'd left her house, and the hospital, and like then, the phone just rang and rang until the sterile voice came on and said this call is being answered by Autotech.

Sage fidgeted the entire bus ride down. Acted three instead of eight. Tried to stick her hand outside of the window, stand up in the seat, run through the aisle, tore a page from the picture book Verdi had opened on her lap. Verdi had to turn a stern face on Sage, something she'd never had to do, and even that didn't settle her down. By the time they walked in through Verdi's door, and Verdi set the bags on the floor and picked up the cordless phone from the foyer table and plopped on the steps to hear who called—Rowe called, said he had driven all night, was halfway to the Mississippi Delta to the spot where he was born, that he was brokenhearted but not blameless, that he'd be gone about a week, would call when he returned to civilly dissolve the holdings they shared—and Sage came at her, hair pulled from her barrettes and standing all on top of her head, eyebrows scrunched, mouth pursed looking like a real badass child, and Verdi took her by the shoulders, pressed her fingers into her forearms. "Settle down," she said, "just settle yourself down."

But Sage couldn't settle herself down. She missed her usual colors, the yellows and oranges and shades of peach that were her mother, her grandmother. And even though being with Verdi was usually as good as a hand-dipped butter-brickle ice-cream cone, she didn't like the way Verdi was right now. Didn't like the sharpness of the silver blue that was like lightning pokes to her eyes. Didn't like the way Verdi wasn't grinning at her the way she usually did when she met her face, didn't like how Verdi kept looking past her to some monster on the wall, not even taking her face in her hands to help her with her sounds. And there were too many sounds getting stuck in her mouth. Too many for her to swallow the way she usually did because she couldn't tie them together in her mouth to make a word, too many to even pick through with her tongue to give a color to. So she ran through Verdi's house to give herself relief, unstrung the videotapes from their reels, marked up her favorite books with black Crayola crayons, pulled out her hair again and again and again because it was too tight against her scalp, didn't Verdi know that it was tight, that she needed for her to take her jaw in her hands and help her make her sounds, that she wanted for her to sit next to her on the couch and put her arm around her while they watched the Reading Rainbow tape so the silvery blues could settle down? But all Verdi was doing was dialing the phone again, and staring out the window and asking Sage over and over what had gotten into her.

SAGE'S BEDTIME came none to soon for Verdi, especially the way she'd transformed herself into the devil's child. And the worse Sage acted, the more Verdi felt helpless. So by the time she'd run Sage's bathwater, and put her in the tub, and came back in to wash her back and Sage threw a cup of water in her face, Verdi started to cry. She threatened to spank Sage then. Told her to get in that bed and not get out of it until morning. Then she went downstairs and poured herself a flute of sparkling cider, put on some Louis Armstrong, and tried Johnson's number one more time.

This time he answered and the sound of his voice went straight to her heart and she couldn't even talk.

"Hello, hello," he said.

And all she could do was let out a solitary sob.

"Verdi? Verdi? Is that you? My God, Verdi. Is it about Posie? How's Posie?"

"Not Posie, me. I'm the one dying here."

"God, baby, Verdi—"

"Johnson, I need you."

"You don't need me."

"Rowe's gone."

"Gone?"

"Yes gone. He left. He knows, he knows about you and me."

"Did you tell him or he found out on his own?"

"He found out on his own."

"Did you ask him to leave or did he just leave?"

"He just left."

Silence. "I'm leaving, baby. Tomorrow morning."

"God, Johnson, please, please don't make me beg."

"Don't beg, Verdi, this is just the way it has to be."

"Why, because it can't be on your terms?"

"No, because it wasn't your decision. Because you're just allowing things to happen for you, because that's how you live, just having things done to you, because last night you could have made the decision to leave him, with some faith, Verdi, that you would get the strength you need, you're the one who was raised in church, I should be the last person telling you that—that you've been caught in an idolatrous relationship all this time giving some old motherfucker power over you that he never had."

"Johnson, please—"

"You know I'll always love you."

"John—"

"I'll call you sometime when it doesn't hurt so much to hear your voice—"

She was listening then to dead air so loud it was deafening as it pushed through the phone, filled the room, obliterating the sound of Louis's trumpet; the ticking of the pewter mantel clock; her shallow breathing; her good reasoning that tried to tell her to just go to bed, curl up next to Sage, everything looks better cast under a morning sun; hope, this dead air even drowned out the sound of her hope; until there was nothing left for her to hear except for that sound that she'd managed to snuff out over the past twenty years, and now there was no Rowe to put his hands over her ears, and the dead air opened up and made like a megaphone and amplified that sound that was always the last sound she'd hear after the sterile point of the metal had punctured her flawless skin and just before the silver pings started firing in her brain, she'd make a sucking sound, drawing her breath sharply as if it would be the last breath she'd take, that sound was always the prelude to her heaven dripping in her brain, or was it her hell, could hell be as magnificent as that rush, or was it the fusion of the two rolling around like a whirlpool that caused that ecstasy, doing it to her, isn't that what Johnson said, she always allowed things to be done to her. Do it to me, she said as she sank deeper in the couch, and realizing what she said, she jumped up, covered her ears, shouted no, no, hell no. But it was too late. That sound of that last sharp breath was all in her ear, like a kiss, whispering, like sound into form now, throbbing, gyrating. The sound had taken hold, amoeba-like reproduced itself, had sprouted a forest by now, too much for her to tame, and wasn't it right upstairs in the nightstand drawer, and wasn't Sage asleep, and just this one more time, awl yeah, to get her through this night, wasn't this the worst night, Rowe gone, Johnson leaving, her aunt Posie still might die? Yeah. She blossomed with unrestraint then and headed for the stairs.

Twenty-two

THE BEDROOM REVERBERATED with Sage's nighttime breaths and the air in here was as soft as velvet. Verdi trod quickly through the softness, her harsh breaths almost gasps now, a stark contrast to the innocence pervading the room. She focused only on the corner of the room as the miniature touch lamp illuminated the nightstand, the brass drawer pulls. She couldn't allow her eyes to fall on Sage's back, her arm that curved under her head, the side of her face. Her Sage whom she thought she could love no more even if she'd birthed her herself, her sister's child—no, no, her cousin's child. She shook her head telling herself to get a grip, even as a silhouette of her father's broken face came at her in this darkened room, the way his face had appeared after he'd finished the story about the roads. Her cousin's child. She said it with finality. Stopped then and held her breath while Sage shifted in her sleep and tossed and turned to the other side. This was such a big-ass room, she thought as she started walking again. Too big to be a bedroom. Why did she even allow Rowe to talk her into making this a bedroom? This was a reception room, Rowe. She said his name out loud, startled the darkness that rippled with the sound of his name, as if this room had already forgotten Rowe, how long would it take for her to forget him? she asked herself as she was at the nightstand now, her hand wrapped around the hard, cold brass pull that could be the handle to a steel-encased coffin. She nudged the drawer open and the sound of wood against wood as the drawer extended out was like a burst of thunder in her ear. And then even the thunderburst dissolved and fizzled into the velvet blackness as her eye found the plastic bag, the substance and the works he'd called it, oh God, how sweet, how sweet of him to do this for her, he'd always been so good to her she thought as she fought back tears and put her hand around the bag as if she were reaching through a flame. She ran into her bathroom then with all power in her hand. She was doing it again, perverting a hymn. She was hell-bound anyhow, she thought now, read her Bible every morning, said her prayers every night, still going straight to hell because Johnson was right, she had no faith. No faith. Johnson, Johnson. She was crying now, in her bathroom, the door pushed shut, running water to cover up the sound of her cries so that her cries wouldn't wake Sage, wishing that she'd been exposed twenty years ago the way Johnson had been exposed, because a lie suppressed can never come back as the truth, comes back like this, she thought, like a junkie leaning over her bathroom counter getting ready to cook. "Oh shit, somebody help me," she whispered as she called on the name of Johnson, now Rowe, now her daddy, always some man taking care of her, saving her from herself, and they never could, no wizards, no white-armored knights, she thought as she cooked it up in a spoon, to liquefy its contents to make it ready for her arm, how generous of him to put it all in this plastic bag. She turned the water off and reached for her white chenille robe that hung on the back of the bathroom door, snatched the belt through the loops then wrapped the belt, tighter, tighter, wrapped it around her arm.

Twenty-three

S AGE WOKE ALL at once with the sensation that a bomb was about to explode in her mouth. As if all the sounds she was so accustomed to holding in her mouth had come together and were now swinging back and forth like a wrecking ball. She needed Verdi. Needed for her to help with her sounds so that they could settle back down in her mouth. She covered her face with the down comforter and breathed gasping breaths because she was afraid of the feeling in her mouth. She wanted to get out of the bed and go look for Verdi but Verdi had seemed so mean all that day and especially when she'd put her to bed and told her to be still, don't dare move, she'd spank her if she got up out of that bed. And the air around Verdi had mixed with even more startling colors like black and turquoise and silver that fought with each other and screeched and Sage had put her hands to her ears and made herself go fast asleep as soon as Verdi left the room.

But now she was wide-awake in Verdi's bedroom with this new sensation that was so hard in her mouth. She thought that if she could give it a color then maybe it wouldn't frighten her so. But this feeling had no color, like the sound she could hear in Verdi's bathroom now had no color. A slapping sound that reminded her of the sound described by the boy who'd had to leave her school because he'd started a fire at his house, but while he went to her school once told Sage how he'd whipped his pet frog to death. "I just slapped hin and slapped hin till hin eyes almost jumped outta hin head, and hin tongue was all bloody and just hanging out," and then he'd slapped his own skin imitating the sound he'd made. And Sage had been so horrified and mesmerized at the same time and now she associated that slapping sound with death, and despite what Verdi said she jumped out of the bed.

Verdi was already tied up, had one end of the chenille belt in her mouth to tighten it, she'd never shot herself up before, Johnson had always been there to do this part so it was taking her a long time and she was concentrating and sweating as she rubbed her finger up and down her vein and slapped at her arm to make a good vein emerge. She was so fixated on finding the right vein that she didn't hear the door creak open, didn't see Sage standing there, her head tilted, looking at Verdi as if she'd just stumbled upon a fascinating oddity. Didn't even hear Sage as she kicked the door to get Verdi's attention to try to let her know that a wrecking ball was swinging in her mouth. Nor did she hear her when she pushed the ball out, finally and there was a great explosion in her mouth, her brain and she let it out, the accumulation of sounds just burst then.

"Veerrdi," Sage said in a husky voice that should come maybe from an adolescent boy who's trying to sound grown.

And maybe if Verdi had already shot up once or twice in the recent past, and had reacquainted her physiology with the rush, and the nod, she would have yelled at Sage to get the fuck out; unable to accept any barrier between this point and her high, she would have shoved Sage out of the bathroom and locked the door. But she hadn't done it yet, it had been twenty years since she'd tasted this brand of heaven and hell. So since she traced her vein now with a level of forgetfulness about how good and bad it could be, she looked up at Sage, in amazement, her heart stopped at what she thought she heard. She ran to Sage with her arm still tied. Grabbed her and stooped to her level, her eyes spilling out tears she said, "Sage, do that again, please do that again for Verdi."

And Sage looked at Verdi and suddenly this new voice felt less frightening with Verdi standing there, her hands gently squeezing the tops of her arms, it seemed to Sage now that maybe this voice could feel as natural as the laughter that always reverberated through her head. She took in a deep breath of air like Verdi had been teaching her to do, she pushed her lower lip slightly under her two front teeth, she curled the front of her tongue, she pulled her breath up from her stomach, from her bowel even she wanted to please Verdi so. "Verdi," she said again. "Verdi, Verdi, Verdi." And then she could barely hear her own voice as Verdi pulled her against her and cried in her ear, "Thank You, Jesus! Thank You, Lord! Sage! Sage! Thank you, thank you, Sage."

Twenty-four

VERDI SLEPT LIKE a lamb with Sage curled up against her. Didn't realize until this morning how disruptive to her sleep Rowe's raucous snoring had been through the years. And now she woke with an appetite too. Felt like a real breakfast, like the kind Rowe railed against always opting instead for bran flakes and fruit. But this morning she was picturing pancakes with strawberries, scrambled eggs with cheese, hot and spicy sausage links, baked cut-up red potatoes sprinkled with garlic and pepper, a little broccoli and sugar snap peas swished in a little olive oil for garnish, nectar of peach juice. She was salivating at the thought. When had she ever cooked like that? She'd never cooked like that. Kitt cooked like that. But she'd watched Kitt do it for enough years.

She jumped out of bed wound up, ebullient. Sage had talked and she was cooking breakfast. Went into her bathroom not at all diminished by the white chenille belt hanging from the doorknob evoking the memory of what she'd almost done. She hadn't. Had not. No matter how close she'd come, she'd been, she'd been, give me a word, she laughed out loud. She'd been delivered. Delivered. She couldn't wait to teach Sage that word. Started to wake her right then to begin working on her *D*s. No, that baby should rest, how hard she'd had to work to say her name like that, no wonder she'd been so incorrigible the day before, she was wild because she was bursting, on the verge.

She ran through the house, half skipping, half jumping, grabbed the phone, dialed Kitt's number, said, "How's Aunt Posie, even though I know she's out of the woods."

Kitt answered in her sleepy voice. "She was asking for her pink lacy lounging set when I left from down there last night. What you do, call down to the hospital?"

"No, girl, I just feel it in my bones, girl. Get your butt up and come on and have some breakfast with me and Sage."

"Who's cooking? I know you not trying to cook for my chile, I know you better just pour her a bowl of Frosted Flakes. Furthermore, what's this Aunt Hortense said that Uncle Leroy said that Rowe left from out of there in the middle of the night?"

"He did."

"Oh no, found out?"

"Yeah, but I'm okay, Kitt. I'm honestly okay."

"Oh, poor Verdi, I was gonna call you, but I was—you know, girl, I was a little umhum, tangled up." Kitt was whispering now. "So if I do come down there for breakfast, you got to set an extra plate."

"No! No! Your big-backed client, Bruce?" Verdi was laughing, shouting, gasping. "Don't tell me you was smelling butter last night."

"Girlfriend, I smelled it, I tasted it, I gobbled it up, I did about everything you could possibly do with some butter before it melts into cream."

"Mnh, mnh, mnh," Verdi said between howls, "Aunt Posie's gonna say she should have had a heart attack long time ago if that's what it took for you to—how should I say it? Go spooning?"

They laughed into each other's ears and Verdi said, "Come on, get up, get dressed, I got a surprise for you that I promise will surpass your last night."

"Can't imagine what can surpass last night, but if you say that *you're* cooking, set our places, we're coming, even though I had promised Leanne and Hawkins a home-cooked once Mama was doing better—"

"Bring them, too, come on, and anybody else you promised a meal, you're always cooking, my turn."

"I mean—you're sure Rowe won't—"

"He won't be here, Kitt, I'm sure," Verdi said as she clamped her mouth so she wouldn't cry, suddenly overcome all over again with a lumpy batter of emotions about Rowe, about Johnson, and now Sage had talked and she wanted to cry about that too. "Hurry," she said, and hung up the phone.

She made up a list then of what she'd need from the store. Got Sage up and dressed and they made a game of pulling and pushing the shopping cart the two blocks to the store and back. And Sage was her slice of sunshine again, smiling, cooperative, hugging Verdi every chance she got. Not talking though, so far this morning she hadn't repeated her name.

And Verdi got busy stirring up pancake mix and cracking eggs and slicing fruit, and peering over directions for heating the brown-'n-serve sausage, and when Sage jumped up from the window seat where she'd been occupied with her crayons and construction paper, and started twirling and laughing, Verdi knew Kitt was here. And not only Kitt, when she and Sage ran out onto the porch to greet Kitt they watched her parents pull up in the car right behind the one Kitt and Bruce and Leanne and Hawkins were in.

"Saw them when I ran into the hospital to take Mama her lounging set," Kitt said as she smooched Verdi's cheek and pressed Sage's head to her stomach. "Your daddy said he knew there was a reason they left church right after the seven forty-five service, so that he could witness this miracle of you preparing a meal."

"Miracles jumping out all over this place," Verdi said as she shook Bruce's hand, welcomed him to her home, hugged Leanne and Hawkins then greeted her parents, fingered her mother's hat that was tilted almost to her nose, lifted the brim, saw her eyes pushing out fresh tears.

"Awl, Mama, you still crying over Auntie," Verdi said as she squeezed her mother to her.

"That, plus she's just overcome with the magnitude of her husband's love," Leroy said as he made circles in Hortense's back.

Verdi pinched her father's cheek and ushered them all inside and was about to go in herself but hung back, just to gulp some more of this new yellow air that was filled with motion that she now recognized as possibilities. And even before she turned around to take in the scene on this block she knew that he'd be sitting there way up the street looking at her through the opened window of the maroon Grand Am, knew that he wouldn't want to get too close to the house.

She walked off the porch then, up to the corner, she swung her arms in wide sweeps and swallowed hard so that she wouldn't cry when she got to the car. And she was crying anyhow when she looked at his face that was stony and intense the way it always was at the first sight of her. She stooped and leaned her arms against the window frame; he wiped her face with his fingers.

"Would you like to come in and have a bit of breakfast before you hit the road?"

"You cooked?" And they both laughed and now Johnson's eyes were filled up too.

"Verdi, I—I can't go in there—"

"You could meet my parents, you never met my parents, you'd always make yourself scarce whenever they came into town."

"But that's where you and he—"

She touched his arm. "I understand, Johnson, I really do. And I'm not begging you; no more begging; no more giving up power that's not even mine to give up, nor yours to take."

He felt a surge move through him when she said that, like a mild eruption of the neurons running through his ear canal, as if their only reason for being right now was to vibrate at this moment and transmit to his brain the utterance she'd just made. His mouth dropped and he was about to ask her what dramatic thing had happened between last night and today to cause this revolution in her perspective; he understood the nature of revolution, knew that it always happened in that pivot between submitting once and for all to the hell of oppression or accepting that there were other possibilities, ready then to fight for the possibilities. Was just about to ask her what hell she'd seen between last night and today, but he stopped then, focused on her house, Verdi too because Kitt had run onto the porch, hollering and dancing, arms flinging like somebody the Spirit had just hit. "Verdi, oh my God, she said 'Verdi,' Lord have mercy, my child just said 'Verdi.' "

Verdi ran to Kitt, arms open, they met on the sidewalk, hugging and jumping and stomping and going in circles as if they were partners in some childhood game of rope. And Kitt started to sob and to weaken at the knees and Verdi sat her on the steps and took her head on her shoulder, and thought how different it felt to take the weight of somebody against her shoulder for a change. Felt good. She squeezed Kitt's shoulder. "Just calm down, cousin, calm down, not sentences yet, but it's a start. It's a word. It's a miracle in a word."

And Kitt said that she had to go in and call Posie. "Mama always said your working with Sage would make the difference."

Verdi stayed on the steps as she listened to Kitt's incantations of "Thank You, Lord" fade behind the ornate wood-and-stained-glass door. She didn't want to stand and look down the street, knew that she'd see an empty hole where the Grand Am had been. She had to though. And a brick dropped in the center of her chest as she followed the fresh tire marks his car had just made, even as the merrymaking from inside the house sifted outside and covered her and she was filled up all over again as she listened to Sage's new voice mixing with the gaiety. "Verdi, Verdi, Verdi," she said slowly, deliberately, her voice so husky, so fresh. And Verdi didn't even notice that the tire tracks made a sudden swerve inward, heading straight for her front door, she felt them though as she walked up the steps, her arms high and wide in a hallelujah way, felt the tire tracks rolling, rolling, gently rolling, nearer and nearer to her heart they came. She heard the gentle squeal of the brakes, the transmission engaged in park, the soulful thump of the car door closing, his footsteps rising out of the concrete, following her up the steps to join the others on the porch. So unencumbered his footsteps were to her now as she swirled around on the porch and basked in the embraces of her family and their friends. It would be different this time she thought, as she heard him clear his throat and say, "Sir, it's an honor and a pleasure to meet you. My name is Johnson and I've been in love with your beautiful daughter for the past twenty years."

So different this time. This time the path to her heart had been cleared.

Perennial

Books by Diane McKinney-Whetstone:

BLUES DANCING

ISBN 0-688-17789-1 (paperback)

A novel that fuses past and present, character and place with a transfixing lyricism that shimmers in its detail. A richly spun story of love, passion, betrayal, and redemption, *Blues Dancing*, grapples with the meaning of faith, forgiveness, and familial bonds, in a narrative that moves seamlessly between the Philadelphia of contemporary times and the city in the early seventies.

"McKinney-Whetstone gives a rhapsodic performance in this story of self-discovery that moves seamlessly between the early 1970's and early '90's... readers (become) passionately involved in the fates of these winning characters."
— *Publishers Weekly* (starred review)

TEMPEST RISING

ISBN 0-688-16640-7 (paperback)

Thrown from the dream life of the black financially privileged, Clarise's three adolescent daughters are forced into the foster care of Mae and her mean-spirited daughter, Ramona. When the girls disappear, Mae and Ramona confront the brutal secret that caused their hearts to lock against each other. This story is told in the shimmering and startling detail that has become a hallmark of McKinney-Whetstone's engaging style.

"McKinney-Whetstone is master at rendering the spaces between people, giving to the air that separates them a taste, a texture, a soul."
— *The Philadelphia Inquirer*

Available wherever books are sold, or call 1-800-331-3761 to order.